"FROM THIS DAY—THIS NIGHT, YOU ARE MINE. YOUR SOLE PURPOSE IN LIFE IS TO PLEASURE ME. COME!"

His voice was imperious; his face as proud as a Roman eagle. Her anger flared immediately. "And have I not told you that I will not willingly become your slave!"

He stood up and pointed to her. "You *are* my slave, as you will soon learn!"

"Perhaps I am your slave, Roman"—she lifted her chin defiantly—"but I am not your *bed* slave. Not without a flogging! Are you savage enough to enjoy me after you have whipped me bloody?"

He descended the steps to her. Though she knew not how, Diana did not retreat from him. Marcus Magnus came so close, they were almost touching. . . . His black eyes bored into hers, mastering her with his dominant presence.

Pick me up and carry me to your bed, a wicked voice inside her cried.

He could smell the Egyptian musk and something else, far headier. His mouth descended upon hers in a kiss that was brutal in its intensity, designed to prove to her that he was the master, she the slave. . . .

SEDUCED

"SEDUCED never loses steam. . . . It's a must read for those who love steamy historical romances. It's bawdy. It's funny. It's a great adventure." —*USA Today*

"The dazzling, decadent and poverty-stricken world of Georgian England comes gloriously alive in *SEDUCED*. . . . A SIZZLING AND SENSUAL DELIGHT, an unabashedly earthy tale that's thoroughly enjoyable and entertaining." —*Affaire de Coeur*

TEMPTED

"A five-star book . . . a classic, a keeper, one I will read over and over again, with memorable characters and an exciting story. . . . Scotland came alive as no other Highlander story has ever succeeded in doing for me. . . . SUPERBLY DETAILED AND RICHLY DRAWN." —*Affaire de Coeur*

"Five stars! . . . As rugged as the Highlands, as feisty as a Scottie dog, and as colorful as a field of heather." —*Heartland Critiques*

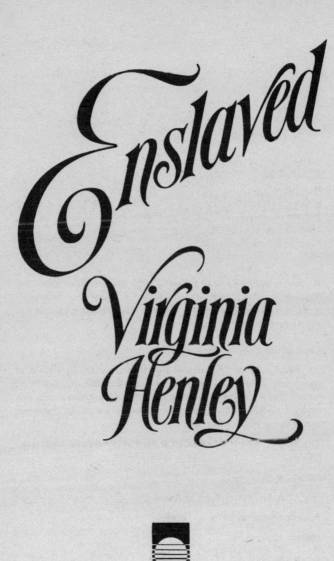

Enslaved

Virginia Henley

Island
BOOKS

ISLAND BOOKS
Published by
Dell Publishing
a division of
Bantam Doubleday Dell Publishing Group, Inc.
1540 Broadway
New York, New York 10036

ISBN: 0-440-21706-7

Printed in the United States of America

Published simultaneously in Canada

January 1996

10 9 8 7 6 5 4 3 2 1

OPM

I've always had the best editors in the business—Page Cuddy, Maggie Lichota, and Tina Moskow.
This book is dedicated to Marjorie Braman.
Once again I've been blessed!

With special thanks to college English instructor Evelyn Finklea, who provided me with such marvelous research books.

Chapter 1

Lady Diana was becoming slowly aroused. Though the hour was shockingly early, she had once again been lured between the sheets to indulge in her favorite pastime. Her behavior had recently undergone a drastic change and she had begun to kick over the traces.

A delicious gasp escaped her lips as the man's sexual intent became clear. He would not take *no* for an answer, and a sensual thrill ran through Diana because he would not be denied. He was dark and dominant and dangerous, exactly the way a man should be, and she felt her very bones melting from his bold advances.

Diana's nipples tightened and began to ache. Her woman's center began to tingle in a most pleasurable way. The hand beneath her nightgown cupped her tender young breast so that her breathing quickened. Though Diana felt very wicked at that moment, she pushed away the tiny pang of guilt, curled on her side, and arched her mons at the pure titillation he aroused in her.

A curse escaped her lips as the candle suddenly went out. Damn, she was right in the middle of the best part of the chapter. She removed her hand from her aching breast and snapped closed the book she had been reading about the intimate sex life of King Charles II.

Diana relit the candle, finished the chapter, then sighed

with longing. She would have preferred living in any other period of history to Georgian times. In this day and age all the men were fops, sporting ridiculous powdered wigs, fans, and lip rouge. Why couldn't she have been born in medieval times when brawny knights stormed castles and abducted the women within, or Elizabethan times when the queen's bold seafarers pirated women along with treasure? During the Restoration, swaggering cavaliers emulated King Charles's devilish way with women, so that life for a young lady of seventeen was exhilarating, exciting, and exceedingly worth the living!

Now the dandies emulated Prince George, or Prinny as he was nicknamed. What the hell sort of a name was Prinny? Actually, the name said it all . . . soft, silly, and stoopid with two *o*'s!

As Diana leaned over to blow out the candle, she caught a glimpse of herself in the cheval glass. She was fair as an English rose ready to bloom. Her pale gold hair fell to her hips in silken curls, her violet eyes were brilliant with expectancy, her body was graceful with long legs and high, thrusting breasts, yet all she saw when she looked in the mirror was the voluminous nightgown she wore. Diana pulled a face, not because the nightdress was hideous, but because it was such a *respectable* garment.

Lord above, how she had begun to loathe anything and everything *respectable*! Respectability was the force that ruled her Aunt Prudence and the measuring stick she used for everything connected with Diana's life.

Two years ago when Sir Thomas Davenport died, he left his daughter, Diana, his fortune, his magnificent library, and his house in Grosvenor Square. It was in trust until she turned eighteen, of course, and her guardians were her father's younger brother, Richard, and his wife, Prudence, who immediately moved into Grosvenor Square to care for her. At fifteen Diana had been a biddable child who never had her nose out of a book. But by the time she

turned seventeen, a wide streak of wilfulness had developed
which clearly alarmed Diana's prudish guardian.

Diana sighed, blew out the candle, and curled under
her blankets, hoping that sleep would bring her dreams of
the more lustful days of King George.

Aunt Prudence was readying herself for bed and bending her husband's ear at the same time. Her frilled night rail
was tied beneath her third chin while her starched nightcap
sat just above her eyebrows. Which was just as well,
thought Richard, repressing a shudder at the thought of her
ever exposing her opulent flesh all at once.

"Far be it from me to criticize our ward, Richard, but
once again Diana has passed up an invitation from Lady
Sefton only to carry one of those infernal books to bed. All
this reading cannot be good for a young girl. Heaven only
knows what could be in some of those tomes. Reading
could give her unsavory . . . notions."

Richard decided it was no bad thing that Prudence was
averse to intimacy and that sins of the flesh stood at the top
of her list of taboos. As he eyed the ocean of white cotton
enveloping his wife, he thought wryly, *It's a wonder she
doesn't wear white gloves to bed, in case she has to handle
the beastly thing!* His mind came back to the topic being
discussed. "My brother's collection is worth a fortune. I
agree the books are a bad influence. I'm trying to find a
buyer for the entire library."

Sir Thomas Davenport had been a chief judge and
baron of the exchequer, who was a learned scholar,
knighted by the king. Richard knew that Diana had been
well educated in the classics and tutored by her father in
French, Italian, and Latin.

"My dear Richard, that is brilliant! Books will not
help her catch the right sort of husband. If rumors get about
that she is a bluestocking, she will sit on the shelf forever. I
shall impress upon her again that she must hide her intelli-

gence at all costs. I don't know what your brother was about, educating a girl beyond what is proper. It's just not *respectable*!''

At the mention of his brother, Richard's mouth tightened. Life was so bloody unfair. How had Thomas risen so high, while he, Richard, remained a struggling solicitor? And why had he left everything to Diana and nothing to his only brother? Not one bloody sausage! He'd thought of a hundred schemes to separate Diana from some of her money, but the girl was so clever he'd have to come up with a plan subtle enough to prevent her suspicions from being aroused.

Prudence sailed toward the bed to turn back the covers. Richard undid his cravat. She eyed him with alarm. ''You're not coming to bed, are you?''

''No, no, m'dear. Just changing my neckcloth. I have to entertain a client tonight.''

Prudence let out a sigh of relief. Richard knew his wife was perfectly aware of just who would be the client and what sort of entertainment it would be and he also knew she was devoutly thankful he sought release elsewhere. She ought to be, and was, thankful that he was such a considerate husband.

Two hours later, Richard descended the stairs that led from the Vaulting Academy to the gaming house known as Pharaoh's Tables. He had thoroughly enjoyed the services of a little dollymop whom he'd delighted in calling ''Imprudence'' while she called him ''Dick.''

A well-heeled youth was descending the stairs at the same time, so Richard struck up a conversation. ''That was a helluva racket going on in one of the rooms tonight. Quite put me off my stroke.''

The young gentleman flashed him a smile. ''Shocking, wasn't it?''

''Sounded like she was being tortured on the rack.''

The young noble shook his head. "Touched up with a riding crop."

Richard eyed him speculatively. While he was not a heavy gambler, not addicted to the gaming tables in any way, he had begun to frequent the more expensive gaming houses where the stakes were high and the play deep. He was on the lookout for a young noble up to his eyebrows in debt. Someone who was already on Queer Street and well on his way to the Fleet.

When both men headed for the faro table, Richard held out his hand. "Richard Davenport, Solicitor at Law."

"Peter Hardwick, one step ahead of the law," he joked.

Richard searched his brain. He felt sure the name *Hardwick* belonged to the peerage. Prudence would know. She was an utter snob and a walking authority on England's nobility. She could quote Burke's Peerage backward.

As he watched Hardwick at the gaming table, Richard began to think he was wasting his time. Surely someone in dire straits wouldn't hazard money with such abandon, nor win and lose with the same devil-may-care attitude. It was obvious to Richard that the young rogue was able to dip his fingers into someone's fortune, if not his own. And yet Richard had a gut instinct that he had found his mark.

Hardwick was just the type who might appeal to Diana. Though his clothes were expensive, he was not a slave to fashion and the slant of his firm jaw showed he was no fop. He had a clean-cut look about him and an easy smile that would disarm the most suspicious nature. He was a well-made, handsome youth who would fit the bill to perfection if he turned out to be both noble and broke.

Richard presented his card and said casually, "I specialize in money matters. I administer the estate of my niece, Lady Diana Davenport, among others. Feel free to call at Grosvenor Square anytime."

Shortly after, Hardwick left with two friends. Richard immediately recognized Richard Barry, the Earl of Barrymore, known as Hellgate. The Barrys were an infamous family. The brothers were all young bucks with more money than brains. Oh well, he'd dangled the bait, and if Hardwick nibbled, he'd reel him in hook, line, and sinker, providing of course Prudence approved him as a *respectable* parti!

Diana's breath was almost gone. She knew if she was squeezed any tighter, she would lose consciousness. "Please, let go, I can't breathe," she begged.

Her pleas were ignored.

If this is what I must endure to be on the marriage market, I'd rather be a spinster, Diana decided. Her breasts were being squashed flat, and she feared her ribs were about to be broken. Anger came to her rescue. "Stop!" she said, firmly pulling away from her tormentor.

The modiste let go of the corset strings and turned to Prudence for support.

"Diana, my dear, a firm foundation garment is absolutely necessary. All grown ladies must suffer these things."

"But I prefer the first one I tried. It merely nipped in my waist and didn't squash my breasts flat as pancakes."

Prudence flushed unbecomingly. "Ladies don't say that word. It's not respectable."

"Pancakes?" Diana couldn't resist. Her eyes sparkled mischievously as she watched her aunt struggle for composure.

"The first one was totally inadequate. This is the one you need," Prudence insisted.

"Why?" Diana asked stubbornly.

"I can see you are forcing me to be indelicate . . . so be it. Your bosom is full and when you dance it will . . . jiggle. And that is not the worst of it. Some dances these days are so scandalous a man actually is allowed to place his hand upon your person. If you were not well corseted, he would think you naked beneath your gown!''

What a lovely idea, Diana thought irreverently. She almost asked, ''Is that an argument *for* or *against*?'' She decided to bite her tongue.

''We'll take a dozen,'' said Prudence.

A dozen will last a lifetime, thought Diana with dismay.

''You may have a few of the lighter ones,'' Prudence conceded.

Diana's hopes began to rise.

''To wear in bed beneath your nightgowns.''

Diana's hopes sank deeper than Davy Jones's locker. She pulled listlessly at the corset strings, digging a whale-bone stay from beneath her top rib.

''Don't dawdle, child. Dame Lightfoot will be here any moment to begin your dancing instruction.''

Diana could already dance. Her body swayed sensually whenever she heard music. She'd watched the Gypsies once when she'd been on holiday with her father and the fast, exotic gyrations had indelibly imprinted themselves on her impressionable young mind. She didn't know the intricate steps to ballroom dancing, however, which were an absolute must for a young lady of the ton. She hoped Dame Light-foot would have music in her heart and passion in her soul. Surely someone who taught dancing for a living couldn't be completely straightlaced.

Diana's hopes were snuffed the moment she set eyes on Dame Lightfoot. She was Junoesque, well endowed in the upper story, but rigidly encased in whalebone. Her iron-gray wig was as severe as her countenance. She carried a tall stick with an ebony knob which she tapped on the floor whenever she wished to emphasize a point.

Obviously the dancing mistress had passed muster with her guardian for Prudence positively beamed upon her. ''This is your charge, Dame Lightfoot. I have no qualms in placing Lady Diana in your capable hands. A few lessons in deportment and etiquette along with the dance steps would not go amiss. My darling niece is rather bookish, I'm afraid. She needs drilling in the do's and don'ts of a successful first season.''

The martinet tapped her stick upon the floor as she scanned Diana from nose to toes. Her hooded eyes were shrewd, they missed nothing.

''I shall leave you to get to know each other,'' Prudence said, closing the French doors of the music room.

''How are you, young lady?'' asked Dame Lightfoot with hauteur.

''Cynical,'' replied Diana truthfully.

The dame let out a bark of laughter that made Diana think perhaps not all was lost.

Dame Lightfoot tapped her stick decisively. ''We shall begin with the language of the fan.''

Diana wondered what in the world that had to do with dancing. When she dared to put the question to her teacher, the dame took on the stance of a military man. Her words came in staccato-like steel-tipped arrows. ''The fan is more important than the feet. In fact, all things are more important than the feet: the hair, the eyes, the mouth, the figure, the manners, the conversation, the appetite, the gown.''

''I think the fashion for young women is execrable,'' Diana dared.

''Indeed?'' replied the dame, the lines of her face seeming to freeze.

Diana almost bit her tongue, but she had begun and she might as well finish. ''Skirts are so voluminous they take up the entire seat of a carriage, assuming you can squeeze through the coach door. Powdered wigs are becoming so tall it's a wonder birds don't nest in them. My personal favorite is the corset. The whalebone stays are so rigid they stab you in the gut whenever you bend over.''

The dame's eyebrows rose so high they disappeared beneath her wig. ''*Gut* is a word a lady would never use. I can see you have had an unorthodox and liberal education.'' The sergeant-major straightened to her full height, gave two raps upon the floor, then vowed, "In spite of everything, I shall make a successful debutante of you."

"That's what I'm afraid of," Diana murmured beneath her breath. She was beginning to enjoy herself, however, and decided to thoroughly shock Dame Lightfoot. "In medieval times ladies slept stark naked! The church condemned nightgowns as scandalous obscenities that would tempt men to commit lewd and lascivious acts. Obviously those first night rails bore no resemblance to the *respectable* garments I wear to bed . . . unfortunately!"

Dame Lightfoot reached into her reticule, unstoppered a small bottle, and sniffed a massive dose of hartshorn. Then, as if she would put a stop to such titillating talk, she whapped out a fan, snapped it open with considerable force, then handed it to her pupil.

Before the lesson was over, Diana learned that the best fans had ivory sticks covered with gauze, lace, or painted silk. She learned the meaning of peeping through it coyly, looking over it, or glancing from the side. It was all she could do to keep from laughing in her teacher's face.

After an hour Dame Lightfoot was satisfied that Diana had learned the art of flirtation.

Comic figures of young beaus flitted through Diana's imagination. "Now that I have mastered flirtation, with whom do I flirt?"

The sergeant-major stared her down. "I shall allow you to answer the question."

"I should like to flirt with danger."

Silence stretched between them. Finally the older woman made an observation. "You have a restless soul, so I shall let you in on a little secret society keeps from unfledged females. Once you have made a respectable marriage and produced an heir, a young matron can have a dashing social life, unconfined by the strictures of an unmarried girl."

"That is the first inducement I've ever heard for the married state," Diana said, tucking away the information.

Prudence returned to the music room, avid to know what dances Diana had learned.

"You go too fast, Mrs. Davenport. Lady Diana is a diamond in the rough. To make her a diamond of the first water will take a little social polishing. I teach the dance steps at my studio in Mayfair, where we have room to do justice to the minuet, contredanse, and the Scottish reel. Here is my card." She rapped the floor with her stick. "Be there at two on Monday afternoon."

Chapter 2

After Dame Lightfoot left, Diana protested, "Aunt Prudence, I didn't learn anything except how to fan myself. This is a total waste of time and money. The woman is a dragon-faced martinet . . . a figure of fun . . ." Diana's words trailed off as she saw the hurt look on Prudence's face.

"I would have given anything for a dancing mistress when I was your age, but my physical condition did not allow me such a luxury. I have been a martyr to pain all my life." Her hand stroked her arthritic hip. "It pains me deeply when you rebel, Diana. It would please me if you would accept dance instruction from Dame Lightfoot."

Diana felt ashamed of herself. "Of course I shall keep the appointment, Aunt Prudence. I didn't realize how selfish it was of me to complain."

"Ah, my dear, it is something you will learn with maturity, to suffer in silence, as I do."

Diana's suspicion that Prudence was a hypochondriac only doubled her guilt. *What if she really is in pain?* "We're invited to afternoon tea at Emily Castlereagh's. Do you feel up to it?"

"As a matter of fact I don't, my dear. I fear I shall be forced to take to my couch this afternoon."

"I'll send a note with our regrets."

Prudence was aghast. "You will do no such thing. Lady Castlereagh is a patroness of Almack's. The young ladies invited to tea today will receive their vouchers. Bridget shall accompany you."

Diana knew instinctively that Prudence didn't feel comfortable with some of the aristocratic hostesses who led society because she had no title. Diana was invited only because Emily Castlereagh had been a dear friend of her father's. Emily was married to the Marquis of Londonderry and her father was the Earl of Buckinghamshire. Though she was at the summit of the social scale, Diana didn't find her in the least daunting. In fact she was an endearing eccentric who adopted an oddity of dress.

"You can wear the chocolate bombazine walking dress; it would be perfect for Lady Castlereagh's tea."

Chocolate my foot, thought Diana. *It's the closest shade to cat ca-ca I've ever seen.*

"And I know I don't need to remind you never to walk along St. James's Street where the gentlemen have their clubs."

"Of course not," Diana replied, deciding on the spot that's exactly what she would do.

Diana chose the most outrageous hat she owned to compensate for the respectable brown walking dress with morocco half-boots to match. The hat sported a full roostertail from some hapless leghorn who had met with misfortune.

Bridget, the maid who accompanied her, asked, "Aren't we going the wrong way, Lady Diana?"

"Yes, Biddy, we are. We are going the long way about so we can walk along St. James's Street."

Bridget McCartney had a face crowded with freckles and a turned-up nose. Prudence would have dismissed the Irish maid long ago if Diana hadn't put her foot down.

Biddy's eyes sparkled with mischief. "Ooh, I'm game if you are."

Diana's lips twitched. "If that remark is prompted by my hat, I assure you I won't start crowing."

When Biddy giggled, Diana thought how lovely it was to have someone share her sense of humor.

Coming out of Brooks's Club at number 60 were two men who looked over the females with an appreciative eye. An occasional whore got up enough cheek to walk along St. James's, but a lady with her maid was scandalous. One drawled, "There goes a prime article."

"And a cunning little baggage with her," the other observed.

With lashes lowered, Diana crossed the street. This was not to avoid the men, but to get a closer look at Boodle's and White's on the opposite side.

The Macaronis lounging about outside the clubs raised their quizzing glasses and tossed about witticisms. One bold fellow in black and white striped pantaloons stepped forward. "If you are looking for a *cher ami,* permit me to offer my services."

Diana's cool glance swept him from head to foot. Then she said to Biddy, "We've inadvertently wandered into the zoo."

The zebra's companions guffawed at the cake he'd made of himself. Diana was in high good humor. She'd worn the cock's feathers for attention and understood that the fop outside White's wore the zebra stripes for exactly the same reason.

Peter Hardwick ran up the steps of 21 Grosvenor Square, presented his calling card, and was ushered into the library by the majordomo.

Richard Davenport had been expecting him and so lost no time joining him, offering the customary wine and wafers.

Prudence, stationed behind the lace curtains of the drawing room, caught a glimpse of the young man and was favorably impressed. The moment Richard had uttered the name *Hardwick,* she had apprised him of Peter's lineage, the title to which he was heir, and the location of the ancestral home. Prudence smiled with satisfaction. The young buck cut a fine figure, one that even Diana wouldn't be immune to.

Prudence made sure Diana was absent each afternoon, hoping Peter Hardwick would show up. Now that he had, Richard would strike the secret bargain behind the closed door of the library, and only then would he present the quarry to Prudence. She waited with great expectations.

Diana told Biddy to go and enjoy herself Monday afternoon while she went for her dancing lesson. "There is no point in both of us being miserable. Meet me at the corner of Grosvenor and Brook Streets at five o'clock."

As Diana made her way toward Shepherd's Market, where Dame Lightfoot had her studio, she spied her Junoesque figure approaching from the opposite end of the street.

"Good afternoon, Lady Davenport, I heartily approve of promptness."

"Good afternoon, Dame Lightfoot," replied Diana, thinking it was a damned good thing she hadn't been early.

The dame led the way into a large studio with mirrored walls. She removed her hat, patted the iron-gray wig into place, then announced, "Make yourself at ease, I shall be with you in a trice."

Diana looked about with delight. Her image was reflected back to her from every side. The room had been designed so that a woman could watch herself dance. How enchanting! Diana removed her hat, then on impulse she removed her powdered wig and shook out her golden curls. She knew her hair was pretty, and she hated hiding it beneath a wig. Suddenly she felt like dancing. Light streamed in through the windows so that tiny rainbows were reflected from the mirrored walls. It made the room warm and welcoming and for a moment Diana felt bathed in magic.

She removed her shoes, tossed them after her hat, and began to twirl about. Her skirts flared out to reveal her legs, her hair cascading about her shoulders in wild disarray.

Dame Lightfoot, about to reenter the studio, paused rigid on the threshold. She stared at Diana for a full minute, then lowered her corseted form to the piano stool and began to play.

Diana did not so much hear the music as feel it. She swirled about madly, matching her movements to the tempo of the music, which went ever faster. She could feel the rhythm in her blood as she gyrated sensually, enjoying it deeply, until she could feel the heartbeats in her throat and the soles of her feet. With a crescendo she fell to her knees and allowed her glorious hair to sweep the floor. Then she opened her eyes and laughed up into the face of the dragon.

The dragon said slowly, "You are a free spirit who has been caged up too long. Your body has a fluidity I haven't seen in years."

Breathlessly, Diana said, "If I weren't wearing this restrictive corset, I could really dance!"

Dame Lightfoot was silent for another minute, then she said, "Why don't we both remove our corsets? Mine is killing me! You can use that dressing room over there."

A surprised Diana was not loath to do the dame's bidding. Inside the dressing room, Diana's eyes widened. Dozens of costumes were hanging on racks. Every color and material the mind could conjure was there, some sequined, some feathered. Diana reached out a hand to caress the irresistible creations, thinking they were dance attire or stage costumes for some theatre. Perhaps Dame Lightfoot was not the old martinet she had thought.

Diana removed her corset, then slipped back into her

gown. She had always longed to make herself a costume; perhaps Dame Lightfoot could help.

It was Diana's turn to pause upon the threshold. The dragon no longer resembled a dragon. She had removed the iron-gray wig to reveal jet-black curls, and now that her corset was removed, her breasts were voluptuous. In fact she no longer looked old. Diana decided she wasn't young either; what she looked was ageless. "Dame Lightfoot—"

"Oh please, call me Allegra."

Diana blinked. Even her voice had taken on a provocative, throaty quality. "Allegra is a beautiful name, cleverly adapted from a musical term."

"Indeed. All my intimates call me Allegra."

"The costumes in the dressing room fascinate me!"

"Try one on," Allegra urged.

"Oh, I shall, thank you. I'll try them all, if I may. But I've been toying with the idea of creating my own. Would you help me?"

"I should be delighted. What strikes your fancy?"

"Diana, Goddess of the Hunt."

"But of course! And what a perfect Diana you will make."

"I picture a white tunic that bares one shoulder," Diana said with much daring, although the goddess would probably have bared one breast.

"Short also," Allegra agreed, "to show off your lovely long legs."

"A golden bow and arrow," Diana added with enthusiasm.

"And gilt sandals with golden ribbons to crisscross up your calves, and your own glorious golden hair, unpowdered, to cascade down your back."

"Golden amulets on my upper arms," Diana added, carried away by the picture they were creating.

Allegra, her head on one side to observe the beautiful girl, alive with animated enthusiasm, said thoughtfully,

"The new Pantheon in Oxford Street is to be opened by a masquerade ball. How would you like to attend?"

"I should love it, but of course it's out of the question. Prudence would think it far too worldly for an unmarried lady."

"Mmm," was all Allegra murmured.

"But I'd still like the costume," Diana insisted.

"Well, let's teach you the steps to all the dances this afternoon, then tomorrow when you come we can devote the afternoon to creating the huntress!"

Diana had such an enjoyable time at Allegra's the following day, she regretted she could not also go on Wednesday. But Wednesdays from now on would be devoted to that holy shrine of the ton known as Almack's.

Prudence chose a gown in the fashionable shade called pomona, an apple green taffeta that emphasized her embonpoint. She beamed such approval at her niece's appearance, it made Diana doubt her attraction. This was her first ball gown and the corset and three petticoats made it feel most restrictive. Prudence had let her make the final choice of color. *Fat choice, allowing me to choose between prissy pink and baby blue,* thought Diana. The gown had a high neckline with rows of tiny frills covering the entire yoke. How ironic that the corset flattened her breasts to such a degree she needed the frills as a bust enhancer.

As she picked up her Kashmir shawl and followed Prudence out to the carriage, Diana admitted to a certain amount of excitement at her debut into society. Her excitement was soon dampened when Prudence took the opportunity of the carriage ride to catalog her rigid rules and regulations. Her aunt concluded, "You must not attract the wrong sort of man under any circumstances. You must be protected from both fortune hunters and rakes at all costs."

Anyone listening would have thought Prudence wished only to protect Diana, but had they been able to read her thoughts, they would have been quickly disabused of the notion. *She is so lovely she will attract a peer of the first*

*water, then Richard and I won't get a smell of her money. I
shall have to watch her like a hawk and discourage any
titled, wealthy suitors. It's a good thing wigs are in fashion,
her beautiful blond hair is enough to take a man's breath
away!*

The coachman knew better than to even drive along St.
James's Street when the ladies were in the carriage, so he
took the circuitous route down Duke to King Street.

There was such a crush at Almack's that there was
actually a line outside. Prudence was most flattered when
Lady Melbourne greeted her. She had her daughter Emily
and her son William Lamb in tow. William immediately
moved close to Diana.

"May I have the first dance, Lady Davenport?"

"Of course you may, sir." It was so ridiculous that she
could not call him William when she had known the
chinless boy all her life. She wrote his name on her dance
card as they entered the foyer and was much relieved to
hear Prudence say, "You young people run along and enjoy
yourselves. My hip doesn't allow me the pleasure of dancing."

Diana joined a group of her friends who were also
making their debut tonight. Hary-O Devonshire, younger
sister of Georgiana, Penelope Crewe, and Fanny Damer had
been brought by their hopeful mothers in expectation of
popping them off in marriage to a wealthy and titled husband. They had been well schooled to employ artifice and
cunning in duping the opposite sex, for all women knew
they must deploy force even though their fathers were willing to pay vast amounts of money for their matrimonial
settlements.

Diana's dance card was filling rapidly. Young Earl
Cowper, rich as Croesus and owner of a Gothic castle in
Hertford, made no bones about fancying Diana, but her
common sense told her his parents would aspire to marriage with the daughter of a duke. *Heaven be praised,* she
thought thankfully.

Caro Ponsonby joined them and Diana decided the young woman always hovered on the brink of hysteria. Her laugh was too loud and she had an intensity about her that was unnatural. "Whoever is that dashing fellow in the Foot Guard uniform?" Caro asked Diana.

"Some young dog with a pedigree, I'll be bound. There are three hundred Foot Guards but only half a dozen have been honored with vouchers." Diana didn't bother to even turn around as she uttered her disparaging assessment, so she missed the pair of striking, dark eyes as they searched the room and then widened ever so slightly as they looked her way.

Peter Hardwick was trying to decide which of the young ladies in the group was Lady Diana Davenport. His experience had taught him the larger the fortune, the plainer the heiress. So the gorgeous creature with the sensual body was obviously not in the running. His gaze wandered about until it settled on a creature with a face like a lump of dough with figure to match. He'd lay odds of ten-to-one she was his target. His courage almost failed him. No wonder his elder brother, the earl, had always joked that Peter would have to be the one to take a bride and beget the heir. But then his dear brother could afford to be cynical about women and marriage. Peter Hardwick could not!

With resolution, he walked a straight path toward the suet pudding, made a leg, and inquired, "Lady Diana?"

A female voice came from behind him. "Yes?"

Peter turned and gazed into violet eyes. He held his breath lest the vision vanish. Nonchalance was an art with Peter Hardwick. "May I have this dance?" he asked smoothly.

"I'm afraid not, sir. I have a partner," Diana informed him.

"Then the next one," Peter pressed.

"My dance card is filled, I'm afraid." Diana's eyes sparkled with amusement and a little regret.

"I don't believe you; let me see," Peter insisted.

Diana did not take offense. She laughed up into his attractive face and presented him with her card.

He immediately wrote his name over the top of two of her partners and gave it back to her.

Diana's lips twitched as she read *Hardwick* written in a bold hand. "Hard cheese," she punned, refusing him.

"Hardwick, darling. Peter Hardwick," he murmured, narrowing his eyes in appreciation.

"Hardface!" Diana replied, reprimanding him for the endearment.

"Among other things," he murmured outrageously. When Diana was at a loss for his meaning, he realized what he should have known all along. Lady Diana Davenport was a virgin. His blood thickened at the thought. Here was unlooked-for sport!

She spied William Lamb coming to collect her. "Here's my partner now."

Peter grinned cruelly. "You cannot prefer that chinless wonder to myself."

Diana examined him frankly for a moment. "Actually, I do." She took William's arm and left Peter Hardwick standing alone. *In a pig's eye!* a voice inside her head protested.

Chapter 3

Over chocolate the next morning Prudence quizzed Diana
endlessly for all the minutiae of her evening. "Let me see
your dance card."

"Er . . . I didn't keep it," Diana prevaricated.

"Didn't keep the memento of your debut at Almack's?" Prudence was scandalized.

"It was quite full. I danced with William Lamb, Lord
Ashley, Lord Granville . . . oh yes, and Peter."

"Peter Hardwick?" Prudence asked avidly.

"No, Peter Cowper."

Prudence was alarmed. Not one dance with Hardwick!
And after she and Richard had him eating out of their
hands. She must say something disparaging to put Diana off
Cowper. "A rather heavy young man."

Diana thought that was the pot calling the kettle black.
"You mentioned Peter Hardwick? Do you know him?" she
asked her aunt casually.

"Er . . . Richard is handling some estate business for
him."

"Oh, I see," Diana replied.

"Did you dance with him?"

"No."

"Did he ask you?" Prudence probed.

"Yes," Diana admitted.

"Then why in the world didn't you dance with him? He's a most respectable young man."

"Indeed?" Diana's lips twitched in remembrance.

"I cannot believe you turned him down!"

"Actually, I wasn't confident enough with my dancing. It didn't matter with William and the others, they seem so young, but Peter Hardwick was different."

Prudence let out a sigh of relief. Diana was definitely attracted. "What you need is more time with Dame Lightfoot."

"Oh, I agree, Prudence. I have a lesson this afternoon. Can you spare Bridget?"

Diana stood mesmerized in the mirrored room. The white tunic felt light as thistledown. Its skirt, made from gauze scarves, fell in points about her thighs. One shoulder was daringly bared, setting off the golden amulets to perfection. A small gilt arrow case was strapped to her back and its golden laces crisscrossed beneath her breasts, emphasizing their round fullness. The sandal thongs were also crisscrossed up her calves, making her slim legs look unbelievably long. At the crown of her head a jeweled fillet held her glorious hair so that it cascaded all the way down her back to her buttocks. She not only looked like a goddess, she actually felt like one.

"The masquerade ball is Friday night," Allegra tempted.

"Oh, I couldn't," Diana refused.

Allegra handed her a winged mask made from the feathers of fantailed doves. When she put it on, she realized that no one would ever recognize her. The seed that Allegra had planted suddenly sprouted. "Will you go with me? However shall I get away from Prudence Friday night?"

"Leave all to me." Allegra waved a dismissive hand as if it were a magic wand.

* * *

When Diana arrived back in Grosvenor Square, the hall table held half-a-dozen calling cards. She skimmed through them quickly looking for a certain name. Her cheeks took on a delicate hue when she found it. When Prudence handed her a nosegay of rosebuds and sweetpeas, her color deepened. "Peter Hardwick, how charming," she said casually, masking her pleasure.

"Rather presumptuous," Prudence remarked shrewdly, hoping Diana would jump to his defense. She was disappointed when Diana agreed with her.

"Yes, he is." She buried her nose in the flowers to inhale their heavenly fragrance.

The next morning Dame Lightfoot paid a call upon Prudence. Her whalebone corset made her as rigid as her ebony-topped cane, lending her the appearance of a dowager duchess. Diana kept her face perfectly straight as she listened with awe.

"Both Lady Melbourne and Lady Bessborough have requested that I give their daughters extra lessons in the hope that they will outshine my other pupils who are making their debuts. However, my code prevents me from being aught but scrupulously fair to all my young ladies. To that end I ask your permission to allow Diana to come to my studio on Friday evening."

"Your ethics are to be commended, Dame Lightfoot." Diana cleared her throat to prevent herself from choking.

"I shall accompany you, Diana. You cannot be out after dark without me."

"I'll take the carriage," Diana offered quickly, "and Bridget shall accompany me. I wouldn't dream of having you sit for hours waiting for me."

Prudence glanced uncertainly toward Dame Lightfoot.

Her code was strict enough to set the standard for what was, and was not, respectable.

"My other young ladies will arrive by carriage. A maid is sufficient chaperon." The dragon had spoken.

When Prudence capitulated, Dame Lightfoot stood to leave. She inclined her head stiffly toward her pupil. "Until tomorrow."

Diana repeated gravely, "Until tomorrow," but inside her, excitement bubbled like frothy champagne!

When Diana arrived at the Shepherd Market studio, she left Biddy with James, the coachman. She was aware they were attracted to each other in spite of the fact that they had to pretend otherwise under the watchful eye of Prudence.

Allegra was radiant in a vivid shade of pinky purple, fashionably known as amaranthus. Diana was happy to see that Dame Lightfoot had been banished for the evening along with her iron-gray wig and whalebone. "Come in, darling," Allegra said. "I was just putting the finishing touches on the old physiog."

When Diana emerged from the dressing room in costume, she watched Allegra in fascination as she outlined her eyes with kohl. "May I try some of the lip salve?"

"Yes, do. Put a little sandalwood rouge on your cheekbones too. I know your mask will cover everything except your lips, but I think a little *maquillage* gives a woman confidence in her charms."

Diana was thrilled with the results of her handiwork and, as a finishing touch, boldly painted her eyelids with silvery violet.

"Voilà! A goddess down to your fingertips," Allegra declared, placing Diana's long cloak about her protégée's shoulders. "We can take your carriage if your servants are discreet."

"We have a mutual understanding," she assured Allegra, who picked up a large ostrich-feather fan, dyed dark purple. Small fans were the fashion, but Diana had to admit Allegra's fan was spectacular. It bespoke a language all its own.

"Oxford Street," Diana told James, as Biddy scurried to hold open the carriage door, unable to keep from staring at Allegra.

The traffic along Oxford Street was backed up all the way to Bond Street. Carriages trying to get close to the Pantheon clogged all the main arteries. "We'll walk from here," Diana decided, rapping on the coach ceiling. "You can have the carriage, Biddy. Be back at Shepherd's Market by ten thirty." Diana fastened her mask in place before she quit the carriage, then she and Allegra stepped out into the throng.

Everyone in London who was anyone was making his way to the Pantheon tonight. They managed to push their way through the crowd until they came up against a large group of gentlemen escorting a sedan chair and holding aloft lighted torches. Allegra touched the arm of one of the gentlemen in evening clothes. He gave her a familiar grin. "Hello, Allegra. Come to watch the fireworks?"

"What are you up to, Sir Charles?" she drawled.

"We got wind that actresses were not to be admitted, so we are giving Mrs. Baddeley our personal escort; a guard of honor so to speak."

"Anything for a lark, eh, Charlie?"

When Diana looked puzzled, Allegra explained, "Sophia Baddeley, who sings at Ranelagh, is Viscount Melbourne's current mistress. His friends are making sure she receives a triumphant welcome."

Diana's mouth almost fell open. Emily and William's father had a mistress? "Lady Melbourne is as straightlaced as Prudence," Diana whispered.

Allegra winked. "There's your answer, my pet. It pays a woman to be flexible and pliant—not quite loose, but accommodating at least."

Diana's thoughts progressed from Prudence to Richard. Could he possibly be unfaithful? After contemplating the notion for a full minute, a giggle escaped her. *He'd be a bloody fool if he wasn't!*

As they made their way along Oxford Street, Diana noticed that all the gentlemen were on familiar terms with Allegra. She recognized both Lord Bute and Lord March, whom Diana had always considered respectable pillars of society. Apparently there was a double standard of behavior.

Allegra poked William Hangar, an intimate of the Prince of Wales, in the ribs. "Sophia enters society, or is it the other way about?"

The men surrounding them roared with laughter at Allegra's bawdy wit, and Diana wondered if perhaps it was only the life of a debutante that was staid and suffocating.

Porters in livery stood at the entrance to the Pantheon, their long staves at the ready to bar the entrance of any undesirables. When the gentlemen championing Sophia Baddeley whipped out their swords in unison, the porters fled. Then to the delight of all assembled, the actress made her grand entrance under the arch made by the crossed swords of her gallants.

Inside was every bit as much of a crush as outside. When a footman relieved Diana of her long cloak, she felt very wicked indeed. It was an absolutely delicious sensation. She received more stares than the eccentric Countess of Cork, who was dressed as an Indian sultana with her face painted dark and wearing a headdress of diamonds.

Cumberland, the wicked uncle of the Prince of Wales, was dressed as Henry the Eighth, and Sir Richard Phillips was resplendent in black and white—half miller, half chimney sweep. As Diana stared and was stared at in return, she realized that everyone wanted attention and she was no exception. People had outdone themselves with their costumes. Every age in history was represented from Restoration to Elizabethan to ancient Greece. Cupid stood next to a lady who looked as if she had just stepped from King Arthur's court of Camelot. The whole room was a mass of swirling color and glittering lights. Diana decided happily it was the most fun she'd ever had.

The Earl of Bath, in town on business, was between mistresses at the moment. He had no illusions about himself and was the first to admit he was both jaded and cynical. The image of his younger brother Peter flashed briefly through his mind. Thank God he could rely on him to uphold the good name of Hardwick. The earl himself had no intention of ever getting trapped by society into marrying and having a family. He knew he was self-indulgent and had the reputation of a rake, but women were attracted by his title alone, so when his wealth was added, the fair sex panted after him like bitches in heat. Had he but known it, his dark dangerous looks accounted for his sexual congress.

The earl had jet black eyes and hair to match, which he refused to powder or cover with a wig. The slight hook in his aristocratic nose lent him the profile of a raptor. Seeking diversion, he surveyed the crowded room for worthy quarry. His dark gaze did not linger upon any female who cast him an invitation; he was a man who did his own choosing for better or for worse.

Bath had not been part of Sophia Baddeley's escort, but had arrived alone from his town house in Jermyn Street. He felt only contempt for those of his peers who were slaves to their vices of gambling, drink, or debauched women. He prided himself on always being in control. But he came very near to slipping when he glimpsed the glorious creature who was surely dressed as Diana, Goddess of the Hunt. His attention was caught and held by this unknown woman who was in the company of the notorious Allegra. He watched in silence as the young beauty threw back her head in appreciative laughter. She had an unaffected quality that lured him closer in spite of her obvious youth.

Unaware of the speculative eyes upon her, Diana was overcome with mirth at the wickedly amusing remarks of Allegra. They were discussing at this very moment one of the more peculiar guests of the ball. When people backed away from the Countess of Cork, appearing here in the Arabian costume of a sultana, Diana said innocently, "She may be eccentric, but surely she's harmless?"

"Actually she's deadly," Allegra drawled. "Punctuates her speech with farts. Her rectal repertoire is amazing. Move over so you can listen."

As Diana bent her ear in the direction of the sultana, she heard her say to Cumberland, "Time they passed the Regency Bill; King's as mad as a damned hatter!!!" Sure enough, the duchess punctuated her sentence with a loud cannonade of exclamation points.

As Diana hastily backed off, Allegra rolled her eyes and wafted the ostrich-feather fan languidly but effectively. Laughing helplessly, she asked, "What advice would Dame Lightfoot give her pupils on the subject of farts?"

Allegra's face took on the stiff countenance of Dame Lightfoot. "The noises are unmentionable, acknowledged by neither the offender nor the victim."

Diana had to lift her mask to wipe away her tears of mirth.

As she did so, the Earl of Bath caught a glimpse of violet eyes that nearly took his breath away. He had been stalking his prey with the confidence of a jungle cat. When he was within striking distance, he reached out with powerful hands to encircle Diana's waist, then lifted her up onto a low platform that stood behind her. "A goddess deserves to stand on a pedestal," he said lightly.

Diana gasped as the dark stranger laid hands upon her. He was so tall she was only slightly elevated above him. She stared down into black eyes that were blatantly assessing her scantily clad charms.

"Introduce us, Allegra," he ordered.

"Not a chance, you audacious devil. She is not a morsel to be devoured by your voracious appetite."

"I promise to savor her. Like a fine wine, I shall sip, hold her on my tongue, then taste her again and again, taking all night to slake my thirst."

Allegra was speechless. She could hardly expose Lady Diana Davenport's identity to the Earl of Bath.

Diana was anything but speechless. Her anger ignited and blazed forth, loosening her tongue in the process. "You lecherous swine! Slake your thirst elsewhere!" Her foot shot out, kicking him on the top of his shin. Alas, her golden sandals offered no protection when her toes struck solid bone and muscle. "Ouch!" she cried.

The earl deftly took hold of her foot, amused that she had suffered the pain she had intended to inflict upon him. With her foot firmly in his hand, his eyes slowly traveled up the contour of her long leg.

Outraged, she snatched an arrow from its gilt case and jabbed it into the hand holding her foot. When he didn't let go, she gave him a second jab, which was more savage. This time he loosened his grip, but proceeded to slide his hand all the way up to her thigh before he removed it.

Diana's face blushed scarlet beneath the mask. Suddenly she was afraid of the powerful male who was handling her body as if she were on display for his personal pleasure. Desperately she looked for Allegra, but that lady was nowhere to be seen. The platform was overcrowded with females in varying costumes. A ballet dancer was pressed up against a shepherdess, who was in turn being elbowed aside by an angel.

Diana looked down into a sea of men's faces, all laughing, leering, and shouting at the fellow dressed as Cupid. Suddenly she wasn't so sure she should be here in this provocative costume. It had seemed such a daring escapade earlier, but now she questioned the wisdom of coming to the Pantheon in disguise or otherwise. Perhaps the place was too worldly for an unmarried lady of her tender years.

The Earl of Bath couldn't take his eyes from the golden-haired girl in front of him. Obviously she was a demirep, but she was so young, she couldn't have been on the game long. He was usually attracted to older women of experience, but this wonderful vision had a natural beauty whose freshness and vitality were somehow a potent lure tonight. Then and there he made up his mind to have her! He raised his hand several times to Cupid as did the other men all about him.

The angel beside Diana reached over and plucked off her winged mask. "This would be perfect with my costume. Do you mind?"

"Of course I bloody well mind," Diana said, aghast that someone might recognize her. "Go play your stupid harp on some other cloud!" she said, grabbing back the mask to cover her identity. Then she looked down into jet black eyes as she felt herself being lifted from the platform.

"What the devil are you doing?" she demanded as her feet found the floor.

He grinned down at her. "I've just bought you, Diana."

"What the hell are you talking about?" she gasped in a total panic because he called her by name, then she realized he was using the goddess's name.

"The auction—Cupid there is auctioning off all the young nymphs on the platform and I just paid the winning bid for you."

"But that is impossible!" she protested, horrified.

"It's for charity, my sweet. It's all for a good cause, I assure you." Smooth as silk, the Earl of Bath lifted two glasses of champagne from the silver tray of a liveried servant passing by and placed one in her hand. "Let's both slake our thirsts tonight."

His deep voice was so dangerously seductive, it affected her in a strange way that shocked her. The suggestive things he said, coupled with the resonant tone, made her body tingle in all its most private places. Close to panic, Diana threw the contents of the champagne glass into his face and fled.

Chapter 4

At the door she saw Allegra had already retrieved her cloak in anticipation of an early escape. Diana covered her costume quickly. "I should never have come."

"Oh, don't go all respectable on me, darling; time for that tomorrow in the cold light of day!"

As they made their way toward Grosvenor Square, Diana began to laugh. "Sorry. Actually I was having the time of my life until that loathsome man forced his attentions upon me!"

"That loathsome man was the Earl of Bath," Allegra drawled.

"Oh lord, and I threw champagne in his face!"

"I daresay that dampened his ardor."

"Thank heavens I was disguised," Diana said with fervor.

As they turned down North Audley Street toward Grosvenor Square, a black carriage halted beside them. The door opened and a powerful hand plucked Diana from the pavement and deposited her against the velvet squabs of the shadowed interior.

Diana screamed.

"Don't be alarmed, we are acquainted, and before the night is over I daresay we shall be on even more intimate terms."

Diana recognized the voice, which only increased her fear. "How dare you accost me? What the devil do you want?"

"I simply want my money's worth, *chérie.*" He paused, then drawled, "And perhaps an apology for the champagne."

"Me apologize to you?" Diana demanded in outrage. "You are the one who should apologize for touching my leg!"

"I'm sorry I touched your leg—I would have much preferred caressing your breast."

Diana gasped. She not only feared him, but was beginning to fear herself and her reaction to this dangerous man. She felt a magnetic attraction to him, yet knew she must repel him at all costs. Then she realized the carriage was moving and she gasped again. "Where are you taking me?"

"My town house. It isn't far."

"Sir, you can *not!* You have mistaken me for a . . . a cyprian. I am actually a lady in disguise," Diana confessed.

He laughed. The sound was rich and dark and enveloping. "I don't think so."

"Why would you say such a thing?"

He struck a match and lit a carriage light. His face was half shadowed, but hers was bathed in the glow of the lamp. "You are certainly lovely enough to be a lady and your voice is quite cultured, but it rather gave the game away when you were accompanied by Allegra. She runs one of the finest riding academies in London. She supplies half the aristocracy with mounts."

For a moment she wondered what he was talking about, but when it dawned upon her that he meant Allegra was a procurist, she blushed to her navel.

He saw the color suffuse her face and knew a need to see the beauty he had only glimpsed beneath the mask. The carriage was drawing up at Jermyn Street, however, and he decided to let her keep her mask in place until they were safely inside.

When he offered her his hand, she said in outrage, "I cannot come into your town house!"

"Ah, at last the light is beginning to dawn. You know who I am and are determined to get the highest possible price."

"No! Yes—that is, I do know who you are . . ."

A cynical smile curved his lips. "Then come up while we negotiate."

A blazing wave of anger swept over her. She had never encountered such an arrogant male in her life. He needed a set-down and she intended to give him one. She began to hastily form a plan.

Like a goddess, Diana gave him her hand and allowed him to assist her to alight. He unlocked the door and waved back the majordomo, who melted into the shadows when he saw the earl was not alone. Her abductor gestured toward the staircase and Diana swept up to the first floor as if she were ascending Olympus, giving the man behind her a full look at her shapely legs.

While the earl lit the lamps in the magnificently appointed sitting room, Diana walked slowly around assessing the furnishings with a critical eye. She glanced at the linen-fold paneling, the rich leather wingbacks, the Van Dyke paintings, and declared, "Rather masculine."

"I should hope so," he said in an amused tone. He went to a Sheraton wine table and poured them two glasses.

"What a courageous man you are," Diana said, eyeing the wine.

"I am gambling that you won't throw a second one." He could no longer conceal his amusement, nor his anticipation.

"You may lose that bet," she warned lightly.

She took a sip, eyeing him over the rim of her glass, then said, "So this is how it is done." She lowered her lashes. "You may open negotiations."

He quirked a black brow. "Are you sure this is your first time?"

"The first time I've been propositioned or the first time I've considered taking a paramour?" Diana was aghast at her own daring, but her inner she-devil was driving her.

He saw her eyes glitter through the mask and knew she was thoroughly enjoying herself. He grew marble-hard thinking about the sport she would provide in bed. He could almost feel her long legs slide up his back. "I'll pay your dress bills and provide you with a ladies' maid," he offered.

Diana set the wine down. "You are wasting both my time and your own."

The earl picked up the glass and handed it back to her. "I'll lease you a *pied-à-terre,* and provide you with your own carriage," he added as an inducement.

Diana licked her lips. Hardwick felt his shaft pulse.

"Your offer"—she paused dramatically—"is insulting," she finished.

Some of the casual amusement left his eyes and was replaced by an intense look of desire. "You play the game very well, little goddess. I am prepared to buy you a house —if you please me in every way."

Diana ran the tip of her finger around the rim of the glass. "Did I hear you say *carte blanche,* my lord?" She was almost carried away by a delicious feeling of power.

"Goddamn it, you strike a hard bargain!" He stared at her for long minutes, his expression grim as his mind argued with his body. His body won.

"*Carte blanche* it is," he agreed, a look of triumph in his eyes.

Diana poured her wine into a vase of lilies. "*Carte blanche* it isn't, I'm afraid."

"What the devil do you mean?"

"I mean *no*. My answer is *no*."

"Why?" he demanded.

Diana looked him up and down. "Because you are too

arrogant, too cocksure, and far, far too old for me, Lord Bath.''

Mark Hardwick, the Earl of Bath, was stunned.

''Don't bother to show me out, I know my way about the streets very well.''

Without even being aware of it, Hardwick crushed the wineglass he was holding.

Lady Diana found her carriage waiting at the corner of Grosvenor Square. When she rapped on the door, it took a few minutes before a disheveled James scrambled out.

Inside Diana threw off her cloak. She was breathless from the deliciously close encounter she had just experienced with the virile earl. When he had made it plain that he desired her, she was filled with a wicked pleasure. ''Quickly, help me off with my costume,'' she begged Biddy. ''How in the world will I get back into my bloody corset in this cramped space?''

Biddy replied blandly, ''It's a bit of a struggle, but it can be managed. Trust me, my lady.''

Early the next morning Diana bathed and washed her hair, making sure every last trace of *maquillage* was erased.

Prudence, chocolate cup in hand, surveyed her with dismay. ''You've washed your head! How tiresome. Hurry and get your hair dried. I accepted an invitation for you to ride in Hyde Park this afternoon.''

''With whom?'' Diana demanded, feeling annoyed at the control Prudence always exercised over her.

''With Peter Hardwick, of course. He has been most punctilious in paying his calls. I must say his manners are impeccable. Which is only as it should be.''

Diana was somewhat mollified when she heard the name and decided the library fire would be ideal to dry her hair. While pacing impatiently in front of the roaring flames, her eyes traveled over the titles of the leather-bound volumes, searching for something that would sweep her away to another time and place. She chose *The Legend of King Arthur* and curled up before the fire in a spacious wingback chair to read.

As always, Diana's imagination took flight. She was transported back to where the swirling mists revealed the earthly paradise known as Avalon. Diana had no notion of time, but all at once she became aware of the fact that she was no longer alone. With reluctance, she lifted her eyes from her book and peered over the top of the wing chair. She withdrew her head immediately like a turtle retreating into his shell, her thoughts in complete disarray.

Except for the crackle of the fire, silence blanketed the room. Diana raised her head to see if her imagination was playing tricks on her. She looked directly into a pair of jet black eyes!

The eyes widened slightly in surprise before they glittered with animosity. "Diana discovered," he sneered.

"How did you find me?" she hissed in outrage.

"I assure you I was not searching. Fate is taking perverse pleasure, throwing you in my path."

"What are you doing here?" she demanded, snapping closed her book and advancing toward him in an aggressive manner.

"I fail to see where it is any of your business, but I'm here to consider buying a library."

His words halted her advance. "Not *this* library?"

"*This* library." His deep voice clipped off the words, clearly showing his irritation.

"That is impossible. This library is not for sale. You have been misinformed, Lord Bath."

He was annoyed that the girl knew his identity without him knowing hers. "Who the devil do you think you are?"

"I am Lady Diana Davenport, the owner of this library."

"Hello, Diana," Richard said, entering the book-lined

room. "I had no idea you were in here, m'dear. Sorry to disturb you."

"Richard, I am more than disturbed. This . . . gentleman is under the misapprehension that I am selling my library."

"I understood the library was *yours* to sell, Davenport," Lord Bath said bluntly.

"Then you understood wrongly, my lord," Diana interjected. "My late father's collection is priceless, at least to me. It is *not* for sale." She glared at Bath, defying him to inform her uncle about last night in retaliation.

The earl had no such petty intent. He spoke to her as an equal. "You are quite right about the worth of this library. I understand perfectly your reluctance to part with it. I thought Davenport had the legal right to dispose of it." His voice was smooth and unruffled yet more than a trifle regretful.

"I *do* have the legal right to dispose of it," Richard asserted. "I am the executor of my late brother's will and my niece's legal guardian and financial counselor until she comes of age. My brother intended that Lady Diana be guided by me in all things."

"How could you even think of selling Father's books?" Diana demanded passionately. "I've grown up surrounded by them. They are part of my life. It would be like cutting off my arm to part with them!"

"Enough theatrics, Diana. It is most ill-bred of you to argue family matters before his lordship." Richard was taken off-guard. Diana had never defied him before.

"Heaven forbid that anyone should act ill-bred in front of the earl!" She could still feel the heat from his ill-bred hand sliding up her leg.

"Leave the room!" Richard was livid.

With flags flying in both cheeks, Diana lifted her chin in the air, flicked aside her skirts as if they would be contaminated if they touched the men, and departed with the *hauteur* of a queen. *Or a goddess,* thought Bath.

*   *   *

When Diana entered the dining room at lunchtime, she fully expected both Richard and Prudence would call her to task over her shocking display of bad manners. She braced herself for the confrontation. Richard, however, was conspicuous by his absence and Prudence was tight-lipped from what appeared to be pain.

Diana was moved to compassion immediately. "Is it your hip, Prudence?"

"Among other things," Prudence accused.

Damn the Earl of Bath to hellfire, thought Diana. At every encounter sparks flew between them, igniting emotions that threatened to consume them. If he hadn't treated her like a trollop last night, none of this would have happened. She would still not have allowed Richard to sell her father's library to him, but she would have at least spoken to the earl in a civilized manner.

Prudence refused to make conversation. Her face was tight with pain, which she was determined to suffer in silence. Diana's lunch was quite ruined. She excused herself to dress for her afternoon ride in the park. She hadn't been sure she wanted to go, but Peter Hardwick's company would be a welcome diversion.

As Diana descended the staircase in an afternoon gown of delicate green carrying a matching pistache parasol, Prudence inquired, "Where are you going, Diana?"

"For a drive in the park with Peter Hardwick. You accepted the invitation for me."

"What makes you think he'll keep the engagement after your appalling manners to Lord Hardwick?"

"Peter isn't a lord," Diana corrected, wondering how Prudence had discovered she had been flippant with him.

"I was speaking of Mark Hardwick, the Earl of Bath."

Diana was stunned. "Peter's brother is the Earl of Bath?"

"Please don't pretend ignorance of the Hardwicks, Diana. You are far too intelligent to play the lack-wit."

"I honestly didn't connect the two gentlemen. I hadn't the vaguest notion Peter Hardwick was related to the earl."

"That is the sole reason I consider young Hardwick an eligible *parti*. It was he who informed the earl about the library."

At that precise moment Peter Hardwick rang the front doorbell. "Oh lord, what will I do?" Diana said, half under her breath.

"Consider yourself one of the most fortunate young ladies in London since he has chosen to overlook your lack of breeding and honor the invitation."

A half hour later, Diana found herself seated next to Peter Hardwick enjoying the fresh air of a beautiful London day.

The blooded pair harnessed to the perch phaeton were impressive animals. Diana made polite small talk as Peter tooled the horses the short distance to Hyde Park. She wondered what he was thinking and what his brother had said about her.

Peter Hardwick, in point of fact, was thinking what a lucky bastard he was. Not only had Diana Davenport exquisite beauty, but she had a yearly income of twenty thousand pounds. The *Vultures,* as he called Richard and Prudence, had only offered him half but he had shrewdly negotiated his cut up to sixty percent, and before he was done, he'd have at least fifteen thousand per annum. Then once he got the ring on Diana's finger, there was nothing to prevent him from dipping into the principal. His eyes ran over her profile with appreciation; what a prize she was.

Diana, feeling his eyes upon her, could bear the tension no longer. She took a deep breath and turned toward him. "I'm afraid I have a confession to make."

His mouth curved good-naturedly, giving the impression he could be indulgent with a woman.

"I attended the masquerade at the Pantheon last night," she said breathlessly. When her companion didn't seem outraged, she continued, "Your brother mistook me for a cyprian because I wasn't properly chaperoned and I'm afraid I threw champagne in his face."

Peter threw back his head and laughed aloud at the picture she painted.

Encouraged, Diana told him the second part. "I have to be perfectly frank, Peter—I'm afraid your brother must hate me. When he turned up in my library this morning trying to buy it, I flew at him in a temper."

"I imagine you are very beautiful when angered."

She looked at him in disbelief. "Aren't you outraged?"

"There are times when I find my dear brother almost loathsome. We have little in common. He has a passion for archaelogy. His inclination to ruins has given him a taste for older women. I'm surprised you captured his interest."

He certainly captured mine, Diana admitted to herself. Why didn't his young brother arouse any feeling inside her?

Diana laughed in spite of herself. Their conversation was most unconventional to say the least. "Well, I thwarted his intent to buy my father's collection, so I'm certain he considers me much worse than loathsome."

"That's a relief. His competition for your attention would be formidable, as he is an earl of the realm."

"I don't care about titles!"

He cocked an eyebrow at her. "What *do* you care about?"

She cared about books, passionately. She would even like to try her hand at writing history, from a woman's point of view, but she had more sense than to tell a gentleman such an eccentric thing. Diana opened her parasol, trying to decide if she should scramble back on to polite ground as befitted a young lady of the ton, or to answer his question honestly. She decided upon the latter. She had certainly not set her cap for this man, and if he found her conversation unconventional, she didn't give a tinker's damn! "I care most about freedom—freedom of choice. I find I have very little freedom now in dress, speech, action, or even thought because I am young and because I am female. I realize I will become older, but I shall remain a woman forever."

"Heaven be praised," he teased, allowing his eyes to boldly assess her delicious breasts. "You'd prefer being a man?"

"Of course not! I want to be a woman with freedom. Only think for a moment: in Georgian society a young lady is passed from her father to either a guardian or a husband and chaperoned every waking moment. Prudence would be in the phaeton with us if it held more than two, but the code is so restrictive I may only ride with you around and around the Serpentine, where there are at least a thousand eyes upon us and hundreds of wagging tongues ready to carry tales if I do not conform."

"Would you like to go somewhere more private?" Peter suggested hopefully.

"No, I would not. You are missing the point, deliberately I might add," Diana said with amusement.

"I'm sorry. I really am listening."

"Celtic women had great freedom. They chose whom they married and were allowed to retain their own wealth and property. A few even became chiefs of tribes. Medieval women were in charge of castles and the entire *demesne* when their men went to war or on crusade for years. Modern ladies are treated as if they have no desires, no opinions, and no brains, while gentlemen are encouraged to achieve, to enjoy, to travel the world, to engage in sports, and do it all with neck-or-nothing enthusiasm!"

"I hereby promise that when you are with me I shall allow you every freedom."

Diana sighed. He was a typical male, thinking he could *allow* her freedom.

"Will you allow me to escort you to the Richmonds' ball tomorrow evening?"

"Thank you for the invitation, but I don't think so," she said coolly.

"I shan't let you escape today without a commitment of some sort."

A commitment was the last thing Diana desired. There was safety in numbers and she hoped for a couple of seasons on her own, free from a husband's control and demands. "I suppose I shall be at Almack's again on Wednesday, if Prudence has any say in the matter, and unfortunately she does," Diana said ruefully.

Peter cursed under his breath while keeping his polite mask carefully in place. Christ Almighty, the sacrifices he must make to get his debts paid off and keep him plump in the pocket were nothing short of excruciating. Ah well, Almack's it would have to be. He could not afford to let this delectable morsel escape. Though Lady Diana Davenport did not give the impression she was panting after him, he hoped her indifference was an act. In any case, he intended to get her to the altar one way or another. There was always one tried-and-true method of ensuring a lady begged for marriage, and planting his seed in this particular lady would be a very great pleasure indeed.

Peter's plans for the evening made his blood surge in anticipation. Though he was loath to ask his brother for money, he had no choice. Deciding to beard the lion in his den, Peter strolled into the library and waited for Mark to look up from a pile of business correspondence.

Without glancing up from the desk, Mark Hardwick said, "In the drawer of the library table."

Peter laughed. "What makes you think I need money?"

Mark raised his eyes. "Don't you?" he asked bluntly.

"Yes, but damned if that was going to be the first thing out of my mouth."

"Oh, I see. First you were going to commiserate with me about the Davenport library, then you were going to inquire where I intended to dine, then you were going to ask me if I got laid last night, as if you give a good goddamn. *Then* you'd get around to the subject of money." Hardwick threw down the quill and stretched. "Look at all the trouble I've saved you."

There was only a thousand in the drawer. It was his brother's way of trying to curb his gambling. Though all he felt was resentment, Peter smiled his thanks, then departed quickly to meet his friends for the planned evening of dissolution.

"Wick, you're late again!" Hellgate complained. "We have a bitch of a night planned. Aren't you eager to get started?"

Peter joined his two friends at the Prospect of Whitby, a pub in Wapping. "Oh, I believe I'm up for it," he leered.

"I ordered for you, just in case," replied Jeremy Montagu, as a barmaid served up a platter of fifty raw oysters.

The Earl of Barrymore had his hand up the wench's skirt in a flash, and when she tried playfully to slap him, he grabbed a handful of thigh and squeezed cruelly. His friends laughed; they were not known as the *Bloods* for nothing. The clutch of extroverts thought themselves daredevils. All three bucks suffered from the infection of bloodlust and the order of the night was brutality.

They made their way into the dirtiest slum in London. The streets were crawling with whores and the three friends prided themselves on choosing the most slatternly. It was an act of bravado to indulge this perverse *nostalgie de la boue* and delight in a sordid escapade in a filthy bed with an unclean whore.

* * *

At the opposite end of London, in fashionable Park Lane, the Earl of Bath followed a maid upstairs and was shown into a luxurious dressing room.

In the adjoining bedchamber Vivian, Countess of Belgrave, smiled at her reflection in the large mirror. She ran her jeweled fingers though her flame-red hair and reached for a large flacon of perfume. As she did so, the black satin wrapper slipped from one shoulder and she knew none would ever dream she was past thirty. This was only the second time Lord Hardwick had accepted her invitation, but already she knew she wanted him. Permanently.

On a sudden impulse she pushed away the perfume flacon, a wicked smile curving her lips. Allowing the black satin to fall open, she slid her hand between her legs, dipped a finger into her slippery wetness, and dabbed it behind her ears. She dipped again, this time tracing her fingertip across her breasts and up toward her white throat. Finally she dabbed behind her knees, in the small of her back, and then inside her wrists for good measure.

She opened the adjoining door and pretended surprise. "Mark, darling, you must be early—I'm not even ready."

They were both aware of the pretense, for in fact Lord Hardwick was late. "You look ready enough for me."

"We could dine here instead of going out," she suggested huskily

"I thought you'd never ask," he murmured, pushing open her bedroom door with his foot and lifting her into his arms. He laid her back on the bed, admiring the effect of her white skin and flaming hair against the black satin cover. He began to undress in a leisurely fashion, mildly surprised at how avidly she watched him. She arched against the pillows at her back and allowed her knees to fall apart in an open invitation to skip most of the preliminaries. He complied willingly, mounting her quickly this first time.

There would be ample time to savor all the nuances of sensuality later.

For the next two hours Mark Hardwick lavished attention upon Vivian. His cardinal rule with a woman was to leave her satisfied. All women were not the same in bed, thank God, and he always focused completely on a new lady to learn her needs and desires, her likes and dislikes, and to show her in no uncertain terms what it took to please and satisfy him.

He had no intention of staying all night, which was rule number two. Her reaction to this would determine how soon he would return or if he would return at all. As it turned out, Vivian was too replete to protest overmuch when he swung his legs from the bed and reached for his shirt.

"Beast! I can't lift a finger, while you're ready to prowl about London."

"Any objection?" he asked lightly, carefully watching her face.

She was far too shrewd a woman with too much at stake to object. And truthfully she had no complaints about the passionate hours they'd shared.

He bent to drop a kiss on her tussled red hair. Her body arched deliciously, her heavy eyelids closed. "Mmm," she murmured.

Hardwick smiled to himself, happy that he had left her purring.

Chapter 5

Diana stifled a yawn. She and her aunt were taking afternoon tea at Devonshire House. The room was both overcrowded and overheated. Her stays bit painfully into her breastbone and she wondered seriously if it was possible to die from boredom. Small talk was anathema to Diana and the people about her seemed to be making it their life's work. She watched the other young ladies simper before the foppish young men in their satin knee breeches while the mamas boasted their lineage.

Lady de Warrenne informed Prudence, "Our ancestry goes back to the Norman Conquest, you know."

Diana glanced at young de Warrenne juggling his quizzing glass with his snuff box and wondered regretfully how the blood could have thinned to such anemic proportions in only seven hundred years. With a polite smile fixed upon her face, Diana allowed her imagination to sweep her away. Splendor of God, how exciting it must have been for a Saxon lady to encounter a Norman conqueror!

She was riding in a meadow when she caught her first glimpse of him. He was enormous, astride a massive stallion. She shivered as she saw him mark his prey, then the chase was on! She fled toward the shelter of the forest, her pursuer more fierce-looking than any male she had ever encountered before. He was closing the distance between

*them so rapidly she could now see the nose guard on his
helm, the chain mail covering his powerful torso. Just as
she reached the trees he swooped upon her, lifted her
bodily from her palfrey, and set her before him on his saddle. In the struggle, her head veil fell off and her mass of
silken gold hair tumbled over his scarred hands.*

*"I claim you as mine!" His voice was so commanding
she wanted only to obey him. He took off his helm and ran
his hand through his dark hair. The look in his fierce eyes
was so intense with desire it took her breath away. Then his
mouth took possession of hers, mastering her with one
long, deep kiss. Her hands went up to push against the
massive chest, but he was so big, so hard, so hungry, it
made her weak at the knees. Pulse racing, breasts tingling,
she heard him demand, "Yield to me." With a delicious
sigh, Diana abandoned herself to the ravishing.*

"Yield to me," the voice came again.

Diana blinked rapidly as a pale hand tried to take the
teacup she clutched. "Oh, forgive me, William."

Young Lamb took the cup and saucer from her and
sighed. "Dare I hope you were daydreaming of me, Diana?"

"You may dare anything you like, William," she replied wickedly. If she had to endure these interminable sessions with society, she might as well have fun!

When they arrived home from Devonshire House, Prudence was surprised to be beckoned into Richard's office.

"Something's come up rather unexpectedly regarding
Peter Hardwick and it's going to take your delicate touch
with Diana."

"She's not easy to handle, Peter. The girl was actually
mocking me in the carriage just now."

"The sooner we can get her off our hands, the better,
m'dear. Hardwick is the answer to our prayers, but I'm
afraid circumstances have changed. His brother, the earl,

has ordered him home because he discovered Peter gambling. He's a tyrant apparently, but a tyrant who controls the purse strings, and Peter cannot afford to enrage him further since he's up to his eyebrows in debt.''

"He wouldn't be in debt if he controlled his gambling,'' Prudence condemned.

Richard said dryly, "If he weren't on Queer Street, m'dear, he wouldn't be aligning himself with us.''

"I take your point, Richard.''

"All you have to do is talk Diana into visiting Bath.'' He held up his hand as Prudence opened her mouth to protest. "Bath has its advantages, as young Hardwick pointed out to me.''

"You don't think he's trying to give us a slip on the shoulder, so to speak?''

"Where do you pick up these expressions, m'dear? No, I don't think any such thing. He's keen as mustard. Well, he'd have to have a few slates missing from his roof if he passed up an opportunity to get his hands on Diana's fortune, to say nothing of getting his shoes under her bed!''

"Richard, there is no need to be vulgar,'' Prudence said squeamishly. "What are the advantages?''

"Well, there are the obvious ones, of course, for a young lady of Diana's temperament. Bath has a feeling of escape from social constriction. Entertainments and activities go on round the clock, making the atmosphere conducive to *amour*. Then there is the singular advantage of Diana being invited to Hardwick Hall. It cannot fail to capture her imagination and make her long to live there. It is a fifteenth-century Elizabethan manor on the River Avon. You know how fascinated she is by anything Elizabethan.''

"I've done my homework on the Hardwicks, Richard. The earl is wealthy as Croesus. He owns stone quarries and a fleet of barges to transport the golden stone up the Avon canal to Bristol. He is a justice of Somerset and a confirmed bachelor. We have nothing to worry about exposing Diana to his 'charms.' ''

"If Mark Hardwick never marries, she could be the mother of the next Earl of Bath. I believe you should convey that vital piece of information to Diana."

"I take it the cost of a season in Bath can be deducted from Diana's money?"

"Absolutely, m'dear—perfectly legal expense."

"Then get on with leasing an elegant house in the smartest part of town and leave Diana to me."

When Diana came downstairs in a cream evening gown trimmed with pink rosebuds, the carriage was waiting to take them to Almack's.

Prudence waited until they were enclosed in its dark privacy before she broached the subject forefront in her mind. "Diana, I've had the most wonderful idea! I think we should take a lovely sojourn to Bath. We will lease a fashionable little house for a month and enjoy a holiday. Bath was on every tongue this afternoon at tea. It seems that no place in England affords so brilliant a circle of good company as Bath."

Diana couldn't believe her ears. *What maggot is eating your brain, Prudence?* "But surely our plans preclude any such thing. I've been invited to the opera, and I'm quite certain you won't want to miss the Devonshire Ball, not with Prinny as its centrepiece? No, no—we will go another time."

Prudence, momentarily speechless, saw the carriage had arrived. She would have to postpone her efforts until later.

Although Diana didn't admit it to herself, she looked forward to seeing Peter Hardwick. He arrived late and walked a direct path to her. He took her dance card and said, "We can throw this away."

"Since when did you start making my decisions?" she asked archly.

"Tonight," he murmured intimately, for her ears

alone. His glance caught and held hers—his brown eyes had a predatory gaze. "Diana, I want you to come to Bath."

Had she heard him right? Within hours she had been pressed to go to Bath twice. What an amazing coincidence —except Diana did not believe in coincidence.

She opened her fan. "You jest," she said lightly.

Peter shook his head. "For once I'm being serious. I must return to Somerset, but I don't want to leave you behind—not when I've just found you."

"Impossible," she murmured.

He swung her into the dance, and when they came together, he said, "Don't say no; please think about it." The figures of the dance caused them to separate again, but his eyes never left her.

Diana felt most flattered to receive Peter Hardwick's undivided attention. Female to her fingertips, she relished the game of pursuit, but she was determined the flirtation would go no further.

When the next dance began, he whisked her away from William Lamb. "I'll show you a fabulous time in Bath. The social mores aren't at all stuffy and regimented as they are here in London."

She could feel his warm breath playing about her ear. "You have no trouble overstepping the rules."

"Too much red blood in my veins for that."

"I thought you were a blue blood."

"Then you *do* think about me."

"Never."

"Liar!"

Diana eluded him until the last dance was called. It began on a light note, but the tension built between them as his arms became possessive and his gaze intense. Diana realized he was becoming too serious and decided she must put a stop to it. In a firm but friendly tone she said, "I'm most flattered for your invitation, Peter, but I shan't be coming to Bath."

The music stilled, but Hardwick held her fast. He had a wild, predatory look that both compelled and repelled her. His voice was low, determined, almost threatening. "You shall, you *shall*!"

When the dance ended, Diana returned to the side of her guardian, who had never taken her eyes off the couple. She saw a look of pure satisfaction cross her aunt's face when she said, "Peter Hardwick invited me to Bath."

"What an amazing coincidence."

"Rather, I suspect collusion," Diana said quietly.

"I swear you are the cruelest girl on earth! How you can suggest such a thing is beyond me. Of course you accepted?"

"Of course I declined. If he is that interested, he will soon come galloping back to London."

"Playing hard-to-get may be unwise. There are prettier girls with greater titles on the marriage market this season."

"But none with a larger inheritance," Diana said quietly.

"Let me tell you, missy, cynicism in one so young is repugnant! I swear you are so perverse that you are rejecting Peter Hardwick simply because I approve of him!"

There's more than a grain of truth there, Diana thought.

"Well, let me inform you that you are cutting off your nose to spite your face! It is common gossip that the earl is disinclined to marry. Peter is his heir and whomever Peter marries will not only be the mother of the future Earl of Bath, she will inherit the Elizabethan hall, the quarries, the lot!"

It was disrespectful and upsetting to argue with Prudence, but Diana refused to be a spineless pawn in her aunt's relentless climb up the social ladder. By the time they reached Grosvenor Square, they were no longer on speaking terms.

Sleep eluded Diana for hours as the events of the evening played over in her mind. She had no objection to Bath; surely it overflowed with antiquity, and the Palladian architecture alone was enough to make it fascinating. She had no real objection to Peter Hardwick's company either. What it boiled down to was her dislike of Prudence controlling her life. She fell asleep determined to be the master, or rather the mistress, of her own fate.

In the morning Diana awoke to an unusual amount of coming and going outside her chamber. When Biddy brought Diana's morning chocolate, she was brimming over with news she wished to impart.

"The doctor's here—mistress had a fall!"

"Oh, no." Diana threw back the covers and dressed immediately. Downstairs Prudence was on the couch with her doctor hovering.

"Whatever happened?" Diana asked with genuine concern, noting the pinched look of pain on her aunt's face.

"I was so distracted over our quarrel that I slipped on the stairs." She fixed Diana with a look of condemnation.

"I am so sorry," Diana murmured faintly.

"It was a very close call," the doctor proclaimed. "You are the most fortunate lady alive not to have broken a bone. If you had, it is conceivable that you might never have walked again."

Prudence covered her eyes, unable to face such a possibility.

"Even with no bones broken, an arthritic hip is a heavy cross to bear. I recommend the medicinal cure of mineral baths. Immersion daily will do wonders for your complaint, Madam Davenport. I vow 'tis the only answer for your affliction."

"How ironic," Prudence said with pathos. "I begged Lady Diana to sojourn to Bath for a month, but she refused out of hand."

The doctor's eyebrows bristled; he stroked his muttonchop whiskers gravely. "Mineral water has almost magical properties. Applied externally, it is antiseptic and antirheumatic; taken internally it is antispasmodic and antibilious. I am sure Lady Diana will reconsider her thoughtless refusal." The doctor then dismissed her. "I should like a little privacy with my patient."

"Did anyone see or hear her fall?" Diana asked Biddy suspiciously as they left the room.

The maid shook her head. "It was me who run for the doctor, but she'd already picked herself up when she rang for me."

Diana sighed. It was all very well to decide your own fate in theory. Reality was another matter. She knew she was being manipulated like a puppet with Prudence pulling her strings, but there wasn't a damned thing she could do about it. She had been outmaneuvered. She had been cast in the role of selfish, heartless bitch. *So be it,* Diana decided.

After the doctor departed, Diana returned to the drawing room to see how Prudence fared. Her aunt could not quite conceal her look of triumph, mingled with pain, of course.

"Prudence, I've been thinking—Bath is a fashionable shopping mecca these days. The Milsom Street shops dress some of the leading hostesses of the ton. If I agree to go, I suppose I could acquire a whole new wardrobe. One more in line with my own taste."

Diana watched a look of real pain cross her aunt's face as she realized Diana was bargaining. What a shrewd baggage the girl was!

Within the hour, plans for the trip were under way. Biddy was rushed off her feet packing for Prudence. Diana packed very little; she would indulge in a shopping spree that would set Bath on its ear! She went to the library to choose a book for the journey. As she ran her fingers across the gilt titles, she paused to think about what effect this trip to Bath might have upon her future. The image of Peter Hardwick came full-blown into her mind as she relived their last exchange of words: "I'm most flattered for your invitation, Peter, but I shan't be coming to Bath."

"You shall!" he had vowed.

Diana shivered at the memory of the look she had seen in his eyes.

"Biddy, take the seat next to Lady Diana. I shall need this one to myself. Just pop that cushion next to my painful hip —carefully, girl, carefully—and we can be under way."

Diana, dreading the trip of one hundred miles confined in a closed carriage with Prudence, had fortified herself with a volume of Ovid from her father's library. Knowing it was overtly sensual, she had tucked it into a copy of the *Bath Chronicle*. She leafed through the book until she found "The Art of Love." She did not exactly learn the things she wished to know, but she certainly learned that the Romans believed woman was created to be man's plaything and considered all females to be unchaste voluptuaries. Ovid's amorous tactics were pure eroticism: the art of enjoying a woman's body as fully and delightfully as possible.

Annoyed that Ovid omitted a woman's mind or personality completely, Diana snapped closed the volume, then inwardly groaned because the noise awakened Prudence. From that moment until they stopped at Reading for the night, Diana listened to Prudence propound on her favorite subject. Respectability!

The following day the drive seemed endless, so Diana allowed her thoughts to drift ahead to their destination. She couldn't wait to see Bath. Its antiquity was legendary. It had been built by the Romans, who had called it Aquae Sulis. The very name conjured pictures that fired her imagination.

When the chaise descended the final hill and crossed

the bridge sporting graceful arches, the sunset had turned Bath into a city of gold. Diana caught her breath, utterly enchanted by such beauty. In that moment she vowed that she would enjoy Bath to the full. She was filled with a thirst for life and she decided this would be the most glorious time she would ever have!

When James paid the toll to enter the city and asked directions to Queen Square, he was informed that Bath was a city for pedestrians and he would have to take the chaise to the White Swan Inn for stabling after he had delivered the ladies to their house.

Though Diana would have preferred a house with a view across the River Avon to the woods and hills beyond where sheep and horses grazed, she had to own that Queen Square was a more convenient location. The fashionable square had been designed by Wood to resemble the courtyard of a palace. Outside, the house had a high facade of Bath stone with pedimented windows. Inside, the elegant house had two communicating L-shaped drawing rooms wrapped around a staircase. The boudoirs and dressing rooms were upstairs while the kitchen and servants' quarters were below the ground floor.

Diana was amused to see that Richard had spent so freely of her money. The house came with a cook, an upstairs maid, and a butler. Prudence began issuing orders the moment her foot was across the threshold. She informed the staff that she was here for the cure and that her condition was delicate, then ordered a dinner that would kill a female with less than a robust and hardy constitution.

When Prudence pleaded exhaustion, Diana and Biddy helped her upstairs, where she proceeded to issue orders from her bed until midnight. She asked so many questions of the staff that the butler finally produced a map that laid out the entire city, row by row. She couldn't understand it, of course, and kept Diana at her bedside for two more hours while she pointed out the Grand Parade, the Pump Room, the Assembly Rooms, the Baths, and the Octagonal Chapel.

When Prudence did not appear for breakfast, Diana seized the moment and set out to explore Bath on her own. She was interested in learning the location of the shops, the subscription libraries, and where the hot springs began down by the river. Diana felt free as a bird escaped from its cage. Excitement tingled along every nerve at the thought of being able to choose clothes for herself.

She sauntered along Milsom Street, gazing into shop windows, carefully reading the signs above the doors, trying to decide which establishment would receive her custom. The largest shop was La Belle Mode; its proprietress, Madame Madeleine, who greeted Lady Diana warmly as she opened the door and stepped inside.

"Is there something in particular you are interested in, mademoiselle?"

"Oh yes, everything really." Diana was entranced at the gowns on display. The shop also had slippers, fans, and every feminine accessory to complete a lady's wardrobe. She glanced about, noting the fine French furnishings, and then she saw it. Easily the loveliest gown she had ever seen, and she knew she must have it or die. It was jade velvet with a heart-shaped neckline and gathered waist. It had classic lines that would have been fashionable in any age.

Diana's imagination pictured herself at Elizabeth's Court wearing the gown, with a magnificent ruff added, of course. It was the vivid color, however, that drew her fancy. "The jade gown—may I try it on, please?"

Madame Madeleine led her into a dressing room and helped her remove her insipid pink daydress. Diana felt compelled to explain to the fashionably gowned Frenchwoman, "I don't care for pastels. I prefer gowns in jewel tones that set off my fair coloring."

"I agree—the jade will be perfect." She stared in disbelief at the old-fashioned corset. "Ah, you will need a new corset perhaps, mademoiselle?"

"Oh no, I hate corsets, but my aunt insists I be fitted for the nasty things."

"No, no—you misunderstand. I refer to the latest fashion, the half-corset. A pretty little garment that merely nips in the waist and uplifts the breasts."

"Really? Well yes, it certainly sounds like an improvement on the garment I'm wearing. I'll try one on."

"*Bon!* What about color—you prefer naughty or nice?"

Diana blinked. "I prefer naughty, every time!"

Madame Madeleine came back carrying a lacy froth of scarlet and began the task of untying the strings of the rigid, cagelike contraption Diana was laced into.

Lady Diana took a gasp of air as her ribcage was allowed to expand and her breasts sprang up from their unnaturally flattened state. She donned the new garment and stared in amazement at the apparition in the mirror. It couldn't possibly be her. The red half-corset made her waist almost disappear, yet her breasts were lush. They were pushed up so that her curves swelled from the top of the lacy garment in the sauciest and most provocative way.

The bell on the shop door tinkled merrily. "Excuse me, mademoiselle, I will be back in a moment."

Diana, completely enchanted with her new look, hardly heard her. She twisted this way and that, posing before the glass. Even her legs clad in her silk stockings looked longer. This corset did not encase her hips, but ended just before the natural swell of her derriere curved outward, exposing her white linen drawers.

Diana looked and felt wicked as original sin and she absolutely relished it. What a pity no one would see such ravishing undergarments. She felt more female than she had ever felt before and longed for the entire world to see how stunning the New Lady Diana Davenport had become. *I wonder if it comes in black?* she asked herself. Then she slowly became aware of people talking.

"Mark, darling, I'd like to try this one."

"By all means," a man replied.

Diana was brought out of her reverie by the familiar

male voice. She would know it anywhere! Its deep timbre sent a shiver up her spine. She was annoyed that he had such an effect upon her.

"Ah, mademoiselle, another lady wishes to try this gown."

"Oh, Mark, only think how the jade will compliment my hair," the plummy voice cajoled.

Diana's anger flared instantly. The Earl of Bath had picked up a woman and was already buying her gowns. Well, one thing was certain—he wasn't going to buy the bloody woman *her* gown!

"Talk the other lady out of it; I'll make it worth your while," Hardwick said smoothly, as if he were used to ordering the world.

Diana hesitated because of her deshabille, then a wicked smile curved her lips as she realized the she-devil inside her was running rampant again. She threw open the dressing room door, stalked into the showroom, and swept the jade gown from the redhead's possessive hands.

"Oooh, how dare you!" Vivian screeched.

"This gown is mine," Diana asserted regally.

Mark Hardwick's eyes narrowed and his nostrils flared in pure male appreciation of the ravishing beauty clad in the provocative scarlet corset.

"I beg to differ!" Vivian hissed.

"You can beg 'til your hair dye tarnishes," Diana said blandly.

"Do you know who this is?" Vivian spluttered, indicating the nobleman who accompanied her.

"Indeed I do," Diana drawled. "The Earl of Bath and I are old adversaries. Do you know who I am, by the way?"

"No, I do not!" Vivian shouted.

"I," said Diana, a delicious smile curving her lips, "am the owner of the jade gown."

Madame Madeleine was wise enough to hold her silence when two bitches fought over the same bone.

Hardwick's countenance was grave, though he did not miss the humor of the situation.

Vivian turned to him for aid. "Mark, do something!"

"I'll buy you *two* gowns to replace the jade one," he soothed.

Lady Diana turned to the redhead and said confidentially, "Have a care, his lordship likes to get his money's worth."

The earl was no longer amused, but he could see by the light in Diana's amethyst eyes that she was thoroughly enjoying herself.

The Countess of Belgrave turned upon her heel and flounced from the shop. Hardwick picked up his hat and cane, having no alternative but to follow her.

"I'm sorry if I've ruined *another* evening for you, m'lord," Diana said sweetly.

Chapter 6

"So many people are in town, I vow, London must be deserted," Prudence declared at breakfast.

As Diana glanced through the calling cards, she saw that Peter Hardwick's was among them. It wasn't Peter's face who sprang full-blown to her mind, however; it was his brother the earl's. He had been ready to throttle her yesterday in the dress shop. She had given him an eyeful and he had certainly looked his fill. Diana had the satisfaction of knowing her looks put those of the older woman with him in the shade.

"Peter was most disappointed that you were not at home when he called. I must say I was quite put out by your behavior, Diana. A respectable lady does not go out walking alone, even in a pedestrian town like Bath."

Diana quickly changed the subject. She realized Prudence would monopolize every moment if she didn't devise a plan to outwit her. "Prudence, I've been thinking, why don't I get you one of these marvelous things they call a Bath chair? I'll push you everywhere and then you won't have to walk."

"Bath chairs are for old people! I wouldn't be caught dead in one. I'm not an invalid, I'm not decrepit. I'm perfectly capable of walking about Bath. In fact, my hip feels better already."

"There must be something in the air, it is most salubrious," Diana said with a straight face. "Well, are we off for a dip this morning?" Diana said briskly.

Prudence hesitated briefly, then squared her shoulders and declared just as briskly, "We most certainly are. Doctors' orders cannot be ignored."

As they made their way across Westgate Street, they were an odd-looking couple. Prudence sailed along in Bishop's blue bombazine, which wasn't blue at all, but a peculiar shade of purple, while Diana wore jonquil brocade. Prudence had insisted they both wear their powdered wigs and large bonnets with ostrich plumes. Since Diana knew they would be removing their clothes at the baths, she had not dared wear the delicious red corset, but had donned an old-fashioned one instead.

Diana was looking forward to visiting the rectangular Cross Bath, where stone faces of Roman gods lined the walls and statues of Apollo and Coronis gazed at the bathers from alcoves set in the walls. Prudence, however, had made up her mind that they would visit the Queen's Bath, and that was that.

She maneuvered the steep narrow steps leading down to the chalybeate springs with amazing dexterity. "Faugh! What is that noxious odor?" she demanded as they walked through a cloud of vapor.

"That is sulphur you can smell," Diana explained.

"Why on earth haven't they done something to purify the water of the stenching stuff?" Prudence demanded.

"It is the sulphur and other minerals in the water that make them medicinal," Diana explained as if to a child.

A female bath guide led them down a covered passage into a room with fireplaces and told them this was where they could leave their clothes. When she brought them long, high-waisted shifts of brownish linen with elbow-length sleeves, the corners of Prudence's mouth turned down. The thought of removing her hat and wig in public was anathema to her, but the attendant assured her all the ladies kept their usual head gear intact. Diana, on the other hand, felt totally ridiculous in powdered wig and ostrich feathers and fervently prayed she would not bump into Peter Hardwick, or worse, his brother the earl.

Prudence shuddered as Diana helped her into the tepid water. Her face had taken on the expression of a gargoyle and the distaste she felt at the whole exercise of a medicinal bath was indelibly stamped upon her countenance for all the world to see.

Diana was willing to bet this would be the fastest cure on record. In fact, Prudence would likely insist it was a miracle. Diana could hardly wait until her aunt visited the Pump Room and tasted the iron in the chalybeate spring water. After today Diana was sure Prudence would divide her time between the Parades and the Assembly Rooms, and to get time alone, all Diana would need say was that she was going to the baths!

By the time they arrived back in Queen Square, Peter Hardwick awaited their return. "Welcome to Bath, ladies. I missed you yesterday," he said pointedly, taking Diana's hand to his lips and lingering over it in a proprietary manner. "I've come to invite you and your aunt to the Wiltshire Assembly Rooms tonight."

"Dear boy, we should be delighted," Prudence accepted immediately. "And Diana is so looking forward to an invitation to Hardwick Hall. The Elizabethan period is her very favorite, is it not, my dear?"

"One of them," Diana murmured, blushing profusely because Prudence was putting him on the spot.

"I know it is highly improper to leave you alone, but I'm sure I can trust you, dear boy."

Prudence was so transparent in throwing them together that Diana blushed once more. The moment she quit the room, Diana apologized. "I'm so sorry, Peter. I have no intention of storming Hardwick Hall."

He looked wounded. "Diana, it is my dearest desire that you will visit the ancestral home. I want you to come tomorrow—early. I want to spend as much time as I can with you."

"What about your brother? Isn't he entertaining at the moment?" Her heart thudded whenever she thought of him, and even though she tried, she could not control the emotions he stirred in her.

"Not that I'm aware of," Peter assured her.

"But I saw him with a charming redhead yesterday."

"That would be the Widow Vixen. Good God, she isn't staying at the hall. She's his—that is, she's—"

"I know exactly what she is."

"Then you're not as innocent as you look," Peter said, his voice growing husky. He captured her hand again and squeezed it. "Only prospective brides are invited to the hall."

Diana could not escape his meaning. Though she was vastly flattered, she could not help feeling the jaws of a trap were beginning to close on her. "Tomorrow is impossible, I'm afraid," she temporized.

"I shan't leave until you promise to come," he vowed.

Her amethyst eyes widened as she saw him bend his head to her with deliberate intent. She only had time to draw in a swift breath before his lips were on hers. She felt no romantic stirrings whatsoever, but she was surprised at the gentleness of the kiss.

When she withdrew her lips from his, he whispered, "When will you come?"

"Soon," she promised.

"How soon?" he pressed gently.

"The day after tomorrow."

Peter shook his head. "Not nearly soon enough." He captured her shoulders and drew her even closer. His lips brushed hers. "Tomorrow," he insisted.

Diana found it difficult to think of a plausible excuse he would believe. "Prudence keeps me on a string. She

came on the orders of her doctor to take the medicinal
waters and I have to accompany her.'' Diana wondered why
in the world she was making excuses. She would much
prefer visiting an Elizabethan manor house to wearing a
hideous canvass robe and standing in tepid water.

''Prudence seemed anxious to come—shall I pull the
bell rope and invite her?'' He took a threatening step
toward it.

Diana's eyes brimmed with amusement that he had
outwitted her. ''You are a devil, Peter Hardwick. I concede
graciously, we shall come tomorrow.''

''And stay overnight,'' he insisted. ''To fully appreciate Hardwick Hall, you must walk along her parapet walls
in the moonlight, ride through her hunting park in the dawn
mists, and of course sleep in the chamber that the Virgin
Queen once occupied.''

Diana's cheeks glowed. ''You win, Peter. I'll bring an
overnight bag, but only on the condition that you spare me
the assembly tonight.''

Peter grinned. ''They are the most god-awful things. It
will be my pleasure to spare you.'' The triumphant smile
reached all the way to Peter's eyes. ''I shall pick you up at
eleven so we'll be in time for lunch.''

When he departed, Diana could hear Prudence in the
kitchen still giving orders and waited until she emerged.
''You'll be pleased to know that Peter issued an invitation
to Hardwick Hall.''

''Did he include me in that invitation?''

''Of course he did.''

''Ah, the dear boy. His manners cannot be faulted.
When are we to go?''

''Tomorrow. We are invited to stay overnight to enjoy
the full hospitality of an Elizabethan hall. Peter didn't
sound too keen about the assembly tonight, so we'll have
lots of time to get ready for tomorrow.''

''An invitation to an earl's home is something that
doesn't come along every day. I shall need Bridget as well

as the upstairs maid to ready my wardrobe and pack the things I shall need for such an occasion.''

The moment Prudence left the room, Diana slipped from the house. She made her way to the river to watch the swans. The Avon was both wide and deep as it rushed on its way to the Bristol Channel and the Celtic Sea. She imagined the sailing vessels of the Celts, the Vikings, and the warships of the Romans with their great oars. She saw two barges piled with golden Bath stone and realized they must be from the Hardwick Quarries. As she looked about her at the magnificent Georgian buildings, she wondered how many of them had been built with stone from those same quarries. *The family must be exceedingly wealthy and it must be old money,* she thought. She'd look up the history of the Earls of Bath when she went to the library and learn how they had come to own an Elizabethan manor.

For the rest of the day it was Mark Hardwick who insinuated himself into her thoughts. He was a dark, dominant, and dangerous man. Just the type of male she daydreamed about. He stood out from his peers in vivid contrast. To Diana he seemed the antithesis of a Georgian fop. In fact, he suited another century far better than this one. He would make a magnificent medieval warrior or an Elizabethan explorer. When she fell asleep that night, it was not the gallant young Peter Hardwick who insinuated himself into her dreams, but the darkly arrogant earl.

As Peter's sleek carriage horses bowled along, following the River Avon as it wound away from the center of Bath and up into the northern hills above the town, Prudence inquired fatuously, ''Will the earl be in residence?''

''Er . . . no, I'm afraid my brother is away at the moment. He is a magistrate of Somerset and was called to Bristol.''

''What a pity,'' Prudence lamented. ''I was hoping this visit would give Diana the opportunity to mend her fences with his lordship. That wretched misunderstanding about the library was most unfortunate.''

Diana cleared her throat but managed to keep a wise silence. There was a good deal more between them than the business of the library! Whenever they met, sparks flew between them, and though Diana wished it were otherwise, she knew she felt a fatal attraction toward the wrong brother. She was vastly relieved that she and the earl would not be spending the night under the same roof.

From the moment they turned in at the ivy-covered gatehouse and swept up the long drive, Diana lost her heart to Hardwick Hall. Peter saw the reverent look in her eyes and knew he was more than halfway home. As the crested carriage rolled to a stop at the front entrance, the major-domo and two footmen hurried out.

''I have a fabulous idea,'' Peter turned to Prudence. ''I shall leave you in the capable hands of Mr. Burke, while I show off the grounds to Lady Diana.''

''Don't worry about me, Peter, I shall make myself at home. Run along, children.''

Diana could hardly believe her ears. As Peter lifted her down from the carriage and led the way toward the formal gardens, she said, ''You have the wretched woman eating out of your hand.''

He stopped and looked down at her. ''I know just how to stroke a female,'' he murmured huskily.

Diana's cheeks felt too warm, and a prickling sensation ran along her spine. Though Peter had a knack for saying things that were wickedly improper, they did not excite her, they caused her to put up her guard. She admonished herself not to trust him too far, but as the beauty of the Elizabethan garden with its herbaceous borders claimed all her attention, happiness filled her heart.

They explored the dove cotes, the orchard with its ancient beehives, the Tudor water garden, and watched the proud peacocks strut about the velvet lawns. When they came upon a privet maze, copied after the one at Hampton

Court, Diana couldn't resist it. Peter sat down on a carved bench. "Go on, explore," he urged. "If you haven't found your way out in five minutes, I'll come and rescue you."

Within the first minute Diana lost her way, which thoroughly enchanted her, of course. The privet hedge was too high to see over and too dense to peek through. After many wrong turns and doubling back, she found its center. There sat Peter awaiting her.

"You fraud," she said, laughing, "you promised to wait outside."

"And pass up the chance to be private with you where none can see my amorous advances?"

Diana knew if she ran it would only issue a teasing invitation for him to chase after her and catch her.

Peter moved toward her purposefully and pulled her into his arms. "I should claim some forfeit before I let you go; it's traditional."

"What sort of forfeit?" Diana inquired, standing perfectly still in the circle of his arms.

"You must remove an article of clothing," he said outrageously.

Without batting an eye, Diana removed a glove and held it out.

Peter couldn't hide a look of disappointment. "You're not playing fair," he complained.

"I'm not playing at all," she informed him.

Christ, she's like an ice queen, he thought. *Any other female I'd have down to her shift by now.* Peter knew it would be so much easier if she were amenable to seduction, but he wasn't going to let that stop him. He'd have to wait until tonight to do the deed. He'd set the stage carefully so there would be no escape. The corners of his mouth lifted in a smile. It would be like leading a lamb to slaughter. He murmured, "I'll settle for the glove, if a kiss goes with it."

When she lifted her mouth to his, he controlled himself. He was going to get a commitment from this woman one way or another and he only had this one night to do it.

Peter knew he couldn't afford to make her mistrust him this early in the game, so he brushed his lips across her forehead. As a reward for his good behavior, she stood on tiptoe and touched her mouth to his. When they emerged from the maze, Peter knew he was one step closer to victory!

The evening meal promised to be a most formal affair served in the paneled dining room with its massive Tudor oak refectory table and carved chairs.

After her bath, Diana donned the scarlet corset, then slipped on the new jade velvet gown. She knew she had never looked lovelier and she had never felt quite as seductively feminine as she did tonight. She could not forget the way the Earl of Bath had looked at her, and crushed a wish that he could see her again tonight.

Dinner consisted of six courses and Diana was impatient for the tour of Hardwick Hall that Peter had promised. At the end of the meal, crystal goblets were set before them and filled to the brim.

Peter stood up. ''Today's mores dictate that the ladies leave the table while the gentlemen enjoy their port, but tonight we shall do things the Elizabethan way. This is hippocras, warmed and spiced the way it was served to the Queen over two hundred years ago. I propose a toast to Lady Diana Davenport. Hardwick cries out for a chatelaine as lovely as you to grace her hallowed halls.''

The wine was full-bodied and its warmth spread along Diana's veins like wildfire. Taking their spiced hippocras, they left Prudence sitting at table while they went off to explore the manor.

He showed her the small lady chapel, the still room where perfume was distilled from Hardwick's own roses and herbs. In the ballroom Peter had had the servants set ablaze hundreds of candles in the chandeliers, and from the minstrels' gallery above them, music floated down from what could only be a virginal.

He held out his arms and Diana went into them. As they danced, she closed her eyes and imagined herself truly in Elizabethan times. She was wearing the identical jade gown with a frothy ruff about her neck. She felt exactly as if she had done this before with another partner who flexed his powerful muscles to lift her high in the gay galliard. She smiled down into his black eyes with happiness, and then his face changed back into Peter's.

As he set her feet back to the polished floor, he drew her against him and whispered, "Let's escape out on the parapet walk." She placed her hand in his, and like two conspirators, they slipped away from the ballroom.

Leaning against the crenellated stones, bathed in moonlight, Diana let the magic of the night wash over her. This small palace was so warm and welcoming, it felt as if it had been waiting for her for two centuries, and now at last she had finally come home. The very atmosphere was charged with romance. Diana knew she had fallen in love, but did not believe it was possible to love the man as she did the house. "You haven't shown me the Queen's bed-chamber," she murmured dreamily.

Diana spoke the words he had been waiting to hear. In the darkness, Peter smiled at his own cleverness. "I've saved the best 'til last. There is a secret passage," he whispered.

"No!" she cried, utterly captivated. One of the chimneys opened to reveal steps leading downward. "Won't we need a light?"

"Just hold on to me, sweet. We'll feel our way along." She clung to his hand and placed the other one on his broad back. She could feel the muscle beneath the material and blushed into the darkness. So much strength he kept under control. What would happen if he unleashed that strength? She shivered at the thought. The darkness and the confined space combined with the excitement of the adventure made her breathless. She was ready to scream, when suddenly a door creaked open and light flooded the passage.

Peter drew her inside and closed the secret door behind them. It was the most impressive chamber Diana had ever seen. It was extremely large with a massive stone fireplace covering one entire wall. Above the mantel was a pair of portraits. One was Elizabeth I in a black velvet gown encrusted with crystals and pearls and the other was a portrait of the first Earl of Bath. His black eyes were brilliant in his darkly proud face.

Before the fire was a pair of "his" and "hers" chairs, hooded against the drafts, and between the chairs was a games table inlaid with ivory and ebony squares. Exquisitely carved jade chessman were set out invitingly.

The far end of the room held bookshelves from floor to ceiling, their leather-bound volumes all embossed with goldleaf. An eight-foot desk with silver inkwells, silver sand caster, and quill holder was covered by letters, documents, and maps as if someone had just been interrupted while hard at work. A four-poster with heavy, velvet bedcurtains dominated the chamber. All was done in the Tudor colors of green and white embroidered with small golden crowns and lions. The entire chamber was fragrant with sandalwood.

"It's simply perfect," Diana sighed. In her green velvet gown she became Elizabeth for one magic moment. She closed her eyes, wishing this chamber could be hers. When she opened them, Peter had poured her a glass of bloodred wine. Diana knew she had already drunk enough to make her a little unsteady, but somehow it seemed right to take the wine and behave a little recklessly. She drained the glass and felt a bloodred rose blossom in her breast.

Peter took the glass from her fingers, then pulled her urgently toward him. His demanding mouth came down on hers, forcing her lips to open for him. He deepened the kiss passionately and moved his hands to the fastenings at the back of her gown.

Suddenly the door swung open and Mark Hardwick stepped over the threshold into his chamber. Diana gasped and pulled out of Peter's arms. Her hand flew to the bodice of her jade gown as the back gaped open.

"Mark! What the devil are you doing home tonight?"

"My business in Bristol was finished," his brother said matter-of-factly. "What the devil are *you* doing?"

"Proposing, actually. Lady Diana and I are engaged to be married."

Diana wanted to protest, but all she could think of in that moment was fleeing from the arrogant Earl of Bath's cynical gaze. It was now palpably obvious that this was his chamber. "Then I suppose congratulations are in order," the earl said smoothly. "Welcome to the family."

Diana knew she was totally compromised. If she denied the engagement, she was admitting playing the whore. Her lashes swept down to her cheeks. "Please excuse me, both of you."

A wave of protectiveness swept over Mark Hardwick. Diana Davenport was so young, so lovely. He wondered if she had any idea that she was sacrificing herself to a brutal young swine.

"Well, are you or are you not?" Prudence demanded as the carriage took them away from Hardwick Hall back to Queen Square.

"Yes . . . and no," Diana replied, her thoughts anywhere but on their conversation.

"Well, that's as clear as mud! And why are we rushing off at the crack of dawn like thieves in the night?" Prudence demanded, mixing metaphors. "It looks like you are running away."

"I suppose I am," Diana admitted. She knew Prudence deserved some sort of explanation for her sudden bolt from Hardwick Hall. "The Earl of Bath returned unexpectedly late last night and Peter told him we were engaged to be married."

Prudence sagged into the corner. "Thank heavens! I thought he'd never get the deed done."

Diana bristled. "The point is, Peter didn't ask and I didn't accept."

"Details. Inconsequential details. Believe me, if the earl has been informed, you are very definitely engaged."

"Perhaps," Diana replied tentatively. She had taken the coward's way out, asking Mr. Burke to have the carriage take them back to Bath and giving him a letter for Peter.

Last night she had been both angry and humilated that he had compromised her, especially before his arrogant brother. It was as if he had deliberately sprung a trap on her. If she had stayed this morning, there would have been a terrible scene, probably involving both Prudence and the earl, and that was the last thing Diana wanted.

This was strictly between Peter and herself. She intended to have it out with him, in private. But before she did, Diana needed time to sort out her own feelings and come to a decision. At the moment her emotions were in too much turmoil to make a rational decision that would affect the rest of her life.

The trouble was that the moment Peter read her letter, he would come. In her present mood she was likely to lose her temper completely and say things that could never be unsaid. She needed time alone, time to think, time to make her own decision without being influenced.

When they disembarked in Queen Square, Diana realized with dismay that in her great haste her luggage had been left behind. At dawn this morning she had struggled into one of her old-fashioned corsets and donned a most prim and nondescript beige dress with panniers before she approached the very proper Mr. Burke. Lord, she had never felt so unattractive in her life.

She tipped the Hardwicks' carriage driver generously, because she was so grateful for the speedy getaway. His jaw almost dropped open. Diana bit her lips as she realized she had committed a social gaffe, but she noticed with cynicism that he did not refuse the money. She picked up Prudence's luggage and carried it inside.

Her aunt was already in the kitchen giving orders for a restorative lunch. "In the meantime you can make me up a posset of madeira and eggs before I take my nap."

Diana's thoughts ran about like quicksilver. If Prudence took a nap, she wouldn't be missed until lunch. An entire morning to wander on her own was more than Diana could resist. Once she had made her escape, she might even stay out all day. What the hell could Prudence do about it if she did?

Diana wanted to change from the beige dress with its hideous panniers, but if she followed Prudence upstairs she would lose precious time. In a flash Diana was out the door heading toward Sion Hill and Lansdown Road.

When she reached the heights and looked down through the trees at the perfect Georgian city, Diana was filled with a sense of freedom. The soft air was resonant with the sounds of water. She could hear ancient springs trickling down the hillsides as well as the rush of the River Avon as it tumbled over the weir at Pulteney Bridge.

She could see the spires of the medieval abbey, where King Edgar was crowned in the tenth century, and the magnificent curve of The Circus, which architect John Wood had built in the style of the Roman Colosseum.

Diana filled her lungs with the delicious fresh air and knew she had reached her decision. It was so simple, really. She and Peter were engaged, but the length of the engagement had not been discussed. If he would agree to a long engagement, say of a year, then she would let things stay as they were. If not, she would call it off immediately. She would come of age in a few months and have the say over her own money and inheritance. She wanted a year's freedom before she submitted to a husband's control. If Peter loved her, he would be willing to wait.

Now that she had made her decision, her cares dropped away like a heavy burden she had been carrying. Her heart was light again. It was a beautiful morning, she was in a magnificent and ancient city, and the best part was she had the entire day to explore its charms.

Diana began to make her way downhill, turning first left then right, where she found herself in a lane dotted with charming antique shops. The articles in the windows were so tempting, she couldn't resist going inside to browse around.

Some things were so curious she couldn't name them. There were dozens of antique brass taps, a painted bathtub with claw and ball feet, ancient stone garden seats, old clocks, spinets, and mandolins. She stopped to admire a medieval tapestry, its colors faded, but still subtly beautiful. Diana was thrilled to her very core to be able to actually see something that had survived since the Middle Ages.

She moved on, then stopped in her tracks as she came upon a display of Roman artifacts. *Surely these can't be authentic?* she thought, her heart beating faster. There was a bronze helmet with decorated side pieces, a shield, swords in scabbards, and iron daggers. *These could be from the first century!* she thought. As she ran her fingertips over the Roman helmet, she imagined it almost burned her. She drew in her breath in wonder that these things had survived for seventeen centuries. "This helmet belonged to a Roman centurion," she murmured in awe.

Diana glanced about the shop, but could not see the proprietor anywhere. On a sudden impulse she removed her hat and decided to try on the helmet. She had momentarily forgotten she was wearing a wig. With a muttered oath she tucked up the powdered curls beneath the side pieces that protected the cheeks.

The bronze helmet was unbelievably heavy and when she tried to remove it she discovered that it was somehow wedged upon her head. She heard a loud drumming in her ears. She felt faint and dizzy and her vision became blurred. Then suddenly she went cold. She felt as if cool air were rushing past her. It gave her the strange sensation that she was moving through space at high speed while standing in one place.

The volume of the noise in her head increased until she felt her eardrums would burst. Her hands went up to cover them, but she felt only the huge bronze helmet making her head ache intolerably. Then she felt herself falling, not just to the floor, but beyond.

Chapter 7

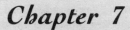

Diana heard men shouting and somehow she was outdoors with the sun beating down upon her face, blinding her to everything. She tried to stumble to her feet, but while she was still on her knees, she saw two huge horses pulling some sort of cart bearing down upon her. Instinctively she fell to the ground to roll away from their hooves. When the horses saw her in their path they reared up screaming and snorting and the wagon they pulled sounded like thunder as it rolled within inches of her head. She heard someone scream, then realized it was herself.

A man's voice was shouting and cursing at her at the top of his lungs. She was vaguely aware of other horses and men gathering about, but her attention was held by the man doing all the shouting. As she stared at him, she thought he bore a resemblance to the Earl of Bath. He had the same black hair and dark eyes, the same hawklike hook to his nose, but a scar ran from his temple to his cheekbone, giving him a saturnine look. His shoulders were unbelievably broad, his chest heavily muscled and completely bare. He was wearing some sort of a costume that left his legs bare too and they were so hard and thick they resembled oak trees.

She glanced at the wheel that had almost rolled over her and saw that it belonged to a chariot. A wave of blazing anger swept over her as she realized she had almost been killed by a bunch of ridiculous men dressed up as Romans racing silly chariots. "You bloody fools! Grown men playing at boys' games. You should be horsewhipped!"

The dark man pointed a finger. "Seize her!" he commanded.

Two huge men carried out his order immediately. Diana's teeth rattled in her head as she was pulled to her feet and held immobile until their leader reached her. He towered above her, gripped by a white-hot rage. "You female bundle of rags! You almost injured my horses. Who are you?" he demanded.

She stared up at him in amazement. Though he spoke a strange mixture of Italian and Latin, she understood every word.

"By Jupiter, you've stolen a helmet," he accused as he reached out a massive hand and wrenched it from her head. He saw that the female's hair was white and thought her an old woman. The filthy, bulky garment she wore covered every inch of flesh from her throat to her heels. She was the strangest-looking female he'd ever seen. "You do not answer me so I'll answer for you. You are a spy—a Druid spy, by the looks of your strange clothing."

What he said made no sense. Diana stared into his dark eyes and watched him gain control of his anger. "Get her off the track and keep her out of the way. Manacle her securely—I'll interrogate her later."

The men dragged her away. "Let me go! How dare you manhandle me? Is that swine Mark Hardwick?" She knew they understood what she said because they laughed, then replied, "No, the swine is Marcus Magnus, the Primus Pilus."

The men handled her roughly, not caring that they were hurting her. Fear began to blot out her anger. They took her to a wooden wagon. One of the men reached for an iron collar, which he snapped about her neck, just as if he were leashing a dog that was being troublesome. "You cannot do this to me!'' she cried, but the men strode off, their minds on other things. She was instantly forgotten. She was a prisoner of these strange, cruel, and uncivilized men. She sank down in the dust and began to cry.

Once Diana began, she couldn't stop; she sobbed until she got the dry heaves. Finally she realized that crying would avail her naught. No one took the least notice of her, so with a few sniffing shudders and much wiping of her face with dirty hands and blowing her nose on her sleeve, her sobs subsided.

She began to watch the panorama stretched out before her. A track had been laid out for racing chariots and every man in sight, whether participating in the races or not, was dressed as a Roman soldier. Regardless of their coloring, height, or weight they were all in superb physical condition. *They are what men should look like, but seldom do,* she thought.

The chariot racers were reckless to a man. Each looked as if he would rather die than lose. They paid scant heed to their physical safety, running the hubs of their wheels together in a supreme effort to win. The poor devils who tipped over their chariots had to scramble to safety as best they could, for no man slowed his horses to avoid inflicting injuries. It was every man for himself and winning was all. Yet Diana could clearly see they were enjoying themselves by the collective noise they made, laughing, shouting, boasting, or cursing.

One man stood out from all the rest. He could not be beaten. That man was Marcus Magnus. His team of white horses was as magnificent as the man himself. Diana's hand went to her neck where the heavy iron collar held her shackled. She was hot and dirty and thirsty, yet there was absolutely nothing she could do about it until she was freed. When she was unfettered, she would bring the authorities to this place and have them all arrested.

She looked about her to see if she could pinpoint her location so that she could recognize it again. How strange everything looked. She was up on the heights, but instead of looking down on Georgian Bath, the town spread out before her was totally different. An area of about twenty-five acres was covered by what looked like a huge military barracks. The rest was comprised of villas and temples. The larger buildings were pillared in the classic Roman style and yet it appeared to be Bath.

She could see the steam rising from the baths, but by the looks of it one of them was being pulled down. No, she was mistaken—it was being built! How could that be? Diana tried to recall what she had been doing before she found herself in this place. It was hard to remember exactly. She had been walking up on Lansdown Crescent. She remembered an antique shop. Had she gone inside? She was almost certain she had, yet the next thing she recalled was the galloping horses bearing down upon her.

Her gaze wandered to the south. The slopes were filled with what looked like flourishing grapevines. Vineyards stretched as far as the eye could see! If Diana didn't know it was impossible, she would have sworn she had been transported back in time to when the Romans ruled Britain!

When the races were finished, Diana could see the sun had begun to sink behind the rim of the hills. Marcus Magnus was coming her way with a younger man who was extremely handsome.

"Your men are getting better at this," she heard him compliment the young man. "As I told you, it's all very well to dish out strong discipline, but if you don't temper that with the outlet of recreation, you are asking for trouble."

"I love dealing with troublemakers, brother. That's why I made centurion before I was nineteen and cohort centurion at twenty-one."

Magnus cuffed the young giant affectionately. "Don't forget, Petrius, you are dining with me tonight."

One of the men who had shackled Diana saluted Magnus. "Shall I dispose of the prisoner, General?"

Marcus Magnus looked at him blankly for a moment, then recalled who the soldier was speaking of. "No. If you put her to death, I'll get no answers."

"You have a prisoner?" Petrius asked.

Magnus nodded toward the woman in the iron collar. "An odd-looking creature. Caught her spying on us." To his soldier he said, "Take her to my villa so I can interrogate her."

"Let me have the woman," Petrius suggested. "I'll soon get the truth from her."

"If I employed your methods, her screams would upset the natives. There's enough unrest at the moment."

"I don't know why the hell you worry so much about the natives. The uncivilized Britons are only half-a-step from barbarians. Fear is a weapon you should use more often."

"Don't tell your betters how to conduct their business," Marcus said with a grin.

The soldier motioned for Diana to get into the wagon she was shackled to. She scrambled up just as he began to drive it downhill. The ride was surprisingly smooth considering the primitive cart she was in. Diana could see the downhill road they were on was very well built. *A Roman road,* Diana said silently.

She kept telling herself that she was dreaming, or more precisely having a nightmare, but she knew as well as she knew her own name that she was not going to awaken. This was really happening to her. She did not know why, she did not know how, but she feared she was no longer in the eighteenth century.

What was worse, much worse, was that she was a prisoner of the man in command. He and his soldier had spoken almost casually of putting her to death! Diana was filled with dread. She also had a sickening feeling that she was the author of her own misery. Of course this should happen to her! How many times had she expressed disatisfaction with the times she lived in? She was forever daydreaming and looking backward to what had seemed more splendid times in history. She had scorned the men of her own generation, thinking them weak fops when compared to the Elizabethans or the mail-clad knights of the Middle Ages. What if Fate had decided to give her a taste of what real men were like? God help her, these Romans would make the Norman Conquerors look like polished gentlemen.

The wagon went through a gate into the walled garden of a villa. It came to a halt at what appeared to be the back door. An older man of medium height and build, dressed in a plain toga with a thonged whip in his belt, spoke with the wagon driver. He glanced at Diana with the hauteur of a prince. "Release her." He made no effort to hide his distaste for what he saw. "Come," he ordered. Diana rubbed her neck where the collar had chafed her skin, but she did not move from the wagon.

He pointed a long finger imperiously. "You—come!" His hand fell to the whip at his belt and the implication was clear.

Diana got down from the wagon and slowly approached him.

"I am Kell, the slave master in this household. You will obey my orders." His eyes were a clear gray, colorless as a stormy sea. All Diana could read from his expression at the moment was excessive pride. "You will follow me," he directed.

He led her down a long corridor with a tile floor. They went through an archway into a chamber that was sparsely furnished with slatted wooden benches. The tile of this floor, however, was laid out in a beautiful mosaic pattern.

Kell clapped his hands loudly and two women immediately obeyed his summons. They were dressed in plain, long linen tunics. They wore their brown hair pulled back and fastened at the nape of the neck. Diana noticed that they were both unattractive, even coarse looking, but they were immaculately clean.

Kell spoke to them briefly in the same lofty manner he had used with Diana. They immediately bowed their heads and went to do his bidding. Kell pointed to one of the wooden benches. Diana sank down with relief. Her knees felt like water. Her nerves were so on edge she wanted to scream, yet she knew better than to expend her energy arguing with this slave master. She would need every ounce of her strength to deal with Marcus Magnus when he came, and come he would. She was sure of that, though she was sure of nothing else on earth at this moment.

Almost immediately the women reentered the chamber carrying food and drink. Diana was surprised that it was intended for her. She lifted the pewter drinking vessel from the tray and drank thirstily. It was a pleasant brew of honey-sweetened grape juice. Her throat felt so parched that she emptied the goblet. The woman refilled the vessel from a stone flagon.

The other woman set the food tray on the bench beside Diana. One plate held artichoke hearts, ripe olives, and soft white cheese. Another plate was heaped with thinly sliced cold meat and crusty white bread still warm from the oven.

Diana felt too apprehensive to enjoy food, but fearing she might be starved as a punishment, she put food in her mouth and began to chew. After a few bites she had had enough and could swallow no more, though the food was well prepared and tasty. She pushed it away and again took up the drinking vessel.

Diana shrank back as Marcus Magnus strode through the archway. A young woman appeared from nowhere carrying an armful of towels. Though she was a tall, well-made female, Magnus dwarfed her when she reached his side. When Kell approached him, the woman stepped back with deference.

"Will you deal with the captive before or after your bath, General?"

Diana saw the look of annoyance cross the general's face. Once again he had momentarily forgotten her. Without wasting further time he addressed her directly in a tone of total authority. His black eyes swept over her with an insulting air of superiority. "Who are you?" His words and manner brooked no hesitation.

"I am Lady Diana Davenport."

He gave a sharp bark of laughter that contained little amusement. "Ha! Diana. You think yourself a goddess?"

"No. Diana is my name. I am not a goddess, but I *am* a lady." Her chin went up, "Who are you?"

He was taken aback at her high-handed tone.

"*I* am the man who decides if you live or die. You are my prisoner, my property. I want answers and I want them *now*!"

Diana jumped in spite of her resolution to stand up to him. She swallowed hard. "You are a brute and a bully," she said quietly.

"Two of my better qualities. What nationality are you?"

"I am English—British."

"Another lie, by Jupiter! The tribes of Britannia are primitive headhunters, so wild and uncivilized they still paint their bodies with woad to frighten their enemies."

Diana was speechless for a moment. She could not deny that ancient Britons were indeed as he described.

"Where did you come from?" he demanded.

"I came from London. I live in London."

"You mean Londinium? Even your speech is strange. And that's another damned lie—Londinium was destroyed by fire a few months ago. What are you doing in Aquae Sulis?"

"Aquae Sulis, of course! That's the Roman name for Bath," Diana murmured to herself.

"You were spying! You are a filthy Druid spy. Is Aquae Sulis the next city to be burned by the wild Britons whom you Druids have under your control?"

Diana's thoughts spun wildly. She had pored over enough history books to know that around A.D. 60–61 Queen Boadicea of Britain had led an uprising of the native tribes against the Romans and had burned London. "I am no Druid," she said truthfully.

"Then what are you, apart from a filthy bundle of rags?"

The uncivilized brute had the ability to maul her pride. She had no answer that would appease him.

"In those mummers' rags I can neither determine its sex nor its age. Disrobe it!" he ordered the women.

The females who had brought the food tried to remove her gown. When she struggled, the tall woman set down her towels and came to their assistance. Diana fled across the tile floor to the far wall.

Kell took the whip from his belt and advanced toward her with clear intent.

Diana's eyes blazed and her lips drew back from her teeth like a wildcat spitting fury. "You cowardly Romans! Is whipping the only way you know how to deal with a Briton?"

Her words amused Marcus Magnus. He smiled a wolf's smile. "Kell isn't a Roman, he's a Briton. In my experience there is no better slave master in the world than another slave."

Diana was aghast. They had her cornered now and began disrobing her. She was left with only her corset and her filthy wig. Everyone in the room stared in disbelief at the sausage-like garment that encased her. Humiliation stained her cheeks.

Magnus looked at Kell and shrugged. "It must be some misbegotten contraption a Druid priestess wears. Get it off."

After much struggling, pushing, and pulling of strings, as well as cursing and scratching by Diana, the corset came off. In the struggle, so did her dusty powdered wig.

Magnus saw a transformation take place that was as

startling as it was pleasing. When the false white hair came off her head, a silken mass of pale gold curls tumbled down her back; a back that was a delicious curve of ivory alabaster. Freed from the distorting garment that encased her, she was indeed a female—all delicate curves and mounds. Her sweet round breasts thrust upward and were tipped by what looked for all the world like pink rosebuds. Her waist was so narrow he could nearly span it with one powerful hand. Her bottom swelled gently before tapering to long silken thighs and slim legs.

Her fair skin was unblemished, her body more beautiful than any goddess. She cowered upon a slatted wooden bench with excessive misplaced modesty. His body quickened in response to the loveliness before him. Beside the other women, the comparison was so marked he could hardly believe his eyes. She was like fine Italian glass set among thick stone jars.

"By the gods!" he murmured huskily. "Have her bathed and sent to my couch." Then he strode from the villa to his own private bathing pool at the end of the garden.

Diana stared at Kell with loathing.

"You are indeed fortunate. The master liked what was hidden beneath your rags. Your body has saved your life—at least for the present." Kell was greatly surprised that Marcus showed such a marked interest in a woman. The general did not normally waste his time with the opposite sex. He was a stern military man with little time for women. He visited a prostitute or used a slave a couple of times a week, but had never shown a preference for any female slave in particular, though everyone in the household was eager for his attention.

"Please give me something to cover myself."

"Romans find no shame in the naked body. In fact they display it every chance they get," Kell said somewhat dryly.

"I am not a Roman," Diana said, using her hair to cover her bared breasts.

Kell said to one of the women, "Summon a bath slave, better send two; the female is capricious."

Two girls entered the room almost as soon as the serving woman had departed. They were young and muscular, their hair shorn close to their heads. They wore short white tunics and sandals.

"Bathe the new slave, then return her to me. I will select a stola for her."

Diana's head went up proudly. "I am no slave!" she said defiantly.

Kell sighed. He approached the wooden bench and spoke quietly, summoning infinite patience. "You need a good flogging. My instincts tell me that if I give you one now, at the outset, I will save myself much trouble. The master, however, will enjoy your body more if it is unmarred by my flagellum."

Diana gasped. "You must be mad!"

Kell continued as if she hadn't spoken. "Life will be infinitely simpler for both of us if you and I reach an understanding. Your speech and your manner tell me you are a highly intelligent female. My position in this household is secure because my word is law. My word is law because I mete out discipline to everyone beneath me. This household runs as smoothly as warm honey, therefore it is a happy household. That is exactly the way the general wants it, and what the general wants, I want. Ergo, what I want, you should want. Am I making myself clear to you?"

Diana answered him in the same tone he used. "Perfectly clear. I find no fault with your logic, but I abhor your gutlessness and your lack of moral fiber!"

His eyes glittered dangerously. "Proceed." His tone clearly told her that if she proceeded, she did so at her own risk.

"I am naked. I refuse to bandy further words with you."

Kell knew exactly what she meant. He was the slave driver of his own people at the bidding of a Roman. Her ideals were most lofty and noble only because she had never experienced slavery. He was interested to see how long her principles would stand up after she'd had a taste of it. He wouldn't have to wait long.

"I hoped we could reach an understanding, but all we have reached is an impasse. So be it." He motioned for the bath slaves to take her.

They did not go in the same direction the general had taken, so she assumed there was more than one bathing area. They took her through a door covered by a heavy canvas curtain. Diana felt a great relief that there were no longer male eyes upon her.

The room, not overly large, was tiled in spotless white; the square sunken bathing pools in turquoise. Steam rose in vaporous clouds from the larger pool. The steaming water looked most inviting to Diana.

"I shall bathe myself," she said imperiously, going down the steps into the water.

The bath slaves exchanged a look but made no protest. One of them poured something into the water from a beautifully shaped flacon. Clouds of scented steam rose up to fill Diana's senses. "What is that?" she asked.

"It is frankincense, an aromatic," came the reply.

The warm water felt heavenly. Diana closed her eyes and leaned her head back against the turquoise tiles. She breathed deeply and it seemed to Diana that the worries and fears that had threatened to overwhelm her began to melt away along with her tension. Suddenly she heard people in the water with her.

Her eyes flew open and she was gripped by fear as she saw a bath slave on either side of her, each holding a dangerous-looking weapon in her hand.

When she cried out, the girls tried to still her fears. "It is only a strigil," one said, holding it on the palm of her hand.

"A strigil?"

When the girl saw she was puzzled, she explained, "It is a scraping tool to cleanse the skin. It won't hurt. Come."

Diana felt too tired to protest. She left the water and lay down on a marble surface as they indicated she should. It sounded like an unpleasant experience to have your skin scraped, but Diana realized she would encounter a myriad of strange customs in this villa and in Aquae Sulis. The quicker she could adapt to new and untried things, the easier it would be for her.

Having to adapt to another time and another culture would be an upheaval of all she had ever known. It would be upsetting physically as well as mentally and emotionally. She told herself that she was more intelligent and more highly educated than any of the people who lived in this household, and coming from the modern world made her more civilized than any of the primitive people who lived in this first century.

She must try to go with the flow of life here. She must accept the smaller differences, which were really of little consequence. She would reserve her energy and her strength to protest the larger issues, which she could never accept. Like slavery! Surely it must be abhorrent to all civilized people?

Diana was pleasantly surprised at the feel of the strigil as it smoothed over her body. The bath slaves massaged her with almond oil, then slicked off the excess with the cleansing tool. Then they urged her back into the hot water, where they washed her hair with handfuls of soft soap.

Finally they urged her to leave the bath and submerge herself in the smaller one. The cold plunge took her breath away and the bath slaves laughed with her as gooseflesh arose on her arms and legs. They wrapped her in a large, thirsty bath cloth and rubbed the wetness from her hair until it was a mass of damp curls.

The pair then stripped off their wet tunics and replaced them with identical short dry ones. They ushered her to yet another room of the villa. The floor was rich mosaic tile, the walls painted cream in contrast. Torches in wall brackets made the room bright. They invited her to sit upon a cushioned stool shaped like a throne. It had exquisitely curved cabriole legs and looked as if it had been created by the famous Georgian designer Robert Adam. Then Diana realized that Adam must have borrowed the design from the Romans.

The mirror before her was highly polished pure silver, which would have been almost priceless in modern times. One girl set to work on her hair with combs, brushes, and hot tongs. The other opened a carved box and set out jars of creams, lotions, perfumes, and face paint.

Diana was woman enough to take pleasure in the adornment of her person. She watched fascinated as her face became framed with tiny tendrils made from the paler silver-gilt hair that grew at her brow and temples. The rest fell about her shoulders and back like a cloud of gold. The other slave dusted Diana's cheeks with color, touched her lips with carmine, and even her eyelids with silver.

Diana gazed at her reflection with bemused pleasure. The bath slaves had worked magic—they had made her beautiful!

Chapter 8

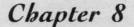

Kell entered the room carrying the robe he had selected for her. Amethyst eyes met gray and held for a long moment. The garment he had chosen was such a vibrant color, Diana lusted for it. He handed it to one of the girls and stood with arms across his chest waiting to see her adorned.

Diana fought down her distaste at having a man watch her dress. She knew no amount of protests would rid her of his presence. She would simply have to think of him as a slave rather than a man. The thought covered her with guilt. Was she already becoming tainted?

The floss silk robe was magenta. Diana had never dared to even hope to own anything in this magnificent shade. It enhanced her coloring a hundredfold, turning her hair to moonlight and her skin to pearl. She wore no undergarments and the irony was not lost upon her. How many times had she wished her body free of restrictive underclothes?

One of the bath slaves bent to her feet and slipped on sandals with high elevated cork soles. When Diana stood up from the stool to see if she could walk in them, she saw the skirt of the magenta silk was slit to the waist on one side to display her leg with each step she took. And an extremely long leg it appeared, atop the high cork soles.

Kell watched with hooded eyes. "The Egyptian

musk," he decided. That particular perfume was so costly the girl brought the alabaster flacon to Kell rather than apply it herself. As he reached out to anoint Diana between her breasts, their eyes locked. His touch was so detached and impersonal that Diana knew they were taking the first tentative steps along the road to understanding.

Diana had managed to keep the words of the general who owned this magnificent villa at bay. Now, however, they came stealing back to her. *Have her bathed and sent to my couch.* Well, the first order had been carried out. She had been bathed and beautified. No longer would he be able to call her a filthy bundle of rags. She thanked God for it. A woman had much more confidence and power when she knew she looked her loveliest.

Now she would be sent to his couch, wherever that was. Well, she was ready for him! All of a sudden the meaning of couch became clarified. His couch meant his bed! My God, how ignorant she was. That is what all this bathing and anointing had been about. They had turned her into an object of pleasure for his enjoyment!

The pupils of her eyes turned dark purple as she looked furiously at Kell. "You are sadly mistaken if you think I will go docilely to the general's sleeping chamber! He may order this household of slaves to his black heart's content, but I am not his slave; I will not obey his orders." She watched Kell's hand fall to his whip and deliberately raised her chin. "Not without one hell of a fight, I won't. I will ruin the tranquillity of this household, I will run riot and cause such pandemonium I will awaken the dead!" She stood defiantly with hands upon hips berating the slave master with her fiery temper. "I will pull this villa down, stone by bloody stone, before I will submit to him."

Kell had his choice of weapons to make her obey. He chose a subtle one. "What transpires between Marcus Magnus and yourself is your own private business. I recognize your high principles and feel sure you will not drag others to their downfall over this affair. If the bath slaves fail to deliver you to his couch, they will be flogged for their disobedience. As slave master of this household, I will be the one ordered to administer the flogging to these young girls. All the while your own precious skin will go unscathed. You possess an eloquent tongue. I suggest you await the Primus Pilus in his sleeping chamber and tell him yourself that you will pull his villa down, stone by bloody stone.''

Diana swallowed hard. What Kell suggested would take a great deal of courage. Yet the alternative was unthinkable. No one must be flogged because of her, if she could prevent it. She knew full well Kell had used his wits to persuade her to do his bidding, yet she could not help but feel a measure of admiration for his clever tactics.

Diana inclined her head. ''Lead on.''

He took her up to the second story of the villa and led her into a large chamber. ''After the master dined, he and his brother went to the amphitheatre. It could be hours before he returns. I suggest you rest while you may.''

His advice did nothing for her morale, but she bit back a retort and allowed him to leave.

Marcus Magnus had been looking forward to spending the evening with his younger brother. They had not seen each other for five years. Now his brother's legion had come here to Britannia and would undergo vigorous training in Aquae Sulis before it ventured into the wilds of Western Britannia, which still lay unconquered.

Marcus waited in the atrium ready to welcome Petrius when he entered the villa. Instead of enfolding him in his arms, he smote him on the shoulder. ''By Jupiter, you look fit. You have filled out considerably from the seventeen-year-old I left in Rome.''

Petrius had followed in his brother's footsteps. Marcus had signed up for twenty-six years of military service at only fourteen years old, becoming a professional soldier for life. Petrius had had to wait until his seventeenth birthday because he did not have the brawn and muscle of Marcus. What he lacked in physique, however, he made up for in ferocity, rising all the way to cohort centurion, commanding over five hundred soldiers.

He ruled his men through fear and would have exchanged his handsome face with Marcus any day of the week. His brother's visage was both dark and stark. The bridge of his nose and the planes of his cheeks made him look hard, severe, invincible. The scar from temple to cheekbone added a touch of savage violence that Petrius coveted.

As he looked about his brother's villa, Marcus' face was not the only thing he coveted. It was almost as grand as their father's outside Rome. The atrium had a glass roof through which he could gaze at the stars. It also had a marble fountain where gold and silver fishes darted about between the fronds of water plants.

They walked between marble pillars to enter the triclinium, where Marcus could dine alone or entertain his dinner guests. The entire chamber was decorated in gold and white. Marble pillars encircled its walls, white marble tables stood between reclining couches, piled with gold and white pillows and elbow cushions.

"Very grand. How many chambers?" Petrius inquired, determined to keep the envy he felt from his voice.

Magnus shrugged. "A score perhaps."

"How many slaves?"

"Thirty household slaves," Magnus replied, eliminating the gardeners and outside slaves who tended his walled peristyle, making it a beautiful sanctuary. He did not wish to sound ostentatious to Petrius.

"You own others?"

Since Petrius would not leave it alone, Marcus gave him the whole truth. "I own hundreds. All taken in battle as prizes of war. I fought a decade in Africa and Gaul before I came to Britannia. I fought here four years before I became Primus Pilus. That adds up to a lot of prisoners."

"I do not take prisoners. The thrill of battle is bloodying my sword in the slaughter of Rome's enemies."

"With the right guidance enemies can become allies. My slaves are all willing workers. They build the roads, aqueducts, and the baths here. Some of them are engineers. They are learning skills they can use once they earn their freedom."

"Freedom? You are a fool, Marcus. When you are done with them, you should send them to the galleys or to Rome to fight in the arena games. Either would soon finish them off instead of letting them live to stab you in the back some dark night."

Marcus changed the subject. Petrius enjoyed bloodlust as did many Romans. Because of it he would rise in the ranks. He might need it where he was going. Marcus had been there. The various wild tribes of the Celtae were head-hunters. The mountains to the west and the Island of Mona were like marching into Hades. "So, has Rome changed much in five years?"

"Surely you jest? Since your last leave to recuperate from your wounds, so much building has gone on, you wouldn't recognize the place. Since Nero became emperor, the entertainments have become spectacular! They are the envy of the entire world. We have beast hunts not only in the circus, but in every part of the city. I admire Nero enormously."

Marcus said bluntly, "He fucked his mother, then poisoned her."

Petrius laughed. "A fate most women deserve!"

Marcus' thoughts flew to the beautiful slave girl he had just acquired. Already he was impatient to possess her. He forced his mind back to the conversation. "I should love to see the chariot races at Circus Maximus. I'd even like to try my hand at racing there."

"I don't frequent the races. I prefer the gladiators and the bestiari, and of course the executions."

Since Magnus could see no entertainment in executions, he thought perhaps Petrius was trying to goad him, but then his brother surprised him with a compliment.

"If you did race there, you would surely win, as you did today."

"I'm not so sure, Petrius. The Britons are the greatest charioteers in the world. 'Tis from them I learned the skill."

"Nero imports all he can get. Why are they better than Romans?"

"Because they still use the chariot for warfare. We gave it up years ago; a mistake, in my opinion. Our foot soldiers are too slow to fight them. They are in and out like lightning. Wait until you encounter them in battle, you won't believe the things they can do."

"The Roman legion is the greatest military machine the world has ever known," Petrius scoffed.

All the time they talked, they reclined upon couches while impeccably trained slaves brought in the many courses of deliciously prepared food. Between each course, other slaves brought in scented water and towels. Petrius almost choked from envy for his plate was made of solid gold.

"Nevertheless our losses are colossal. But don't worry, I'll teach you all the tricks. That's why you were sent to Aquae Sulis."

"Acceptable losses are just part of the price we pay for conquering the world."

"Indeed they are," Marcus said grimly.

"How have you endured it here, all these years away from Rome?" Petrius asked curiously.

Marcus' mind swept back to when he was twelve years old. Emperor Claudius had just invaded Britannia and it had fired his ambition to become a Roman general and conquer new lands. Because of his size and strength, the army had taken him at fourteen. "I like Britannia, especially Aquae Sulis. Under Claudius, people flocked here from all over the empire. They intermarried with Britons and became extremely civilized. They speak Latin as well as you or I; they have adopted Roman dress. Merchants from the far corners of the world have set up their shops so that any commodity or luxury can be purchased. Here we have the best of all cultures, theatres, amphitheatres, temples. We are close to the sea, and we are not overcrowded as is Rome. We are far away from the corruption of politics, and best of all are our hot springs that bubble from the earth at a constant temperature of one hundred and sixteen degrees!"

When the food was cleared away, the wine was served.

"Well, I may not admire the place as you do, but I find no fault with its oysters or its wine," Petrius said affably.

"Let's be off. How would you like to spend the evening?"

"How about the theatre? But none of your dreary poetry by Sophocles, thanks. A bawdy play might suffice. Then a visit to a luxuria might be stimulating. You do have fornices here?"

"They are known here as brothels. We have prostitutes from as far away as Asia and Arabia."

"Do you suppose they have Nubians? Can I purchase the services of a male *and* a female?"

"A good thing I served oysters tonight," Marcus said dryly. He had looked forward to spending the evening with his brother, but now that it was here, he would have rather stayed home a thousandfold. He thought fleetingly of the lovely creature he had ordered to his couch. His taste for a coarse and lewd prostitute diminished by the minute.

Petrius chose a mime theatre. It was a roaring farce where a lover was surprised by the return of a jealous husband and forced to hide beneath the bed. Then it showed his great suffering as the husband performed numerous sex acts with his wife upon the very couch the lover hid beneath.

The language was exceedingly gross. The posturing of

the actors and actresses was indescribably vulgar. All was accompanied by loud music and florid dancing. The theatre was packed with men, most of them Roman soldiers, but also merchants and a vast number of the youth of Aquae Sulis.

Marcus was bored to death, but was thankful that Petrius laughed throughout. His brother's only discontent was that at the interval they did not enliven the audience with a bear or bull baiting.

The play seemed to go on interminably, with the grossest parts receiving the loudest applause. Finally, it was over, and as they filed out of the theatre, Marcus searched his mind for an excuse not to visit a brothel tonight.

"You should see the fornices that have sprung up outside Circus Maximus. Bawds solicit from morning 'til night."

"That's because the sadistic pleasures of the games raise sexual excitement to a high pitch," Marcus explained, hiding the distaste he felt.

"Every bakery and cookshop owner in Rome now keeps slave girls for sexual purposes to entertain their customers. Females can be had for two pennies."

"We are behind times here in Aquae Sulis," Marcus said, silently thanking the gods that it was so, and wondering why it was that Rome was losing her glory as she became more degenerate.

They took a litter to the seamiest street in Aquae Sulis, where Magnus took his brother into a fornice that catered to depraved appetites. He paid five gold sesterces to the whoremaster, then bid Petrius goodnight. He said, grinning, "I must be getting old. The chariot races today used up all my excess energy and dawn comes early."

"Indulge, brother, you can sleep when you're dead!" Petrius insisted. "Or could it be your seraglio of female slaves that draws you home? Come to think of it, you have been distracted all evening. I shall return to see what the great attraction is."

Marcus laughed. "Come anytime, Petrius. My villa is yours while you are in Aquae Sulis."

"I accept your generosity. I prefer to sleep at the barracks with my men as they need watching, but I just might avail myself of your peristyle and your private bath."

Relief swept over Marcus as he made his escape. Tomorrow would be a long, hard day, dominated by lessons of vicious swordplay. Then he grimaced. Marcus wasn't deceiving himself for one minute. The strong lure that drew him home to his villa was a fascinating female who called herself Lady Diana.

Though she dreaded the arrival of the brute whose orders held her captive, Diana was enthralled as she gazed about the general's sleeping chamber. It was so large it must have taken up one whole side of the villa. The shutters were open to reveal glazed windows, which surprised her. Hadn't the early castles and watchtowers built centuries after the Romans left Britain used hides to cover arrow slits?

The longest wall boasted a marble hearth. Above it the entire wall was painted in a fresco. Diana went over to study it and saw that the figures depicted on the plaster were Roman gods and goddesses, most of whom were naked! Diana was fascinated; she had never seen nude bodies depicted in art before.

The dominant god at the top, gripping a golden thunderbolt, had to be Jupiter. The female below him and to his right, whose belly was swollen with child, had to be Juno, the goddess of women and childbirth. There were many others Diana did not recognize.

At the lower left of the wall was a feast, a drunken feast by the way the limbs of the bodies were wrapped about each other! Diana blushed and decided the artist was depicting Bacchus; the feast a Bacchanalia. The male bodies were magnificent with broad backs and chests, all heavily muscled with limbs like treetrunks. The females were grossly overweight with large breasts, bellies, and thighs.

Only one female had a lithe body. She stood in a grove of trees with her hand upon a stag. She had golden hair, long bare legs, and one bared breast. The entire fresco was most disturbing. She lowered her eyes to the marble fireplace, which was black with gold veins. Beside the hearth was a huge saucer-shaped bronze brazier. Diana puzzled over its use.

Then her eyes fell upon the bed, which dominated the room. It was massive and sat high upon a platform with steps up to the dais. She supposed it could be termed a four-poster, except the posts were ceiling-high Roman columns whose tops were decorated by curled rams' horns. The bed itself was covered with animal skins whose fur was deep-piled and glossy. On top of the furs were a dozen pillows and cushions embroidered in black, gold, and purple. It, too, was disturbing. She deliberately turned her back upon it.

In an alcove toward the back of the chamber was an ebony desk and a massive chair to go with it. There were parchments and papers with what looked and felt like heavy linen content, but the things that filled Diana with awe were the wooden and wax tablets and styluses. She ran her fingers over them reverently. She had read of such things, but never dreamed she would ever actually get to see and touch them.

Behind the desk, maps were displayed upon the wall. Three were of Bath, or Aquae Sulis as it was called. She studied them and saw that one map showed how it used to look, one how it looked at the present time, and the third showed improvements that were planned. She traced her fingertip along the Roman road known as the Fosse Way. Another, larger map, encompassed Northern England and parts of Scotland, while at least four maps depicted Wales.

The moment Diana saw the book scrolls, all her attention became focused upon them. Obviously he read the Greek philosophers. Here were Homer and Sophocles translated into Latin by someone called Suetonius. She selected a leather box holding a scroll of Satires by Horace and, unrolling it, read at random.

> "And when your lust is hot, surely
> if a maid or pageboy's handy to attack
> you won't choose to grin and bear it?
> *I* won't! I like a cheap and easy love!"

Diana let the scroll reroll itself. What a disgusting philosophy! She found a history about Julius Caesar when Rome was a republic rather than an empire. She sat down in the great ebony chair and began to read. She became so absorbed, she lost track of time.

Suddenly, she heard a man's deep voice. My God, he was come!

Chapter 9

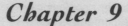

Marcus' powerful body filled the doorway as he paused on the threshold. His black eyes swept over her, from her golden hair to her cork-soled sandals, and back up to her silver eyelids. Then he entered his sleeping chamber and secured the door. He came halfway across the room toward her, where the light from the torches illuminated her loveliness.

In contrast, his shadowed face looked dangerously dark. His jet black eyes missed no finest detail. He saw how the magenta silk turned her hair the color of moonbeams. Saw how it molded the globes of her upthrusting breasts, revealing their diamond-hard nipples.

He watched her jump up from the chair, saw her lips part with a tiny gasp, noticed how her delicate hands fluttered as she dropped the scroll she held. *Can she actually read?*

When she stood, he watched the clinging material caress her curves. It revealed the place where her navel dipped in, and even more temptingly, where her high pubic bone raised the magenta silk to show off her delicious Mound of Venus.

His ebony eyes traveled down the slit skirt, along her slim leg to her delicate ankle and small foot. Then he slowly reversed the direction of his gaze, allowing it to trace her body from her toes to her temples.

She was like a rare gift from the gods. Had he done something exceptionally noble and courageous recently to receive such a reward? His arousal was most pleasurable. He could feel the pulsebeat in his shaft match the one in his throat.

"Walk for me," he said softly.

Diana was startled, both at the request and at the soft tone of his voice. Her chin went up, her eyes blazed violet fire. "Where shall I walk?" her voice dripped with sweet sarcasm. "All the way to your bed?"

"That would be my choice." His words were direct, but the tone was low and husky. It made her belly and breasts contract with a quiver. His dark eyes saw.

"Well, it wouldn't be my bloody choice!" she challenged recklessly.

"You *have* no choice. You are my slave," Marcus said quietly. His look told her he would consume her, devour her. She knew deep in her bones and her belly it was inevitable. She knew in his eyes she was beautiful. She knew he desired her above all other women at that moment and the knowledge was melting her insides to molten hot lava.

It was his total masculinity that did it. He was more male than any man she had ever known or conjured in her fantasies and the innate femaleness at her core cried out for him. He had asked her to walk for him and unbelievably that is what she yearned to do. She began to pace in front of him sinuously, provocatively, sensuously, placing one high-soled foot before the other, undulating her hips, knowing the magenta silk clung to her bottom cheeks, molding them possessively.

Eve-like, she wanted to set his blood on fire. Her wicked juices were bubbling out of control, running like wildfire along her veins, all flowing to her hot woman's center between her legs. "Your slave? What happened to your preposterous notion that I was a spy or Druid priestess? Has all your fear of me vanished?''

He gave a sharp bark of laughter. ''I am a Roman. Romans do not fear women. I care naught for what you were before today. Today, whatever you were, ceased to be. From this day forth you are my slave, my property. You have only one reason for living and that reason is to please Marcus Magnus.''

As she undulated before him, displaying her fire and passion, the glint in his black eyes told her that she pleased him inordinately. The newfound female power within her surged. ''Well, Roman, if it pleases you to think me your slave you may do so, but let me disabuse you of any notion that I will be your *willing* slave. Before I submit to your demands, you will have to use your whip.''

The verbal foreplay served only to whet his appetite, making him hungry for her, then ravenous. ''I am a Roman. I do not need to whip my chosen slaves.'' He climbed the steps to his bed, then sat upon it to remove his shin guards and sandals. The muscles of his powerful calves bulged like lumps of iron. His bare thighs looked even harder.

Diana ran her tongue over lips gone suddenly dry. She stopped pacing. She stood before him with hands on hips and mimicked him. '' 'I am a Roman!' Such bloody arrogance. You are less civilized than a savage!''

He unfastened his wide leather belt, then laid aside his short, wide gladius sword and his dagger. ''Is that what you are hoping?'' he asked softly. His quiet question was more menacing than if he had shouted, promising that he could be more savage than any man alive.

''My God, no,'' she whispered, showing a vulnerability that deeply thrilled him, making his cock pulse savagely.

He unfastened his ornamental breastplate and the segmented bronze girdle of his cuirass, then removed them. He wore only a short white linen tunic now. He spread his knees wide, then rested his elbows upon them as he leaned toward her. ''Come to me,'' he ordered softly.

Marcus Magnus sat upon the high bed covered with furs as if it were a throne and he, Emperor of the World.

"No, I cannot." Diana trembled slightly. Her refusal was no longer defiant, but it was firm.

"Give me a reason why you cannot," he said, his eyes caressing each trembling curve.

"I am a virgin," she blurted.

He stared at her in disbelief. "Now you are telling me you are a vestal virgin?" His voice was incredulous.

"No, not a vestal virgin—just a virgin."

He smote his thigh and laughed. "Impossible!" His laughter ceased. She looked as if she were serious. "You have known no man before me?" The thought that it might be possible did strange and glorious things to him.

"No, I have never known a man."

"But that is ridiculous. It makes no sense. You are female; a female's only purpose is to give pleasure to the male. Why are you not experienced in the ways of Venus?"

"Because I am unmarried," she explained.

"So?" he asked, still not comprehending.

"Where I come from, a girl must remain virgin until she becomes a bride." Diana's cheeks were flushed with the intimacy of the subject.

"Why?" Marcus demanded. "It serves no purpose to preserve a hymen. There is no logic, no benefit." *If that is true, why does the possibility that she is virgin drive you to the edge of madness? Why is your manroot ready to burst?*

"I don't know," Diana whispered. "I only know that in my culture no man would take you for his wife if you were not intact. If an unmarried female is physically ruined, she is worthless and disgraced. It is the single most important thing in a young woman's existence."

It angered him when she spoke of her culture and her previous life. "Have I not told you that from today your past existence is wiped away? From this day—this night, you are mine. Your sole purpose in life is to pleasure me. Come!"

His voice was imperious; his face as proud as a Roman eagle.

Her anger flared immediately. "And have I not told you that I will not willingly become your slave!"

He stood up and pointed to her. "You *are* my slave, as you will soon learn!"

"Perhaps I am your slave, Roman"—she lifted her chin defiantly—"but I am not your *bed* slave. Not without a flogging! Are you savage enough to enjoy me after you have whipped me bloody?"

He descended the steps to her. Though she knew not how, Diana did not retreat from him. Marcus Magnus came so close, they were almost touching. "I shall bloody you, but my weapon will not be my whip." His black eyes bored into hers, mastering her with his dominant presence.

Pick me up and carry me to your bed, a wicked voice inside her cried.

He could smell the Egyptian musk and something else, far headier. His mouth descended upon hers in a kiss that was brutal in its intensity, designed to prove to her that he was the master, she the slave.

Her mouth was deliciously soft and compliant beneath his, then suddenly she fastened her sharp little teeth into his bottom lip. He had to give her golden hair a vicious tug to force her to let go.

She drew back panting, a victorious light glittering in her amethyst eyes. " 'Tis I who bloodied you, Roman."

He drew back his arm to knock her to the floor. Then it was as if the gods held back his fist to prevent him from felling her. Marcus realized with a sickening twist of his gut that if his blow had connected, he would have smashed the delicate bones of her face. He strode to the portal, flung it open, and bellowed, "Kell!"

Within a minute the slave master entered the sleeping chamber. He lowered his eyelids so that the general would not see the light of admiration that he felt for the new slave. He knew instantly that Diana had not yielded to him. Knew also that she had kindled a towering desire in Marcus that he had never experienced for another woman. His enormous arousal lifted his linen tunic. He seethed with anger and lust, a fatal combination.

"This *lady* thinks she is too fine to come to my bed. She is not convinced that she is my slave. I am sure that between the two of us, we can persuade her to the truth that I own her. Together I know we can prevail upon her to accept her fate."

"I will do my best, General," Kell said. His hand fell upon the handle of his flagellum, but before he could brandish it, he was surprised to see Marcus Magnus blanch at the punishment he threatened. *He wants her desperately and he wants her unmarked. I wonder if she knows how much power that gives her?*

Marcus Magnus' face was a bronze mask. "Replace her fine silk with an ugly brown toga and cover her fancy hair with a plain head cloth. Scrub her face so that it is free of flattering lip salve and eye paint. Give her only bread and water."

"I've worn ugly clothes all my life," she cried defiantly. "It matters not one whit to me!"

"Ah, but now that you have had a taste of looking exquisite, your female vanity will not put up with ugly rags for long."

Damn you, damn you, Marcus Magnus, you know exactly how to attack my pride.

"At five tomorrow morning put her to work scrubbing my tile floors. I believe there are at least a score in my villa. It should take her until nightfall to make every last one spotless. Then you will bring her once more to my couch and we will see if the *lady* has had a change of heart."

Her chin went up with the hauteur of a goddess. "I shall deny you throughout eternity."

His black eyes blazed into hers. "One way or another, I will have you on your knees to me!"

* `*` *

If I do not put space between them, their sparks will set the villa ablaze, Kell thought.

Diana followed the slave master down an upper hall. He selected a small airy sleeping chamber for her and took her inside. Blazing torches showed her it was plastered in an apricot color with a terra-cotta tiled floor. A design of the Celtic Sun God, Sul, was at its center. The head of the bed was made from wrought iron, painted gold with a design of a many-rayed sun upon it. The covers were cloth of gold that looked like woven sateen and brocade.

There was a corner hearth with the same sort of oval dish atop a brazier that she had seen in the general's chamber. There was also a dressing table with a mirror of highly polished bronze. All in all, it did not look like the room of a slave.

Kell summoned house slaves, who appeared immediately even though the hour approached midnight. In a low voice he issued his orders. When they returned, one carried in scented water and towels; another brought a plain brown linen toga and matching head cloth. A female slave stripped the bed of its fine covers while another remade it with coarse-fibered sheets. The slave set down the water bowl and stood waiting with the towel.

Kell said, "Wash your face."

After a moment's hesitation, Diana obeyed him.

Kell thought her skin so fine, she was lovely without the aid of paint.

A slave held out the toga. "Remove the magenta silk," Kell said quietly.

Diana bent to remove the cork-soled sandals, then she flung them across the room. They thudded into the wall with a crash. Then she snatched up the ugly brown toga and flung it after the sandals.

Kell's hooded gray eyes showed no emotion. He turned

to a female slave. "Remove the magenta silk." The slave obeyed him immediately.

Diana stood tall and proud while she was deprived of her finery. Then like a prideful cat she walked to the bed and slipped between the coarse sheets.

"Leave us," Kell ordered the house slaves. When they were alone, he spoke low. "Do not be a fool. Give him what he desires. He prides himself on his self-control. I have never seen him lust so for a woman before. Give him what he asks—it is so little. He will be more than generous to you."

"I cannot," she replied.

"Will not, you mean. You were so exquisitely lovely tonight, you could have seduced him with the flutter of an eyelash." When she made no reply, Kell extinguished the torches and withdrew.

Diana lay in the darkness reflecting upon her encounter with the Primus Pilus and then Kell's words of advice. Cleopatra had gone down as one of the greatest women in history because she had conquered Caesar and seduced the Roman general, Mark Antony. Marcus Antonius—Marcus Magnus. If she were willing, perhaps she could rival Cleopatra!

Kell thought it such a little thing. Even the great Roman himself put no value upon virginity. When she closed her eyes she could see his magnificent body, hard with bulging, rippling muscle. She could see his eagle's face, so strong, so proud, with the slash of scar from temple to cheekbone making his deeply bronzed face almost irresistible.

She saw the black eyes glittering with lust, the coal black hair curling upon the thick column of his neck, the powerful shoulders and the arms bulging above and below his golden amulets. Diana often lied, but never to herself. As she lay there, she admitted that she lusted for him. She wanted this magnificent Roman general to initiate her into the mystical rites of womanhood. All she had to do was place her hand in his.

And acknowledge that I am his slave, a voice inside her said. *Only think,* another voice said. *No other woman of your time will have an opportunity such as this. Diana, if you are suddenly swept back to your own time and you have not shared his bed, you will regret it for the rest of your life! But how could I return no longer a virgin?*

Sleep finally claimed her. After an hour she began to dream. She dreamed that someone had tied her hands to the head of the bed. She struggled in vain against her bonds. The wrought iron symbol of the sun on the bed's headpiece laughed down at her. *Dear God, even in my dreams I am a slave in bondage!*

Chapter 10

Marcus Magnus lay naked atop the furs of his great pedestal bed. His massive arms were folded behind his head, his black eyes staring up at nothing. His body was still aroused from his encounter with his new slave. He was a man of great self-control and he willed his body to be quiet.

The trouble was he had been lying here for the best part of an hour, and if anything, his rampant male member grew harder by the minute. Even his sac and testes were taut and aching.

Impatiently he threw his legs over the edge of the bed and stood up. His erection stood up too, all the way to his navel. He cursed and reached for the bell pull to summon a female slave who would ease his body's lust. He cursed again and let his hand fall. He had no taste for a quick in and out. Tonight he had no desire for any female save one.

He took the small torch that still burned and lit all the lamps in the chamber. His eyes fell upon the wall fresco depicting the gods. They widened as he realized the female's likeness was painted on the wall of his sleeping chamber. The other goddesses were almost grotesque when compared to this one. Diana of the Grove. Her delicate hand rested upon the neck of a stag. The two females were identical from the golden hair to the long bare legs. Even their name was the same: Diana.

He felt her hand upon his neck; it turned him into a rutting stag. Diana of the Grove wore a tunic that bared one breast. He would order Kell to adorn his Diana in such a garment. He wanted her company at the evening meal each night when his day's duty was done. Until he tamed her, he would have her seated on the floor beside his dining couch, close under his hand.

Once she accepted her role, he would have her recline upon her own dining couch opposite his, so that she could entertain him with civilized conversation. When she became his concubine, she would share his dining couch, so they could recline together, intimately touching and tasting.

His marble-hard phallus jerked and bucked. He knew if he touched himself at that moment, his seed would spurt forth simply from thinking of her. Diana the Huntress? No. Diana of the Grove? Doubtful. He dismissed the idea that she was a goddess, but the idea that she might be a gift from the gods lingered in his thoughts. Diana the Virgin? He almost spilled!

Had he really been gifted with a virgin? It was highly doubtful. Marcus laughed at himself. It was nothing more than wishful thinking. However, he must thank the gods for this gift! He would make them a sacrifice. He took a small cake of salt from a silver casket and broke it into the shallow bronze dish. He sprinkled the salt with frankincense and myrrh, then lit the incense in the brazier beneath the dish.

Marcus poured himself a flagon of bloodred wine and lifted it high. Then he rubbed the gold coin, bearing the head of Caesar, that he always wore about his neck. "Jupiter Optimus Maximus, best and greatest, I offer thanks for the gift of the female slave." Marcus then thanked the Greek god Eros, silently, so that he would not offend the Roman gods.

He quaffed the wine, then splashed some into the bronze dish. "I ask a boon. I ask that she be virgin." Then he drained the goblet. His blood was on fire, but it was not wine that affected him, it was woman!

Smoldering, aromatic scents filled the air, yet all Marcus could smell was Egyptian musk. She had saturated his senses. He paced about sacrificing his sleep time for visions of her. He gave no thought to the heavy day ahead of him, to the endless hours of training men before their fighting skills were honed enough to send them into the dark wilds of the savage west country. All he thought of was Diana.

If he was not careful, she would become an obsession. Were the gods playing with him, laughing at him? Finally he knew he would have no peace until he learned her secret. Marcus knew he must learn if she was indeed a virgin. There was only one way to find out.

At a certain point in her dream, Diana's eyes flew open. Perhaps she was not dreaming! All she could see was darkness, but she sensed that someone was there in the room with her. She tried to hit out, but her hands had been tightly secured. So, it was no dream, she was bound in very truth!

She closed her eyes tightly as the sudden flare of a torch blinded her. Instinctively, she used the only defense she had and kicked out wildly to keep her predator at bay. Her ankles were suddenly seized in a viselike grip. When she opened her eyes to see who attacked her, she was frozen with fear. It was the all-powerful Roman general who towered before her at the foot of her bed!

The hands gripping her ankles felt like iron manacles. His gigantic shadow loomed up the wall, making him appear even more massive. And he was naked.

Diana tried to swallow, but she could not. She tried to breathe, but found it impossible. She had always wondered what a man's parts looked like. Now she saw. She saw, but she did not believe. Parts like these could not be concealed in the satin breeches of Regency men!

His sex organ was far too big, far too hard, rising like a Roman column from a nest of blue-black curls. A nest that held two swan's eggs! He had obviously come to rape her and she knew that when he impaled her, he would kill her.

Diana found her voice. It was a low, breathless whisper. "Please, do not do this thing."

His black eyes caressed the curves and mounds of her alabaster beauty spread before him. She was totally different from other women. She was so much finer. It was as if she had been refined, then re-refined for eons until she had reached perfection. She had soft down upon her belly, giving her skin the texture of velvet. The skin that covered her luscious breasts, however, was almost transparent, revealing delicate blue veins. She looked ethereal as an angel. Her mons was domed high like an arch crowned with a hundred pale gold tendrils. When he finally opened the petals of her female center, he hoped the color would be the same rose pink as her soft mouth and the aureoles that crowned the tips of her breasts. With her wrists tied above her head, her breasts thrust up like luscious fruit, ripe for tasting.

As he stood transfixed, drinking in her loveliness, drowning in desire, she found the courage to beg him again. "Please, Marcus, do not do this thing."

"I am riven with need," he said low.

"If you rape me, you will kill me," she whispered.

"I have not come to rape you," he said hoarsely.

"Then why are you here?"

"I seek only the truth."

"What do you mean?" she cried, desperately trying to understand.

"I would know if you are truly virgin," he said huskily.

Suddenly she understood. It was like a revelation. "My God, you wouldn't!" Yet incredibly, she knew that he would. He wanted proof of her virginity. A blazing anger dispelled her fear. "You Roman swine! I thought virginity meant nothing to you. You said it served no purpose to preserve a hymen. You said there was no logic in such a thing, no benefit!''

''I want the truth.''

Diana knew he was a man of his word. In that moment he had more determination than any man alive. No plea on earth would sway him from his intent. And then she had another revelation. He was doing this because he didn't believe her!

She lay before him completely helpless and yet somehow she possessed all the power. She held the power because she was still in possession of her maidenhead. Diana began to tremble. Though he perceived each tremor, it did not stop him.

Her fear stemmed from being hurt and Marcus had no desire to hurt her. He wrapped one arm about her legs above the ankles and lifted her knees. The fingers of his other hand reached out to touch her woman's center.

Diana flinched, then swallowing hard, she fixed her attention on the golden coin that hung about his neck.

She was so hot and dry to the touch, he wished he had lubrication so he would not hurt her. His eyes fell to the swollen head of his phallus where he saw a huge drop of glistening clear body fluid. He caught it on his fingertip, raised her knees higher and slowly, carefully, slipped his finger up into her sheath.

He heard her gasp. It was a delicious feminine sound. She was extremely tight, but still he doubted she was intact. And then, suddenly, there it was. The barrier. Marcus was exultant!

Diana, too, experienced exultation. Then with the power that only a beautiful woman possesses she said, ''I shall never gift you with it.''

''You shall! You shall!'' It was a vow. Deliberately, he found the tiny bud of her woman's center and traced a circle about it with his fingertip.

Diana's eyes widened in shock as she felt a delicious frisson shoot up inside her. Then her sheath gripped his finger with a tiny convulsive shudder. When he withdrew it, he did so slowly, drawing his finger along her pink cleft with a sensual caress that made her pulsate. Up inside she suddenly felt hot and wet. At all costs she must not let him know that fondling her had excited her body, making her feel deliciously wanton.

He stood up from the bed and removed the thongs that bound her wrists. Diana resisted the impulse to rub them. Instead, she locked her gaze with his. "I would like some sleep, General. I have many floors to scrub tomorrow."

The fact that she chose the work of a menial slave over him enraged him. Only his iron self-control prevented him from slapping her, hard. Perhaps the *lady* did not believe that he would actually order her to do such hard, demeaning work. When dawn arrived, she would learn otherwise!

A female house slave awakened her before dawn. She brought a jug of cold water for laving, then picked up the brown toga and head cloth and stood waiting patiently.

"I will not wear those," Diana said haughtily.

"It is all you have to cover yourself. Kell will not relent," the slave informed her quietly.

After a moment's reflection, Diana reluctantly used the cold water, then donned the ugly garment. A young boy of perhaps eleven or twelve brought in a small loaf of bread and a cup of drinking water. Diana almost flung the offering at the wall, but a small voice inside her told her it might be all the food she would see that day.

The youth was on the thin side and had obviously not yet reached puberty. His dark eyes seemed far too large for his small face. "You must hurry," he urged.

"I shall do just the opposite," Diana informed him.

His thin shoulders sagged.

"If you do not hurry, Sim will be flogged," the female slave told her.

Diana's anger flared. "Take me to Kell!" she ordered.

The trio made their way to the first-floor kitchens, then into a rear kitchen with a huge hearth, big black ovens, and an enormous cistern with steaming water. When Kell saw her coming, he ordered a slave to fill a bucket with hot water. "You are late. You may start with the bathing rooms. First you scrub the tile with the lye soap, then you rinse thoroughly, and wipe dry with a chamois cloth."

"And if I refuse?" Diana demanded.

"Let me introduce you to Sim. He is to be your whipping boy."

For a moment she thought Kell had given the boy permission to whip her if she did not obey, then the terrible truth dawned upon her. If she did not do exactly as she was told, the boy would be flogged instead of her!

Her eyes flew to Sim, to his thin shoulders and large, sad eyes. "That is monstrous!" In an accusing tone she demanded, "Is he a Briton?"

Kell raised his eyebrows. "Do you suppose they let me flog Romans?" he asked dryly.

Diana took the wooden bowl of lye soap and bucket of steaming water and took them through to the rooms where she had bathed last evening.

When Kell was sure she was out of earshot, he winked at Sim and said, "You evoke pathos so well. Go to the kitchen and get your reward."

"That was a devious trick," a woman's voice accused.

"Mind your own business," Kell said coldly.

"What happens in the general's household is my business," replied Nola, a freedwoman the general had brought with him from Gaul while she was still a slave. These two were ever at odds regarding the running of the household. When Kell had first arrived, Nola was in charge, but once Marcus had freed her for good service, Kell had been appointed to her post. He had authority over everyone in the household, save Nola, and womanlike, she delighted in her ascendency over a male.

"You are only happy when you are poking your nose

into men's affairs. Women, whether they are slaves or not, should be seen and not heard!''

Nola laughed in his face. ''Are we such a threat to you, Briton? If I were you, I would treat the new female with a little more respect. Once she gains favor with Marcus, she could make your life a living hell.''

''You already do that, woman of Gaul!''

''Really?'' Nola drawled. ''I had no idea my barbs pierced your thick hide. Be so good as to have my breakfast sent up to my chamber.''

Diana worked off her fury scrubbing the tiles, then as her anger began to dissipate and she moved on to the floors of other chambers, the beauty of the mosaics caught her imagination. She took pride in her work, making the vibrant colors spring back to life, rinsing off the lye soap until they were spotless, then polishing them with the chamois cloth until they gleamed.

After she had completed six floors, however, her scraped knees hurt, her back ached, and her hands were puffy and stinging. With dogged determination she traipsed back to the outer kitchen to change the cleaning water, then made her way to the atrium, which was in actuality the magnificent entrance hall to the villa. She had never been in this chamber before because she had been brought to a back entrance when she first arrived.

It had rained in the night, but now the sunshine flooded through the glass skylights, making rainbows dance about the splashing fountain. Brilliant flowers spilled from huge terra-cotta pots around the oval room. A fresco of birds, from waterfowl to brilliantly plumed exotic varieties, adorned the pale green wall. With a sigh of appreciation for its beauty, she washed the floor, making the entire chamber sparkle like a jewel.

Suddenly, two great mastiffs came lunging through the front door. They were so big and ferocious, Diana screamed. Her fear quickly turned to anger when she saw that their huge paws were covered with black mud, which they were tracking all over her freshly scrubbed tile.

"Romulus, Remus—heel!" a deep voice thundered. The pair of mastiffs rushed to the side of Marcus Magnus, panting with adoration for their master. Diana sat back on her heels with utter disbelief. All her painstaking work was undone in seconds!

The general's black eyes swept over her without interest, as if there were nothing to distinguish her from any other female slave in his household. Last night he had looked at her as if she were a prize to die for. Then, later, when he had come to her sleeping chamber, even though he had done an obscene thing to her, his hands had handled her as if she were a piece of priceless porcelain. Now, he looked through her as if she didn't exist!

Diana wanted to fling her bucket of dirty water around the delicately painted walls. She had the urge to kick his dogs and hold the Roman's head beneath the water of the fountain until he gurgled his last breath. What she did was sink back on her haunches and clench her fists in impotence, as her eyes slowly filled with tears. When he swept back out with a map in his hand, he did not spare her a glance.

Kell was right. She was an utter fool. He had told her that last night she would have been able to seduce the Roman with the flutter of an eyelash. Because of pride she had let her opportunity slip through her fingers and now Marcus Magnus was completely indifferent to her. She would be scrubbing floors for the rest of her life!

She dashed the tears from her eyes and set to work cleaning up the mud that the ugly beasts had tracked all over the atrium. With each pawprint she obliterated, she became obsessed with the need to get back at the arrogant Roman who thought he ruled the world.

She knew she would do almost anything to gain power over him, to have him at her mercy. She wanted to enslave him as he had enslaved her. She decided she would pay any price to reverse their roles so that she was the master, he the slave.

She needed some measure of control, but a Briton had none under Roman rule. Diana began to understand Kell's situation. His position gave him power and control, even if it were only over his own kind. Without a small measure of power over your own destiny, life was not worth living.

When she thought about it, she was surprised at the similarity between this time in history and the eighteenth century. Men had ruled the world since time began. Men controlled the government, the army, the wealth, the land, the property, the economy, the arts, the family, and they also controlled women. She thought of all the wives, all the daughters, all the female servants who had cowered under man's total authority down through the centuries.

The only women who had power and manipulated men were mistresses, courtesans, and favorites. A woman could only achieve power through a man. If a woman was clever, she would choose the most powerful man of her acquaintance and make him fall in love with her. Then she would possess all his power.

Diana's resolve hardened. She was beautiful, intelligent, and sophisticated compared with the women she had seen here. If she could not seduce the Roman, she deserved her miserable fate!

Her fertile imagination began to concoct a plan. Her mercurial mind added details. As she scrubbed, she even formed carefully worded speeches and worked out actions as if she were rehearsing a part in a play. The first thing she must do was regain his attention in some spectacular fashion. Her plan was so audacious, it had to work. If she played her role well, she would gain power over the Roman, and once she had him on a leash, she would never let him off it. She would control him completely!

Diana decided this was the last floor she would ever scrub in her life. She got up off her knees, picked up the bucket, and made her way toward the outer kitchen. Before she got there, she saw Kell directing the household slaves in the inner kitchen. The moment she spied him, she staggered with the weight of the bucket. Her hand fluttered to her head as if she were dizzy and managed to drag the ugly brown head cloth from her pretty hair. She knew her pale golden tresses were unique in Aquae Sulis; she had not encountered another fair-haired person since she arrived.

Diana straightened her shoulders as if she were making a valiant effort, took a few more steps, then sank down upon her knees, knowing that Kell's eyes were upon her.

She felt a hand on the back of her neck. "Keep your head down until the dizziness passes," Kell ordered.

After a couple of minutes, Diana raised her head, gave a tremulous sigh, and allowed her eyes to flutter open. Kell helped her to her feet. "Have you had enough?" he asked quietly.

"Perhaps," she temporized softly.

"Perhaps! That is no answer; either you capitulate or you do not!"

Diana smiled a secret smile. "Kell, you think the world black and white, but I have discovered the world encompasses a multitude of gray. 'Yes' and 'no' are good words, simple words; uncomplicated and unexciting. But the word 'perhaps' is mysterious, tempting, and exciting with a hundred nuances implying that the possibilities are endless. Let us say that I am ready to negotiate." Diana held out the bucket.

Kell ordered Sim to take it away. The smell of freshly baking bread from the ovens filled the kitchen. Diana perched on a stool and said, "The bread smells heavenly. Could I have a little honey with mine?"

Kell took a stool also. A female kitchen slave brought them oat cakes, freshly baked bread and honey, a stone jug of milk, and a basket of fruit. They ate in silence. Kell's hooded eyes watched the graceful movements of her hands and the delicate way she chewed her food. Here was a most enchanting female. He could understand exactly why Marcus Magnus wanted her to grace his table and share his bed.

Diana sighed with repletion, then bit into a ripe black plum. "Kell, may I put a few things on the table for our consideration?" She was careful to seek his permission for everything. When Kell nodded, she proceeded. "You said that the general lusted for me. You said that if I gave him what he asked, he would be more than generous to me."

Kell waited for her to go on.

"*If* I become his concubine and *if* he is well pleased with me, it will give me a great deal of power."

So, she does know she possesses power, Kell thought.

"There would then be two of us with power in this household. I believe it would be folly for us to be rivals. A power struggle between the two of us would mean one winner and one loser. If we become allies, not friends of course, but allies, we could both win."

She knew Kell was shrewd enough to recognize the truth in her words. "*If* I do this thing, I will do it on my own terms. I know that you do not need me, Kell. But oh, I am aware that I shall need you." Diana was purposely touching on his vanity, but nevertheless her words spoke the truth.

"Your advice to me has been both wise and sound. In the days ahead, I will need your advice, your guidance, your help, and possibly your protection. My relationship with you will be as close as the one I hope to have with the general."

Kell digested her words. If this woman did gain power, he wanted her on his side. Nola could so easily become her confidante, and the only thing worse than a woman with power was two women with power! Finally Kell spoke. His gray eyes looked deeply into hers. "We have already declared a silent truce. Let us build upon it."

Diana smiled. "Good. I have an idea. Rather than wait until day's end when he returns to the villa, then summons me to ask if I am ready to submit to him, I think that I should seize the initiative!''

As Kell listened to her audacious plan, he wanted to tell her it was impossible. But as he watched her animated face light up with feminine mischief and her voice come alive with passion, her boldness caught his imagination. She was a most daring female; one who could ensnare a man and hold him captive in the palm of her hand. She was as shrewd and clever in her way as he himself. She was also a Briton. How could they be aught but allies?

Chapter 11

"The first thing I shall need is a scented bath. Then, if you will be generous enough to open up your treasure trove of feminine garments, we will choose something that the Primus Pilus will not be able to resist."

Diana soaked in the delicious hot water for the better part of an hour. When the ache in her back from scrubbing tiles melted away, the bath slaves wrapped her in a large towel, then set to work on dressing her hair.

Kell brought a carved cypress box with a selection of hair ornaments and pieces of jewelry.

"To whom do these belong?" she asked with curiosity.

"Everything and everyone in this villa belongs to Marcus Magnus, but if you are asking if there is a female here who owns these, the answer is no. They are mostly gifts from the merchants of Aquae Sulis. There are many Celtic artisans here who make beautiful ornaments. The general has many amulets, some gold set with amber, some silver set with cabochon emeralds. The general collects Celtic jewelry. He has an eye for a fine piece."

Diana's eyes met Kell's and they laughed together at his unintentional joke. She chose a gold filigreed hair ornament that gathered her hair high, then allowed it to fall down her back in a pale mass of curls. The female who had styled her hair the previous evening once more created tiny tendrils that spiraled about her face.

Diana selected a deep violet silk from an armful of stolae Kell showed her. She had an unerring instinct for the dramatic. The deep jewel tone contrasted with her pale coloring, making her look delicate and ethereal. She touched her lips and eyelids with a lighter shade of violet face paint that was mixed with silver, giving her an iridescent glow.

"In the general's collection there is a piece that would set off your beauty to perfection. Wait here," bade Kell.

Diana slipped the high cork-soled sandals on her feet and practiced walking. The beautiful stola was designed in slim classical lines to follow the curve of a woman's body, but it had a small train that she wanted to learn to kick aside dramatically when she stopped walking.

When Kell returned, he held out a Celtic torque encrusted with amethysts. It was magnificent, except of course it looked exactly like a slave collar. Diana took a great fancy to it, not only because it complemented her violet silk, but because it made her neck look long and elegant. The ironic symbolism was not lost on her either.

"I shouldn't let you wear it without permission," Kell said doubtfully.

"I will take the responsibility. If he is angered, tell him I stole it! I need more than jewelry from you, Kell. I need a horse."

"Impossible."

"I must go to him, in front of his men. I will not wait until he comes to me."

Kell's brows drew together in total disapproval. "You may be both beautiful and desirable, but you are still a slave. How much power do you think you have?" A thought suddenly occurred to him. "Do you have some secret power?" he demanded.

A smile lifted the corners of her luscious mouth. "Yes, I do, Kell."

"What is it?" he asked suspiciously.

"It is a secret," she said, smiling.

"Does Marcus know the secret?"

"Yes. It drew him irresistibly to my sleeping chamber in the middle of the night."

Kell blinked. He had no idea Marcus had left his chamber to visit the female slave. "What is this irresistible lure you possess?"

Diana hesitated. She needed Kell on her side. She would be completely honest with him. "My irresistible lure is my virginity," she said softly.

Kell's gray eyes widened in astonishment. Then he shook his head and began to chuckle. "Such a simple device," he murmured, "yet so rare, it is priceless."

"I need a horse, Kell."

He shook his head. "There are no horses we can ride. I have a small chariot I use to take messages to the general," he said doubtfully.

Diana considered for a moment and liked the picture that sprang to mind. "That will be just as good, perhaps better. Before we leave, can you order his favorite food be prepared for the evening meal?"

"It is done. I am one step ahead of you."

"Good heavens, I hope not," she teased lightly.

A slave brought Kell's chariot with a sturdy pony harnessed between the shafts. With Kell's aid she climbed in carefully. "I've never ridden in one of these, but as I understand it, I ride standing up and hold on to this wooden rail?"

"I do not drive like a madman," Kell informed her.

"Marcus does. He almost drove over me," Diana said, remembering.

"I'm amazed he drew rein for you."

"I stopped him in his tracks. With any luck I shall do the same again."

"I hope you understand that you will have to answer to him for what you do today. The responsibility for this is yours, not mine," Kell warned.

Diana closed her eyes in trepidation for a moment. What if she enraged him and he heaped humiliation upon her, or worse? She straightened her shoulders. So be it. She would cast her fate to the winds. Marcus Magnus was only a man when all was said and done, and she a woman. The odds were definitely in her favor.

Kell drove out slowly through the gate of the walled garden of the villa and headed down the sloping hills toward Aquae Sulis. The afternoon sun was hot upon Diana's bare shoulders as the guard waved Kell's small chariot through the gate of the fortress. She glanced up at the ramparts, which had a foundation of stone, then turf from the surrounding ditch stacked like bricks to a height of about eighteen feet. All the soldiers on the ramparts gaped down at her.

Diana was surprised at the size of the fortress. Inside the walls was like a town with many streets and buildings. At the junction of the two main streets was a complex of buildings around a courtyard, which included the principia or headquarters, storerooms, and offices. When Kell stopped to inquire where the general was, the guards informed him the Primus Pilus was out in the external annex.

They drove past stables, workshops, and finally long rows of barracks where the Roman soldiers ate and slept. They looked quite spacious and were fronted by colonnaded walkways. As they proceeded toward the annex, men everywhere stopped what they were doing, stared after them in disbelief, then began to follow on foot. Kell's chariot was a common sight at the fort, but not since it was built had a woman been inside.

In the center of the back wall a gate opened into the annex. This vast amphitheatre was used for weapon training and parades. There were at least a thousand soldiers on the field, all wearing segmented armor of metal strips and plates. The sun blazed off the bronze and iron helmets and breastplates of the legionaries who stood in regimented lines around the perimeter of the field.

As they stood at attention with javelins and shields, all eyes were focused on the century in the center of the field who were taking weapon practice. The fighting was vicious. The soldiers were not play-acting.

Marcus Magnus intended that every man present would be totally proficient with the gladius, the short, double-edged sword, before he left Aquae Sulis. It was a stabbing rather than a slashing weapon, designed for use in close fighting and held in a leather and bronze scabbard beneath the right hand. On the left of the body was a pugio dagger in an iron scabbard, suspended from the same weapon belt. Medics stood by to carry the wounded off the field to the hospital.

Behind Marcus stood two Celtic tribesmen in native dress, which consisted of a brief leather loincloth, an axe, and a knife. Each had long, black hair, their naked limbs tattooed with woad in frightening patterns. Both came at him at once. The first was dispatched immediately with a gladius straight into the gut. Marcus grabbed the second man by his long hair, yanked his head back viciously, then cut his exposed throat.

The general hadn't even taken time to toss his scarlet mantel behind his shoulder so that it wouldn't impede his sword arm. A great cheer arose from the men. It was followed by embarrassed laughter when the two tribesmen got to their feet unhurt. They thought he had actually slain them. The Celts had been doing this for two years now and still they were not fast enough to take him. Only once had they nicked him deeply enough to draw blood; after that first time he could have killed them each and every time he used them to demonstrate effective weapon skills.

As Diana's chariot came into the sight of the warriors, all eyes swung toward her unexpected arrival. A great murmur arose in the ranks, which the leaders failed to silence because they, too, were remarking upon the spectacle unfolding before them.

The general stared in disbelief as Kell's chariot rolled

toward him with the beautiful female slave at his side. As it came to a halt, Marcus sheathed his gladius and strode to the vehicle. He glared at her in astonishment, his black eyes smoldering with fury. Before he could bark an order, Diana held out her delicate hand to him. "Help me down, Marcus, or your men will think you most uncouth." She spoke softly, intimately, for his ears alone.

"You will learn just how uncouth I can be," he promised, but she noticed that he kept his voice purposely low.

"Smile at me. Surely you want every man here to think you have ordered me to visit you."

Her beauty almost took his breath away. He showed his teeth in a wolf's grin, ignored her outstretched hand, and lifted her down from the chariot by the waist. A great cheer went up from the ranks when his powerful hands closed about her tiny waist and he lifted her to his side. The general ignored them, giving his full attention to the beautiful woman who had actually been bold enough to seek him out before a thousand men.

She smiled up at the dark man who towered above her. "They think I am your new concubine," she murmured seductively.

At the thought, his shaft filled instantly, hardening and lengthening him to a marked degree. His black eyes glittered with victory. "Is that what you have come to tell me?"

"Of course not, you brute," she teased.

A blazing hot desire almost consumed him. He wanted to push her to the ground, mount her, and give her the fucking of a lifetime before all these Roman soldiers. He wanted to put his brand upon her to show them all that this exquisite female was his, and his alone! He took her possessively by the shoulders. "Then by the gods, what in Hades are you doing here?" he demanded fiercely.

She reached up and traced a delicate fingertip along his scar. Every man watching sucked in his breath. "I am here so that you may invite me to dine with you." She made a little moue with her mouth. He longed to cover it with his own. Lust pounded inside his temples. "You are my slave —I *order* you to dine with me."

Diana shook her head provocatively. His hands tightened on her, needing to master her.

"If you *invite* me, it will be my greatest pleasure to accept. Then when we have dined, I have a proposition to lay before you," she whispered.

"You will lay before me, make no mistake," he murmured fiercely.

"Perhaps." She said the word filled with mystery, promise, and excitement. Marcus felt the effect of that word all the way to the tip of his marble-hard phallus.

He smiled inwardly. She had turned the tables on him. This morning he had deliberately allowed his dogs to muddy the tiles she had scrubbed, just to provoke her, but when it came to being provocative, this female won, hands down!

"Go now, before I use my weapon on you, here before all these rough soldiers." His dark eyes glittered. "I *order* you to dine with me tonight."

Diana smiled a secret smile. "You silver-tongued devil, how can I resist such a charming invitation?" She went up on tiptoe to whisper in his ear. "Seeing you command and control all these rough soldiers is like an aphrodisiac to me." She stepped away from him toward the chariot.

His powerful hands scooped her up by her bottom cheeks and he deposited her beside Kell. The men roared and whistled their appreciation. "Enough!" he thundered, his dark face prouder and fiercer than any eagle's. Silence blanketed the entire field.

As they drove back to the villa, neither Kell nor Diana could quite believe she had gotten away with it. She had deliberately whispered words that would seduce him, words to flatter his male vanity, words he'd wanted to hear. But she admitted to herself that the words she had spoken were true. Being close to him, having his hands on her, was an aphrodisiac.

It gave her a heady feeling to know that when she moved close to him, Marcus Magnus could not resist touching her. She would test her theory again this evening. She would go close to him to prove that he could not keep his hands from her. Diana glanced at Kell. "He did not censure you."

"He did not even see me, lady."

Diana was pleased with Kell. He was showing his admiration for her by calling her lady. She felt lucky to have him for her ally because he had earned the general's complete trust. She must do the same. She had discovered that it gave her pleasure when she saw Magnus' dark eyes light with amusement. Men loved to laugh. She must try her best to entertain him.

By the balls of Jupiter, thought Petrius as he stood before his sweating legionaries, watching the drama between his brother and his exquisite slave play out, *no wonder my brother enjoys Aquae Sulis!* With a villa of slaves such as the golden-haired female to do his bidding, to obey his every command, to satisfy his every craving, what man wouldn't be content? His brother had kept his female slaves well hidden last night at dinner. No wonder Marcus had not needed the services of the fornice. A slave girl aroused far more lust in a man than a prostitute, and this particular slave girl was exceptionally beautiful. *Whether Marcus knows it or not, he will entertain me again at dinner. And this time it will be share and share alike, brother!*

As the sun blazed down, the heat became almost oppressive. The general knew how much the men sweated beneath their armor and iron helmets. He divided the field into quadrants to practice various offensive and defensive skills. One group practiced with the seven-foot pilums or javelins. He designated half the group as attackers, the other half as targets. Before now their javelin practice had been limited to hitting wooden butts. The human targets became immediately drenched with sweat, from fear now, rather than heat.

Marcus Magnus moved on to the next quadrant. "Remove your armor," he commanded. Every man was eager to relieve himself of the heavy bronze breastplate, cuirass, and iron helmet until the general issued his next order. "Half of you buckle on your pugio, the other half your gladius. You will fight each other without the protection of armor. You will be amazed how quickly your defensive skills become honed."

He ordered half of the third quadrant to strip naked and practice their wrestling skills. "The wild tribes to the west fight naked. You had better get used to it. They are more vulnerable to your weapons, of course, but they move like greased lightning. Those still wearing armor will discover just how much it impedes you and slows you down when your enemy is totally free of all encumbrance."

The men of the fourth quadrant were issued weapons they had never used before. Long swords called spatha, usually given only to cavalrymen, and bows and arrows were distributed by mule-drawn carts. Then Marcus Magnus and the two Celtic tribesmen gave them a lesson in archery followed by a demonstration in the correct use of the spatha. Straw dummies were set up at the far end of the quadrant.

"First, you will learn to put an arrow through the center of every head, then you will learn to sever each head from its body with one slash of the spatha."

Marcus knew that by the time the legionaries left the field they would be dog-tired. He glanced at the western sky and saw thunderheads gathering in the distance. If the storm was heavy enough to swell the river and make it rage, tomorrow might be a good time to give them their swimming lesson. If not, they could practice mounting and dismounting from high-speed war chariots.

Marcus was impatient for the light to fade from the sky, though he did not allow it to show. The anticipation of his evening with Diana set up a heavy pulsebeat that made his blood throb. He was careful to mask his mounting excitement and his towering impatience before the Roman soldiers he trained. They deserved his total attention. His pride would not allow him to give them half-measures when it came to survival tactics. With an iron control, he put all thoughts of his beautiful female slave aside, until he could give her his complete and undivided appreciation.

When they arrived home, Diana followed Kell into the kitchens. Both males and females were employed in preparing the evening meal, working at long scrubbed tables beneath copper utensils that hung from beams.

"Why are you here?" Kell asked sternly.

"I want to make sure everything is perfect for him."

"Do I not do that every day of my life?" he asked with *hauteur*. "You need rest; take it while you may."

Diana blushed prettily. It had indeed been a long day, but she felt so alive, so filled with a mixture of apprehension and excitement, that she knew she could not lie down and sleep.

"It is so hot in here. Go out into the peristyle, the garden. It will fill you with tranquillity. Just stay out of the master's private bathing pool; slaves are not allowed in it."

The gardens were lush with scented flowers and lovely shade trees. As she strolled down its winding paths, she came upon small yew arbors with stone seats, sundials, and ornamental ponds. As well as oaks, there were towering walnut and chestnut trees and smaller, fruit-bearing trees of pear, quince, apricot, and damson. Red squirrels dashed about gathering acorns, crested kingfishers swooped over the ponds, while thrushes grubbed for insects beneath the flowering rhododendrons.

As she rounded a bend in the stone path, a pale aquamarine bathing pool stretched out before her. At the far end, water spouted from great stone dolphins, and when she drew closer, she saw that the pool had a border of jade mosaic water lilies and water hyacinths. A long wooden bathhouse stood on one side of the pool covered by climbing purple wisteria and ornamental grape vines. If Marcus Magnus had designed this oasis, she realized he must have a deep appreciation of the beauties of nature. Diana sat down on a carved stone bench and allowed the tranquillity of her surroundings to calm her.

An older woman in a plain linen toga came toward her carrying a cool drink. Diana smiled her thanks.

"I have decided to look after your needs, child."

She was a motherly woman with a comfortable, rounded figure and graying hair. Diana felt guilty. How could she accept the services of a slave? "Thank you, but I can look after myself."

"My name is Nola. I shall ease your way and you shall ease mine, if you accept me."

"Please sit down, Nola. I cannot accept the services of a slave. It is against my beliefs."

Nola beamed at her. "You are a Christian; I knew it! I shall mother you. Everyone needs mothering, even the great man himself. He is no more than a boy, really. His responsibilities make him stern and harsh. But sometimes in the evening he sheds his cares with his armor. I've seen him chase about with his dogs and play in the pool like a boy. He is lonely, though he does not even realize it. Will you assuage his loneliness?"

"I . . . I will try," Diana said, realizing she had learned that he was vulnerable. It could be a powerful weapon. "How can you feel affection for him when he owns you?"

Nola laughed. "He freed me long ago. I stay from choice. Who else could keep him in line and protect him from the machinations of Kell?"

Aha, Kell and Nola are obviously adversaries. Perhaps I can use this to my own advantage.

When Diana tasted the drink, she was surprised. "This is cider. It's good!"

"Romans drink wine incessantly. Some of it tastes no better than vinegar. Britons prefer cider." Nola studied Diana's face as she sipped her drink. "You have a most impetuous nature. It has been held in check for far too long. It is as if you have been sleeping, waiting for the moment when you could emerge from your cocoon, spread your beautiful wings, and fly. That moment is at hand."

"How do you know these things?" Diana asked, recognizing the truth of her words.

"I know all—deep down in my bones. You are longing to throw off your clothes and splash in the bathing pool. Learn to indulge your desires, child. I will get you a towel to wrap up your pretty hair. I will hold your lovely stola and keep the slaves away from the pool while you refresh yourself."

"It sounds like heaven, but Kell forbade me to use the pool."

"A little power and it has gone to his head. Marcus allows me to use it anytime I wish and I invite you to be my guest. Water is magic. It will help shed your cares and inhibitions. Promise me you will bring him here often to play."

For the life of her, Diana could not picture a playful Marcus Magnus, yet when she considered for a moment, had his hands not been playful when he picked her up by the bottom cheeks this afternoon? Perhaps she *could* succeed in finding the boy in the man. Then she might truly have him under her spell—and in her power.

Chapter 12

Marcus Magnus could not remember a twelve-hour day that had lasted longer. He often walked home, climbing the hills that stretched from the fortress to his villa, but tonight he rode one of his white stallions. Bruise-colored clouds were piled one on top of another and low thunder had begun to rumble by the time he reached his own stables.

Always, he tended his own animals as any career legionary worth his salt would. Yet tonight he turned Trajan over to the care of a stable slave. "Have a care," he warned. "Trajan bites and the approaching storm will make him restless."

As he had ridden, the very rhythm of Trajan's hooves had drummed out Diana, Diana, Diana. When he entered the atrium, he curbed his impatience that it was not she who greeted him.

Kell bowed his head. "I hope you had a productive day, General."

"Yes, it was most fruitful."

Kell kept a straight face as Marcus said, "I'll bathe in the villa tonight. The storm will break any minute."

Kell often disagreed with the master, simply on principle. "I believe it will build slowly, then climax with a bang." He added silently, *You being the thunder, she the lightning!*

The pointed analogy was not lost on Marcus Magnus. "Would it be asking too much to have you serve us tonight?" he asked Kell.

"Such was my intent." Usually the bath took at least an hour, sometimes two. Tonight, however, Kell thought he had better bring the lady to the dining room in about thirty minutes.

As Diana sat before the polished bronze mirror in her own chamber, she said to Nola, "I don't think I will change my gown. Marcus seemed quite taken with the violet silk."

"Did you know that the color purple is magic?" Nola asked. "That particular shade changes color with the light. In the shadows it is almost black, but in the lamplight it glows rich and vibrant. It will lend you power, as will the amethysts about your throat. You need violet-scented oil between your breasts and at the base of your spine."

"I have never applied perfume there before."

"It will not go to waste, trust me."

"Last night I wore Egyptian musk."

"Musk can be cloying. Tonight the violet is better."

When Nola opened the door to a light tap, Kell stood at the portal. "I see you have wasted no time currying favor, woman of Gaul. I have come to escort the lady to him."

Nola's eyebrows elevated. "This morning you called her slave, tonight you call her lady. I am delighted you took my advice to show her respect. You can learn a lot from your betters."

"One Briton is worth ten women of Gaul." Kell pushed his way into the chamber and spoke to Diana. "Are you ready?"

Diana knew a moment of total, blinding panic. She felt like a prisoner being taken to her own execution. How could she do this thing? How could she subjugate herself to a dictator? How could she abase herself to a master? The ancient tale of Scheherazade came to her rescue. Had that female not kept the sultan enthralled for a thousand and one nights?

*All I need do is negotiate. I shall simply trade inno-
cence for power. A fair exchange when all is said and done.*
Yet deep down, in the depths of her mind where reason
didn't quite reach, she knew she had to do more than negotiate. She must enchant, enthrall, enslave!

Diana smiled her secret smile and held out her hand to
Kell. "I am more than ready."

He placed her small hand upon his arm and took her
downstairs. His gray eyes hid a smile as he saw Marcus was
already in the oval triclinium. Kell took her through the
pillars. "Lady Diana," he announced with far more ceremony than she had received when she had been announced
at court, a lifetime ago.

Marcus came forward to greet her. His black eyes
touched her everywhere. Diana kicked aside her small train
dramatically, then took one token step toward him, with her
head held proudly high. Marcus clasped her small hand
firmly, then chided, "You obey my orders regally, like a
goddess bestowing a favor."

"That is because you issue them arrogantly, like a
master ordering a slave."

"That is precisely what I am." His grip tightened painfully.

"Unfortunately, I am not a goddess. I am mortal flesh
and blood. Will you crush my very bones?" she asked
softly.

Her reminder that she was flesh and blood did wanton
things to him. "Are you ready to accept that you are my
slave?" he demanded huskily.

She reached up to run her fingertips along his jaw
where he had just shaved and said intimately, "I came to
amuse you. If it amuses you to play master and slave girl,
you must teach me the game."

His eyes glittered. "It is no game."

Diana looked at his mouth, then ran the tip of her
tongue over her top lip. "Marcus, between a man and a
woman, it is always a game."

His erection lifted the linen of his tunic.

He had not given her permission to use his first name, yet it sounded wondrous on her lips. No one ever called him Marcus, and he realized he was hungry for such intimacy.

"This afternoon you said you would yield to me tonight."

Diana slanted him a teasing glance from beneath her lashes. "I said no such thing, as you very well remember."

"You *intimated* that you would yield to me!"

She laughed up at him. "Do you delude yourself every night, or is tonight special?"

He showed his teeth like a wolf and growled, "You are doing it again."

"Doing what?" she asked innocently.

"Alluding, hinting, intimating that tonight will be special and it cannot be any such thing unless you capitulate and yield to me!"

"That's part of the game. Alluding, hinting, intimating is how men and women play, I believe. What I said was: *When we have dined, I have a proposition to lay before you.*"

"And what I said was: *You will lay before me.*"

Diana placed her hand in the center of his chest and splayed her fingers. She could feel the gold coin beneath his tunic. It was warm from the heat of his body. She moved slightly closer to him. "And what was my reply?" she asked huskily.

"*Perhaps,* was your reply," he said, devouring her mouth with his black eyes

"A tantalizing word filled with promise, is it not? If I told you *no,* it would anger you and make you bend me to your will. If I told you *yes,* it would take away all the anticipation, all the speculation. So I tell you *perhaps,* and that preserves the mystery, draws out the suspense, and heightens the desire."

He was riven with the need to taste her. Her lips, so temptingly close, whispering such arousing words, made him want to fill her mouth with tantalizing desire. He claimed her lips, slanting his mouth against hers, slowly exploring the softness, the lushness, tasting her sweetness, drawing the tip of her pink tongue into his mouth.

Something hard touched her belly, making her gasp. He shuddered as the head of his shaft touched her silken body. She lifted her lips so they were a pulsebeat away. "Are you hungry, Marcus?" she whispered.

"Ravenous!"

The thunder crashed above their heads.

Kell entered the room carrying a heavy serving tray. Diana took immediate advantage of the interruption and put space between her and the Roman. Now she would test her power. She would see how long it took her to make him close the space between them.

"Kell has had your favorite dishes prepared. You are so fortunate to have him. He is a marvel of efficiency."

"Thank you, Kell," Marcus said low.

"Mmm, the aroma of the food is tantalizing."

All Marcus could smell was violets until Kell removed the heavy silver covers. "Would you like me to carve?"

"I'll do it, Kell."

As Kell left the triclinium, she said, "Dining in such a fashion is new to me."

Marcus was beside her immediately, his hands lifting her to the couch opposite his. "Let me show you. Recline on your side so that you face my couch. Now tuck this small pillow beneath your elbow."

The corners of her mouth lifted with feminine satisfaction. Once Kell had left the room, it had taken only a heartbeat before his hands were on her. Diana rolled onto her tummy, resting her weight on both elbows.

Marcus traced the curve of her back with his calloused hand until it rested lightly on her bottom.

"How wise Nola is," she whispered.

"Nola?" he murmured thickly.

"She told me to dab perfume at the base of my spine. She said it wouldn't be wasted."

His fingers moved in small circles until he found the spot exactly. The scent of violets made his nostrils flare wide.

"The food cools," she murmured.

"My lust does not," he said bluntly.

"The sooner we eat, the sooner we can negotiate," she reasoned.

Before he removed his hand from her bottom, he pressed down hard so that her pubis rubbed against the cushion. A frisson of her first sexual arousal spiraled between her legs.

Outside, the brilliant lightning flashed and was immediately followed by a crash of thunder that made the very roof shake.

Marcus moved to the serving table set between the two couches. He carved the haunch of roast boar, selected the most perfect artichokes, the tiniest green peas, the thinnest spears of asparagus, along with a pot of warm herbed olive oil, and placed it close by her hand.

Also on the table, Kell had set out salad greens with cresses, fine lettuce, and edible mallows. A huge platter of cheeses, olives, grapes, and nuts sat in the center of the serving table. Marcus moved a finger bowl and towel beside her before he reclined upon the opposite couch.

They lay facing, with their bodies curved toward each other. Small gold cushions were propped beneath their elbows. The storm within raged as wildly as the storm without.

Marcus had a man's healthy appetite, doing justice to everything set before him, but if he hadn't been informed that he was being served his favorite wild boar, he would have had no idea what he ate.

His dark eyes were on Diana throughout the meal, seeing the graceful movements of her hand, watching her delicately lick her fingers and sip her wine. He saw how the violet silk clung to the curve of her hip and molded the swell of her breasts. Above all else he thought about her maidenhead. If he hadn't proved to himself that she was still intact, he would never have believed it. She was so seductively feminine and wise in the ways of women. She was ripe for lovemaking.

Diana dipped her fingers into the scented water and dried them on the towel.

"Have you finished?" he asked impatiently.

She picked up a ripe plum and bit into it lustily.

Marcus shifted on the couch to ease his arousal.

"Finished? I've only just begun," she purred.

Marcus decided she had teased him long enough. "I am ready," he stated emphatically.

"I won't ask you to show me the proof of that. I'll take your word for it."

He was momentarily shocked at her erotic innuendo, then he threw back his head and laughed. The column of his neck was corded with muscle. A crack of thunder prevented him from hearing her swift intake of breath.

"So, I do amuse you. I almost despaired of making you laugh."

He swung his legs to the floor.

"No!" she cried, putting out her hand. "I want the table between us until we have concluded our bargain."

His black eyes glittered their challenge, but then he reclined back on his elbow, waiting, banking the fire in his blood.

When she licked the juice from her plum, Marcus closed his eyes and grit his teeth against the sudden pulsing of his phallus.

She began quietly. "You want me to acknowledge that I am your slave. You want me to obey you implicitly. You want me to yield to you willingly. You want me to gift you with my virginity."

An eerie silence filled the chamber. Marcus could hear his own heartbeat as he waited for her answer.

"I am ready to acknowledge that I am your slave. I will obey you implicitly. I will yield to your orders willingly, *but* . . ." Diana paused for emphasis and Marcus held his breath. She continued, "*But* only in front of others. When we are alone, you will treat me as a lady, not a slave."

He stared at her as if she had lost all reason. "In other words, you will only *pretend* to be my slave?" He was dangerously close to violence.

"For all intents and purposes I will be your slave, your property. Every legionary, all of Aquae Sulis, and your entire household will know me for your slave, but when we are completely private, our relationship will not be that of master and slave. Our relationship will be that of a man and a woman . . . of lovers."

Marcus could see no difference. It was a woman's duty to obey the man, whether she be slave or concubine. The man's will must always prevail, else he would not be a man! He noted that she had left out the part about gifting him with her virginity. Whether she was agreeing to *willingly* join her body with his or not was still unclear, and when it came right down to the fine point, this was the crux of their bargain.

"Do you agree to *willingly* yield your body to me?" he demanded.

"Only when you have wooed and won me. Not on demand," she said softly.

"When will you *allow* me to begin this wooing, my fine lady?" he asked with heavy sarcasm.

She glanced across at him provocatively. "You and I both know your wooing has already begun. . . . I enjoy it excessively!"

A crack of thunder rent the heavens and the deluge began. There was a sudden commotion in the atrium and then Kell stood at the entrance to the triclinium. "Your brother, Petrius, General." Kell stepped aside and the handsome young cohort centurion stood between the pillars, drenched to the skin.

Diana fled across to Marcus' couch and sank to the floor at his knee.

"Is aught amiss, Petrius?" Marcus demanded.

"I am come to dine, brother. The storm took me unawares."

Though he had not been invited and though his timing played havoc with Marcus' plans, he extended his hospitality. "We are finished eating, but there is food in abundance. Bathe and change into dry clothes while your dinner is prepared."

Petrius swayed on his feet, then advanced into the chamber. "I shall forgo the food and join you for the drinking." He left a puddle of water with every step.

Marcus frowned. He could see the young devil had already been drinking.

"Don't worry about the water, brother, you've plenty of slaves to clean it up." He poured himself wine from a flagon, then filled up the two glasses that were half empty. "Drink with me, or is the great general of Aquae Sulis too high and mighty to share his wine with a lowly centurion?"

His tone was so belligerent, Marcus placed his hand on Diana's shoulder to reassure her that he would control the situation.

"My wine is your wine, Petrius; my food and my villa at your disposal. Be seated, take your ease."

Petrius reclined on the white and gold couch, soiling everything he touched. He held up his wine. "To Rome, glorious Rome." He drained his glass, then waited for them to do the same. "You may like this country, but I think it the arsehole of the empire. Even the gods are pissing on it!" Petrius spied Kell on the threshold. "Slave—more wine!"

The eyes of Marcus and Kell met in quiet understanding as Kell brought another flagon of wine and refilled Petrius' goblet. Once more he drained it, but this time his eyes roamed over the female who sat quietly beneath his brother's hand. "Does your hospitality not provide me with a couch slave? Or will we share this one?"

Diana shrank back and Marcus stroked her silken hair. "This slave is my private and exclusive property, Petrius, tonight and every night. Your drunken behavior insults me and brings shame upon you. Tomorrow you will regret the wine you have consumed when you will be required to teach your men to swim the river wearing full gear."

Diana turned to face Marcus, her eyes filled with admiration. She spoke softly. "May I come and watch you?" Her hand touched his knee in supplication.

She was everything he desired. She had played the slave girl to perfection the moment they were no longer alone. He searched her face; their glances touched and held. "You may come. The bargain is sealed," he murmured.

Petrius staggered to his feet. "I'm not drunk!" He drew his pugio. "I'll fight you for the girl."

Marcus sighed heavily and got to his feet. "Go up to my chamber now," he directed Diana. "Come on, old man, I think we'd better sweat you until you are sober. Can't have your men see you in this condition." He easily disarmed Petrius and threw a brotherly arm about him to keep him upright.

Kell came to the general's aid. As they walked him toward the baths, Petrius passed out.

"By the gods, he has a skinful. What in Hades prompted this?"

Kell answered silently. *Envy. Envy of you eats him alive.*

"We have our work cut out for us," Marcus said with calm resignation. First, he took him into the cold plunge to revive him. When Petrius regained consciousness, he fought like a young bull. Marcus had him under full control at all times. When he finally hauled him from the cold water, he helped Kell administer an emetic, then held his brother's head up while he spewed out his guts.

The fight has gone out of him now, Kell thought with satisfaction.

Marcus took Petrius into a small room that was heated to a high temperature by steam. As sweat poured off Petrius, Marcus made him drink copious amounts of water so that he would not dehydrate. Marcus, too, had to drink so he would not lose body weight in the heat.

After three hours, Petrius was cold sober. Marcus ordered a bath slave to give his brother a massage, then he accompanied him back to the officers' quarters. As they rode to the fortress in the drizzling rain, Petrius was much subdued. When he left him at the gate, Petrius mumbled, ''Thanks.''

Marcus replied, ''That is what brothers are for.''

In Marcus' sleeping chamber, Diana stood before the fire that had been lit against the damp night. All her fine plans had been spoiled by the intrusion of Petrius. She giggled. He had been drunk as a lord. She admitted she wasn't quite sober herself. By now, Marcus must be furious to have his drunken brother on his hands. His desire had been rampant by the time they finished eating; she could not imagine what state he was in by now!

Diana yawned. It had certainly been a long and eventful day. The corners of her mouth went up. She had no doubt that Marcus would agree to her terms. She had told him that when they were alone, she would not be his slave. What she hadn't told him was that slowly but surely, he would become hers.

The amethyst torque was becoming too heavy for her slender neck. She unfastened its clasp and laid it on the table beside his bed. She sat down on the steps that led up to his bed and removed her sandals. She yawned again.

It was amazing, but somehow she had lost all her fear of the Roman. He was the strongest, most powerful man she had ever known, but that strength would protect her not harm her. She laid her head down upon the furs and smiled sleepily. Marcus thought she was his, but in truth, he was hers!

Kell awaited Marcus in the atrium with a pair of towels. He handed Kell his wet mantle and stripped off his soaking tunic. Then he wrapped one of the towels about his hips and rubbed his black hair vigorously until it was dry.

Kell took a torch from its bracket and lighted Marcus through the dark, silent villa, up to his sleeping chamber. The door swung open to reveal Diana lying on the steps with her golden head resting on the bed. As Marcus gazed with longing at the sleeping beauty he asked, "How many floors did she scrub today?"

"Seven," Kell replied.

"Seven must be my unlucky number," Marcus murmured.

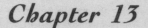

Chapter 13

Diana came up slowly through the layers of a deep sleep. When she opened her eyes, she saw the tops of the Roman pillars with their curled rams' horns. She realized immediately that she was in the great pedestal bed of Marcus Magnus.

A thrill of excitement shot through her, curling her toes, then she summoned the courage to turn her head. She was alone in the bed. Did she feel relief or regret? She experienced both at the same time and wondered how that was possible.

Marcus must have found her sleeping and taken her into his bed. Had he awakened her? Had he made love to her? She searched her memory, but recalled little beyond sitting on the steps and laying her head on the bed. She remembered the fur beneath her cheek, the scent of Marcus filling her senses, but nothing beyond.

Diana sat up and saw that she still wore the violet silk. She stretched and then ran her hands lightly down her body. It felt no different than it had yesterday. With a certainty she knew he had not touched her, for once Marcus Magnus made love to a woman, surely her body would never feel the same again!

Sitting up in the bed, she gazed at the place where he had lain beside her, so close and yet so very far away.

Nothing had happened and because of that she knew so much more about him now than she knew before. He had accepted her offer, the bargain was sealed, and he had not violated their agreement. In spite of the fact that this Roman general controlled thousands of men and had the strength and the power to impose his will anytime, anyplace, and in any way he chose, he had not awakened her to demand she yield her body to him. Apparently he was a man of honor; a man of his word. Yet his abstinence told her more. It told her that somewhere, deep within, the Roman had a spot that was soft and kind and gentle. Diana vowed to exploit that tenderness she had discovered.

She felt exultant because she knew the balance of power had tipped her way. She must be very careful to play the role of slave in front of others, even Kell, so that when they were private Marcus would allow her to enjoy the full and complete power of a woman.

Nola brought her breakfast. "May I join you?"

"Oh, please do."

Nola set the serving tray of crusty rolls, honey, and fruit upon the bed, then perched on the steps. "You are special to him."

Diana lowered her lashes, not quite knowing how a slave behaved. "How do you know?" she asked shyly.

"He kept you with him all night. He has never done that before."

Diana realized that in a household of one master and thirty slaves, there could be few secrets.

"The entire villa is buzzing with talk of you."

She raised her lashes. "Nola, I realize a slave has no right to privacy, but Marcus is a most private man. I am certain he would not want the details of our intimacy in the sleeping chamber gossiped about."

"You would have more success holding back the tide than keeping slaves from gossip. You will have to have Marcus cut out their tongues."

"You jest?" Diana asked with apprehension.

"A little," Nola admitted, "though it is practiced in some Roman households. What I meant was that Marcus is so fervent he would likely do anything you asked of him."

Diana licked the honey from her fingers. "In that case I should have asked for clothes. I have nothing to wear."

"Before he left this morning, he asked me if I would take charge of your wardrobe. I was never so surprised in my life that he, of all men, would take such an interest in dressing a female."

"What sort of interest?"

"A fervent interest, filled with detail. He wants you in robes that will bring him pleasure, garments that will enhance your delicate beauty."

Diana wanted to curse. Always, someone had chosen her clothes for her. Had she escaped from Prudence only to find she still had no choice in what she wore? She was about to protest, vehemently, when she remembered that she was his slave. He could dress her any way he chose!

Diana made a token protest. "I know best what colors suit me."

"Marcus is more interested in style and texture. He desires only the costliest materials for you. There will be much leeway for you to select things that please you too."

"Will I be fitted here in the villa?"

"Yes, but we shall buy outside as well. A profusion of shops spreads itself along the streets of Aquae Sulis. Merchandise spills out onto the colonnaded walkways. Shopping is one of life's pleasures for a female. There are perfumers, jewelers, goldsmiths, floras, cookshops, ornatrices—"

"Ornatrices?"

"They fashion and arrange the hair," Nola explained.

"One of the female slaves has been dressing my hair. She is most talented."

"That is Sylla. You may take her for your personal slave to do your hair and makeup." When Nola saw Diana hesitate, she said, "It will elevate her to a higher status in the houschold, and if you choose her to serve you, it would please her so much.''

"Then I would love to have her," Diana said, accepting her first slave.

"Have your bath, then you can be fitted for some new stolae and robes.''

On her way to the bathing suite, Diana sought out Kell. Before she told him she wished to watch Marcus instruct the men at the river, he said to her, ''The general left orders for me to take you to him after lunch.''

"I will obey," she said softly. Diana was delighted that Marcus had remembered her request. He must have wanted it too, or he would have forgotten it. It would be a thrill to be taken to him before all the legionaries under his command. It showed how much he valued her, and how much he wished to show her off. It also showed that he needed to see her at some point in his day and that night was too long a time to wait.

She must wear something to make her beautiful. Something that would heighten his desire for her!

After her bath, Nola took her into the solarium. She had never been in this chamber before, but it was as lovely as all the rest of the villa. One entire wall from floor to ceiling was windows. On impulse she asked Nola, ''How is the glass made?''

"It is made by casting in flat molds. It is one of the many Roman skills that they have taught the Britons.''

The decorative floor was spectacular. It depicted a life-size Bengal tigress lying amid tall grasses. It was made from pieces of brilliant orange, black, and green marble. The couches in the room were covered with fine linen, interwoven with gold thread and dyed to pick up the colors in the floor.

Two merchants awaited them and each had female slaves to assist them because their customer was female. They had brought their wares in large trunks made of basketweave so they would be light to transport. The first was a cloth merchant, the second a jeweler.

One by one the baskets were opened and the lengths of cloth within were displayed before her. Every color, every texture, every material, some from as far away as Egypt and China, were spread about the couches. As Diana caressed the silks and stroked the fine wool, Nola ordered the garments Marcus had requested.

"I need something to wear when I go out today. Can it be made in time?"

"Of course," Nola replied. "The toga is simply a length of material, draped in various ways and fastened with a brooch. A mantle, even a hooded one, takes little more than draping and fastening. A simple stola and matching palla can be sewn in minutes by an experienced cloth slave."

"I would love a scarlet mantle like Marcus wears," Diana decided. "This white silk would make a lovely classical toga. A garment we imagine a goddess would wear," Diana said wistfully, rubbing the heavy silk between her thumb and forefinger. She drew in her breath as the lid of another basket was lifted to reveal lustrous material in a shade she could not begin to describe. "What color is this?"

"It is ultramarine. The vivid blue pigment comes from powdered lapis lazuli."

"May I have a stola made of this?" she asked Nola.

"Of course you may. The cloth merchant has recorded everything you have ordered."

"Ah Nola, look at this. The design is copied from the skin of a tigress, but it is as fine as a spider's web." She draped the transparent material across the marble floor and seemingly it disappeared.

"Exotic animal prints are the very latest fashion. There is much demand for them in Rome," the merchant told them proudly.

From the jeweler, Nola and Diana selected brooches,

clasps, hair ornaments, and a wide golden girdle to define the waist and emphasize the breasts. When she admired a pair of amulets fashioned after snakes with ruby eyes, Nola nodded to the jeweler. Then he opened a cypress box holding things Diana had never before seen. There was a set of rings attached by fine chains to matching bracelets. There were anklets, some with bells, and finally there were toe rings set with jewels. To Diana the jewelry was so exotic it seemed decadent and she absolutely lusted for all of it.

"The general asks that you leave your goods so he may select what appeals to him in particular. We will need one of the stolae and a fine wool mantle in about two hours," Nola told the cloth merchant.

As they walked through the villa, Diana asked Nola, "As a slave of this household, what are my duties?"

"Your sole duty is to obey and please Magnus. Your day should be spent at leisure doing pleasurable things so that you are in a receptive mood to spend your evening entertaining the general. He has a heavy workload and crushing responsibilities and needs diversion from constant duty. I myself am going to have a relaxing body massage before lunch. I'll send Sylla to your chamber so she can do your face and hair."

When Diana stepped into Kell's chariot, she drew the scarlet wool mantle about her closely. She was glad that it had been fashioned with a hood, for today a chill wind was blowing in from the coast. Up on these heights she could tell that autumn approached. Perhaps the storm last night had signaled the end of summer. For Diana it also signaled the end of innocence. She did not regret it. She felt more alive than she ever had. Life was filled with challenge and excitement, all centered on that driving force known as Marcus Magnus.

"Am I ordered to the fortress?" she asked Kell.

"Nay, we go straight to the river."

Diana shivered. "The weather has turned cold. Surely they won't go into the water today?"

"Inclement weather never stopped the general."

She glanced at Kell from beneath her lashes. "What would stop him?" she asked lightly.

"Naught in this world, lady."

Diana shivered just thinking of him.

"He's been waiting for a storm to swell the river. He'll be in his glory, never fear!"

Kell stopped the chariot in a meadow that looked down upon the River Avon. The banks of the river, about forty feet below them, were lined with more than a thousand legionary soldiers, each wearing full armor, bearing a full complement of weapons, and carrying a backpack of supplies. Across every soldier's back was slung his shield and a pack of provisions for making camp.

Diana's eyes easily picked out the powerful form of Marcus. He was about to give the men a demonstration of how to cross the river. She watched him secure his weapons, hang his shield across his back, then hold up his two javelins together in one hand.

Diana caught her breath as she watched him wade into the water, using the javelins as a staff, then when the water was deep enough to close about his breastplate, he used the javelins to push himself away from the bank, out into the river's swift current. He began to swim using only one arm to stroke. His other arm held the javelins parallel with his body so they would aid, rather than impede, his sidestroke.

Diana was terrified that the heavy armor and the bronze and iron helmet would drag him beneath the raging waters. "Why is he risking his life?" Diana cried out to Kell.

"He must set the example," Kell told her.

"He is attempting the impossible!" She pulled the wool mantle close about her, to try to keep from shivering.

Kell shook his head. "To Marcus Magnus nothing is impossible."

Diana did not dare take her eyes from the helmeted head that bobbed up and down in the raging torrent. All her thoughts and concentration were focused upon him as he battled the current, and she realized by the shouts of the men that they, too, were eager for him to win against the odds.

He was more than halfway now, and she realized he would beat the river. How much strength and determination such a feat must require! When he reached the far bank, her heart was pounding with joy for his victory. A great cheer arose from the throats of the legionaries and their centurion officers. Then, incredibly, Marcus Magnus waded back into the water to recross the river.

He was all brute strength. Watching him made Diana weak at the knees. Her mouth went dry remembering his powerful hands on her body. He must have taken her in his arms last night and lifted her into his bed, then stretched his magnificent body alongside hers as he watched her sleep. Watching him was like an aphrodisiac. Now she wished with all her heart that he had awakened her last night.

Marcus was once more successful in crossing the river. He waded out and handed his javelins to an officer. *Does he know I watch him?* The moment she asked herself the question, Marcus Magnus turned and looked up at her. Her heart overflowed with pride. She threw back the hood of her scarlet mantle and let the wind blow through her gilt tresses until it was in wild disarray. He was laughing and he lifted his arm to hail her. She waved back, then threw him a kiss.

Now it was the turn of the ten centurion officers and the two cohort centurions to duplicate the feat of the Primus Pilus. It took them twice as long, with many false starts, but with encouragements and dogged determination, half the leaders made it across. Six of them had to be dragged out and would have to attempt it again once they had rested.

Now it was the soldiers' turn to attempt the crossing and not all of them could swim. Fortunately Marcus had his own permanent legionaries to aid the newcomers. They had passed their leader's swimming tests before he had accepted them at the permanent base of Aquae Sulis.

Diana watched Petrius drag himself from the water and stalk toward his brother. He looked just as dangerous as he had last night.

"Freezing my nuts off in cold water is not my idea of training soldiers." He spat a mouthful of river water at his brother's feet.

Marcus looked him directly in the eye. "Your nuts will be the size of peas when you ford the icy rivers awaiting you in the western wilds. If you want your men to survive, you had better make sure they learn their lesson well today."

Petrius followed his brother's gaze to where Diana stood above them, her long golden hair blowing in the breeze. His loins clenched painfully. "How much do you want for her?" he asked.

"She isn't for sale," Marcus said evenly.

Petrius grinned at last. "Too bad. She won't get much fucking from you tonight, brother. The legionaries want another demonstration from you of how the standard bearers get their gear across."

At a signal from Marcus, Kell said to Diana, "He wants us to leave now."

"I'm glad I came to watch him!"

Kell knew she played some kind of game with the Roman, one that hid what she really thought and really felt about him. He did the same himself. But Kell knew Diana was coming to genuinely admire Marcus. She accepted his protection and she craved his admiration whether she was aware of it or not.

It would be most diverting to watch the relationship unfold beneath his very nose. Would the balance of power shift? In a subtle way, perhaps it already had. Should he foster their relationship or jeopardize it? He smiled to himself. Kell would do whatever was best for Kell!

When they returned to the villa, Diana was surprised at how lovely and warm it was inside on such an inclement day. When she removed her woolen mantle, she was quite comfortable in a silk stola with nothing beneath it. "Kell, how is the villa heated?"

"We have raised floors with ventilation. Heat comes from hot water pipes laid beneath each and every floor. You may go barefoot inside in the dead of winter and still be comfortable. Romans like their comfort."

Diana marveled that such an ancient civilization could be so advanced. Georgian houses were damp and drafty places in winter, depending on heat from a small fire in every room.

She knew it wouldn't be too many hours before Marcus arrived home. A bubble of excitement inside her was growing. She wanted to see how her new wardrobe was progressing and also she would have to have Sylla redo her hair because the wind had turned it into a wild tangle.

The merchants had departed from the solarium, but the cloth merchant had left his female assistants to make up the new garments and Nola had set two household slaves to help with the sewing. Diana was delighted with the numerous stolae in different colors and fabrics.

"Thank you, Nola, they are exquisite. I thank all of you for your hard work and generosity." She took an armful of gowns, including the ultramarine, the tigress print, and the classical white silk up to her own chamber, where Sylla showed her how to fold them in a special way that would prevent creasing.

Diana decided she would wear the white silk tonight for Marcus. As she sat before the mirror watching Sylla thread seed pearls onto strands of her golden hair, her excitement grew at the thought of being alone with her Roman tonight. She had never felt this way over Peter Hardwick, and that told her how attracted she was becoming to

Marcus Magnus. In fact, she realized that she was infatuated with him.

When she pictured him swimming across the raging river and then imagined those powerful arms about her, she could have screamed with excitement. She smiled to herself. She would be willing to bet the general would make sure they had no unexpected guests this evening.

When Kell tapped on her chamber door and came in with more new garments, Diana was disappointed to learn that Marcus had already arrived. "Oh, I wanted to be in the atrium to greet him when he arrived home!"

"He needed a hot bath immediately to unthaw his bones." Kell lifted one of the garments he had brought up. "The general has requested you wear the short white tunic to dinner."

Diana was amazed at how much it resembled the costume she had worn to the opening of the Pantheon. It came only to the thighs, its hem falling in points and its fastening on one shoulder. "Oh, I'm afraid this has been made wrong. I won't be able to wear it tonight." She felt somewhat disappointed, for the tunic would have made her resemble the goddess Diana.

"It has been especially designed this way," Kell informed her.

"The bodice will only cover one breast," Diana pointed out.

Kell nodded. "This is one of the tunics the general especially requested and he asks that you wear it to dinner tonight."

Diana was stunned that he would ask such a thing. How could he possibly expect her to join him for dinner wearing a tunic that displayed one bare breast? Everyone in the household would be able to look their fill at her nakedness. Her bubble of excitement evaporated and was replaced by a tight little knot of anger.

He was treating her like a prostitute! Was he doing it on purpose to insult her, or was his lust so great that he desired her to sit almost naked before him? If she reclined on a couch in a tunic that barely covered her thighs and left one breast fully exposed, she could guess how long it would be before his hands were all over her body!

Diana put the garment on the bed and said firmly, "I shall wear the elegant white silk stola. Would you be kind enough to wait outside until I am dressed, Kell?"

Kell's gray eyes held hers for a moment. "I have agreed to advise you, lady, and I do so now. Wear the garment the general has selected."

"I thank you for your advice, Kell. I will explain to him myself why I cannot wear such a garment."

Kell deferred to her decision and stepped outside of the apricot chamber, waiting to escort her to the triclinium. When she was dressed, Diana carefully examined her appearance in the polished bronze mirror. The white silk fell in a graceful straight line over her slim figure. Her upthrust breasts clearly showed the outline of her diamond-hard nipples through the delicate material. The seed pearls in her silver-gilt hair emphasized her delicacy tonight. She chose a gold wrist bracelet and matching gold anklet and decided to go barefoot tonight so she might display a pretty toe ring.

Diana placed her hand on Kell's arm and walked down the stairs with her head held high. She was confident that she looked exceptionally lovely.

Once again, Marcus had reached the triclinium before her. Household slaves were busy carrying in serving dishes. On Kell's arm she paused dramatically between the two pillars and awaited Marcus' response.

It wasn't long in coming. His dark face was unsmiling. His black eyes swept over her coldly. "You are not wearing the gown I requested."

Diana took a step forward. "Marcus, I refuse to wear such a scandalous garment!"

The slaves stopped what they were doing to stare at her.

Marcus strode toward her purposefully. "Refuse? I

don't believe I heard you correctly.'' His tone was harsh, forbidding.

Diana swallowed hard and lifted her chin. Foremost in her mind was her promise to obey his orders implicitly before others. If she violated their agreement, he was free to do the same. In fact, by the look of him he would welcome the excuse to do so, even relish it!

When he spoke again, it was as the all-powerful Roman. ''You will return to your chamber and change. When you return, you will fulfill your sole purpose in life: giving me pleasure!''

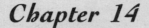

Diana's lashes swept to her cheeks. Her fingers dug into Kell's arm in frustrated fury. If she lost her temper and berated the Roman before his slaves, she would lose what little power she had gained. She knew she had little choice but do exactly as he commanded.

With quiet dignity she turned and left the room. She was grateful that Kell did not remind her that she should have taken his advice. Sylla awaited her with the brief tunic ready. She had known Diana would be sent back. The general never allowed disobedience.

Diana decided she would have to overcome her shyness. Modesty was not allowed in a Roman household. She had no choice but to be obedient in front of the other slaves, but once she and Marcus were private she would give him a piece of her mind and show him just how outraged she felt at being forced to display her nudity before others.

Diana removed the lovely white silk and allowed Sylla to slip the tunic over her head. It, too, was white, but the material was more diaphanous, allowing the color of her flesh to show through. As Sylla fastened it on one shoulder with a huge ruby brooch, Diana stared at her reflection in amazement. She had never even imagined herself in a garment that concealed one breast while totally revealing the other. It was a most erotic garment. Nay, it was more, it was decadent.

She felt her cheeks become warm and saw the blush that suffused them in the mirror. Well, she might as well get all her blushes over with, for in a moment Kell would see her, then Marcus and the slaves who served tonight would be able to observe her at leisure all through the evening meal.

Sylla handed her a pair of sandals with long, golden ribbons. Diana removed the toe ring, the golden anklet and bracelet, then crisscrossed the ribbons up her bare legs. Finally, she selected a pair of gold and ruby amulets. When she clasped them about her upper arms, she felt decidedly un-Christian. She felt and looked like a Sybarite. Before Diana left her chamber, she dipped a towel into a bowl of rose water, then held it to her burning cheeks to cool them.

Once more Kell escorted her to the triclinium, his hooded gray eyes concealing his thoughts completely. This time Diana held her head even higher. Marcus Magnus behaved as if this were the first time she had come down to dine. His face was no longer grim, his voice had lost its icy tone.

"Greetings, my lady. It is a pleasure to be home at last."

"Greetings," she murmured, without using his name or lifting her lashes from her rosy cheeks.

Diana circled away from him and sought her couch immediately. She sat down, lifted her legs to the couch, then carefully arranged the hem of the tunic so that it completely covered her thighs, for she wore no undergarment beneath its diaphanous skirt. She did not tuck the small gold cushion beneath her elbow because she did not wish to recline. She noticed that the couch had been completely recovered and new gold cushions set out to replace the ones that Petrius had soiled.

Two male slaves served them tonight. Because of the tremendous energy Marcus had expended during his rigorous day, his appetite was enormous. Tonight there was a whole turbot with fennel sauce, followed by a steaming venison pie, and an assortment of roast partridge and peacock.

Tonight they drank calda made from mixing wine, spices, and hot water. It was the same recipe as hippocras and Diana thought fleetingly of Peter Hardwick. He would have been the first man to make love to her if she had not gone back in time. She shuddered at the very thought. In one way she had had a lucky escape. She glanced across at Marcus and realized that in spite of the gulf that separated them in attitude, in thought, word, and deed, there was no other man she would rather have make love to her.

"Did you enjoy the demonstration at the river today?"

"May I please tell you when we are private?" she begged softly.

"Of course you may." He wanted her to say his name. It gave him untold pleasure to hear it on her lips. He wished she would entertain him with conversation while they dined. He had thoroughly enjoyed last evening until Petrius had ruined it.

"You were asleep when I came to my chamber last night. Did I disturb you?"

"May I please tell you when we are private?" she again begged softly.

His dark brows drew together. She was deliberately trying to annoy him. "No, damn you, you may not. You will answer whatever questions I put to you."

"May I have permission to answer your questions truthfully?"

Marcus knew this was some devious female trick. His black eyes narrowed. "You may answer my questions any way you like, so long as your reply gives me pleasure."

Diana bit her lip. He knew they were playing a cat-and-mouse game.

"We shall begin again. Did you enjoy the demonstration at the river today?"

"I enjoyed it above all things, master."

Marcus grit his teeth at her subservience. "Did I disturb you last night?"

"Your nearness always disturbs me, master."

His patience snapped. "Leave us," he bade the serving slaves. "Close the door behind you."

He did not speak until they were alone. "Once more . . ." His tone warned her that he was at the end of his tether with her. "Did you enjoy the demonstration at the river today?"

Diana tucked the gold pillow beneath her elbow and reclined provocatively. She cast him a sideways glance and replied outrageously, "I did enjoy it, but not nearly as much as you did, Marcus. You were showing off to the legionaries, and especially to the cohort centurions. Poor Petrius, he doesn't stand a snowball's chance in Hades of measuring up to you."

"Mea culpa," he said, grinning like a boy. His eyes licked over her. "Have you any idea how breathstopping you look tonight?"

"For a slave, you mean?" she asked sweetly.

"You don't look like a slave! You look like a goddess. I had the tunic made exactly like the one Diana of the Grove wears. All you need is an arrow in your hand."

"I expect you will soon rectify that," she murmured suggestively.

Marcus threw back his head and his laughter came rolling out. "You are delightful."

"My only wish is to please you." Her words dripped with sarcasm.

"If that is true, come and recline on my couch so we may share the same plate, the same goblet."

Diana's pulses quickened. If he got her on his couch, all food would be forgotten and she would become the main course. She must give him an answer that would buy her some time.

"You promised to woo me before I must yield to you."

"How better to woo you than on my couch?"

"If I was not wearing a garment that bared one breast, I would not object to sharing your couch. Perhaps tomorrow evening?" she offered.

"Tomorrow. Swear it!" he commanded, not trusting her.

"I promise, Marcus," she said softly.

His black eyes glittered as a diabolical idea came to him. He would take full advantage of her vow. "Would you like me to ask Nola to serve us tomorrow, instead of the male slaves?"

"Yes, that would preserve a small shred of my modesty. Thank you."

"Your modesty is misplaced, Diana. You have the loveliest female form I have ever seen."

"I thank you for your compliment, Marcus, but can't you understand that I have no wish to display my body?"

"That is ridiculous. When a woman has beauty, it should be displayed. It is the only thing of value a female possesses." His dark eyes caressed her, adding emphasis to his words.

"You are wrong! Beauty is only a small part of a woman!"

"No, it is everything. Beauty is all I, or any other man, want in a woman; beauty and obedience, of course."

"That is blind arrogance—a totally dominant male concept!" Diana tossed her hair back impatiently as she spoke with passion. Marcus couldn't take his eyes from her. Anger certainly increased Diana's beauty tonight. "What else is there?" he asked bluntly.

"A woman's intelligence, of course, and her strength of character. What about her sense of humor? Humor is at least as important as beauty. A woman should be appreciated for all her attributes. Any slave can give you obedience, Roman!"

"We Romans did not invent slavery, Diana. The Celtic

tribes of Britannia have traded slaves with Rome for years.''

"That doesn't make it right. Slavery is wrong. It has always been wrong.''

"The economy depends on slaves. Slavery will always be with us. You must accept it.''

"No, Marcus, you are quite wrong. Slavery will be abolished, thank God.''

"I have no intention of debating the merits of slavery. You are here to entertain me. It is your exceptional beauty that interests me, not your intelligence.''

"That is too bad. I had planned to entertain you with my intelligence tonight, not my beauty.''

"That would be impossible.''

"What a challenge you are, Marcus Magnus.''

He grinned at her. "We shall go upstairs now and continue our game,'' he said decisively.

"Is that an order or an invitation?''

His grin widened. "Since there is no one to overhear us, it is an invitation.''

"I am happy that you play by the rules.''

"The beauty of being in command is that I can change the rules at any time.'' He came over to her couch and towered above her. His nearness made her pulsebeat erratic.

"It would give me pleasure to carry you up.'' Before she could protest, she found herself lifted in his arms. Her bare breast was pressed against his wide chest. The raw linen of his tunic brushed against her nipple, making it instantly erect. Her naked thighs rested on his great muscular forearm and the heat of his body seeped into her, almost melting her bones.

As Marcus climbed the stairs, she felt his marble-hard phallus brush against the bare cheeks of her bottom. Desire spiraled from her buttocks to her woman's center and beyond into her belly. Every step he climbed increased the intensity of the feeling. She clung to him, feeling his muscles ripple beneath her hands. All the sensations she felt were highly charged and deeply sexual. She was beginning to discover that arousal was a most pleasurable activity.

He carried her into his sleeping chamber and kicked the door closed with his foot. The desire to yield herself to him was almost overwhelming. She wanted him to cover her mouth with his so that she could taste him. But instead of kissing her, he carried her to his big silver mirror, so she could see what she looked like in his arms.

Their reflection was overtly sensual. He held her legs high so that she could see the golden tendrils covering the pink center between her thighs, and there, just below, was the bulge of his manhood, erect and straining toward its goal. He lowered her body slightly so they brushed against each other.

When she drew in a quick breath, he smiled knowingly. He let her body slide down his until her feet touched the carpet, but he did it with her facing the mirror. Diana couldn't believe the disparity in the size of their bodies when he was standing this close behind her. Their coloring, too, was a startling contrast; hers so fair, his so dark and swarthy.

She watched, mesmerized, as his powerful hand cupped her bare breast and his calloused thumb toyed with her nipple. Threads of molten fire ran from the tip of her captured breast and plunged downward into her belly, then moved even lower. Marcus pulled her back against him so that she could feel the hard length of his shaft against her bare buttocks. She gasped and slipped her hand between their bodies where they touched, but he pressed her even closer so that her hand was now trapped, with her fingers curving about his swollen manroot. As his thumb teased her nipple, she felt him grow longer and harder in her hand.

Then with his other hand, he lifted the short tunic so she could watch him trace her high mound of Venus and let his fingers thread through her pubic curls. Diana was gasping with the things he was doing to her and the sensations his powerful fingers aroused. Her free hand covered his, in an effort to make him take it from her woman's center, but her small hand was totally ineffective and fell away of its own volition as he searched her cleft with a calloused fingertip until he found the sensitive bud within.

Then Marcus moved his finger in a slow, circular motion, until she moaned with pure pleasure. As Diana watched herself writhe beneath his fingers, she became so aroused she wanted to scream from excitement. She began to pant and felt his phallus buck and pulse beneath her hand.

He began to squeeze her bare breast with a slow, rhythmic motion that matched the rhythm of his encircling fingertip. She wanted to beg him to go faster, but the words stuck in her throat so that she could only moan her pleasure. Sensations were coming in waves now, setting up pulsations that were intensifying. With a female knowledge as old as Eve's, she realized that if he quickened his finger, her pleasure would soon be over. Moving in slow, steady, rhythmic circles made the pleasure go on, and on, and on.

She arched back against him and her head began to thrash about against his wide chest. When her climax came, it was so hard and fast, she cried out and thrust into his hand wildly. He cupped her firmly, intensifying the sensual pleasure each pulsating contraction brought her. Then he lifted her back into his arms so he could possess her trembling mouth.

She clung to him sweetly, allowing him to plunder her mouth as he had plundered her senses. When at last he lifted his mouth from hers, he murmured, "That is just a foretaste of the pleasure we will share. Now that I have entertained you, it is your turn to entertain me. Do you imagine your intelligence can hold my interest, or will you have to resort to your beauty?" he challenged.

He carried her up the steps and deposited her on his bed. Then he threw off his linen tunic and stretched his length beside her, propping his shoulders against the pillows and cushions.

Diana's curious eyes examined him with awe. He was indeed a splendid male specimen. His torso was covered by thick black curls that were dense across his chest where the golden coin reflected the light from the silver lamp. The hair was sparse across his ridged belly, then bloomed again at his groin. His male sex, still in a state of arousal, stood erect as a column of marble crowned with a head of vermilion velvet.

She tucked her knees beneath her and clasped her hands. In an almost kneeling position, she began to talk to him quietly. "Marcus, my name is Diana Davenport. I was born in London, Londinium, in the year A.D. 1772. I traveled to Aquae Sulis, which we call Bath because of the ancient Roman baths built seventeen hundred years before. One day I went into an antique shop, a shop that sells old antiquities. I was amazed to find a Roman helmet of iron and bronze. I couldn't resist trying it on, but when I did, I felt strange, ill almost, and I experienced a sensation of falling through space.

"Now I realize I was somehow being transported through time. I think I fainted, and when I regained consciousness, I was here in Aquae Sulis, almost beneath the wheels of your chariot. In my ignorance I thought that some men, of my own time, were dressing up as ancient Romans and playing silly boy games. However, when you put a slave collar on me, I realized it was no game."

Marcus watched her lovely mouth as she talked. He was the luckiest man breathing. He had a slave girl who was not only exquisitely beautiful, but one who could bemuse him with stories and entertain him with her humor and intelligence. And the best part was that no man had touched her before. Not a single one. His eyes began to close. As the music of her voice went on, the day's work began to take its toll on the general and he fell asleep to the sound of Diana.

Diana lifted her lashes to gauge his reaction to the things she was telling him. Her eyes widened in disbelief—

Marcus had fallen asleep while she talked! Still on her knees, she leaned forward to get a closer look at him. In repose, his features still had the pride of an eagle, but he looked so much younger. His wide chest rose and fell with his slow, even breathing. His neck, arms, and shoulders were corded with heavy muscle, while the swarthy skin across his belly was taut as a drum.

His shaft, no longer like a ramrod, lay against his thigh, its head withdrawn inside its cowl. It still looked a dangerous weapon, however, its size alone intimidating. Her eyes drifted down his thighs and calves. He had the most muscular legs she had ever seen. Modern men were not built this way. He was like a Colossus.

Finally, she looked at his hands. They were large, capable, powerful hands, both calloused and scarred. She marveled that they had brought her such pleasure. They had been strong yet tender at the same time. She looked at her exposed breast, the one he had stroked and fondled, and was surprised that he had left no mark upon it.

She placed one of her hands beside his and discovered it was only about one third its size. Though he was enormous, there was nothing clumsy about him. He had the strength and lithe power of an animal. In swordplay he was quick on his feet, moving with the speed of lightning and striking with the same deadly surety.

Diana wondered why Fate had sent her to the arms of this man. There was no answer. Yet deep down, in the recesses of her heart, she was secretly glad that she had been given such a fantastic chance to experience this time, this place, and this man. She experienced a tiny flicker of fear that she might be snatched away from him. She was surprised at her own emotions and admitted that she would be loath to leave him.

She knew if he opened his eyes, she would yield to him in a heartbeat. Then she felt guilty. He had had an exhausting day and needed his rest so that he could arise at five and start all over again. With one last reluctant glance at him, she quietly tiptoed from his chamber.

Chapter 15

"This is outrageous!" Diana cried. "I refuse to wear this, I refuse to go downstairs, and you can bloody well tell him so!"

"The general told me you might be unreasonable. I am to remind you about the promise you gave," Kell said stonily.

Diana was so angry, she couldn't think straight for a minute. Then her own words came back to her: *If I was not wearing a garment that bared one breast, I would not object to sharing your couch. Perhaps tomorrow evening?*

"Tomorrow. Swear it!" he had commanded.

I promise, Marcus. Her thoughts ran about like quicksilver. He had tricked her. Deliberately tricked her! He had diabolically used her own words to trap her. The garment he had chosen for her tonight did not bare one breast, it bared both!

"You can go down and tell him all promises are off. In fact, our bargain is off!"

"You mean the one where you agreed to be his slave only when others are about?" Kell asked with a straight face.

"How did you know that?" Diana demanded angrily.

"The walls have ears," Kell said dryly.

"The entire household knows?" she asked in outrage.

"Knows what? That in return for pretending to be his slave, he has to keep his cock to himself until you agree to yield willingly?"

"Ohmigod!" Diana covered her blushes with her hands. She had never been so embarrassed in her life. Then she decided the shame was not hers, it was Kell's for violating her privacy. "Are you taking bets as to when he will bed me?" Diana asked in outrage.

"Actually, it won't be long if you call off your bargain," Kell warned.

"Get Nola up here!"

"A slave cannot issue orders."

"I'm a pretend slave, remember? Get Nola up here before I have your flagellum removed."

"That could be painful, Briton," Nola said from the doorway.

"Woman of Gaul," Kell said, rolling his eyes ceilingward, "that's all I needed."

"Nola, does everyone in the household know my secrets?"

"No. Only the Briton knows, and I'm shrewd enough to put two and two together, but Marcus is a most private man and it is Kell's job to preserve that privacy, so you can rest assured none know your secrets."

"Thank you for undermining my authority. Perhaps you can persuade the lady to dress and go downstairs to dine."

"Look at this!" Diana cried, holding out a garment of bloodred crimson.

"It is a loin dress. You will look magnificent in it."

"I will look naked in it! One of you will have to go and tell him I refuse to put it on."

"This will take diplomacy. The Briton would be useless; I'll go." Nola had spoken simply to disparage Kell. Why did she get herself into these things? She walked into the triclinium, hiding the trepidation she felt. "The loin dress you chose would look exquisite on her, General, but you forget she is extremely modest and has never seen a garment like that before.''

"She has promised to obey my orders. Is she refusing to do so?"

"No, no. But I think it would be most thoughtful of you to clear this part of the villa of male slaves. She would feel more at ease if only your eyes observed her charms.''

"Have Kell remove all the males. Will you serve us tonight, Nola?''

Nola inclined her head. She had a delicate task before her and did not quite know how to accomplish her mission. When she returned to Diana's chamber, Kell said, "Ah, Woman of Diplomacy, did you tell him the lady refuses?''

"I explained that she is extremely modest and has never seen a garment like this before.''

"And?" Kell pressed relentlessly.

"And he wishes you to remove all the male slaves from this part of the villa. That, of course, includes you, Briton!''

Kell heaved an exaggerated sigh of relief. "The gods are with me tonight. I will have no trouble obeying my orders, while you, dearest Nola, are faced with an insurmountable task.''

When he left, Nola said, "Just once I would like to wipe the smug look from his superior male face.''

"You didn't tell Marcus," Diana accused.

"He has made a great concession to make you feel more comfortable," Nola pointed out.

"Still, he expects me to wear this thing! Have you seen it? It is a lewd and scandalous garment.''

"Scant perhaps, but not scandalous. Romans honor and worship the body. There is nothing more beautiful than the naked female form. To think there is lewdness connected with it is an obscenity in itself. Try on the garment and you will see for yourself that it only adds to your beauty.''

Reluctantly, Diana removed her stola and allowed Nola

to drape the crimson loin dress over her hips. It dipped down at the front all the way to her pubic bone, where Nola fastened it with a huge pearl brooch. When Diana looked in the mirror, all she could think was that if Prudence saw her, her aunt would die from shock!

A deep voice from the doorway said, "You have admired yourself long enough, now it is my turn."

"Marcus!" Diana gasped. "I cannot walk about like this."

"Then I shall carry you," he said implacably. He picked her up as if she were thistledown and, completely ignoring all her protests, carried her down to the triclinium. Diana turned into his body so that only her back would be exposed should any eyes be spying on her. This, however, was not without its consequences. The tips of her breasts brushed against his chest with every step he took. She could feel the heat from his body and smell the male scent of his dark skin.

She expected him to take her before the mirror again, but instead, he set her down upon her own couch in a reclining position and tucked a small gold cushion beneath her elbow. Then he crossed to his own couch and let his eyes roam over her at his leisure.

Diana had stopped protesting. Marcus Magnus' will would always prevail. He was the ultimate dominant male and no force on earth would ever alter him. She had a choice: Either she accepted him or she rejected him, and she knew it would be in her own best interests to accept him. Also, deep down at her core, she did not really want him any other way. If she admitted her true feelings, she was inordinately flattered that he found her irresistible.

They were highly attracted to each other, and the anticipation of seeing and touching and tasting was like a fire in the blood. They tempted each other so much that they were in a constant state of arousal. Diana knew it was inevitable that he would make love to her and the thought of it made her want to scream with excitement.

Nola followed them into the triclinium. "Will I serve you separately?" she asked, knowing full well that Marcus wanted Diana on his couch, reclining with him.

"You may serve the main courses separately and then you may withdraw, Nola."

There were huge prawns, small shrimp, and baby scallops in a sauce of lemon butter, followed by a larded and crisped goose, stuffed with chestnuts. The salad had chick peas, cucumber, and beetroot with a tangy honey and aniseed dressing. Diana had never had anything at the Roman's table that was not delicious. The Prince of Wales would have been green with envy had he been able to dine here.

"Do you forgive me for falling asleep last night?"

"The fault was mine. I obviously bored you."

"Nay, I was highly entertained. You have a fertile imagination."

"I didn't imagine it, Marcus. It really happened."

"I want you to continue your story. I want you to tell me everything—after."

Diana found it difficult to breathe. "After?"

"Yes, after. Not only tonight, but every night I would enjoy being entertained by your stories."

"After what?" she whispered, her throat suddenly dry, her voice husky.

"After the needs of our bodies are satisfied. After we have eaten and quenched our thirst, and after we are sated with lovemaking. Then we will talk."

Diana lowered her lashes to her cheeks. If Nola didn't leave them alone soon, she would die of longing. It was highly erotic and titillating to recline before this virile Roman general clad only in a garment that covered her loins. And its purpose was clearly designed to do more than cover, it was designed to emphasize her pubis, which was adorned with the great pearl. Finally, Nola cleared away the first courses and brought in a tray of desserts and fruits, then she withdrew.

Marcus' black eyes glittered. He held out his hand to her and said, "Come over here and see if there is aught that tempts you." The sexual tension in the room was so tangible, he could taste it and smell it.

Diana slid from her couch and came to him slowly and sinuously. When she was close by his couch, she gave him a sideways glance and said provocatively, "I see much that tempts me. Choose your dessert and I will serve it to you."

"I choose you," he said hoarsely.

Like a houri who had been trained in a harem for her sultan's pleasure, Diana sat down upon his couch, lifted her legs, and in one fluidly graceful movement curled her body against his. He had been lying on one elbow with his knees bent. She leaned back against his knees, facing him, so that he had complete access to the breasts his eyes had caressed throughout the meal. But his need to taste her lips first was so overwhelming that his arms enfolded her against his heart and his mouth came down on hers in total possession.

Once they had begun, they could not stop kissing. They had been starving for each other. Her lips opened to his fierce demands and he thrust his tongue inside the dark honeyed cave to plunder her sweetness. Her senses were overflowing with the scent and taste and feel of him inside her. He stroked her tongue with his, playing out the male-female game of domination and submission until he mastered her, and she clung to him, allowing him to ravish her until she was mindless. He took her close to the edge of madness until she was panting and biting and digging her nails into his flesh in blind ecstasy.

After a while his kisses became less fierce and brutal, but much more sensual and erotic. His tongue traced her lips, he nibbled and sucked her mouth, taking endlessly until her lips were swollen with an excess of kissing. Yet still their mouths hungered for more. He gave her tiny kisses, quick hot kisses, and slow melting kisses.

Then Marcus held her away from him so he could look his fill at her lush breasts, which were slowly hardening at the lust he aroused in her. He dipped his head to lick a taut pink nipple, then drew the whole luscious crown into his mouth. She arched backward so that her breast thrust into his mouth and he almost devoured her.

Her mouth was ravenous again, so Diana let her lips and tongue slide up the column of his throat. She felt insatiable. She would never get enough of him. His linen tunic had wide armholes so she slipped her hands inside to caress and fondle the great slabs of muscle that covered his wide chest.

This did not satisfy her for long. "Remove it," she begged, and when he eagerly complied, she ran her fingertips through the dark curls and set her mouth to licking and sucking his copper nipples. A deep craving began inside Diana. She needed more voluptuous love play. She needed to wrap her long legs about his magnificent body. She needed his fingers to play with her, even go inside her. Now she knew exactly what Marcus had meant when he said he was riven with need!

Marcus, however, now chose to do teasing, playful things to her. He dipped his finger in his wine and anointed the tips of her breasts, then curled his tongue about her diamond-hard nipples to catch the bloodred drops. Then he sipped the wine and set his mouth to hers to give her wine-rich kisses.

"Please, Marcus, please!" Her whisper was so intense, he realized that at last she was ready to yield to him, oh so willingly.

"Come," he said, rising from the couch and taking her hand. When her feet touched the floor, her knees were like water. She clung to his hand and followed where he led. He was naked, save for the gold medallion he always wore, and at that moment she thought him beautiful enough to always go naked.

Suddenly, Diana felt very overdressed. When they reached the bottom of the stairs, he lifted her before him and unfastened the pearl. "Wrap yourself about me." Her arms slipped around his powerful neck, and as her legs encircled his torso, the crimson loin cloth fell onto the bottom step.

As Marcus slowly mounted the staircase, their desire also mounted until it burst into flame. The length of his shaft rested in her cleft, hard as a battering ram and she writhed upon him until she was creamy with craving. She kissed him hard and slipped her tongue into his mouth. Diana was ready to make some demands of her own.

He ignored the steps leading up to the side of the bed and instead went to the foot. His powerful hands lifted her by the waist and stood her on the high bed. His mouth was on a level with her knees and he rained kisses upon them, then rubbed his cheek against her velvet-soft skin.

"Marcus, I need to touch you," she whispered hoarsely, gazing down at him. "I am Diana, I need your arrow in my hand; I need your arrow inside me!"

"I want to savor you. I have decided to keep you virgin awhile."

"No!" she cried, in a fever to gift him with her maidenhead.

"Go on your knees to me."

For a moment she thought he was asking her to abase herself in homage. His hands slid up the backs of her thighs and he pulled her on her knees so that his mouth was in close proximity to her woman's center. Then it was Marcus who was paying homage to her. He gently blew his warm breath on the golden tendrils that crowned her high mons. Then he began to kiss her. His hands cupped her bottom, his fingers splayed in the cleft between her cheeks, then he lifted her forward so his mouth could work its magic.

Diana was shocked at his actions. What he did was wicked and far too intimate even for lovers. But as his lips nuzzled her, then his tongue sought her tiny bud of pleasure, she lost all her prudish inhibitions and arched herself into his glorious, glorious mouth.

By the time he plunged his tongue inside her, she was

crying her pleasure with such wild abandon, it filled his
sleeping chamber and echoed throughout the villa. When
she reached her peak, she arched back onto the furs and
then collapsed limply in a delicious sprawl, with her legs
dangling over the end of the bed.

Marcus came over her in a heated passion. His needs
had never been so great, yet he did not want to spoil her this
night. His weapon could no longer be described as an arrow, it was now a gladius sword lusting for blood. He
curbed his hunger with an iron will and thrust himself between her luscious breasts. His powerful hands came up to
cup them and make a deep cleft where his marble-hard
phallus could stroke in the velvet softness of her flesh.
When he spent, his cries made hers seem like mere whispers.

Marcus brought scented water and bathed her breasts
tenderly, then he lifted her beneath the covers. When he
joined her, he pulled her against his side. "I don't want to
sleep, I want to hold you close all night so we can touch
and talk and kiss."

She sighed with contentment. "So this is *after*?"

"Afterglow," he corrected, burying his face in the perfumed tangle of her pale hair. "Mmm, you are so different
from other women—so much finer, so delicately boned."
For a fleeting moment he was almost ready to believe she
was a goddess. "Where did you really come from, Diana?"

"I came from the future, Marcus."

"And what did you do in this Londinium of the future?"

"I lived with my aunt and uncle after my father died.
He left me his house and the most wonderful library filled
with books. I read everything I could get my hands on.
History was my favorite subject. I've read a lot about when
the Romans occupied ancient Britain. In modern times,
Queen Boadicea is a great heroine."

"Boudicca was a wild, uncivilized madwoman who incited the Iceni to rebellion, once her husband died," Marcus corrected her.

Diana raised her eyes to his. "She was driven to it by the Romans."

Patiently, Marcus said, "Tell me what you have heard, then I will tell you what really happened."

"Well, she was Queen of the Iceni, a wealthy Celtic tribe with much gold and silver. I believe it was the Procurator Catus who plundered their wealth. When poor Boadicea objected, he had her publicly whipped. His men raped her two daughters and enslaved her people, so they rose up in rebellion and burned London. She was so brave that she took her own life rather than be taken alive by the Romans."

"First of all, Boudicca was not a queen. She was, however, married to the King of the Iceni. When Emperor Claudius came to Britain, he and the king came to peaceful terms and he agreed to allow the Romans to build and occupy military camps. For sixteen years we lived together in peace and prosperity. We built roads and towns whose populations were mostly Britons who had become civilized. The king outlived Claudius, then had the same arrangement with Nero. We increased trade so that people from all over the world came here to settle.

"When the king died, he bequeathed half of his vast wealth to Emperor Nero and the other half to his daughters. The monstrous Boudicca was so jealous that she paid some soldiers to destroy her daughters. Then she proclaimed herself queen and incited the tribesmen to revolt against Roman rule.

"My legion and the other three stationed in this region were fighting in the west country under Governor Paullinus. Only token garrisons were left behind. The wild Iceni overran the new administrative capital that was being built at Camulodunum. They set ablaze the half-built town and massacred two hundred defenseless stonemasons and builders.

"Having seen what they could do, they became gluttons for destruction. They looted the richest towns where defense was weakest. Paullinus brought the legions back at double speed, knowing the beautiful and wealthy trading port of Londinium would be her target. We arrived before the barbaric tribes, and rather than risk Londinium's population, we evacuated them. It was a town of merchants, aristocrats, retired legionaries, administrators, and clerks. Many were left behind—the old, the sick, those too stubborn to leave their homes.

"Boudicca and her wild tribes looted, burned, and beheaded everything in their path. When we went back in, we found they had destroyed the basilica, the forum, the baths and temples, but that was not the worst part. The rivers ran red with blood. We were a month picking up severed heads, and most of the victims were civilized Britons, not Romans. Put all romantic visions of *poor* Boudicca from your mind, Diana. She was huge and terrifying, with a loud coarse voice and a filthy mass of bright red hair."

Diana clung to him. "This happened only a few months ago, Marcus? I thought Aquae Sulis such a beautiful place."

"It was almost a year ago. Aquae Sulis is a beautiful place," he told her firmly, "but some of the Celtic tribes are still unconquered. They have retreated into the west country and the legionaries are trained here before they go in after them."

"Marcus, I'm afraid," Diana whispered.

He kissed her and soothed her. "How can you be afraid with me beside you?"

"But I am afraid for you," she said, clinging even tighter.

He began to tease her to dispel her anxiety. "You've seen the size of my weapon, little one, I'm invincible."

She curled against him knowing he would protect her with his life. All life was uncertain; each day an unknown quantity. To be held warm and safe in someone's arms was the best anyone could ever hope for.

Chapter 16

Diana awoke and sat up in the bed. When she saw Marcus at his desk, she said, "Oh, I thought you had left me."

Marcus came up the steps, sat on the edge of the bed, and took her hands in his. "I didn't want to waken you and yet I couldn't make myself leave."

"It's lovely to wake up and find you here."

He enfolded her in his arms and gave her a lingering kiss. Her breasts were crushed against his metal breastplate and he whispered, "Damn, I cannot feel your soft flesh against mine. How will I get through the day without seeing you?" His fingers dipped inside his tunic and he drew the gold chain over his head. "Wear my Caesar coin today." He slipped it over her head and saw the goldpiece rest in the valley between her breasts. He hardened instantly, recalling the feel of that deep and delicious valley intimately. "All day long I shall know that the coin that covers my heart is covering yours today."

"It's still warm from your body," she murmured.

"Keep it warm for me and return it tonight."

"Marcus, if I had a horse, I could ride out to you sometimes."

"You know how to ride?" He could never remember seeing a woman on a horse. Horses were for cavalry and warfare. Women rode about in litters. "A horse could be dangerous. They are very strong, Diana, and need a great deal of controlling. Have Kell bring you in his chariot. I must go.''

Below, as Kell picked up Marcus' tunic in the triclinium, he raised his eyebrows. Never before had the general discarded his clothing before he reached the bath or the sleeping chamber.

At that precise moment, Nola picked up the crimson loin dress from the bottom stair. As the two met, each saw what the other held, and came to different conclusions.

Nola thought, *She holds him in the palm of her hand.*

Kell thought, *He has claimed the prize.*

They were both right.

By the time Diana bathed and had her breakfast, Marcus was back. ''Get your mantle and come out to the courtyard. I have a surprise for you.''

As Diana stepped into the peristyle and pulled her red wool mantle about her shoulders, she saw Marcus leading a milk white steed. It had a saddle with four pommels, two in front and two behind, to aid a rider to stay put.

''It's a mare with a fairly good nature. Do you think you can handle such a huge beast?''

''Oh, Marcus, she's beautiful,'' Diana said, taking the reins and stroking the mare's muzzle. ''Let me show you that I can indeed manage a horse.''

He lifted her into the saddle and watched her sit sideways rather than straddle it. He was impressed when she cantered about the courtyard with total confidence. She trotted the mare back to him and held out her arms so he could lift her down. He brought her against him so he could whisper in her ear. ''I didn't get you a stallion because the only male I want you to ride is me.''

Diana blushed almost as deep a shade as her mantle. ''Thank you for such a lovely, thoughtful gift, Marcus.''

''I've ordered one of the stable slaves to ride beside you at all times. Will you come to me this afternoon? We will be on the heights at the chariot track.''

She reached up and offered him her lips. When at last he found the strength to withdraw his mouth from hers, she murmured, "You know I cannot stay away from you for an entire day." She watched as he mounted his own stallion in a running leap and rode off into the wind, his scarlet mantle billowing out behind him.

Marcus Magnus was such a vital force, she had sudden misgivings that she would not be enough woman for such an all-powerful man. He seemed enchanted with her at the moment, but was not that because of her virginity? Perhaps once he had performed the mystic hymenal rites, he would lose interest in her.

In that moment, she wished with all her heart that she had more knowledge of sexuality. Unmarried Georgian women were deliberately kept in ignorance about the intimate behavior of men and women. Perhaps that was the reason there were so many unhappy marriages. Most wealthy titled men kept a mistress and perhaps this was because of the marked distinction between good women and bad women, imposed by society. If ladies were taught how to behave wickedly once in a while, perhaps their husbands would remain faithful.

Diana sighed and went back into the villa. She had no choice; Marcus would have to teach her about her own sexuality. At the moment, he seemed happy enough to do so. A frisson of excitement ran down her spine. Tonight he would probably teach her all there was to know.

"Nola, I have a problem. I want to ride the horse Marcus just gave me, but all my stolae are too tight. Some do have slits up the skirts, but that would bare my legs and they would be cold."

"When the weather turns very cold, some legionaries, especially the cavalry, wear leather trousers, but most of them, including Marcus, wear the short tunic with long fur boots. But women don't ride horses, I'm afraid."

"Well, I do. Leather trousers are a wonderful idea. Have some sewn up for me. It's not too cold yet, but it will be in winter. How will I keep my legs warm today?"

"We have woolen stockings," Nola suggested.

"Oh good! I'll wear them with a short tunic and some boots, if you can find any small enough."

Nola brought her the stockings and turned the problem of the boots over to Kell.

"She will look scandalous!" Kell said with marked disapproval.

Nola rolled her eyes. "Only a male would object to such an outfit while totally approving a gown that bared a female's breasts."

"You should not encourage her to ride about like a man. She should have a litter or let me take her in my chariot."

"Oho, Briton, you don't like the idea of being usurped by a strapping young stable slave."

"Get your mind from the gutter, Woman of Gaul. I know most females are faithless bitches, probably including yourself, but the lady is different." Kell looked down his long nose at Nola and said with great superiority, "I happen to know she is virgin."

"After finding their clothes strewn about the villa, I doubt that very much, Briton."

Kell smiled smugly. "I know what I know." He did not tell her how carefully he had examined the sheets when he changed them that morning.

By the time Diana pulled on the woolen stockings and the short tunic, Kell arrived with a pair of soft leather boots that came to the ankle and had leather thongs that wound up the calves. But he also brought her some fur leggings that wrapped about her legs and were held in place by winding the thongs about them. When Diana looked in the mirror, she laughed. "Oh, I look like a Viking!"

"You look very fetching," Nola said.

"Retching!" Kell retorted. "Lady, I will come to the

stables and have a few words with the slave who escorts you.''

Diana threw on her mantle and preceded Kell, trying to keep from bursting into laughter at the faces Nola was making behind his back. When Diana entered the stables and saw the slave for herself, she thought wickedly, *If my grooms had looked anything like this one, I might have been tempted to a roll in the hay!* Then she realized how liberal her attitude toward men and sex were becoming. The slave wore a short leather tunic and leather wristbands. His brown hair came to his shoulders and was tied back with a thong. Tor had a merry face and laughing eyes.

''Wipe that damned smile off your face. You are being entrusted with the general's personal favorite. If aught befalls her, I will personally castrate you!''

The young slave blanched white.

''Watch her every minute, but avert your eyes if the wind blows her mantle aside.''

Her young groom looked so confused, Diana felt sorry for him. ''Kell, I'll be just fine, but thank you. It feels good to know that you worry about me.''

''I worry only because you are the general's property,'' he informed her, but she knew better.

As Diana rode from the villa to the track where her unbelievable adventure had begun, she could tell just where Georgian architect John Wood would build his Royal Crescent and The Circus. Both were extremely Anglo-Saxon versions of the classic Roman style. When she passed the vineyards, the grapes were being harvested. She saw that the vines had all been planted facing south and realized with awe that some of them would still be flourishing in the eighteenth century.

She saw the dust rising up from the track before she saw the chariots. There was no recreational racing today, however. The legionaries were being given a demonstration of how the Celtae used their chariots for warfare. These were small square vehicles with wicker sides, open at both ends for easy access. As Diana watched, the men ran along the chariot poles, stood on the yoke to throw their spears, then got back in and rode off before the legionaries could retaliate.

The bloodcurdling cries of the Britons, combined with the noise of the wheels, were almost enough to inspire terror in the enemy. Diana's hand flew to her mouth as she saw Marcus, without armor, run along a chariot pole to hurl javelins. If he slipped, he would be trampled beneath the hooves of the thick-set shaggy horses pulling the chariot.

"I can't watch!" she cried, covering her eyes.

"It's all right, lady, the general has leaped clear of the chariot," the stable slave informed her.

She saw that Marcus was addressing the officers. "The Celtae combine the mobility of the cavalry with the power of the infantry. Their charioteers can control their horses at full gallop even on steep inclines. They bring in their men, who engage on foot, and meanwhile they line up their chariots for a quick retreat. Before the day is over, you will learn how to combat them so that they will be no more than an annoyance. Your first target will be the horses that pull the chariots!"

Marcus was aware of Diana's presence and came to her once he had given the centurions specific tasks. They smiled into each other's eyes. All seeing them knew they were pledged lovers. He came to her side and rubbed the mare's nose. One black brow arched like a raven's wing as he took in her attire. "You look nice and warm."

She bent down from her saddle and whispered in his ear, "My legs are warm, but my bum is freezing!"

His black eyes glittered. "If we were more private, I would take you into my lap and warm you," he murmured.

"If we were more private, you would rub me until I was hot."

"You are a wicked lady," he accused. He took the mare's reins and led her a few paces away from her escort so he could speak privately. "We have a guest for dinner tonight. A message arrived from the procurator that he will be in Aquae Sulis today."

"The procurator is an important official of some kind?"

Marcus nodded. "He holds the highest office in Britannia. He is the administrator in charge of finances and all else. I don't want him to know you are a slave. I'll make up a plausible tale."

"It won't be a tale; I'm not your slave," she teased.

His powerful hand came down possessively on her thigh. He turned hard as marble the moment he touched her.

She stopped teasing. "Would you like me to stay in my chamber, Marcus?"

"No. I want you beside me. If we have confidential business to discuss, you can withdraw. I've already sent a message to Kell. He will see to everything."

When Diana arrived back at the villa, Kell had assembled all the household slaves and drilled them on everything from their dress to their specific duties. Nola was giving instructions to a group of female slaves. When the slaves went off to perform their assigned tasks, Diana said to Kell, "Marcus wants me to dine with him when he entertains the procurator, but he doesn't want him to know that I'm a slave."

"I see," Kell replied.

Nola explained to Diana, "The procurator, Julius Classicianus, is like the emperor here. He is all-powerful. If he knew you were a slave, he could ask for you for a night, or permanently, and Marcus would have to oblige him."

Kell said, "The procurator is no voluptuary. He has never used one of our slaves."

Nola said dryly, "Nevertheless he is a man. Marcus realizes Diana's temptation if you do not, Briton."

Kell ignored her and addressed Diana. "Dinner will be served later than usual because they will enjoy the ritual of the bath first. I will come for you when it is time to come down.''

"What do I do?" Diana asked helplessly.

"You will simply grace the triclinium," Kell said, far too busy to explain further.

Nola said, "Come upstairs, I will answer all your questions."

"You have more gall than grace," Kell accused.

"And you have more arrogance than a Roman!" Nola replied.

"I am a Briton. I have more to be arrogant about."

Diana laughed outright. "Kell won that round."

"Just once I'd like the last word with that man!"

"Nola, take a lesson from me. You catch more flies with sugar than vinegar."

"I have no doubt you have Marcus eating from your hand. Don't hurt him, Diana. He is a good man. There is no evil in him."

"I have discovered that for myself, Nola."

Marcus and the procurator arrived together in a litter. Kell had set a slave with a torch as a door guard, and when they entered the atrium, they saw that it was filled with urns of late-blooming flowers from the garden. Both men gave a burnt offering to Vesta, Goddess of the Hearth, then Marcus took his guest out through the peristyle garden to his private bath suite.

Since the night was chill, they decided to bathe inside. The long wooden bathhouse, covered by wisteria vines, was anything but rustic on the inside. It contained a caldarium that was hot, a tepidarium that was warm, and a frigidarium. They disrobed, entered the hot room, and lay upon marble slabs to sweat. As the temperature and the steam began to rise, Julius began to talk.

"At last Londinium is being rebuilt. The Forum, with its council chamber and administration offices, is complete, and the Temple of Jupiter is also finished. It has massive altars and fine mosaic floors, much like yours, and it is surrounded by ornamental gardens. This time, the entire city will have a ten-foot defensive wall with crenellated parapets and four towers with gates.''

"It was madness to destroy such a fine city, Julius. It was our greatest trading port and will be again. Once it's rebuilt I'm sure it will be bigger and better than ever.''

"Marcus, I received a communiqué from Emperor Nero. He's reassessing Britannia's importance to the empire. He is considering withdrawing all Romans and handing it back to the Celtae, whom he fears will never be conquered.''

"That would be a colossal mistake, Julius," Marcus said, his heart plummeting into his feet.

"So say I!" the procurator said decisively. "For monetary reasons alone, it would be foolish to abandon this corner of the empire. The profits from silver and slaves alone will pay for building dozens of new cities.''

"You are an honest man, Julius. The last procurator held the rank of speculator, which meant that when he executed prisoners, he kept their possessions. Perhaps the profits from silver and slaves found their way into his own coffers as well.''

"I'm afraid they did, Marcus. Now I must convince Nero that this country has everything: lead mines, iron, bronze, timber, even gold to make our own coinage. The fields are so fertile, we grow enough grain to feed the population, the legions, and still have some left over for export. Agriculture is organized on a massive scale and it's backed by a substantial fishing industry.''

"This country is thriving," Marcus agreed. "Have you told Nero in your reports?''

"Ad nauseam," Julius lamented.

"He must be getting negative reports from some other source," Marcus decided.

"You've put your finger on it, I believe."

Bath slaves began to oil and scrape their skins with strigils, but the Procurator was not distracted from the subject at hand. "I feel I can be blunt with you, Marcus, because we think alike on some matters. I think it's Paullinus. We have the wrong man at the head of the army. Oh, I know he is determined to stamp out all insurrection of the Celtae tribes, but he has exterminated the Silures entirely and the Iceni are being massacred instead of transported to Rome as slaves. Now he is systematically wiping out the Druids."

"I have known for a long time that when we desecrate sacred Druid places and massacre their priesthood, it incites the native tribes to more and more insurrection," Marcus said flatly.

"When Claudius was head of the army, we had peace. Britons were eager to become Roman citizens. They adopted our toga, learned to speak Latin, built arcades of shops, and as a result, prosperity for all rose steadily because of the demand for consumer and luxury goods."

"Aquae Sulis has been unaffected, but I know the rest of the country has suffered under Paullinus."

They moved from the hot room to the warm bath. "You've fought under him. What is he like, Marcus?"

"He is infected with the Roman disease of bloodlust. He slaughters women and children and even the pack animals when the madness is upon him. He practices *decimatio* to punish his legionaries, killing one in ten regularly for disobedience. These are counted as *acceptable losses*."

"No wonder none dare speak out against him," Julius concluded.

They took the cold plunge, were wrapped in huge towels, and moved on to the dressing room.

"Well, one step at a time. First, I must persuade Emperor Nero to keep Britannia in the empire. My last report was accompanied by a large shipment of money and silver ingots, which will go a long way in convincing him, but I'd like you to submit a report on Aquae Sulis, not only regarding the fort and the training of the legionaries, but about the thriving town itself and how the natives have become Romanized over two generations and are now productive builders, weavers, potters, goldsmiths, engineers, physicians, etc.''

"I'll do it tomorrow, Julius," Marcus promised.

"Good man. I knew I could count on you. Now, let us dine. My belly thinks my throat has been cut!''

Diana decided to wear the elegant white silk stola with the golden girdle. Nola had brought her an emerald and gold torque from the general's collection, and Sylla had fashioned her pale hair in a heavy bun at the nape of her neck. Kell escorted her to arrive at the triclinium entrance the same time as Marcus and his guest.

"Julius, may I present Diana, who is often a guest at my table.''

Diana extended her hand to the procurator and he raised it to his lips graciously. "Forgive an old man for staring at you, my dear, but you have a rare classical beauty.''

Marcus saw he was openly curious about her and explained, "Diana's father was a scribe for the government who married a Briton.'' He implied that she was half Roman and Diana simply smiled at the procurator. He was dressed in a long white toga with a wide purple border and actually wore a laurel wreath upon his graying head. Diana lowered her lashes to prevent herself from staring. She couldn't believe she was actually dining with such a high-ranking official of Rome.

They moved into the triclinium, where three dining couches were arranged about the table. "Here is a perfect example of a blending of Britannia and Rome. If Diana graced the emperor's table, she would stand out as an exquisite blend of beauty and culture. She is living proof that Britons are highly civilized.''

"Thank you, My Lord Procurator."

"Oh please, call me Julius."

Diana gifted him with a brilliant smile as she reclined on her couch and tucked a gold elbow cushion beneath her arm.

As the leisurely meal progressed, both Marcus and Diana felt the sexual tension build between them explosively. Though three dined, two of them were being driven mad with desire. Whenever Marcus' black eyes caressed her, they smoldered with the dark fires of anticipation. Neither of them could wait for their guest to leave. When Julius finally stood up to depart, Diana was weak with longing.

Chapter 17

Marcus walked with the procurator to the atrium and saw him into his litter. Julius always slept at the praetorium, a spacious residence within the fort, but he had informed Marcus that he would be leaving at dawn for Glevum, where most of the retired legionaries now lived.

"You dog, Marcus. Where have you been hiding her and however did you find her?"

"I think of her as a gift from the gods," Marcus said wryly.

"She said she came to Aquae Sulis to take the waters, but I think she stays for more personal reasons. You'd be a fool to let her escape, Marcus."

"I'll hold her captive, never fear," Marcus said, laughing, as the litter moved off.

When he went back inside, Diana was leaning against one of the pillars. His arms encircled her waist and he held her imprisoned against the marble. "You were a charming hostess, *amor*."

Diana knew that *amor* meant love. She lifted her lips to his. "And Julius was a charming guest, but you didn't discuss your business."

"We did that when we bathed. Steam not only opens the pores, it often loosens the tongue. Clothing is a barrier, and once it is removed, all reticence disappears."

"So I've discovered," Diana murmured wickedly, moving against him sensuously to unfasten his toga.

His mouth claimed hers in a passionate kiss that sent chills and then fire running along their veins. With his lips still against hers, he said huskily, "Do you think we can keep our clothes on long enough to get upstairs tonight?"

"It will be very hard," she murmured wickedly, stroking his shaft with her fingertips.

He lifted her against his hard length and proceeded to kiss her on each and every step of the staircase. When they finally reached the sleeping chamber, Marcus said low, "I want to carry you to bed every night for the rest of my life."

He was so earnest, Diana melted against him. Never one to lie to herself, she believed they were falling in love. She pushed the problems love would entail to the back of her mind. Nothing must spoil this special night for either of them.

Kell had lit a fire for them in the huge hearth and they stood before it now as Marcus disrobed them both. Then he took infinite pleasure in taking down her hair, allowing his fingers to become entangled in the silky mass, as he lifted it to his face to explore its texture, its smell, its very taste.

Marcus tossed the purple cushions from the bed before the fire, then pulled her down to him so she was cradled in his lap. He held her back to the fire and massaged her bottom cheeks. "I've been waiting to warm your bum all day."

Diana clung to him as he kissed her deeply, then she took the chain from about her neck and put it over his head so the gold Caesar coin lay amidst the dark curls. "From my heart to yours," she whispered.

Marcus watched the firelight turn her hair and skin to flame. His fingers traced over her flesh reverently, then his lips followed. "Diana, it occurred to me today, when I saw you astride the mare, that I have given you the means to escape from me."

Her eyes widened. "I wouldn't run away from you, Marcus. I have no desire to leave you."

His arms tightened about her as a wave of protectiveness swept over him. "You might after tonight. I'm afraid I will hurt you."

"Yes, I know you will. You are far too big for me, but your hands and your mouth work magic. They arouse me to such a frenzied peak of desire that I hunger and lust for us to join our bodies. My need becomes so great that fear of pain is nothing beside it. It must be the same for you. We become riven!"

"I'll go slowly; I'll stop at any time," he pledged.

Diana pushed him back upon the cushions. "I won't!" She straddled him with her silky thighs, then brought her breasts down upon his chest, so that his huge, swollen phallus was trapped between their bodies. The flames from the fire added to the heat in their blood, and as always, once they began to kiss, they could not stop.

It occurred to Diana that once their loveplay reached a certain point, Marcus displayed much more control than she. She knew he had an iron will, but tonight she wanted to make him lose all control. She wanted to test the outer limits of his resistance. She knew she had a certain power over him, but tonight she wanted to test her allure to its depths.

She lifted one of her long golden curls and teased the corners of his mouth with it, then she touched the corners with the tip of her tongue, tickling him until he laughed helplessly. Then she trailed her curl down the column of his throat, then followed with her tongue, leaving a hot, wet path to dry by fireflame. Diana sat up so that her knees gripped his narrow hips and her bum cheeks rested on his muscular thighs, then, using the same golden curl, she stroked his flat bronze nipples until they became erect.

By now, Marcus was anticipating her moves and knew her tongue would soon follow where she played. He relished the attention she was lavishing upon him, wishing they had met long ago, but he was wise enough to realize that all things came at their appointed time. He was also wise enough not to waste thoughts on what might have been but to focus on seizing the moment and squeezing every last drop of pleasure from it. Until Diana came along, he had no idea there was something missing from his life, but if she left him now, he realized he would be inconsolable.

When she tickled his belly by dipping her pretty hair into his navel and around it, all he could think was that soon she would dip her tongue into the sensitive indentation, to lick and nibble at him. When she did it, her tongue felt rough, causing a delicious shudder to run down the entire length of his backbone.

Diana loved it when she could make Marcus laugh and she noticed that he laughed easily these days. He stopped laughing, however, when she trailed her curl from his navel, down his ridged belly to the engorged head of his phallus. When she looked into his black eyes, she saw how intense he had suddenly become. Was he hoping that her mouth would follow to tongue the spot that her hair tantalized? Did she dare to do such an intimate thing to him?

Marcus drew in a great shuddering breath. And in that moment she knew he hungered for her to taste him. She gazed at him provocatively for long minutes, drawing out his anticipation, then slowly she lowered her lips to touch his velvet head. Her mass of silken hair fell forward, hiding what she did from his view. His hands came forward to part and lift her tresses so that he could see her luscious mouth upon his rigid sex.

The tip of her pink tongue flicked the tip of his manroot. The contrasting colors alone were enough to send deep thrills through him. Pink against vermilion; they complemented each other to perfection. Then her hot wet tongue curled around the heart-shaped head so she could taste him fully. Marcus tasted of salt and almond oil and pure male sex. She lifted her head to watch the pleasure register on his strong, dark face. As she knelt before his prone figure, his seeking fingers found her woman's center and discovered that what she did to him had made her creamy.

"Do you think you are ready to take me inside you?" he asked hoarsely.

"I don't think I will ever be more aroused than I am at this moment," she whispered.

Of course, Marcus knew that she most assuredly would be. She had never even experienced coitus yet. He did not delay matters by taking her to the bed, but laid her on the floor and opened her legs so that the fire warmed the inside of her soft thighs and heated the pink cleft until it was scalding hot.

"Wrap your legs about me," he ordered, and as she obeyed him, he miraculously began to slide inside her, slowly, inch by inch. Her creamy liquid felt like molten lava to Marcus. Never had he experienced anything so hot, so tight, and so blatantly sexual in his life.

Even if Diana begged, Marcus knew he would not stop now. He was obsessed with a driving need to possess her totally. He wanted to put his brand upon her so that she would be his forever. When he came to the barrier, he thrust through sharply. If he was brutal, then so be it. She must endure the pain before she could become a woman who could give and receive pleasure endlessly.

Diana cried out in pain, but Marcus thrust into her powerfully until his bloodthirsty weapon was seated to the hilt. Then he went still to allow her to get used to the fullness inside her. Diana moaned that her sheath was stretched so tautly about his engorged cock.

"Mea amata, are you all right?" he asked, low.

When she tried to speak, her muscles contracted upon him strongly. Marcus moaned deep in his throat from pure pleasure and suddenly Diana experienced a wave of power and pride that she could affect this all-powerful, virile Roman so profoundly. Compared to her, he was like a colossus, and she had worried that she would not be woman enough for him. Suddenly, she knew that she was more than woman enough. Diana bit his shoulder and raised her legs so they clasped him high across his back, then she arched her mons into him and he slid even deeper until she molded the entire length of him like a velvet glove.

Then Marcus began to move his stunning body in and out of her. Each time he buried himself hard, then withdrew in hot, sliding friction. He was marble hard, throbbing, hot and hungry. She could feel his heavy testes thud against her bottom with each deep thrust, then tiny tremors of pleasure began in the sleek heat he created inside her. She became all liquid fire, all smoky-eyed, sultry sensuality, then love slick as his strokes became almost violent, going deeper and faster in a rough, elemental mating that brought surging waves of pleasure crashing upon deep thrills, until she experienced a profound hedonistic enjoyment.

The sensations built higher and higher; they moved together, reaching the peak, then flung themselves heedlessly over the precipice. Diana screamed, from pure bliss this time, then Marcus' cries drowned out hers. She kissed his heart, which beat so strongly she could feel it inside her as his erection pulsed, then exploded, spurting his white hot seed high into her vault.

They both relished a hot, shuddering release, then lay motionless, sprawled together in surfeit. When Marcus withdrew, he saw that semen and blood stained her silken thighs and a pain twisted his gut that he had hurt her so brutally.

"I'm sorry," he said ruggedly.

"No, no," Diana murmured softly, touching his face. "It was cataclysmic; the way it should be between a man and a woman."

"I love you," Marcus whispered.

Diana's heart stopped beating. God help her, she knew she loved him too.

He brought scented water, washing her delicate flesh tenderly. Then he lifted her in his arms and carried her to his bed. His arms came about her to lift her onto his body. Her limbs were so heavy and languid, she felt too exhausted to lift her eyelids. She wondered how he could stand her weight upon him, then realized he was so muscular and strong, she such a lightweight, that his armor probably weighed more.

Diana curled against Marcus so perfectly, it was as if they had been made for each other. Her hands lay upon his wide shoulders, her cheek rested on his furred chest, feeling his heartbeat. One of her long legs lay between his. His male sex, now only semihard, grazed her thigh. She straddled one of his muscular limbs with her long silky legs. It was so firm and unyielding, it felt wonderful pressed against her sensitive mons.

As she drifted off to sleep, she thought she heard an intense whisper. "I'll never let you go back." What a strange thing to say when she knew Marcus did not believe her unlikely tale. Perhaps she was only dreaming.

When Diana lifted her eyelids, she looked directly into a pair of glittering black eyes. "You never moved all night."

She smiled dreamily. "That's because I was where I wanted to be."

Marcus pulled her up on his body so that his lips could touch her temples and her eyelids.

She asked sleepily, "Shouldn't you have left by now?"

"We are not leaving this chamber today. I don't want us to be more than three steps from the bed."

"But what about the men's training?" she asked, blushing prettily.

"I have more important lessons to give here, now."

Marcus slid his body from beneath hers so that she lay facedown on the bed. Then he straddled her, lifted her golden hair from the nape of her neck, and nuzzled her there. His playful lips sent shivers down her spine and she began to squirm with a tingling arousal. She arched her back so that his hands could slip beneath her body to claim her breasts. They felt so full and lush in his big calloused palms. She realized that her squirming bottom was brushing against his manhood, hardening and lengthening it to an alarming degree.

"Mmm, sword practice, I believe. But I have no weapon," she teased.

"I'll lend you mine. This morning we will practice sheathing the sword." His fingers began to stroke her soft buttocks, sliding in the cleft to arouse her.

Diana was amazed at the sensations that began to build deep within her woman's center. It was as if threads of fire were connected from her bottom, all the way up the front of her body, through her belly and up to her tingling breasts. When she began to pant with feverish desire, Marcus murmured, "Go up on your knees for me." She was so highly aroused, she would submit to anything he desired, trusting him to give her unknown pleasure.

He arched his great body over hers and entered her from behind. As before, her muscles spasmed upon him and actually drew him deeper. He paused to let her get used to the fullness and experience the new sensations of his position. When Marcus began to thrust, she cried out her pleasure immediately. The head of his shaft kissed her sensitive bud each time he stroked in. The sensations felt entirely different than when she lay on her back. His cock slid so much farther forward, rubbing her bud with a sleek rhythmic friction that made her build so quickly, she felt wildly uninhibited. Diana had seen a stallion cover a mare once and realized Marcus was taking her in the same way.

He was able to unleash his great sexual energy without restraint in this position. Marcus knew if he thrust too savagely, Diana was free to pull away. She did not, however. She arched herself to match the curve of his lithe body, so that he could surge into her with powerful strokes. She built to such a pitch of excitement, she clawed at the bedcovers, thinking her need was unquenchable. Then Marcus bit her neck exactly as the black stallion had done and Diana climaxed with an eruption that sent tremors down to her toes.

The moment he felt her contract upon him with her pulsations, Marcus exploded inside her. He rolled on his side, taking her with him, and they lay curled together experiencing the "little death" that always follows a magnificent mating.

When Diana could again think coherently, she asked, "Marcus, won't you be missed at the fortress today?"

"I'll send a message telling them I am doing a report for the Procurator."

When Kell brought breakfast, he was loath to disturb them for something as mundane as food, but a naked Marcus proclaimed he was famished and gave him a message to be sent to his highest-ranking officer. Kell kept his eyes from the high bed where Diana perched with the covers pulled high beneath her chin. Without setting his eyes upon her, he knew she was blushing deliciously.

Marcus brought the tray to the bed, set it down between them, and proceeded to feed Diana, making her try everything that had been brought.

"Your food is the best I've ever tasted. The Prince of Wales would kill to have your cooks."

"The Prince of Wales?" Marcus questioned, quaffing from a goblet of honeyed mead he had just held to her lips.

"Our king's son. The heir to the throne always holds the title Prince of Wales. Wales is the western country that gives you so much trouble. It was eventually conquered, but not for hundreds of years."

Marcus cocked a quizzical brow. "Your stories fascinate. I almost want to believe you are who you say you are."

"Almost, but not quite," she teased, taking the goblet back from him and setting her lips to the spot where he had drunk.

"What is this prince like?" Marcus demanded.

Diana laughed. "He's fat and parades about in military uniforms because of his frustration at never being allowed to fight in a war. His father, the king, is mad as a March hare and the prince is holding his breath until they make him regent. In the meantime he wears satins and lace, paints his face, writes silly letters to his mistress, and plays ridiculous practical jokes with his equally ridiculous friends."

"Males who wear lace and paint their faces are not men, Diana. They are playthings for the debauched. There are many such at the emperor's court in Rome. What are normal men like in your London?"

"The young ones slavishly copy the style set by the prince. 'Tis the fashion to wear tight satin knee breeches and powdered wigs. They are extremely effeminate and that is why I refused to consider marrying any of them."

He pulled her down into his arms. "You are making all this up so I won't be jealous of the men you know."

With the tip of her finger she traced the vicious scar that slanted down to his cheekbone. "It's all true. I spent my entire life dreaming of the real men of other ages."

"Like Romans?" he asked, taking her breasts into his possessive hands.

"No, I never daydreamed of Romans. That's why I find it so strange to have been transported to your time in history. I would have loved to have gone back to Elizabethan times or the medieval period."

"Tell me about these medieval men you daydreamed about," he growled with mock ferocity.

"Well, it's a long story and I'd love to tell you all the intimate details, but why don't we wait until after?"

"After?" he asked huskily, hoping she meant what he thought she meant. Happily for both of them, she did.

Chapter 18

When Diana opened the shutters, sunlight flooded into the chamber. "Oh, it's a beautifully warm autumn day."

Marcus came up behind her, wrapped his arms beneath her breasts, and dropped a kiss on top of her head. "And here are we, wasting it in bed," he teased.

"You need a rest; you work too hard."

"Yes, you are rather exhausting," Marcus teased.

"You Roman devil, I meant a rest from your legionaries."

"You promised to tell me about these medieval men you dream about."

She leaned back against him. "They were great warriors, just like you. They invaded Britain in the year 1066 from France, the place you call Gaul, and that was the last time this island was ever conquered."

"So, you were enslaved by the Gauls?"

"No, no, they didn't enslave us. The kings, a dynasty of Plantagenets, and their nobles, ruled for over three hundred years."

"If there were no slaves, whom did they rule?"

"The peasant class. It was a feudal system where the nobles fought the battles and the peasants worked the land."

"In effect, they were slaves," Marcus pointed out.

"In a way, I suppose they were, but medieval men certainly did not buy and sell people."

"You have great admiration for these men," Marcus said wistfully.

"The reality of those times was no doubt horrendous, but the legends of those Middle Ages have been romanticized in books and songs. It was an age of chivalry where a knight pledged himself to a lady, not only to protect her but to remain faithful to her, even though most times they could only love from afar."

"Lip service," Marcus scoffed. "They pledged constancy, then fucked the first female they encountered under a hedge."

Diana ignored his coarse comment. "Their armor was very different from yours."

"How?"

"Well, their helmets had visors on the front to protect the face." She touched his scar.

"It offends you," he said.

"Oh no, Marcus. I consider it a badge of honor. It adds to your attraction, though it's wicked of me to think such a thing."

"Did they not fight with shields and swords?"

"Yes, and they had archers who used bows and arrows. But knights covered their entire bodies with steel armor."

"How could they maneuver in hand-to-hand combat?" he asked skeptically.

"Not very well, I'm afraid. They progressed to chain mail shirts with a coif to protect the neck and replaced the visor with a fixed nose guard on their helmets."

"Mmm, a nose guard isn't a bad idea," Marcus acknowledged.

"They were magnificent builders. They changed the face of Britain, and their great castles are still standing after a thousand years."

"Castles?"

"Let me show you." Diana took pieces of parchment

and charcoal from his desk and brought them to the steps that led up to the bed. She perched on the steps while Marcus lounged beside her and Diana proceeded to draw a castle. "They were huge, built of stone, much like your fortress. The walls could be fifty feet high and ten feet thick. They were built around an open bailey or courtyard. They had either round or square towers at the corners and the whole thing was surrounded by a deep moat of water. There was only one entrance for defensive purposes, with a bridge across the moat that was drawn up every night."

"This is where the king and nobles lived, but what about the other citizens?" he asked with interest.

"Well, the peasants had only thatch huts, and when an enemy threatened, they went into the castle bailey for safety. But merchants and craftsmen lived in towns and built shops, much like we have here in Aquae Sulis."

"They copied from us," Marcus said with satisfaction. "Our temples and our forums are probably still standing after nearly two thousand years."

She looked at him and wondered if she should tell him. Almost gently she said, "No, Marcus, they are not."

"This is where your story falls apart! Are you saying that nothing we Romans built remains in your Britain?"

"Your roads remain and your baths. The rest are ruins that are being excavated by people called archaeologists. We know that beneath a lot of our modern cities, Roman cities lie buried. Beneath London is Londinium; beneath Bath is Aquae Sulis."

"Is that all that remains of the world's greatest civilization?" he demanded arrogantly.

"Of course not! Your language, law, literature, art, customs, and architectural styles have passed into everyday life. The thing that most amazes the modern world is your technology. Your aqueducts, your engineering, your heating and drainage systems were far ahead of your time. In fact, we still haven't caught up to them."

Marcus trailed his fingers down her leg. "What about

love? Romans make far better lovers than your modern men, you admitted that yourself, and we likely make better lovers than these medievals you dream about.''

"As a matter of fact I just finished reading a book by your great learned scholar Ovid on the subject of love, and I didn't think much of him,'' Diana teased.

"Well, we have better writers and philosophers than Ovid,'' he said, waving his arm toward his book scrolls.

"Ah yes, let me see if I can find some very clever lines I read the first night I was here.'' She ran lightly to the shelves behind his desk that held the leather canisters of scrolls and searched through them for a minute. Marcus was mesmerized as he watched her. He would like to keep her naked forever.

"Here it is,'' she said triumphantly, unrolling a scroll. She quoted:

> " 'And when your lust is hot, surely
> if a maid or pageboy's handy to attack
> you won't choose to grin and bear it?
> *I* won't! I like a cheap and easy love!'

"That is your great philosopher, Horace!''

"But that is a satire,'' Marcus explained. "Do you know what a satire is, Diana?''

"You arrogant devil, of course I know what a satire is!''

"Then tell me,'' he insisted.

"A literary work that holds up human vices or follies to scorn.'' As soon as the words were out of her mouth, she understood Horace's motive.

"Very good. I am impressed.'' He took the scroll from her hands and returned it to the canister. "Now, do you know what hot lust is?'' he asked, lifting her high and letting her slide down the hard length of him.

"Only since I met you, Roman,'' she said, laughing.

"Good. Let me see if I can obliterate your fantasies of these medieval men of yours.''

"Ooh, that would take something very special."

"Mmm, then perhaps it's time for *tantra*."

Diana went still in his arms. "That sounds too exotic for a lady with little experience."

"Sweetheart, don't be afraid. I want to love you, not hurt you. Tantra is slow and sensual, and every part of your body receives pleasure. And furthermore, I won't burden you with my great weight."

"I love your weight, Marcus. I love your bigness. When you are on top of me, I'm in no doubt that a real man is making love to me."

He cupped her face in his calloused hands and lifted it to his mouth as he would a delicate porcelain vessel from which he longed to drink. Within minutes their kisses enflamed them and they sank to the rug.

"For tantra you must sit in my lap, face to face."

Diana sat upon his muscled thighs and stretched her legs out behind him. Enfolded in each other's arms, their bodies touched from hips to lips. When she became aroused enough, Marcus lifted her onto his rampant sex and he began to thrust. His mouth commanded her to open her lips so that his tongue could delve deep into her scented alcove. With a matching rhythm of tongue and tool, he thrust wildly so that their passion built hot and strong, but before they climaxed, he stopped and allowed his hands to roam over her skin until she felt she would go up in smoke.

Since he was buried so deeply, it took a long time before the throbbing and pulsing slowed. When his hands had traced every inch of naked skin and she had explored every magnificent muscle, he began to thrust again, taking them ever higher in their fevered quest for fulfillment. The fourth time he repeated this sensual ritual, neither could hold back any longer. Marcus spent at the same moment Diana let down her love juices to anoint the full honors of his manhood.

As he gathered her against him to stroke her silken hair, Diana experienced a moment of panic. What if she were suddenly snatched from Marcus, back to her own time? The thought was unendurable and she clung to him tightly until she could banish the frightening idea.

Later, when they could think coherently and talk again, Marcus teased, "Now that I've proved to you that Roman men are superior lovers, what other medieval fantasies can I lay to rest?"

Diana was gazing out the window, thinking how lovely the forest looked bathed in sunshine. The leaves had just started to change color and she hoped it would be a glorious autumn. "I always wanted to go on a royal hunt in medieval times," she said dreamily.

"Is there no hunting in your time?" he asked, towering behind her with his powerful palms cupping her shoulders.

"Eighteenth-century hunters are pathetic. Three or four dozen men with great packs of hounds run one pitiful fox to earth. I should like to go on a boar hunt where the prey has a fighting chance equal to that of the hunters. I don't suppose I'd enjoy the kill, but the chase would be exhilarating beyond my wildest dreams."

He dropped a kiss onto her soft shoulder. "I'll take you on a boar hunt."

She turned to face him. "Are you serious, Marcus, or just teasing?"

"I'm perfectly serious, but you'll have to wait until Seutonius Paullinus takes the newly trained legionaries on campaign. I'm expecting him back from the western territory tomorrow, but he only ever stays about a week."

"Oh Marcus, I would enjoy it above all things!"

"Not above *all* things, I trust?"

"Stop that. I need a bath; I'm all musky from too much loving."

"There's no such thing. The more you make love, the more you want to make love."

"Like a compulsion?"

"Like a narcotic," he said intensely. "We'll go for a

swim in the garden pool," he said in a lighter tone. "We can't waste the sunshine."

"I can't swim," Diana said with regret.

"I'll teach you!" He was suddenly filled with great enthusiasm.

"You won't make me wear armor, will you?" she teased.

"No, I'll make you swim naked. Come on," he urged, threading his fingers through hers.

"Marcus, we can't go out there like this," she protested.

"Why not?" he asked blankly. "What a waste of time to get dressed, only to get undressed. Then repeat the ridiculous ritual to get back here."

"Humor me," she commanded, wrapping her red mantle about her nakedness. Marcus, too, draped his scarlet mantle about his shoulders, but his jutting manhood thrust out from between its folds.

"I said humor me, not convulse me," she said, laughing at the outrageous spectacle he made.

Marcus glanced in the mirror. "Now *that* is rude. Stark naked would be much more respectable."

"May the gods preserve me from respectability," Diana murmured reverently. With hands clasped, they emerged from the sleeping chamber displaying all the dignity they could muster, and descended to the peristyle.

The water in the beautiful bathing pool was warmer than the air. They spent two hours playing in what seemed to Diana their own Eden. Marcus, with iron determination, resolved not to let her escape from the pool until she could swim. With much laughing, splashing, ducking, and kissing, he finally accomplished what he set out to do.

With great daring on her part, Diana agreed to allow Romulus and Remus into the pool with them, and the four frolicked with abandon. They made so much noise that the entire household, including the gardeners, gathered to watch their master with disbelief. The coming of the new female slave had wrought such an amazing change in the master, they were astounded. He had never revealed this side of himself before. Only Nola had caught a glimpse of the fun-loving boy who dwelt within the man.

The dogs tired before Marcus, climbing from the water and shaking themselves to dry off. When Diana climbed out, she saw a pair of eyes watching her through the leaves. She didn't want anyone to be punished, so decided to keep quiet, but when Marcus emerged from the depths and tried to take her in his arms, Diana panicked. She picked up her cloak and fled toward the villa.

Marcus followed in full pursuit. She glanced over her shoulder as she sprinted up the staircase and saw that he had already gained the bottom step. "When I catch you, I am going to . . ." She turned into his arms and put her hand across his mouth. "Hush, darling . . . they are all watching and listening to us."

Marcus grinned. "Ask me if I care?"

As her red mantle fell away, suddenly Diana didn't care either. There was absolutely nothing shameful about love. It was a glorious thing to behold.

Kell had changed the sheets and tidied the chamber. Clean towels replaced the bloodied ones and fresh scented water had been provided.

Now that Diana was out of the warm water and sunshine, she began to shiver. Marcus knelt to build a fire and she rubbed herself against his broad back to warm herself. "I'd better put some clothes on," she said for the sheer pleasure of having him forbid her.

Marcus turned to gaze at her naked splendor. "Why don't you put on those fur leggings? I can't think of anything more erotic than making love to you with your legs clad in fur." His suggestion appealed to the vixen inside her. Every time Marcus made love to her, Diana gained power over him, but a curious thing was happening to her heart. She had set out to deliberately enslave him, but somehow she had fallen in love with the magnificent Roman and relished the male-female game of domination and submission so much that she did not wish to rule him. She wanted him exactly as he was. So long as his was the power, hers was the glory!

They dined abed, and Diana decided that since Marcus had enjoyed such erotic pleasure from the leggings, she would keep them on all night. When they were finally replete from indulging in all their favorite things, they slept curled as they had the night before with Diana facedown on top of him.

When she awoke at dawn, he was gone, but she stretched sensually in the big bed, immediately aware that he had left her two things. While she still slept, he had slipped his gold coin over her head and he had also left her covered with his virile male scent.

Diana and Nola decided to go into Aquae Sulis to shop. They were gone all morning, and when they returned, their litter was filled to overflowing with Diana's purchases. She bought perfume, makeup, a board game with ivory counters, some red Samian pottery, and a supply of wooden writing tablets and a stylus.

The leather riding pants she had ordered were finished and waiting for her when she returned, so Diana decided to wear them when she visited Marcus in the afternoon.

She rode to the fortress with her trusty stable slave at her side, but Tor was made to wait for her at the fort's entrance. Though he was from the general's household, the guards were not about to allow a Briton to wander about unescorted. As well, Governor Paullinus was back and they knew his hatred for all Britons.

Since rules were rules, Diana decided to leave the horses with Tor and proceed on foot. She noticed immediately that the fortress held a lot more men than it had on her previous visit. Paullinus must have returned with his legionaries from Wales. She received so many stares from strange men that she was relieved when she saw the familiar face of Petrius. He came to her side immediately, his handsome face wreathed in smiles at their chance encounter.

"My brother is a lucky man to inspire such slavish devotion, Diana."

She gave him a brilliant smile. "Do you know where he is?"

"Extremely busy, I'm afraid. Paullinus is returned with his army and Marcus is at the Valetudinorium with all the wounded legionaries. I shall be your escort in his stead. Have you toured the fort yet?"

Diana realized he was speaking of the hospital. "I've been here before, but I didn't stay long. If Marcus is busy, I had better go."

"Don't leave. If Marcus learns I didn't take you beneath my wing, he will mete out a fine punishment." Petrius grinned boyishly. "And I'm still in his bad books for arriving drunk at the villa."

Diana blushed prettily. She didn't really want to stay, but she didn't want to cause bad blood between brothers. This brave young man would be leaving to fight in Wales within the week, and she could not bring herself to rebuff him.

"Let me think what would interest you. I live in the officers' quarters, but they are unremarkable. There is a good view from the turrets of the watchtowers, but that wouldn't be of much interest to a beautiful female. Have you visited the temple?"

"No, I've never seen a Roman temple."

"You Britons worship Sul, the sun goddess, do you not?"

"Oh no. I am a Christian," she explained.

Petrius stared. "A Christian?" This was the strange sect of troublemakers whom Nero delighted in persecuting. In Rome it had become the custom to blame everything on the Christians and punish them accordingly. Romans loved to watch the spilling of human blood, so Christian prisoners were always in demand at the games. Petrius tucked the knowledge away, knowing instinctively that knowledge was power.

"Here in the fortress there is one massive building that houses many temples." When they entered on the ground floor, there were different doors to choose from. One had the name JUPITER OPTIMUM MAXIMUS carved above it and another had MITHRAS. A third was inscribed MARS, whom Diana knew was the god of war, and the last door was inscribed FORTUNA, whom Diana assumed was the goddess of luck and good fortune.

"Marcus worships Jupiter, but most men in the military worship at the altar of Mithras. It is a male cult. Mithras is an unconquered god who represents courage. In legend, Mithras was ordered to catch a primeval bull. From its body spring plants and herbs, from its blood come new forms of life, from its semen comes all procreation."

He led her through the door marked MITHRAS and they began to climb, then they entered the temple and were able to look down upon a massive altar. Below the stone altar was a pit where a few centurion officers had gathered. Petrius pointed to a man who resembled a huge bear and whispered, "That's Seutonius Paullinus. He must be here to give thanks for his victories over the Celtae."

A well-muscled, bare-chested youth in a white loincloth walked onto the massive stone altar. He carried a huge iron hammer and a sword. Then suddenly there was a great roar and a pure white bull ran onto the altar, snorting and tossing his head with rage. The young acolyte lifted his heavily muscled arms high and brought down the iron stunning hammer onto the bull's head. The moment it dropped to its knees, he drew his gladius and plunged it into the bull's neck, ripping it open. The blood spurted everywhere, then poured down onto the sacrificial worshippers in the pit below, who became drenched in seconds. Diana watched in horror as Paullinus lifted a bowl to catch the bull's blood while it was still warm and raise it to his lips. Diana turned and fled blindly through the door.

Petrius was at her side instantly. "What is it?"

"Get me out of here," she demanded.

He saw that she was white-faced and trembling. The spilling of blood had sexually aroused him and Petrius had hoped that it would have the same effect on Diana. He had taken her there so that they could couple. But now that he saw her vulnerability, he realized his desire to fuck her while she trembled was growing by the minute. He picked her up and carried her through two more doors until they were in the temple of Fortuna.

He set her down beside a pillar and knelt beside her to remove her mantle. He pretended concern. "I should not have taken you to the temple of a god. I should have brought you to the goddess Fortuna. She will give us anything we desire."

A tiny black lamb came gamboling up to Diana. Its baby horns had been gilded and it wore a garland of flowers about its neck. "Oh, the dear little thing," she said, reaching out her hands to cradle the adorable baby.

Before she knew what he was about, Petrius ripped open its belly with his knife and filled her hands with the lamb's entrails while they still pulsed with life.

Diana felt herself going down in a faint, and suddenly she knew that Petrius was about to ravish her.

Chapter 19

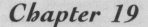

Diana did not dare to faint. She hung on to consciousness like a drowning woman would cling to straw. She threw the lamb's bloody entrails into his face, but rather than repel him, blood excited Petrius. He was on top of her in a flash, ripping the silk tunic from her body.

In the end it was the leather pants that saved her. In his struggles to tear them from her, she got her booted foot between his legs and kicked him sharply. Petrius went down, much as the bull had done when stunned by the hammer. The only difference was that Petrius howled in agony.

Diana was up and running immediately. She did not hesitate for one second, not even to look over her shoulder. She was almost crippled by a stitch in her side, and her lungs felt as if they were on fire by the time she reached the guardhouse. The blood of the lamb had been absorbed by her scarlet mantle and so the legionaries at the gate saw only that she was in a great hurry to leave.

Diana was in the saddle before Tor could help her mount.

"Is aught amiss, lady?" he asked in a worried voice.

"Just get me home," she said.

He saw that she was unwilling or unable to speak further and assumed that the general had ordered her back to the villa.

When she arrived, Diana went directly to the bath suite to bathe. Kell, seeing her agitation, sent Sylla in to her. The slave found Diana vomiting down the latrine. Diana bathed and put on a cream-colored robe made of fine wool, then she climbed the staircase and went directly to her own chamber. She put the heavy wooden bar across the door to assure her privacy and began to pace about in distress.

Diana frantically pushed away all thoughts of what had happened in the temple. It was so disgustingly abhorrent, she couldn't even bear to think of it. But the more she tried to make her mind go blank, the faster her thoughts crowded in on her. Finally, she sat down and relived every horrifying moment.

She would never forget the metallic smell of blood mingled with incense. The worst moment for her was not when Petrius tried to rape her, but when he slashed the innocent little lamb and inextricably involved her in the sick sacrifice. Her eyes flooded with tears and she began to cry softly.

Diana had no idea how long she cried, but when she looked from her window, darkness had fallen. She washed her face and felt better for having shed the cleansing tears. But underneath, a sadness had pervaded her consciousness that she could not dispel.

It was quite late when Marcus arrived home. He had been at the hospital all afternoon trying to cope with the inordinate number of wounded legionaries Paullinus had brought back to Aquae Sulis to recuperate. He knew that less than half of them would survive. At the end of the day his garments were soiled with blood and other foul matter, so he bathed at the fort before he went home.

Marcus thanked the gods that Diana awaited him. She could dispel the darklings more effectively than any wine or opiate he'd ever tried. He knew she was more than a lovely female body where he could lose himself. He savored her intelligence and her humor and something else, more difficult to define. She had a sweetness and innocence that was untainted and that made him feel as protective as he was possessive; possibly more protective.

When Diana was not in the atrium to greet him, he was disappointed. He told himself the hour was advanced. He hoped she had waited to dine with him, but he would understand if she had already eaten. Marcus did not go through to the bath as was his custom, but went straight to the triclinium. Only Kell was there to greet him. After a moment's disappointment, his heart lifted. Diana was awaiting him upstairs. "Kell, have my dinner brought to my sleeping chamber."

Marcus took the stairs three at a time. When he opened his door and found the chamber empty, his heart sank. Where in Hades was she? There were no slaves about; the hallways were deserted. Marcus strode along to the apricot chamber where Diana used to sleep. The door was closed. When he tried to open it, he found it barred.

"Diana, I'm home," he called. He could not conceal the irritation he felt at having her door barred against him. When he received no answer, his irritation turned to anger. "Diana!" he said sharply.

"Go away," she said quietly.

Go away? Am I hearing her correctly?

"Open this door!" he commanded. His anger was turning to fury. *This is what I get for indulging her!* When Marcus heard no movement inside the room, he realized incredibly that she was not going to open, as he'd commanded. In a blazing rage he set his shoulder to the door and crashed against it until the heavy bar on the inside splintered and fell away. The door swung open and Marcus stepped into the room, his black eyes blazing.

When he saw how quiet and pale she was, he knew there was something wrong. His heart constricted with fear as he rushed to her side and went down on one knee. "Are you ill?" His voice was ragged with emotion.

"I . . . I was sick, but I'm better now."

For one split second his heart soared, thinking she was breeding, but then logic told him it was too soon. He reached out tenderly to take her hand.

Diana flinched from him. "Don't touch me."

"Don't touch you?" He repeated her words in a tone so quietly ominous, it warned her that she was on very dangerous ground. Diana ignored the warning.

"There are too many differences between us," she cried. "I hate Rome; I abhor everything it stands for! I detest Romans!"

"What maggot is eating your brain? Rome is the center of the world. It stands for excellence in government, learning, culture, and philosophy. And as for Romans, we are not like the ordinary masses, we are patricians! We are the most educated, civilized, courageous, and honorable men who have ever lived."

Diana recoiled from him. "You are a race of brutal, primitive degenerates." She had been holding the golden coin in her hand. She thrust it at him. "Take it, it defiles me."

Marcus ignored the chain and swept her up into his arms. "I will defile you, by the gods I will!"

Diana struggled in vain. His arms were steel bands; his chest like the stone wall of the fortress. The more she tried to resist him, the more his anger and his lust became enflamed. He threw her down onto the bed and tore open the cream robe. Then he threw off his mantle and lifted his tunic over his head.

Diana's gaze challenged his as she lay trembling with fury. "If you force me, like a master takes a slave, it will kill my love for you. It will prove you a brutal, primitive degenerate and we shall be everlasting enemies." Her voice was low and so intense it gave him pause.

Marcus ran his calloused hands through his hair in

complete frustration. "What happened today? What has wrought this change in you? Talk to me, woman!" he thundered.

Diana drew the soft robe about her nakedness and sat up, curling her feet beneath her. Marcus, a tower of virile frustration, loomed at the foot of the bed. She chose her words carefully. "When I came to the fort today, you were busy, so I went into the temple. The brutal pagan sacrifice I saw sickened me."

Marcus sank down on the foot of the bed with relief. "Is that what this is all about? Diana, you should not have gone there. You are too gentle and tender-hearted to understand these things. Why do you think I've never taken you to the temple?"

Diana shook her head. "It's not just the blood sacrifice of animals. It's the vast differences between us. I can never be reconciled to the Roman way of life. I can never accept your beliefs and practices." She hugged herself, her arms crossed in protection. Her palms felt the soft wool of her robe. "The clothing, the food, and the language are small differences, easily overcome. It's the way you think, your beliefs, your ideals that I'm totally opposed to. You think you rule the world by divine right. Your entire empire is based on power and oppression. Romans are sadistic by nature. The differences between us are too great to overcome."

"The only difference between us that counts is that I'm a man and you're a woman! Our bodies fit together so perfectly, we become one when I make love to you. Our differences are gone the moment we are joined."

"No, Marcus. We set aside our differences so we can indulge our lust. When that is slaked, our differences are still there, larger than life!"

"What I feel for you is *love*!"

"Can you honestly say you feel no lust for me?" she demanded.

"Yes. I feel love and lust. A combustible combination.

Most men and women would sell their souls to experience what we have!''

''I fear that is what I have done,'' Diana said quietly. ''Take this back.'' Again she held out the chain.

''Julius Caesar was the *greatest* patrician, statesman, and general who ever lived.''

''Caesar was a conqueror, seizing land that didn't belong to him and enslaving proud free people by the thousands.''

Reluctantly, Marcus took back the Caesar coin and slipped it over his head. He knew she was accusing him of these things, not Caesar, and it was true.

Marcus lifted his head, proud as an eagle, and with all the courage he possessed, asked, ''Do you love me?''

Diana stared at him aghast. An unbearable lump came into her throat and her eyes flooded with unshed tears. She came up onto her knees before him. ''Marcus, I love you so much I am heartsore.'' Her arms went around his neck, and as he cradled her against him, her tears wet the column of his throat.

''Don't cry, beloved, I can't bear it,'' he murmured, pressing her heart against his.

In the warm, protective circle of his arms, the horror of her afternoon receded. She would not tell him about Petrius —it would serve no purpose, and in any case, he would be leaving in a few days.

''I don't care if you are Christian, Druid, Briton, or Celt. To me you are simply Diana—my heart, my life. Does it really matter to you that I am Roman? Can I not just simply be Marcus?''

Before she could answer, they were interrupted by the sound of a soft cough. Looking up, they saw Kell standing in the doorway among the shattered wood of the door. He was carrying a tray of food, and he had a look of cautious relief. No doubt he hadn't known what to expect after seeing the general's handiwork.

When Diana saw the food and realized Marcus had not

eaten, she felt guilty. "It's so late. Please eat your dinner, you must be exhausted."

Marcus set the tray on the bed. "Share with me," he tempted her. "My food always tastes so much better when you share it with me."

Diana nodded and dried her eyes. Marcus scooped her into his lap and fed her all the choicest morsels, between his own mouthfuls. The desire to make love to her was like a torment inside him, but he banked the fires of his passion with an iron will. He had her gentled now and did not want to destroy the fragile bond that he had only just managed to reestablish.

After they had eaten, they talked together quietly. He told her of his day, minimizing the horrendous wounds and the high death toll. She showed him the things she had bought in the shops and he promised to show her how to write with a stylus. Then he tenderly tucked her into bed with a light kiss. "You look pale. Get some sleep, love. I just want to have a word with Kell, then I'm for bed too."

Marcus had a nagging problem that had just multiplied a hundredfold because of Diana. He sought out Kell and they went into the solarium. Kell poured the general a goblet of wine and Marcus told him to pour one for himself. He indicated that Kell should be seated, but Marcus remained on his feet. He could always think better when he paced.

After he had walked the length of the mosaic tigress three or four times, he said, "I have a problem regarding the feast I throw for the governor and his centurions before they go to fight."

"It has never been a problem before. As always, I will keep out of the governor's way."

"No, Kell, the problem isn't with you, it's with Diana."

"I see." And Kell did see, clearly. Feast was a euphemism for the Bacchanalia the general threw, which had become a tradition. The centurions and the cohort centurions who had successfullly made it back, and the ones who were about to take their place, joined Seutonius Paullinus in what could only be described as an orgy. They feasted until they disgorged, drank until they spewed, and fucked until they were delirious. "She should be safe enough from the men's lechery, locked in your chamber. For extra measure you could post guards at the door."

"It's not her safety that worries me. I shall always be able to protect her." Marcus paced across the tigress, then walked around her through the long grass.

Kell hid a smile. The general was skirting the tigress as if it were Diana. The analogy was most apt, for Diana would behave like a tigress if she got wind of the debauchery that occasionally took place in this villa. She didn't even condone public nudity, so he could only imagine her shock at the multiple copulations, carnality, and perversions practiced by Julia Allegra and her prostitutes when they got together with the Roman legionaries.

Kell was surprised that Marcus Magnus worried about what a female slave thought of him. Was he no longer master in his own house? Had the general handed her his balls along with his heart? "Could you hold the feast at the fort?" he asked tentatively.

"No. I'm not supplying two thousand men with prostitutes. It would destroy discipline forever."

Kell knew it was useless to suggest that he not throw the usual feast. That swine Paullinus had come to expect it, and if he thought the general was withdrawing his hospitality, he would take it as a personal insult.

Marcus spoke again. "Perhaps you could remove the lady from the villa that night, but where you would send her and on what pretext, I have no idea."

Kell drained his goblet to give him courage for what he was about to say. "General, it seems to me that you worry unnecessarily. Not because she is your slave, but because she is your woman, she should know her place. A woman will take advantage of a man anytime he is foolish enough to allow her to do so. In my own case, Nola takes advantage of me every day, simply because she knows I have a soft spot for her.''

Marcus was well aware of the currents between Kell and Nola. ''What you say is true. If a man does not lead, he is led. If he does not rule, he is ruled. If the man is not the master, the woman will hold him in contempt. The feast I am obliged to give has nothing whatsoever to do with Diana. It is none of her business and she must not concern herself with it.'' Marcus finished his wine. ''Thank you, Kell.''

''The decision was yours, General. However, I believe it to be a wise one.''

As Kell watched him climb the staircase, he wondered what had prompted him to take the Roman's side against a Briton. Then he realized there was more at stake here than nationalities. It was a far older struggle—man against woman. How could he not take the male side?

As Marcus slipped into bed, he decided he must take a firmer hand with Diana. Perhaps he should have given her a sound thrashing tonight when she rejected him and flung their differences in his face. He was far too indulgent with the little vixen. He had dried her tears and fed her, then tucked her into bed, keeping his lust in check in case she sulked. Now he decided he must make up for that mistake. If she showed even the faintest reluctance, he would slap her beautiful little arse until her teeth rattled!

He reached out with ungentle hands and pulled her to him. His mouth crushed hers in a savage kiss. If he didn't force her to yield to him, now, this minute, he would lose the whip hand.

Diana melted against him. Lying between his marble-hard thighs, she became all soft, all womanly compliance. Her luscious breasts lay upon his chest, her soft belly caressed his rampant sex, and her scented mouth opened to his with an invitation that was irresistible.

He plundered her mouth with his thrusting tongue, and when he withdrew, she held her lips to his and whispered, "Marc . . . Marc . . . Marcus."

When she whispered, it did the most glorious things to him. She traced the scar on his face. Her faintest touch brought full-blown passion to him. Then unbelievably she rose up upon him, grasped his shaft firmly in her hand, and plunged down voluptuously. She felt like hot silk. Marcus was drowning in need. She began to ride him slowly, seductively, lifting high, then plunging hard until he was anchored deep. Then she increased the tempo, making him buck powerfully.

Their union became a wild, driving tempest, primal and shocking in its intensity. Heat leaped between them as they made love sounds in raw whispers. They shattered together and Marcus held her imprisoned upon him long after the last liquid tremors stilled. He held her there until he became half aroused again and decided to stay inside her all night.

Marcus felt all-powerful after he had mastered her in the ultimate act of domination and submission, but as Diana lay upon him in silken splendor, it felt like she was purring. He smiled into the darkness, wondering wryly which of them was enslaved.

Chapter 20

Marcus told Kell to order the food and wine for the feast and paid a visit to Julia Allegra to arrange the entertainment. He did not broach the matter with Diana until the day arrived, then before he left for the fortress, he sat on the edge of the bed and cleared his throat.

Diana loved to see him in his polished breastplate. Whenever he touched her while wearing his armor, it made her go weak all over.

"Paullinus leaves with the legionaries tomorrow. It has become a custom for the governor and his officers to dine here before they depart."

Diana looked alarmed. "You mean he'll be here at the villa tonight? Oh Marcus, can I not go somewhere else?"

Marcus' spirits lifted. She was not going to prove difficult at all. "Perhaps that would be best. Paullinus detests Britons and so I like to keep even Kell away from him. Why don't you and Kell go to the theatre tonight? When you return, you must come straight up here and bar the door. You saw what my brother was like when he'd been drinking and I'm afraid when the men get together, they carouse until they are legless."

"The theatre is a lovely idea. Paullinus disgusts me." She shuddered delicately, remembering the hirsute giant who resembled a great mangy bear.

Marcus kissed her goodbye. "I won't see you today; you'll be asleep by the time I come up, but once the legionaries leave tomorrow, I'll have more time to spend with you. I'll take you on that boar hunt." He stood and fastened on his leather weapons belt. "Enjoy the theatre."

"Enjoy your feast," she replied innocently, which only made him feel wretched about deceiving her.

Wearing her ultramarine stola and matching palla, Diana received more attention at the theatre than the performers. Her blond tresses attracted the eye of both men and women. Whispers of *Who is she?* were answered by those with the privileged information that General Magnus had taken a concubine. The men were instantly envious of the general, while the women would have paid any price to take Diana's place.

She was amused that Kell kept one hand upon his flagellum as a warning to the masses to keep their distance. She and Kell had chosen a musical entertainment that turned out to be like an extravagant ballet. Diana enjoyed herself immensely watching the singers and dancers in their elaborate costumes and masks. It got a little raucous when a troupe of female acrobats tumbled across the stage, for they wore little more than wide black leather bands—one to cover their breasts, the other their groins.

The entertainment wasn't over until quite late, then Kell took her into a vintner's, which was a traditional after-theatre stop where patrons were served either hot or cold drinks. Diana chose calda, which was warm, spiced wine, while Kell preferred Setinian, a choice old wine imported from Italy. He grudgingly agreed that Roman wine was superior to that of his native land.

Diana returned in a litter with Kell walking at her side so they could converse about the evening. She felt very pampered, almost wicked, that she had had a night on the town while Marcus was obliged to play host to the military

leader and his centurions. "Thank you for escorting me,
Kell. I enjoyed it so much. I shall be sure to tell Marcus
about the female acrobats he missed." Diana giggled.
"Poor Marcus."

Litters were lined up outside the villa when they arrived home, so they knew that the general's guests were still
there.

"I think we should go through the peristyle garden
rather than the front entrance," Kell advised. "They may
be discussing military business." *May the gods forgive me
for the lie,* Kell thought.

Diana slipped into the walled garden through the gate
and stood rooted to the spot. Half a dozen naked females
rode on the backs of men who were equally naked. Other
nude revelers held blazing torches or carried small whips to
flagellate those playing stallion. "Military business?
Bloody funny business, you mean!"

Kell took her arm and pushed her toward some steps
that led to the second story. At that moment, Marcus
stepped from the villa with a naked woman clinging to his
arm. She had jet black hair and was amply endowed with
heavy breasts and wide buttocks. Diana couldn't believe her
eyes. The woman with Marcus looked exactly like Allegra.

"What the devil are you doing here?" Diana demanded, her amethyst eyes blazing purple fury at Marcus.

"She's here because I invited her. Go upstairs," he
ordered. Marcus glared at Kell. Where in the name of
Heaven and Hades were his brains to allow Diana to see
such a debauch?

Diana set her hands on her hips and dug in her heels.
"Go upstairs, did you say? Are you sure *you* won't be
needing the sleeping chamber for your fat whore?"

Marcus gave her a sharp slap across her face and
swung her into his arms. Then he carried her kicking and
swearing up the stone steps to the upstairs balcony. He
thrust her inside his chamber and closed the door. "Stop

that cursing immediately. Anyone hearing you could mistake you for one of those whores!''

"They wouldn't be mistaken! That's all I am to you— your whore! One of many, apparently. That's all any woman is to a Roman! Why don't I put on my loin dress and join your games?''

Marcus ground his teeth. She was deliberately goading him to violence. He opened the door and found Kell hovering outside. "Get in here. Make sure she doesn't leave this chamber tonight.'' Marcus raked Diana with his black eyes. "If you've quite finished making a spectacle of yourself, I'll get back to my whore.''

Diana picked up a silver lamp and hurled it at the door. Then she threw herself onto the high bed and began to sob.

Kell let her cry for a full five minutes, then said dryly, "Your tears are quite wasted on me, lady. Save them for the general.''

"Oh, shut up! This was a damned conspiracy to get me out of the way so he could throw a bloody Roman orgy!'' Diana sat up and dashed the tears from her eyes.

Kell thought he had better try to smooth her very ruffled feathers. Marcus Magnus wasn't too happy with him at the moment. "The general wanted to spare you. The men always act like rutting animals.''

"You mean this sort of thing has happened before?'' Diana cried.

"It's that swine, Paullinus. If the general didn't open his villa for the feast, the governor would be his enemy, and Paullinus' enemies don't live long. The general only invites Julia Allegra and her bawds so the men will not abuse the household slaves.''

"Julia Allegra is the bawd mistress?'' Diana asked. "She reminds me of someone I used to know who was also called Allegra.'' *When she wasn't calling herself Dame Lightfoot,* Diana thought miserably. Her bottom lip trembled. "Oh, Kell, what am I to do?''

"Stop being ridiculous, of course.''

"What do you mean?" she asked woefully.

"Come over here to the mirror."

Diana came slowly and stood gazing at her reflection with big sad eyes.

"Look at yourself . . . really look at yourself. You are one of the most beautiful women I have ever seen, and no doubt that the general has ever seen. One look at you and he was stunned as if he'd been hit with a thunderbolt. When he has you waiting for him, why would he even look at another female?"

She sniffed back her tears. "What about Julia Allegra?"

"He wouldn't swive her with another man's prick!"

"Really?" she asked in a small voice.

"Well, I ask you to use your own eyes. If he put a bag over her head, he still wouldn't fuck her."

Diana laughed in spite of Kell's coarse language. "Perhaps he's saving her for Paullinus."

It was Kell's turn to laugh. "A sow for a rutting boar!"

Diana reasoned that it was far more honorable for Marcus to provide prostitutes than allow the legionaries to run amok among his slaves. It was, after all, his villa and he could do as he pleased, but she could not dispel an overwhelming jealousy that encompassed every female he had ever touched. When he came up to bed, she would punish him dearly. She would play the Ice Queen and it would take a thousand apologies to thaw her.

Marcus, however, did not come to bed. He stayed away and she did not see him until the following evening. Diana spent the entire day alone, for the entire household was busy from dawn to dusk clearing up the mess and the debris of the night revelers. Everything needed cleaning—floors, walls, rugs—and every couch in the villa needed recovering.

Diana's emotions ran the gamut from hate to jealousy and anger. Her pride was involved; Marcus had shamed and embarrassed her. She would let the punishment fit the crime. But by afternoon, longing accompanied loneliness and she had to crush the desire to ride to the fort just to catch a glimpse of him. By the time evening crawled along, she had decided that she would pretend total indifference. She would greet him normally and pretend that nothing at all had happened. And certainly nothing to upset her. Of course, she would wear something extra special.

When Marcus arrived home and Diana was not in the atrium to greet him, he was disappointed, but not surprised. He hadn't expected her to be there. He anticipated trouble and envisioned a confrontation that would be so explosive, it might erupt into violence if he didn't keep an iron control on his temper.

He heard female voices coming from the solarium and his ear easily picked out Diana's silvery laughter. She drew him like a lodestone. She was wearing some exquisite creation that made her look like the tigress in the mosaic that lay resplendent at her feet. Her beauty was breathstopping.

"Oh Marcus, you must be early. The afternoon has melted away. But you are just the man I need to make a decision for me."

The hours away from her had been endless and his return was anything but early. Where were her accusations, her angry words, her threats, her tears?

She gifted him with a smile of adoration. "I cannot decide about a winter mantle. Shall I have it lined with black fox or red?" She held a sample of each soft fur to her face. "Nola thinks the red has more fire, but I favor the black because of my fair coloring."

Marcus looked from Diana to Nola and back again. She had thrown him completely off balance. "Why don't you have both?" he suggested smoothly, but he was wary as a wolf.

"I told you he was brilliant," Diana said to Nola, then she came to him and raised her lips for his kiss.

Magnus' eyes sought Nola's and signaled for her to leave them private. One part of his mind told him to leave well enough alone, but after Nola had departed, his perverse streak prompted him to bring up the subject of the previous night. "Did you enjoy the theatre?" he asked after a tentative kiss.

"I loved every moment of it. Thank you for suggesting I attend." Diana was being gracious. Perhaps too gracious?

"You look lovely tonight; very much the tigress."

She spun away from him and turned full circle to give him a chance to appreciate the full impact of the sheer gown. He could clearly see the swell of her luscious breasts with their rosy pink nipples as well as her navel and the golden tendrils covering her high mons. When she turned around, even the cleft between her bottom cheeks showed through the material.

Diana knew the effect she had on him and Marcus sensed it was totally calculated and deliberate. She closed the gap between them, but not all the way. She left a tempting few inches between their bodies, knowing he would pull her against him. When he did so, she teased, "Ooh, is that your sword, or are you just pleased to see me?"

"Are your claws sheathed?" he murmured.

"Of course," she said sweetly.

"That disappoints me. I thought you might be seething with jealousy about last night."

Her laugh was like a silver bell. "Jealous? I haven't a jealous bone in my body."

Marcus grabbed her and pulled her hard against him. "Then what the hell is this performance all about? You are shamefully displaying yourself and acting brittle as glass." He ground his mouth down on hers to let her know she had succeeded in tempting him beyond his endurance.

"Damn you, Roman, damn you to hellfire!" She

grabbed his black hair in both fists, then bit his lip until she drew blood. "I wanted to kill you!"

Marcus grinned with deep satisfaction. "You little bitch, I love you so much I suspect you have bewitched me with your sorcery. By the balls of Jupiter you have spoiled me for all other women. Surely I don't have to tell you these things?"

She clung to him wildly. "Yes, I want you to tell me every day and every night—not only tell me, but show me!"

Marcus took her down to the marble floor and laid her back upon the tigress, spreading her hair about her into the tall grass. Then very slowly and deliberately, he told her and showed her exactly how much she meant to him.

When Paullinus departed for the west, taking the newly trained legionaries with him, Marcus had a couple of weeks respite before two more cohorts would arrive to be trained. His own men, who were stationed permanently in Aquae Sulis, had a change from their military duties also. The corps of engineers went back to building roads and aqueducts and erecting public baths where the hot springs bubbled naturally from the earth.

Marcus decided the time was ripe to take Diana on her boar hunt. One morning, he kissed her awake at an ungodly hour, and when she curled against him and opened her arms, he teased, "God of Thunder, is that all you ever think about?"

Pale amethyst eyes looked up into devilish black ones. "Am I too much woman for you, darling Marcus?" she asked, stretching sensually for the pleasure of brushing against the hard length of him.

"If you want to go on that boar hunt you've been nagging about, you'd better get dressed before I change my mind."

Diana jumped up immediately. "Today? The hunt is

today?'' She didn't even try to hide her great excitement. She had had a doublet made in the style she imagined they wore in medieval times, which she would wear atop her leather riding pants. It was emerald green embroidered with a great golden eagle, which she decided would have been Marcus' device if he'd had one. She had even bought a gold hunting horn to wear about her neck.

Sylla fashioned her hair in a braid as thick as a mooring cable and wound it about her head in a coronet. Then she used emerald and gold hair ornaments to fashion a small crown. After all, this was her fantasy of going on a royal hunt and most likely would be the closest she would ever come to such an experience.

Tor had her mare saddled and ready for her when she arrived at the stables. She let him lift her into the saddle when she heard the dogs barking. Marcus was astride Trajan with Romulus and Remus circling him with excited yelps when she rode into the courtyard.

"Diana, the huntress, you are indeed a goddess today."

"Where are the others?"

"What others?"

"You can't hunt boar alone, 'tis too dangerous!"

"I have the dogs, I have an extra pack horse. That's all I need to hunt boar."

A frisson of fear curled inside her belly. He had no gun, no crossbow, no pack of hounds, no attendants.

"Don't be afraid, love, I'll protect you," he vowed with unconscious arrogance.

Diana straightened her shoulders. "Afraid? I'm not afraid! With all my heart I trust you to keep me safe." She wished she felt as brave as her words. "I love adventure!" she cried, taking off like the wind toward the forest.

Marcus easily overtook her before they reached the trees, and once they entered the forest, their pace was slowed considerably. Sunlight came through the tall trees in great shafts, setting the red and gold autumn leaves ablaze.

Where the trees were too dense for the sunlight to penetrate, it was dim and shadowy.

Diana stayed as close as she could to Marcus. She realized the forest must be filled with unseen danger for she could clearly hear animals crashing through the underbrush and also detected strange rustlings in the fallen leaves. Marcus controlled the pair of mastives with sharp orders or they would have taken off after the first deer they scented.

The air, heavily scented with pine and bracken, was filled with bird calls, some twittering, some screeching their warnings that danger approached. Marcus seemed to know where he was going so Diana swallowed her apprehension and followed. They came to a clearing surrounded by massive oak trees and there, large as life, stood a wild boar with its head down rooting out acorns.

Marcus spotted it long before it saw him. He gave the dogs a hand signal to keep them quiet, followed by another signal for them to take chase. Diana stopped breathing. The beast was so ugly, fear gripped her throat. In that terrible moment she wished she hadn't come. More, she wished she had never suggested this terrible thing they did. Marcus didn't need a weapon, she thought wretchedly; his dogs would tear the boar apart.

They took up the chase immediately. It ran well, despite its heavy belly and short legs. She watched in horror as it tried to gore the dogs with its viciously sharp tusks. Her mare was so nervous it began to toss its head and blow through its nostrils. Her hands tightened on the reins to keep it from bolting. Marcus was out of the saddle in a flash, running close on the heels of his baying dogs.

In horrified fascination, she watched them run the entire length of the clearing. It slowly dawned upon her that Romulus and Remus were only nipping at the boar's ears, while warily keeping their distance from its vicious tusks. The mastives were well trained to prevent the boar from escaping into the forest. It was their job to keep it in the

clearing. Finally, with one on either side, the dogs brought
it down.

Marcus flung himself on top of it and grasped its tusks
so it could not gore him. The boar, now maddened by anger, fought like any enraged wild animal would whose life
was threatened. Diana's hand was pressed to her breast. She
felt as if her heart were ready to burst. She no longer feared
for herself, or even the dogs. All her concern was focused
on Marcus. His bare arms and legs were already bloodied
from deep scratches and she feared he would be badly
wounded any second. Her heart pounded so heavily, she
heard it inside her eardrums until she became faint. She
loved him so much she could not bear to see him hurt and
bleeding!

Chapter 21

As Marcus wrestled with the boar, sweat glistened on his face and the bulging muscles of his bare arms, then mingled with the blood from his scratches. Incredibly, the boar's struggles lessened and Marcus took a rope from his belt and bound its back legs together. Then he wrapped the rope around its tusks and pulled its head down to its front feet, securing it in such a way that it was totally immobilized. He left it on the ground and came to her across the clearing, grinning with satisfaction.

"You didn't kill it," she said in a stunned voice.

His grin disappeared. "Are you disappointed?"

"Oh Marcus, no! It was the bravest thing I've ever seen." She reached out her arms so he could lift her down to him.

"I stink," he said bluntly. "A boar's odor is disgusting."

"I don't care," she said, flinging herself upon him so that he was forced to catch her. "You are so reckless! My heart stopped beating, I was so worried for you."

He let the dogs go off after a hare, while they sat on a fallen log so that Marcus could catch his breath. "I couldn't do it without the dogs," he explained. "I've trained them to go for the ears so they won't damage the boar. I take them back to the fortress, to a large boar enclosure where we breed them. That one is a little female.''

"Little?" Diana repeated in astonishment.

"Males are much larger, but not nearly so valuable.''

"Am I hearing you correctly, Marcus Magnus? Are you actually admitting that a female is superior to a male?''

He grinned at her, tucking an errant curl behind her ear. "It takes only one or two males to keep a score of females impregnated and breeding litters.''

"What happens to the males?''

"We eat them, of course.'' He took his axe from his saddle and built a temporary holding pen from sturdy branches, then set sharp stakes about it, explaining, "I don't want wolves to get it while we hunt the next one.''

"Wolves?" Diana cried, hoping he was teasing her. When she saw that he was perfectly serious, she said, "Why don't we take the boar back? My desire for a boar hunt has been well satisfied.''

"Do you suppose your medieval men would stop after just one?''

"Oh, I'm certain they would, Marcus.''

He grinned. "Then all the more reason why I can't stop until I've outdone them.''

Her heart overflowed when she realized he was doing this all to impress her. He was actually jealous of "her medieval men" as he called them. Marcus Magnus had nothing to worry about. He would have outshone other men of any age. And she would tell him so, but not until they were in bed tonight, where she could reward him for bravery, strength, and endurance above and beyond the call of duty.

When the hunt was finally over, they emerged from the forest with three boars. The two females were tied onto the packhorse, while Marcus had slung the male about his own shoulders. Romulus and Remus, dog tired, trailed behind them and as the small hunting party neared the villa, Diana blew her hunting horn with gusto. Though it had not been what she envisioned, she realized that no hunt in any time of history could have surpassed the one she had experienced at the side of her magnificent Roman general. At that moment she would not have changed places with Cleopatra or the Virgin Queen herself!

During the week that followed, Marcus took Diana with him all over Aquae Sulis as he went to check on the progress of various projects designed to improve the town and the outlying district. They rode out on a Roman road that was being extended toward the coast. Diana knew that beyond Bath was Bristol and the great Bristol Channel, which Marcus called the Sabrina Aestuary. They came to a crossroads that led to the northeast.

"I'm very proud of this particular road. My own engineers designed it and my slaves built it. It runs all the way to Lindom over two hundred miles distant."

To Diana, Lindum sounded very much like Lincoln and she suddenly realized this road that went from Bath and Exeter, all the way to Lincoln, was still used in Georgian times. She dismounted and placed her hand reverently on one of the paving stones.

"Oh Marcus, this is the great Fosse Way—it's probably the most famous road in Britain. Only a couple of days before I tumbled back to your time, I remember standing on the Fosse Way and feeling this incredible sense of timelessness, that something the ancient Romans built was still in use."

Marcus stared at her, slightly uncomfortable at some of the things that went on in her head. Most of the things she said made sense. Only once in a while were the things she spoke of beyond the realm of possibility, but he could never accept her story as truth. For once he did, the possibility of her disappearing back as quickly as she had arrived would haunt him.

"This stone is such a beautiful color. It's native to Bath, I mean Aquae Sulis."

He laughed at her. "I know that. I own most of the stone quarries."

Diana stood up slowly and stared at him as if she were seeing a ghost. When he said the words "stone quarries," something clicked in her brain. Was it possible that Marcus Magnus could be the Earl of Bath?

"What's wrong?" he asked.

"Nothing. Nothing at all," she said quickly. The idea was so bizarre she could not possibly tell him. She tried to dismiss it, but whenever she stole a look at that dark, proud profile, the impression was still with her. She suddenly recalled that the first time she laid eyes upon him bearing down on her in the chariot, she mistook him for the Earl of Bath, playing ridiculous games. Mark Hardwick . . . Mark . . . Marcus . . .

He took her down to the river and pulled out a folded parchment. "The next project is a permanent bridge across the river. Let me show you my sketches."

"No! Don't show me." Diana considered both banks of the Avon for a moment, then said, "It will span the water down there where you have built the weir. It will be a high bridge with beautiful stone arches. I can tell you the precise number of them."

"You've seen my sketches!" he accused.

"Marcus Magnus, you have an explanation for everything! I have *not* seen your sketches. It still stands in modern times. It is called the Pulteney Bridge. A Georgian designer takes credit for it, but obviously he stole your ideas."

His eyes narrowed. "*These* are modern times," he said flatly.

Diana looked at him and understood his reluctance to believe the things she said. They were too much in love and too possessive of each other to accept the idea that anything could separate them, especially a thing like time, which was so frighteningly ephemeral.

It was a glorious autumn day, possibly one of the few remaining to them this year, so they continued to ride along the riverbank until they found a secluded spot where nature seemed to be having a last mad fling before the long sleep of winter blanketed the world.

"I brought food," Marcus confessed.

"And I brought a writing tablet and stylus!"

Marcus groaned. "That isn't what I had in mind."

They dismounted, tethered the horses, then Diana spread her cloak on the grass and sat down with her back to the bole of a copper beech. The water sang as if it were happy to rush over the stones of this blessed place. Bees droned endlessly as they collected pollen from the Michaelmas daisies, and fork-tailed swallows swooped across the river catching insects.

Marcus unfolded a big linen napkin that held cold venison and a couple of roast pigeons. He also had bread and cheese and olives, which no Roman meal was complete without. They had no goblets, so Marcus showed her how to drink from a wineskin, which of course turned into an hilarious game, whose laughter became intimate, turning their thoughts to love.

They stretched out full-length so they could enjoy their kisses completely. When Marcus' hands removed the brooch that fastened her tunic, she demurred. "Marcus, I cannot lie naked out here in the open."

"You won't be naked. You can wear my Caesar coin."

"I'm sorry I criticized one of your heroes. Do you forgive me?" she asked, tracing Caesar's noble profile with her finger.

"Only if you wear my coin, and nothing else!"

She laughed up into his eyes. "You are so persuasive. How can I deny you anything?"

"*Veni, vidi, vici,*" Marcus quoted.

"No. *I* came, *I* saw, *I* conquered," Diana said slowly,

challenging his manhood, knowing he would master her before their loveplay reached its tumultuous climax.

Later, she sat between his legs as he showed her how to use the stylus. When she learned how to make legible letters in the thin lead that covered the wooden tablet, she took up a fresh one and said, "I'm going to put down our names and bury this so that our lovely day will be recorded forever."

He laughed at her. "It's common practice to bury these things, but they usually contain curses."

"What sort of curses?" she asked curiously.

"Oh, wives who have unfaithful husbands write nonsense such as: 'I curse his life and mind and memory and liver and lungs' and then they bury them in the superstitious belief that the curse will work."

She glanced over her shoulder to look up into his black eyes. "And what if it is the wife who is unfaithful?"

"The husband would bury the wife, not some writing tablet."

It sounded as if it could be a veiled warning. "Perhaps I am lucky that I have no husband," she said lightly.

A look of contemplation came into his dark eyes, but Diana, intent upon holding her stylus at just the right angle, did not see the longing writ clearly on his face. He watched from over her shoulder as she wrote:

Marcus Magnus,
Primus Pilus
and General of Aquae Sulis.
Loved Forever by
Diana Davenport, A.D. 61

His finger touched the numbers. "What is this?" he puzzled.

"That is the date, the year we are in."

Marcus shook his head. "This is the eighth year in the reign of Nero."

"Yes, I know that, my love, but future generations date

everything from the birth of Jesus Christ. So the year is either B.C., before Christ, or A.D., anno Domini.''

Marcus accepted her explanation without demur. He was too filled with love for her to argue and spoil their precious time together.

They buried it among the roots of the copper beech like two children intent on burying a treasure. When it was time to return, Marcus lifted her before him in the saddle while her own mare followed. Though they had spent the entire day together, he was loath to let her go from his arms.

Upon their arrival at home, Kell presented Marcus with a message that Julius Classicianus was to arrive on the morrow, which meant Marcus had to rush off to see that all was in order at the fortress, in preparation for the Procurator's visit.

As Diana lay alone in the pedestal bed with its towering columns, her thoughts wandered back to the time before she had come there. Her other life seemed a thousand years and a million miles away. Like another lifetime. Her thoughts touched for a moment on the Earl of Bath. It was amazing how much he and Marcus had in common. What if they were one and the same man? Were such things possible? Now that she was a woman in the full sense of the word, she realized that she had been sexually attracted to Mark Hardwick's dark, arrogant maleness. Sparks had flared between them every time they met.

A smile curved her lips as she drifted off to sleep. What a comforting thought it was that Marcus might live again and again, down through the ages, in the place that he loved. Yet if it were true, seventeen hundred years of civilization had not altered his dominant, arrogant personality. Thank God. Marcus would be Marcus forever!

* * *

"It's official," Julius told Marcus. "Emperor Nero has decided to keep Britannia in the empire." They were sitting in the map room of the principia at the fortress.

"I imagine your shipment of gold and silver ingots stamped DE BRITAN made it impossible for the Emperor and the Senate to even consider giving up such a lucrative source of income."

Julius came straight to the reason for his visit. "I am recommending that Paullinus be replaced. We need a governor who is a statesman, not one who massacres the native tribes by the thousand."

"To exist here and prosper, we Romans need the support of the Britons," Marcus agreed.

"Yes, and Paullinus fosters hatred wherever he goes. His determination to eradicate whole tribes of Iceni and Trinovantes incites more rebellion. We need a man of diplomacy. Only a statesmanlike attitude can restore the full support of the Britons."

"You will have to return to Rome to present your ideas to the emperor and the senate. Messages are easily intercepted, lost, or ignored."

"We are of like minds. I want you to come to Rome with me, Marcus. Two voices carry more weight than one. You are the best advocate for this country that I have. I will personally see Nero, but I would like you to speak before the senate."

Marcus' emotions warred within him. He would love to visit Rome, to see his father again and the villa and lands to which he was heir, but he no longer thought of it as home. This was his home, this was where his heart was, and the thought of leaving Diana behind was unimaginable. Still, he was a man who had always put duty before personal considerations. He was incapable of sacrificing his honor for gain, for gratification, or for any other temptation. "Julius, you have presented me with a dilemma."

"Weigh it carefully, my friend. I don't need your decision for a couple of days. I intend to sail next week, though,

There won't be much time until the gales make the sea crossing hazardous.''

"Come to dinner tonight. There's something I've been hesitant to ask you about, and the questions will come easier on a full stomach.''

"If your lady, Diana, will be there, it will be my pleasure to dine with you,'' Julius accepted with twinkling eyes.

"If you are to be my guest, Julius, I am certain she will accept my invitation,'' Marcus said graciously.

Before they dined, Marcus and Julius relaxed in the bath suite for the daily ritual that was so socially significant. They had been oiled, cleansed, and massaged and finally Marcus' tongue was loosened enough to bring up the subject that had been foremost in his mind. Before they took the cold plunge, Marcus said, "I am a career soldier, you know. I signed up for twenty-six years and have served sixteen of them.'' His glance met that of Julius. "It is taken for granted that a life soldier will not marry.''

Julius knew immediately what Marcus had in mind. "That rule has been relaxed in the last couple of years. You will need permission, but if I recommend it, it will be given almost automatically.'' Julius could smell victory. "If you come to Rome with me, it will expedite matters considerably.''

"Well, that is certainly an incentive,'' Marcus admitted

"So, your relationship with the lady Diana is serious, I take it?''

"Yes. I would like a son and I grow no younger. Until now I was content to have my brother be my heir, but at thirty I have suddenly decided I want a wife and a legitimate heir of my own.''

"Good for you, Marcus. It is a big step but a wise one, I think. With maturity comes the realization that none of us is immortal, and when we see a chance for happiness staring us in the face, we should grab it with both hands and never let go." He winked at Marcus. "I'm ready for the cold plunge when you are."

Some hours later, Kell escorted Diana to the triclinium, where both men welcomed her with a chaste kiss of greeting. She wore a pale lavender stola with a deep purple palla draped and fastened over one shoulder. Her golden curls were piled on top of her head to show off the amethyst torque she wore about her elegant neck.

The conversation was politely impersonal while the serving slaves moved about the couches and table quietly and efficiently, but the moment they withdrew, Julius spoke of his journey to Rome. Without warning he turned to Diana and said, "I must convince the emperor and the senate that Britannia's army should be turned into a peacetime force whose main function is to police her territory and defend her frontiers."

"Your mission is most noble, Julius. I hope with all my heart that you succeed."

"If Marcus adds his eloquence to mine, I am sure we shall convince them. But the decision is his."

Damn you, Julius, why couldn't you let me tell her? Marcus thought.

Panic spread its wings inside Diana's chest and fluttered wildly. The procurator's words told her that Marcus was needed in Rome, but that he had not agreed to go. By telling her that the choice was his, Julius was hoping she would influence that choice. Diana did not want to be separated from Marcus, did not want to be left alone. Marcus was her world, her life, her reason for being. The food in her mouth turned to ashes. She did not dare to look at Marcus for fear of what she would see in his eyes.

Julius dipped his fingers into the perfumed water and

dried them on a linen napkin. "Perhaps Diana would like to see Rome."

Marcus' spirits soared. He could clearly see that Julius was making it impossible for him to refuse. He issued Diana an invitation because he guessed Marcus would not go without her. Of course Julius had no idea Diana was a slave who had no free choice, but would come or stay as Marcus commanded. And he did not want Julius even to suspect she was his slave. Romans did not marry slaves!

Diana no longer followed the conversation. Dimly she heard them speaking of Marcus' father and the lands he would inherit from him. Her pale countenance was remote and calm as a moon goddess, as if she were completely detached from the subject of the conversation floating about her. But inside she was in turmoil, her thoughts filled with Rome, the Eternal City. The suggestion that she might visit ancient Rome was so startling, she was thrown completely off balance.

The thought of Rome was terrifying, though it wasn't the magnificent city that filled her with dread. It was the people of Rome. It was Romans!

Of all the emperors who had ruled, Nero was the cruelest and most degenerate. *Nero is a madman,* Diana thought, with a shudder of revulsion. Julius would take Marcus right into Nero's court, which was nothing more than a seething den of depravity. Her history books had taught her well what Nero did to Christians, so a visit for Diana was out of the question. Yet in her heart she knew that Marcus would consider it his duty to go. And if he went, would he ever return?

No! No! her heart cried. *Make this day start over without Julius' visit!*

From beneath her lashes she observed Marcus. Her eyes secretly caressed his noble profile, his heavily muscled torso, his powerful hands gesticulating as he talked with Julius. It dawned on her that the procurator spoke openly before her because he suspected she had total influence over Marcus Magnus. She prayed that it was so. She would use that influence to stop him from going to Rome. She would keep him beside her if it was humanly possible to do so. Had she not set out to enslave him? She would use her powers of persuasion to influence his decision, and if they did not work, she would use her body. Playing harlot to Marcus was a small price to pay to protect what they had found together, here in Aquae Sulis!

Chapter 22

Diana retired to the sleeping chamber, leaving Marcus to bid the procurator goodnight. She removed the brooch that held her palla in place over her shoulder, but she neither undressed nor took down her hair. She would leave these intimate enticements for Marcus.

The general accompanied the procurator outside to his litter. "I'll give you my decision tomorrow, Julius." As he reentered the atrium, Marcus became introspective. He was a decisive man. He had made instantaneous decisions all his life and regretted few of them. Why was he hesitant about returning to Rome? The answer came back immediately, of course. Diana. Diana was the reason.

He paused with one foot on the bottom stair, his black eyes unseeing as he gazed upward. How did he go about this business of proposing to a woman? He ran a distracted hand through his hair. What a fool he was! Before he asked her to marry him, he would have to free her. But what if Diana refused to go to Rome? As his slave she would have no choice. Perhaps he should not be in such haste to free her.

Yet in his heart he knew he should have done it long ago, and he would have, if he hadn't been afraid she would leave him the moment she was free. Trust. That's what it boiled down to. There should be complete trust in a marriage, and before trust could be shared, truth must be shared. Marcus squared his shoulders and ascended the staircase.

Why in the name of Jupiter was he worrying? As his slave she must obey him, as his wife she must obey him, and as his concubine she must obey him. If she rebelled, he would simply bring her to heel. She was a mere woman and would have to learn her place, which was at his side, in silence and obedience.

The moment he stepped into the chamber and saw her before the mirror, his body responded as it always did. His heart skipped a beat, then his pulse throbbed so heavily he could feel it in his throat, his groin, and the soles of his feet. Blood flowed hot and strong through his veins, pumping into his shaft so that it shot out of its cowl like a predator would spring from its cave to devour unwary prey. Marcus faced a difficult truth; Diana was not an ordinary woman.

It was not just his body that responded to her either. His mind took great delight in her intelligence, and when he was not making love to her, his favorite thing to do was talk. There were times he had the fleeting impression that their spirits touched. Marcus could not imagine spending his life with anyone else. He had a gift tucked away for her, but he would wait until the right moment presented itself. He wanted it to be intimate, special, and meaningful when he gifted her with a symbol of sharing their love and their lives.

Diana cast him a provocative glance from beneath her lashes; it drew him as the moon pulls the tide. His hands removed her palla, exposing one bared shoulder, and she shivered with pleasure as his calloused fingers touched her soft skin. As his hands lifted to take the pins from her hair, he murmured, "I wish Julius had let me tell you about Rome."

"Marcus, I—"

His fingers covered her lips, staying her words. "Let me talk. I have many things to say tonight."

Diana's heart contracted. *Goodbye. He's going to say goodbye!*

Her nearness scattered his thoughts. He moved to the hearth to poke the banked fire into a small blaze and to collect himself. With his back to her, he gazed into the flames. "I want to free you, but before I do, there must be truth between us, Diana."

She stiffened. "I thought there was nothing but truth between us."

He turned to face her, his dark eyes intense. "Your tales amuse me, my love, but it is time for the truth. Trust me, I will not punish you."

A curl of anger spiraled inside her. His arrogance was intolerable. "Punish me? You actually still consider our relationship that of master and slave!" In the space of a heartbeat her anger burst into a fine rage. "Let me disabuse you, Roman. Where I come from, there is no such thing as slavery. You cannot free me for I have never been your slave. I am not your slave now, nor will I ever be in the future!"

In two quick strides he had her shoulders gripped in his powerful hands, shaking her until her teeth rattled. "Since you will not confess the truth to me, I will tell you. I know you are a Druid who was sent here to spy. Credit me with some intelligence. I do not fear your secret rites, that is not where your strength lies. It is Druid control over the Celtic tribal aristocracy that must be broken. The Druids are the strongest unifying force in Britannia. I know Druid priests and priestesses educate the children of the Celtae kings and nobles and that you are influential advisers with strong anti-Roman feelings, bent on holding back the influence of Rome. They sent you to me because you were beautiful. Your job was to seduce me."

Diana, already flushed with anger, blushed deep rose; had she not just been planning to seduce him?

"Can't you see that I made you my slave to protect you? If Paullinus had the slightest suspicion about you, you would have been condemned to death. Have you ever seen a public execution? An enemy of Rome is not allowed simply to die. Death is an escape. An enemy must suffer torture." His voice was harsh, trying to bring home what could befall her if she did not cleave to him.

"I have seen prisoners flogged until their flesh fell from their bones in bloody strips. Then seen them staked and set on fire." In a much quieter voice, he asked, "Have you ever witnessed a crucifixion?"

"Stop!" She pulled away from him, her eyes glittering with outrage. "I am not a Druid. I am a Christian. The Romans crucified Christ, so I have been taught all about such abominations!"

"Christianity is an unpopular eastern cult whose converts are considered atheists. You are too intelligent to be a Christian."

"And you are too ignorant even to carry on an intelligent conversation about Christianity. We believe in one supreme being, one God. How can that be considered atheist?" she demanded.

Marcus hung on to the last shreds of his temper, knowing that if he lost it, violence would reign. "They are atheists because they renounce all other true gods," he explained, as if speaking to a stupid child.

Diana stared at him, speechless for a moment. Then with quiet dignity she said, "The gulf between us is so wide and so deep, it can never be breached. Time separates us, Marcus. Between your time and my time, Christianity has spread so that it encompasses most of the civilized world. And the ironic part is that the highest Christians are known as *Roman Catholics* and *Rome* has become the heart and soul of Christianity."

"Rome is too cultured and civilized for such a thing to ever happen," he sneered.

"Romans are about as cultured and civilized as wild

boars. You have the intelligence of donkeys, the stubbornness of mules, and the arrogance of hairy, blue-arsed baboons!'' Her beautiful breasts rose and fell with her deep agitation. ''I shall never come to Rome with you!''

Marcus stepped away from her as if she were a viper. If he laid hands upon her, he would not be responsible for the damage he might inflict. She deliberately incited him to savagery. ''I shall never ask you,'' he vowed.

Diana snatched up her palla and swept past him with the contempt a queen would reserve for a leprous beggar.

Kell dismissed the slaves who had cleared and tidied the triclinium. He did not want them to overhear Diana shouting at the general.

Nola descended the stairs. ''They are at it again.''

''Eavesdropping, woman of Gaul?''

She ignored the taunt. ''I will go to her; you go to him.''

Kell nodded. When he tapped on the chamber door it was thrown open with such violence, Kell stepped back in alarm. Marcus, still fully dressed in a purple-bordered toga, ran a distracted hand through his short curls with impotent fury. ''I offered her her freedom and she threw it in my face. By the bloody balls of Mithras, what is wrong with women?''

''It is my fault, General. I knew she needed a beating from the first day she arrived, but I left her chastisement to you. I was too much of a coward to mar her beauty.''

''She *is* exceptionally beautiful, isn't she?'' Marcus asked wistfully.

''Yes, she is. But between us we have created a monster, for now she is willful and spoiled as well as beautiful.''

''What do you suggest I do? Put her back to scrubbing floors?''

''She would relish the punishment so she could throw

that too in your face. My advice is to shun her. Neither look at her nor speak to her. Her vanity will not allow such a thing to continue and she will be instantly contrite.''

Marcus paced about the chamber, grim-faced. ''Gather her things and take them to her.''

In the apricot chamber Diana catalogued her grievances to Nola. ''He thinks me a spy sent by the Druids to seduce him. He refuses to believe I am a Christian. He refuses to believe anything I've told him. If he loved me, he would believe me!''

''What did the procurator want?'' Nola asked.

''He wants Marcus to go to Rome. Well, good riddance. If he has to do without me, he might come to appreciate me.''

Nola was startled at the news. Had Kell been keeping this visit to Rome secret? ''Keep to your own chamber. If you shun him, he will soon be contrite.''

Kell scratched on the door before he entered Diana's room.

''Thank you for sharing the news that the general is returning to Rome,'' Nola said with sarcasm.

Kell's mask was in place, so the shock of the news did not register on his face. He put Diana's gowns and hair ornaments on the bed. ''The general forbids you his sleeping chamber. He asked me to return your things.''

Diana was outraged. ''What the hell is the matter with men?''

Nola explained sweetly. ''When they are young, their brains are too soft and their cocks are too hard. When they reach Kell's age, they suffer from hardening of the brain and softening of the cock.''

''Woman of Gaul, you are enough to induce limpness in any man, regardless of his age.''

''That depends on how I wield my tongue,'' Nola said suggestively.

"Your tongue is so sharp, it would draw blood."

"Briton, my tongue could drain you dry," Nola retorted, refusing to let him have the last word.

Diana lost her patience with both of them. "I thought this was about my problem, but obviously it is about yours. The pair of you need to go someplace private where you can work off your sexual energy."

Nola and Kell stared at each other in horrified silence as the truth was brought home to them. Kell bowed stiffly and withdrew. Nola threw her a quelling glance of accusation and followed him.

For the next two hours Marcus paced about his chamber. The pendulum of his emotions swung all the way from self-righteous outrage to self-blame. He had botched it plain and simple. He should have taken a firm hand with her long ago. He should never have agreed to let her say whatever she wished when they were private. The first time she was insolent to him he should have put her across his knee and made certain it was the last time she dared challenge him!

The pronouncement she had flung in his teeth galled him like a burr on his backside. *I shall never come to Rome with you!* The echo of her taunt lingered in his ears. By the splendor of Jupiter, Kell was right. She needed a beating. She had asked for it and she was going to get it. He was in the right bloody mood to slake his temper!

Marcus selected a short leather flagellum from among his weapons, then hesitated. If he went to her in a roiling rage, he would damage her. She was so delicate and finely boned that he might kill her if he struck her. He reflected for a moment. Where in the world *had* Diana come from? She was so different, he was almost ready to believe she *was* from another time. Did he love her enough to believe in the impossible and accept what she told him? For his sake as well as hers, he realized he had no choice. The only way there could be truth between them was if he accepted *her* truth.

To vent his blood's heat and achieve a measure of calm, Marcus went to his desk and opened maps to plot his journey. They would likely sail from the closest port of Silarum on the Sabrina Aestuary into the Oceanus Britannicus, then into the Oceanus Cantabrius, past Gaul and Hispanic. Then they would pass through the narrow strait by the towering rock into the vast Mare Internum and thus to Roma.

It would be good to see his father again. Though Titus Magnus was of noble ancestry, he was not above making money through trade. His olive groves alone brought him vast wealth. His father had always been a shrewd businessman as well as a total authoritarian. Marcus grimaced. He had had discipline knocked into him at an early age, but it had served him well in his military career.

Marcus wanted his father to meet his beautiful bride. Though it was no longer necessary to Marcus to have his father's approval, it would be pleasant to have his blessing. Marcus stood up and stretched, then he let his glance travel about the chamber, seeking a way to make it more inviting. He turned down the fur covers on the bed and slipped a small ivory box beneath Diana's pillow.

He was tired of waiting for her to return. He considered himself a patient man, but his patience was not endless. This was ridiculous! He could feel the small measure of calm he had achieved desert him. Marcus cursed under his breath and strode to the door. He would wait no longer!

Diana lay abed feeling utterly sorry for herself. Why was she cursed? Why did she have to sleep alone? Even Kell and Nola were likely sharing a bed by now. She shivered. She fully expected Marcus to come and beat her. Beat her to a jelly for the insults she had flung at him. Why hadn't he come? Why was he drawing it out? Why didn't he come and get it over with? Suddenly, she heard him at the door and closed her eyes in pretended sleep.

Marcus saw that Diana had fallen asleep with the lamp blazing. He dimmed it to a soft glow and looked down at her. His gut twisted as he saw her eyelashes were spiky from tears. What a brute he must seem to a little girl like Diana. Yet she stood up to him with all the tenacity of a terrier. A wave of protectiveness almost engulfed him. Still wearing his tunic, he got into bed beside her and very gently slipped his arms about her. "I cannot sleep without you," he whispered against her ear.

As if she were rousing from slumber, Diana turned in his arms, lifted her lashes, and looked up at him. A sigh trembled on her lips.

His dark face softened as he looked down at her with adoration. With gentle fingers he lifted the teardrops from her lashes and lightly stroked the fine hair from her temples, then he bent his lips to feather tiny kisses across her brow. His lips touched her eyelids, her cheekbones, the corners of her mouth so tenderly it made her throat ache. He brushed the back of his fingers across her chin and cheeks as if she were made of fragile porcelain that must be handled with a delicate touch.

Her breath caught in her throat. She never dreamed her fierce Roman could be so tender and gentle. She lifted her hand to stroke his cheek, then softly traced his jagged scar with a fingertip. When he quivered at her delicate touch, she realized how sensitive his face was. She never realized such a strong man could be sensitive.

Marcus enfolded her in tender arms to cradle her against him while he whispered and crooned words of love. His gentleness allowed her to see how affectionate, softhearted, and sensitive he was capable of being. "I love you more than life," he murmured. Diana melted against him, entwining her arms about his neck. "When you cling to me so sweetly, it doubles my strength. It makes me feel invincible," he whispered. "Will you let me carry you back to our chamber? I never want to spend a night away from you as long as we live.''

His whispers were so intimate and private, she knew he had never uttered those words to anyone else in the world. In these moments there was no one in the entire universe, except the two of them, sweetly clinging. She yielded herself up to him. ''Take me back. It's where I belong.''

Marcus lifted her from the bed and held her tightly against his heart. When he held her like this, in a warm cocoon of love, she realized she had never felt happier or safer. When he carried her into their sleeping chamber, the immense bed looked most inviting with the furs turned back.

Marcus climbed the steps, placed her gently on the bed, then sat down beside her. He made no move to take off her nightrobe nor divest himself of his clothes. Instead he covered her hand with his, then lifted it to his mouth to kiss each finger. ''From now on I will believe whatever you tell me. I love you and I trust you, Diana.''

''Marcus, I love you too. I am devastated when we fight.''

He pulled her against his side, then with gentle fingers tilted her chin so that their eyes met. ''I know you love me, my heart, but do you trust me?''

''I would trust you with my life, Marcus,'' she vowed.

''That is what I am asking you to do, beloved. I am asking you to marry me. I am asking you to come to Rome to meet my father, while I get permission from the military authorities. When I have spoken to the Senate about replacing Paullinus, we will come home to Aquae Sulis where we are happiest.''

Her bottom lip trembled as she looked up at him with joy. Her heart was overflowing with the love she felt for this man. He wanted her for his wife, and surely she wanted him for her husband more than she had ever longed for anything in her life. She was terrified to go to Rome, but she would never hurt him by refusing. He had asked her to trust him with her life. How could she not when she loved him and trusted him with all her heart and soul? She smiled tremulously. "Yes, I will marry you, and yes, I will come to Rome."

Marcus lifted her into his lap and hugged her tenderly. "Oh, Diana, thank you. I was so afraid you would refuse me. You have made me the happiest man alive." His lips traced her ear, then moved softly across her cheek until they found her mouth. He did not devour her; instead, his lips touched hers with heartstopping gentleness.

She reached up to caress his face and let her fingers drift down the column of his neck. His gentleness almost undid her. How could such a physically powerful man show such infinite tenderness? Her throat tightened with unshed tears. She pressed her face against his chest and felt the gold chain beneath her cheek. When she glanced down, she saw that something was wrong with his Caesar coin. "What happened to it?" she whispered huskily.

"I had it cut in half," he murmured. Marcus reached beneath her pillow and pulled out the ivory box. He placed it in her cupped hands and held his breath.

Diana opened it slowly, and there upon a cushion of silk lay the other half of his Caesar coin with a fine gold chain attached to it. "Oh, Marcus," was all she could say before the teardrops slipped down her cheeks.

"No tears, beloved, I beg you," he pleaded hoarsely.

"They are tears of happiness. So long as I wear this against my heart, you will always be with me."

He let out a long relieved sigh that it meant as much to her as it did to him. He gently lifted the chain over her head and watched it fall to rest in the valley between her beautiful breasts. "Wear it as a symbol of my undying love for you."

She took his half of the priceless gold coin and fitted it to hers. "We fit together to become one whole." She lifted a tremulous mouth to his in sweet seductive invitation and

Marcus slowly made them whole with the tenderest love-making they would ever experience. They fell asleep en-twined together, knowing they had committed totally to one another, for better or for worse.

Chapter 23

The following day, Diana resolutely thrust away all apprehension as she busied herself with preparations for the journey. As she and Nola packed her clothes, jewels, toilet articles, and cosmetics, she realized how many beautiful things Marcus had given her. She smiled ironically. How she had hated the restrictive fashions of Georgian times. Now she had the most seductive and erotic garments ever designed throughout history. Each and every item was made to enhance the female body for the sole pleasure of the male. When she analyzed it, Diana realized the concept was barbaric and yet, in reality, it was delicious to flaunt her femininity and exercise the power nature had bestowed upon the female sex.

Marcus decided he could manage without Kell while he was in Rome; his services were better employed here in charge of the villa and the household in Aquae Sulis. Marcus told Diana she could take Nola with her if she wished, but when she learned that Kell was to remain behind, she thought it would be a splendid opportunity for Nola and Kell to spend time alone together to explore the boundaries of their newfound relationship.

Marcus insisted that Diana have a bodyguard with her at all times, both on the journey and while they were in Rome. There would be many times they would be separated and Marcus knew of her fears, though she valiantly tried to keep them hidden. He appointed Tor, who had acted as her groom, to be her personal slave and instructed him to stay at Diana's back, as close as her shadow.

Tor could not believe the honor bestowed upon him. The other slaves envied his elevated status of bodyguard to the general's lady, whom it was rumored was soon to become the general's wife! Kell immediately began instructing Tor on everything from personal hygiene to how to prevent Diana from being jostled in a crowd. By the time Kell had finished with him, Tor's head was spinning with the myriad duties he would be expected to perform and with the monumental responsibility of protecting Diana.

Kell presented him with his own leather flagellum and instructed him never to hesitate to use it on anyone who did not make way for his lady. Then Marcus took Tor to the fortress for lessons in the short sword. The general, of course, would take ten of his best soldiers as his personal guard, but lessons in weaponry wouldn't be amiss for Diana's personal body slave.

Only two days remained before they sailed. Marcus knew he would be late at the fort, packing supplies for the journey, selecting the centurions he would take with him, and instructing his second-in-command to take charge of the fortress in his absence. He would dine with his men and instructed Diana to eat without him.

When he arrived home, however, and found the triclinium in darkness, he realized how much he had missed her stimulating company over dinner. He strode into the bathing room intending to cleanse himself quickly and was overjoyed to find Diana awaiting him in the water.

"Have the gods gifted me with a water sprite?"

"I've seen so little of you these last two days, I thought I'd act as your bath slave tonight." Her words were seductive as her beautiful body, as she floated naked in the pale green water.

He grinned down at her. "You'll soon see more than

you bargained for,'' he promised, growing enormous with anticipation.

"No! Don't undress, master, let me do that."

She came out of the water to stand before him and unbuckle his breastplate. She stood much closer than was necessary. A bemused Marcus murmured, ''You always refused to serve as my slave, yet now that I have freed you, it amuses you to play slave girl!''

"Amuses me and arouses me, master," she said, running her hands over the great slabs of muscle in his bare chest. He removed his cuirass of leather strips himself, leaving her to strip him of his linen undergarment. When she did so, she jumped back in pretended alarm as his swollen phallus sprang free of the garment. "I am an ignorant bath slave, master, instruct me in my duties."

"Minister to my needs," he ordered huskily.

"How?" she asked innocently.

"Touch me," he commanded.

"Like this?" Diana slipped her hand between his powerful legs and allowed the tips of her fingers to trail up the inside of his thigh. His shaft stood up rigid at her touch. "And like this, master?" She cupped his heavy sac in the palm of her hand, moving it up and down with a slow rhythm. Then her fingers squeezed on him until she discerned the two spheres within the sac, and she rolled them one against the other.

He moaned with the sweet, heavy ache her manipulations provoked. With her other hand she placed one finger on the underside of his cock at the base and slowly traced its full length. His foreskin stretched, allowing him to lengthen another inch until the head was fully exposed and straining to lengthen further. When it could not, it began to pulse and swell until it was a bloodproud shade of vermilion.

" 'Tis a formidable weapon, like a great gladius sword. What shall I do with it, master?''

"Sheath it!'' he ordered, his voice thick with desire.

His hands cupped her bottom cheeks to pull her to him, but she slipped from his grasp in mock outrage. With her hands on her hips, she demanded, "Is this what your bath slaves do for you? You need a damned cold plunge!"

She slid into the water and in a flash he followed her, and caught her. From behind, his arms encircled her and he pulled her back against him so that his hard length rested in her woman's cleft. She wanted to torment him further by rubbing herself back and forth upon him, but to her dismay she realized she was suspended on him and her feet could not touch bottom.

She smiled a secret smile, refusing to be thwarted. He was so long, the tip of his phallus protruded from the golden curls of her mons. With a deliberate finger, she encircled the swollen tip over and over until he thought he would go mad. Marcus grit his teeth against the erotic sensations.

"Two can play this game, little cocktease." He held her immobile with one arm about her waist and unerringly placed his finger on her sensitive woman's bud, directly above the tip of his cock. What he did with his finger made her squirm, then wriggle, then arch in frenzied arousal. He stopped abruptly and she cried out in protest.

"Finish me," she gasped.

With his mouth against her ear, he ground out, "My will prevails. I will finish you when *I* am ready." He hoisted her from the water, then with powerful arms elevated himself from the bath. He swept up a big towel and a flacon of oil, fully prepared to chase her down. But Diana did not run. She came against him and rubbed her soft body against his hardness. "Selfish brute," she whispered playfully.

"Not selfish, beloved. I'll be more generous than I've ever been in my life. I'll give, and keep on giving until you can't take any more."

He swooped her up into his arms and carried her upstairs to their sleeping chamber. Then he spread the towel before the fire and pulled her down to him. He poured the almond oil into his palms, warmed it at the fire, then began to massage her with long, powerful strokes.

"Your skin is so fair and so smooth, I hope the bitter winds of the sea don't roughen it."

Diana stretched like a feline who was being stroked. "You can do this every night to prevent it," she purred.

He laughed at her naiveté. "A ship isn't conducive to long, playful sessions of lovemaking. A quick in and out against a cabin wall perhaps."

"Mmm . . . that, too, might be interesting."

"Enough to warm the blood perhaps, until we sail into the Mare Internum where the glorious sun shines every day."

"We call it the Mediterranean," she murmured, barely able to carry on a conversation when she would rather give herself up to blissful arousal.

"Means exactly the same thing: inland sea," he said, dipping the fleshy pads of his blunt fingertips into her cleft. He traced over each pink fold as if they were the petals of a flower. The fragrance of almonds was heady as the heat of the fire made the oil release its scent. She was gasping now, trying not to beg as her senses all became heightened.

"Why did you choose almond?"

"Because I love the flavor," he said huskily, bending over to lick each nipple, then covering them with his mouth to feel them spike into sharp little spears. His tongue licked a burning wet path from her breasts, across her belly, and down to her high mons. Diana dug her nails into the palms of her hands to prevent her from screaming as his wicked tongue licked the almond from every petal of her flower.

"Marc . . . Marc . . . Marcus." His name was a supplication, and as much for his sake as hers, he thrust his tongue deep, unable to deny himself another moment. He plunged and curled, plunged and curled, stroking her bud until it swelled to the bursting point.

Her fingers were buried in his thick hair, urging him on

to devour her. From beneath languorous eyelids she watched his black head between her legs and realized with a deep sexual thrill, it was the most exciting, intimate thing a man could do to a woman. She could contain her climax no longer and arched into his mouth with a piercing cry of pleasure.

Marcus immediately moved over her body so that his mouth could capture her cries. She tasted herself on his lips and it immediately began a new cycle of desire, only hotter and fiercer, that no teasing tongue could assuage.

The urgency of her need paled in comparison to his. He drove into her savagely, the powerful force of his penetration moving her dangerously close to the fire. She became so wantonly greedy with lust that she opened her legs wider and arched herself higher to take every fraction of his hard length inside her.

Marcus was ravenous as he drove into her voluptuous body with all the power of a virile male body at the peak of its strength. Yet still, Diana craved more, demanded more. Finally she lifted her legs high enough so that her ankles lay against his broad shoulders and she was wide open to him. He thudded into her over and over, endlessly, until they were love drunk, then love mad. The sensations each of them experienced were so heightened in intensity, their cries began a full half-hour before the volcanic eruptions of their orgasms began.

When coitus was finally complete, they collapsed together, spent in mind and body and emotion. They lay motionless for long minutes while the world stopped spinning and righted itself. Then some devil provoked Marcus to whisper, "Can you take more?" She was utterly slaked and knew he, too, was completely spent from the ferocity of their lovemaking. She couldn't yet speak, so slowly shook her head.

"Neither can I," he admitted, with a deep sigh of pure satisfaction. The same devil now pricked Diana and smiled her secret smile.

"That's too bad, Marcus darling," she whispered, "for I suddenly have a craving for the taste of almonds." She sat up in one fluid motion and appraised his male beauty from beneath eyelids heavy from passion. With alarm, he watched her hand reach for the flacon of oil. He knew he could not achieve another erection without a protracted rest.

She knelt above him and trickled the oil into his navel, then with delicate hands, spread it downward across his ridged belly and onto his muscled thighs. With wicked fingers she stroked his flaccid member, which lay peacefully slumbering after its labors, and to his amazement it awoke immediately. It did not stir sleepily, but sprang to life with a vengeance, ready for any assault.

She dipped her head, running her tongue over her lips in anticipation as she said, "I want to play slave girl again." She started at the base and ran her tongue up the entire length of him. When she reached the head, she licked delicately, then swirled her tongue beneath the crest, then dipped the tip of her tongue into the tiny opening to taste the drops of clear juice that flowed upward so readily. Then she repeated the sequence, managing to do it more erotically each time.

Her tongue slithered about him like a sensual snake, making him pulse and quiver in ecstasy. Marcus closed his eyes and opened his mouth to emit the sounds of pleasure that built in his throat. When she took him inside her hot mouth, he cried a warning to her. "I'll come."

She lifted her mouth from him only long enough to give him back his own words. "My will prevails. I will finish you when *I* am ready."

When they awoke in the morning, they lay entangled before the ashes of the fire. Diana blushed profusely as Marcus murmured, "We didn't even make it to the bed last night." He kissed her nose. "I adore you." He loved it when she blushed, and she always did when she thought their lovemaking had been erotically wicked.

A message came that Marcus Magnus was needed urgently at the fort. When he saw Diana's worried frown, he said lightly, "This is our last day. I'll soon dispose of the problem, whatever it is." On his arrival at the fort, he realized the problem could not be disposed of so quickly. His first cohort centurion awaited him with disquieting news.

"General, your brother, Petrius, rode in early and fell unconscious from his horse. He was carried to the valetudinarium to have his wounds tended."

Marcus rushed to the hospital, fearing the worst, but when he arrived he found Petrius conscious, telling the procurator of his misfortunes.

"Where are you wounded?" Marcus asked with deep concern.

The physician who attended him spoke up. "A fractured arm I am about to set. We thought his shoulder was broken also, but it was just dislocated. His head was drenched in blood, but when it was washed, it proved only a minor scalp wound."

"What in Hades are you doing back here?" Marcus demanded.

Julius spoke up. "It's an outrage. He was left for dead. When he regained consciousness, the army was long gone. Paullinus is a piss-poor leader of men!"

Marcus looked at Petrius with disbelief. Why hadn't his own men tended him? At last Petrius spoke up. "Paullinus is a swine. He ordered the wounded legionaries put to the sword so it wouldn't slow down his army."

Marcus had served under Paullinus, and though he detested the man, he knew the things his brother said were untrue. Paullinus would only put a legionary to the sword to put him out of his misery, if naught could be done to save him, as Marcus himself would do. Paullinus brought his wounded back to Aquae Sulis. It was highly unlikely a soldier would be left for dead, especially a cohort centurion.

Marcus suspected his brother had deserted, but since the penalty for such cowardice was death, he kept his mouth shut.

As the physician set the broken bone in Petrius' arm, Julius said, "Why don't we take him to Rome with us? One more advocate for ridding Britannia of Paullinus can't hurt our cause, and unfortunately your brother's fighting days are over for a while."

When he saw the wild look of hope on Petrius' face, Marcus did not disclose that Petrius was left-handed.

"Rome? You're going home?" Petrius asked joyfully.

"Since the procurator thinks you might aid his cause, I will sign you out of combat on sick leave. Get some rest. We sail tomorrow at dawn."

The general visited his corps of engineers to make sure the bridge across the river would be built as planned in his absence. Once he was away from Petrius, he chided himself on his uncharitable suspicions. What was it about the handsome young devil that made him think his brother was less than honorable? He set aside his misgivings, thinking how happy their father would be to have them both beneath his roof at the same time.

In the late afternoon Marcus arrived at the villa with the ten legionary guards who would accompany them to Rome. They took the trunks and baggage to load on the barge that would take them to the coast, where they would board the ship for the voyage to Rome.

Marcus wanted to put off telling Diana about his brother's return. Though she had never said anything to disparage Petrius, Marcus knew she had a dislike for him. The only alternative was to tell her tonight and that might ruin her evening and his as well, so he slipped his hand over hers and drew her out to the garden.

Thinking he wanted to be private so they could exchange kisses and love words, she warned, "One kiss only. You know that once we start, we cannot stop, and I still have a dozen things to do."

He looked down at her tenderly, lifted her hand to his mouth, deposited a kiss within her palm, and closed her fingers about it. "Diana, my brother Petrius has returned with a broken arm. Since he cannot fight until it heals, Julius asked him to accompany us to Rome."

Marcus saw the blood drain from her face. "Darling, I know he has treated you with disrespect in the past, but when I tell him you are to be my wife, I know he will treat you with every honor." He smiled down at her. "I promise you he will be on his best behavior." Silently he added, *If I have to strangle the young bastard!*

Diana forced herself to smile back at Marcus, but the moment he returned to the fort, a wave of nausea engulfed her. She had thought she was well rid of Petrius. Surely this was not some sort of omen that her journey to Rome was fated to disaster before it had even begun? Perhaps she should have told Marcus what happened that day at the temple, but she had not wanted bad blood between the brothers then, and she did not want it now. Marcus was taking her to his father's home, so it was doubly important there be no discord in the family because of her.

She thought of confiding in Kell, for she found him very easy to talk to, but telling Kell was probably the same as telling Marcus. The two men had few secrets. Finally she decided to have a word with Tor. Since it would be his job to protect her, she would have to confide in him. She found him with Kell, listening patiently to last-minute instructions regarding everything from strange drinking water to *mal de mare.*

"I think it's time for us to become better acquainted, Tor. Walk with me in the garden where we can be private."

Tor looked uncertainly to Kell for approval. Kell rolled his eyes heavenward. "Dolt! The number one rule is to obey your lady before any other—even me!"

As Diana led the way into the garden, Tor's eyes were no longer merry. "I fear I am a sad choice, lady."

Diana was appalled. Tor had been stripped of his self-confidence and she knew she must restore it at once. "Tor, you are the best possible choice. You are *my* choice. Please don't be distant with me. I want us to be friends; I want to be able to confide in you. In fact, I want to be able to tell you anything."

The frown disappeared from his brow. "You can, lady. I will serve you in any way you wish. Please correct me when I do things wrong, lady."

"Call me Diana. Please don't concern yourself with unimportant things like manners or dress, Tor. Come and sit by the pool so I can confide my fears."

Tor seemed much relieved that she was not overly concerned with manners for he had never been trained as a house slave. "Tell me your fears, Lady Diana."

She bent toward him confidentially. "I hate Romans and fear them." She saw his look of astonishment. "Oh, I love Marcus with all my heart. He is seeking permission for us to marry, but I have this unnamed dread inside me that disaster will befall if I go to Rome."

"I won't let anyone harm you, Lady Diana," Tor vowed.

"I am a Christian but I prefer to keep that hidden while I am in Rome. The Romans do terrible things to Christians. Marcus doesn't want it known I was a slave in his household, either."

"I am a Briton, like you, Lady Diana. Your secrets are sacred to me."

"Thank you, Tor. There is a delicate matter I must confide to you that no one else knows. My husband's brother, Petrius, was here recently for training. He left with Paullinus' army, but he has returned and will accompany us to Rome." Diana's lashes swept her cheeks. "He tried to rape me in the temple."

Tor's hand flew to the handle of the gladius sword Marcus had given him. "I will protect you from Roman slime, lady," he swore intensely. "I am strong. I can lift a horse. My muscles are iron—feel them!" He flexed enormous biceps and Diana placed her hand upon one in amazement.

A sound made her look up at that moment, and there stood Petrius, watching her lay hands on the handsome, half-naked young man who was her personal body slave.

Chapter 24

The two young men glared daggers at each other. "You overstep yourself, slave."

"No, he does not, Petrius," Diana said firmly. "He was chosen by Marcus and acts on his orders. He is sworn to protect me from any and all danger."

Petrius changed his tune immediately. He adjusted the sling about his neck, setting his right arm in a more comfortable position, and gave her a disarming smile. "Marcus has shared the knowledge of his good fortune with me. Let me be the first to welcome you to our family." He took her hand to his lips so gallantly, she could not believe this was the same man who had behaved like a drunken lout or a bestial ravisher.

"Thank you, Petrius. I am sorry you have been injured."

"These things happen. Marcus told me to ask for Kell. I haven't a stitch to my back other than my armor."

"Of course. I'll show you where you may find him." She refrained from pointing out that Marcus was taller and broader than he was. She believed Petrius was well aware of his shortcomings when compared with Marcus. She turned to Tor with a conspiratorial smile. "I'll see you at dawn."

"I will be ready, Lady Diana."

* * *

The barge that left Aquae Sulis at dawn was over-crowded with people and baggage, but when they reached the Bristol Channel and boarded the Roman sailing ship, everything was stowed below and Marcus took Diana to the tiny cabin where they would sleep, which was sandwiched between a similar one for the procurator and a cubbyhole for Petrius. Marcus' legionary guards and the two dozen who traveled with Julius slung hammocks belowdecks and Tor stationed himself outside Diana's door, deciding instantly that was where he would sleep.

The wind was bitter cold and Diana was thankful for her fur-lined cloaks with their warm hoods. When the ship reached the Bay of Biscay, however, it was far too rough for her to be up on deck. Unfortunately, when she retreated below to the small cabin, she experienced seasickness.

Marcus tucked her into the bunk, cleansed her, and ministered to all her needs as tenderly as a mother would a babe. He held her and comforted her as well, and coaxed her gently to put something on her stomach each and every time she retched and emptied it.

She did not begin to feel better until they were well down the coast of Spain, but she managed to recover completely by the time they approached Gibraltar. She stood at the rail with Marcus' arm about her as they sailed through the strait, basking beneath the warm Mediterranean sun. Though she had not thought it possible, she loved Marcus more every day.

Tor was at her side as she walked the decks whenever Marcus was absent. She was both surprised and thankful that Petrius treated her like a princess whenever they came into contact, but she noticed cynically that he spent most of his time cultivating the procurator, who had obviously taken a fatherly interest in the disabled young brother of Marcus Magnus.

One day when the blue sea was calm as a millpond and

the sun beat down gloriously, Diana decided to explore the Roman vessel. It was designed along the lines of Greek ships, except it had a long iron spike mounted on its prow. Tor told her the spike was used to ram into enemy ships, so they could let down a boarding plank for Roman soldiers to fight their way aboard. Diana shuddered, feeling thankful they had encountered no trouble.

She opened a heavy door and descended a flight of wooden steps. She stopped, aghast at what she saw. Rows of men, naked to the waist, sweat dripping from their well-muscled backs, were pulling on huge oars. Her hand covered her mouth in horror, her eyes widened to the size of saucers. Tor took her forcibly by the shoulders, turned her about, and pushed her back up the flight of steps.

On deck she took in great gasps of air, clinging to Tor as if he were a lifeline. Marcus strode along the deck, curious to know why Tor had his arms about Diana. When he was close enough to see that something was wrong with her, Marcus lifted her in his arms and felt her recoil from him.

"Galley slaves!" she gasped with loathing.

He carried her to their cabin and set her on the bunk before he answered her. She looked up at him with such accusing eyes, Marcus threw up his hands. "I cannot believe you are so naive. In the name of the gods, how did you expect our vessel to make the journey from Britannia to Rome? They are not all Britons," he said defensively. "Some of them are Gauls, some Nubian—"

"They are *men,* Marcus, no matter their race. Dear God, how can Romans be so indifferent to human misery? How can you condemn men to a lifetime of slavery in the galleys?"

"It's not a lifetime. It's ten years. Men need to be in their prime to row a galley." When he saw that made it no more acceptable to her, he went down on one knee and took her hand. "Beloved, if I could right the wrongs of the world for you, I would do so. Perhaps there is no slavery in your time, but can you honestly say there is no suffering or injustice? In return for their labors our slaves are well fed and decently housed, and they are so numerous that none are overburdened.''

She thought of London, where the conditions of rich and poor were so disparate. The wealthy ton had an inexhaustible appetite for pleasure and luxury, while barefoot match girls quietly starved on street corners and children were sent down chimneys to sweep them, and often burned to death. Diana reasoned that Marcus could not be blamed for conditions of his time, any more than she could be blamed for the poverty and hunger of hers.

She touched his face. ''By coming to Rome, you are striving to improve conditions for all Britons. I can ask no more of you.''

''We should arrive tomorrow,'' he told her. ''Come up on deck, where you can enjoy the sea and the sunshine.''

That last night aboard, as she lay in his arms, Diana told Marcus what history had recorded of Emperor Nero. ''Avoid him if you can. He is a madman whose reign degenerates into cruelty and tyranny.''

''He murdered his own mother; I know all about Nero,'' Marcus assured her.

''You don't know that three years from now he will burn Rome so that he can build a vast new capital upon her ruins.''

''The City of Rome burns?'' he asked incredulously.

''Yes, but the new Rome will be magnificent and will last down through all the centuries. Nero will blame the fire on the Christians, but he will become so hated there'll be a massive revolt against him and he'll commit suicide before he is thirty-two.''

Marcus stared at the beams in the cabin ceiling and wondered if Diana really had lived in the future or if she simply had prophetic visions like many others claimed to have. He drew her against his heart. So long as they were together today, the past—and the future—didn't matter to him.

Though she had dreaded coming to Rome, now that she was so close, Diana decided to let go of her fear. She had made her decision to be with Marcus and she wanted neither of them to have regrets. She would embrace his city wholeheartedly, as she did all things. Half measures were simply not in her nature. She would look upon it as a gift from the gods. To be able to see and experience ancient Rome was like a miracle. She vowed not to waste one moment in fear or regret.

They disembarked at Ostia at the mouth of the Tiber. The famous river, which would take them to Rome by barge, was wide with turbid yellow water. Marcus stayed by Diana's side so he could point out all the landmarks of the area.

As she had read, she saw that Rome was indeed built upon seven hills. All was a confusion of enormous buildings, gilded roofs, domes, stately phalanxes of marble columns, and private homes with red-tiled roofs. Some were built in the valleys, others on the summits, and still others clinging to the slopes of the hills. Marcus pointed out temples, forums, amphitheatres, and the long hollow that was the great Circus Maximus.

"My father's olive groves lie to the south," he said, pointing out the chain of Sabine hills that stretched in a golden haze toward the horizon. "Our quarries are to the north, in the Apennines, where the River Tiber begins."

"Are they stone quarries as in Aquae Sulis?"

"No, we quarry marble. The marble trade is Rome's greatest commercial enterprise, as you shall see," Marcus said proudly.

"Is your father's villa here in the city?"

"Yes, it is on the slopes of the Esquiline. By now my messenger will have informed him of our arrival. When our river craft docks, horses will be awaiting us, and I requested a grand litter for you."

"Oh, I thought we could walk through the city," Diana said with disappointment.

"Darling, over a million people live here and most of them will be on the streets. Our progress will be so slow, you'll see more than you care to from your litter. We have to pass through some squalid districts before we start to climb the Esquiline, where the patricians' villas are located." He looked into her eyes, his face set in serious lines. "Rome is the crucible for everything good and bad in the world. There is no other city where the divine and the bestial are in such evidence. Don't let it overwhelm you."

When she gave him a reassuring smile, he brushed his lips across her brow, then beckoned Tor. "Find her a seat in the shade on the quay. It will take some time to unload and locate my father's slaves with our horses and litter. The Procurator will be going to his own home from here, so I must go and coordinate our plans before I bid him farewell."

Though Marcus had warned her, Diana was unprepared for the throng of humanity that choked the streets as she gazed in fascination from her ornate silk litter, with its four sturdy litter bearers in pale yellow livery.

Hundreds of small shops were packed together, their counters jutting out onto the pavement to display what looked like their entire stock. Bakeries, vegetable stands, wine shops, and cheap restaurants vied with pottery stalls and clothing stores. At every crossroad were religious street shrines and fountains where water spouted from an eagle's beak, the mouth of a calf, or the breasts of a goddess. The overflowing basins carried away the filthy rubbish, thrown out recklessly from the shops and upper windows.

It seemed that every inch of stuccoed wall was painted with messages and advertisements. Mercury, the god of gain, was painted on the wall of a money-changer, and crude serpents were painted everywhere as guardians. She saw a *celer,* or notice writer, with a noisy crowd gathered about him as he wrote with a piece of red chalk about a gladiator fight in the Amphitheater of Taurus. Everything was written on the walls, from love notes to curses to rude verses. The walls were obviously the writing paper of the masses. If a slave was for sale, his name and attributes went up on the wall. If a garret over a store was for rent, it was also advertised on the wall.

The only thing that Diana found offensive was the incessant noise. People screamed at one another so they could be heard above the racket of corn grinders, builders' hammers, costermongers' cries, schoolmasters who gave their lessons on the streets, and dozens of would-be poets spouting endless diatribes.

Suddenly came the shouts of a dozen Praetorian guards in gilded helmets and breastplates. "Make way, make way," they bawled, pushing slaves and hucksters aside with their spear butts. Even Marcus and his guards had to dismount while the Praetor, a magistrate of the people, passed by.

At the next street they met a procession of priests and priestesses banging drums, blaring trumpets, and waving hands holding castanets and bronze rattles. The women were dark-skinned Syrians, whirling in wild dances, hair flying, on their way to the Temple of Cybele to spend a day of orgy.

Suddenly, Diana's litter came to a halt as another vast procession took precedence. Marcus rode back to her, cursing.

"It must be someone important," she ventured.

A filthy epithet fell from Marcus' lips. "She thinks she's important. Her old husband is a millionaire. There should be a law against such vulgar ostentation."

Diana watched in awe as a great concourse of handsome slaves marched past with boxes and packages on their shoulders. Next came a group of pretty Levantine slave girls in gaudy veils, then an Egyptian boy holding a pet monkey, and a slave girl carrying a yapping lapdog in its basket. Next came the great lady's troupe of musicians, followed by a hundred slaves and freedmen carrying caskets and trunks of valuables and costly garments.

Finally, "Her Magnificence" appeared in a litter borne by eight identical Nubians. She leaned back upon her cushions, bored with the world, indifferently fanning herself with a jewel-handled ostrich fan. Her dark hair was sprinkled with gold dust and Diana's mouth fell open as she saw that the woman wore only a loin dress below her waist and pearls above.

"She's likely moving from her palace to one of her country villas. Even the Praetor had his litter set down while he greeted her," Marcus said with disgust, "which proves that even official rank must yield to the conquering flash of gold."

Diana could feel his outrage at being kept waiting. She smiled up at him. "It gives me a chance to observe everything at my leisure. Look, there's a dice game on the pavement!"

He looked with arrogance at the swarms of people. "Idlers and parasites! Mostly slaves of the wealthy. Their tasks are so few they have too much time on their hands, which they spend gambling and indulging in coarse sexual encounters."

Marcus was embarrassed at how much his city's mores had degenerated. People did things openly in the streets that should have only taken place in privacy. Men pissed in the gutters and whores serviced their customers in doorways. He thanked his gods that Aquae Sulis would never sink to this level.

Finally, they left the more commercial districts behind as they ascended the hills. They now passed larger public buildings such as the baths and temples, and establishments that catered to wealth. Imposing triumphal arches spanned avenues and heroic statues in prancing chariots turned this section of the city into a showplace.

The architecture was in the Greek style, but rather more embellished, and in Diana's opinion, rather vulgar. Each and every column was overdone in the ornate, florid Corinthian style, and the garish blue, green, and orange marble was in rather poor taste, with far too many scrolls and floriated designs.

When they arrived at the villa of Titus Magnus, however, Diana could find no fault in its superb taste, though she was staggered when she contemplated what it must have cost. Its unremarkable exterior only added to the shock of her senses when she stepped through the lofty Ionic pillars of the portal.

All the chambers were built around open courts, each with its garden, pool, and fountain. Light and sun streamed in everywhere. The rooms leading from the first court were both numerous and spacious. An open balcony encircled the upper story. A dozen slaves met them at the entrance, while another dozen entered the atrium, carrying cooled drinks and sweetmeats. All wore pale yellow togas with ram's head insignias on their shoulders.

Diana hung back, watching Marcus and Petrius stride into the first court and greet the older slaves who had been with the family for years. Marcus turned back and brought her forward.

"How many slaves?" she whispered.

"A hundred and fifty when I was here last." He squeezed her hand. "Don't let it overwhelm you." He led her down a magnificent, light-bathed hall until they entered a second court, even larger and handsomer than the first, with another array of dependent chambers. The floors were made of mosaic tile, the walls and pillars of pale Luna marble. In the center, graceful dancing nymphs shot great jets of crystal water into a circular white marble pool, edged with luxurious water plants. Sculptures and fine art objects upon carved pedestals were scattered throughout the villa.

The majordomo, Lucas, greeted Marcus warmly.

"Your father is in his chamber and asks that you go to him. He is not as young and vigorous as you remember him," Lucas cautioned him, "but his pride is still intact. He sends greetings to your lady and will see her at dinner."

Lucas clapped his hands and a dozen olive-skinned slave girls came forward. "I chose these female slaves for your lady. They will have no other duties but to attend her. I have taken the liberty to choose a suit of rooms for her overlooking the peristyle garden, not too distant from your own chambers, General."

Marcus' eyebrows rose with amusement. "The arrangements are rather formal, as is your address, Lucas."

"Now that you are a general, it is only proper to use your formal address. After the wedding you and your bride will require a larger suite."

Marcus' lips twitched as he thought of the separate sleeping arrangements. He would try to be discreet until they were married, when he could openly take Diana to his bed.

"Put yourself in the girls' hands," Marcus told Diana. "I know you are longing to bathe and change your clothes. If you don't have enough maids, there are plenty more female slaves with idle hours to fill."

The girls led Diana away and Tor followed doggedly, his hand on his flagellum. Once they were all inside her sleeping chamber, they giggled and touched his muscles with delight. Tor looked as though he'd died and gone to heaven.

One of the slave girls turned to Diana to speak. "My name is Livi, my lady. Do we have your permission to see to your bodyguard's needs, as well as yours?"

Tor rolled his eyes in supplication toward Diana. The corners of her mouth went up with the wickedness of her thoughts. "I want you to keep him happy. Do you suppose you could take turns? He will sleep in the adjoining chamber. Does it have a couch?"

The girls opened the adjoining door to show them that

indeed the chamber was furnished with a sleeping couch. She stepped into the room with him for a moment.

"Thank you, Lady Diana," Tor said fervently.

"Keep your weapon ready at all times," she cautioned with a straight face.

"I will, lady," he assured her.

"I feel sure Livi and her girls will be able to keep you reasonably happy. The question is, are you up to keeping them happy?" Laughing, Diana went through the door into her own chamber, leaving Tor grinning from ear to ear.

Chapter 25

Petrius coveted his father's wealth. He had always been wildly jealous that Marcus was firstborn and the heir. But at least until now he had been Marcus' sole heir. As Primus Pilus, then general in the Roman army, the odds were against his brother surviving past his prime. Until now all Petrius had to exercise was patience, and everything would be his. Now that Marcus was about to marry, however, all that would change. Marcus' children would become his heirs and Petrius would receive only a small share of the family wealth.

On the voyage to Rome, he had done his utmost to persuade Marcus against marriage. He had vilified women in general as faithless bitches who sold themselves to the highest bidder. He pointed out that a concubine could be controlled; a wife could not. But when his insinuations moved from women in general to Diana, Marcus had not taken it kindly. Especially when Petrius hinted of impropriety with her virile young bodyguard. His brother's black eyes had glittered dangerously.

"I think I am capable of controlling my woman, Petrius. Keep your vile tongue and your vile thoughts from her, if you wish to remain healthy."

"Marcus, you mistake me. It's the shackles of matrimony I warn you against, not Diana. If your mind is made up to marry, you couldn't have chosen a more beautiful bride."

Petrius had only one avenue left open to him, before he would be forced to do something quite drastic. When he went in to greet his father, he was dismayed to learn that the old man's brain had not deteriorated along with his body.

"There is a most serious matter I must bring to your attention, Father. Marcus is a love-sick fool who cannot see that this woman marries him for gain. She cannot wait to get her hands on your wealth. I swear to you she was his slave. Your grandsons will be the offspring of a slave!"

Titus closed his eyes to ease the pain Petrius' words brought him. After a moment's silence he opened his eyes and looked at his handsome son. "You think I should change my will." It was a statement, rather than a question.

"Yes, I do, Father. If he is determined to bring shame upon the House of Magnus, he should not receive the lion's share of our wealth. The woman is a slut who fornicates with her own bodyguard. She even accepted my advances."

"She must be very beautiful to tempt you, Petrius."

"She is. She tempts every man who glimpses her."

"Beauty can be a curse, Petrius. I believe your beauty is a curse. I shall change my will. But I'm afraid it won't make you very happy. You see, I, too, am cursed, Petrius. Cursed by one son while being blessed by the other. I had hoped a military career would at least cure you of cowardice, but even that was too much to expect. Get you from my sight!"

Petrius flung from the chamber, and then the villa. So be it. The old tyrant had sealed his doom. Petrius was being forced to do something drastic, and do it soon before his father had a chance to change his will.

Though he was very sick, Marcus' father had one of his personal body slaves lift him from his couch into a chair. He was too proud to receive his firstborn son in bed.

But even so, the pallor of his skin and the amount of weight he had lost betrayed to Marcus the extent of his father's illness.

Marcus was shocked at how much his father had aged, but he was relieved to see that the burning intensity of life still glowed in his dark eyes. Marcus dropped to his knees so they could embrace.

A blunt, unsentimental man, Titus said baldly, "I have lost the use of my legs, but as a result my brain is twice as sharp."

Marcus grinned at him. "You always were the most intelligent and astute man I ever met. I am happy to see the years have not altered that."

"So you have brought a bride home at last. I quite despaired of grandchildren. She must be something special to meet your exacting standards."

Marcus raised an eyebrow, a protest on his lips.

Titus lifted a commanding hand to stay his words. "You are too much like me. You have such lofty principles, you expect the same from others. Duty before pleasure; death before dishonor. Your gods are truth and justice."

"You make me sound insufferable."

"We both are. Wherever did you find a paragon worthy of you?" he asked with amusement.

"She is a Briton, as intelligent as she is lovely. I hope you will give us your blessing, Father."

Titus' black eyes met those of his beloved son's and held. "Marcus, your choice is my choice."

Marcus knew they shared a bond that nothing could ever tear asunder. Their love for each other was unconditional and absolute.

"Now, tell me of this mission you and Julius Classicianus have. If you are to persuade Nero and the Senate to aught, it won't hurt to have unlimited bribes at your disposal. My wealth is your wealth, Marcus; you know that."

Marcus told him of the plan to bring about a change that would benefit the entire nation of Britannia. He deeply appreciated the offer of his father's wealth for the noble cause and assured Titus he would never use it for personal gain. When he took his leave, Marcus felt assured his father knew he did not covet his wealth, as his brother Petrius did.

When Marcus went up to Diana's suite to take her down to dinner, he was delighted that she had chosen an elegant stola of jade green with a gold tissue palla and gold sandals with high cork soles. Her hair looked prettier than he had ever seen it, except when it was spread across his pillow. It had been fashioned in a cascade of curls that fell down her back and was threaded with green ribbon and seed pearls.

When they reached the triclinium, the white-haired Titus Magnus already reclined upon his dining couch, and Marcus was glad that he had not mentioned his father's disability to Diana. She was so tenderhearted she would have treated the older man with an overabundance of kindness, when Marcus knew he much preferred to be treated as a man.

Marcus brought Diana forward with such pride that his father knew how deeply he felt about this woman. Titus liked her immediately. Not only was she beautiful enough to steal a man's breath away, but there was a delicacy about her fair coloring that reminded him of an alabaster sculpture of a goddess. Was it Venus? No, it was Diana, her namesake. "A thousand welcomes, my dear. I hope my son will make you happy."

"He has done that already, my lord." The swift glance she cast Marcus told Titus how much she loved his son.

"Sit by me. A beautiful woman is better than any tonic for an old man."

As Marcus watched them, it amused him that his father was actually flirting with Diana and it warmed his heart that she was kind enough to flirt back, just a trifle.

The food and the service were impeccable, as only upper house slaves were allowed to prepare and serve food in the villa of Magnus. When the meal drew to a close, Diana smiled at her future husband's father. "You have a magnificent home. Thank you for making me feel so welcome."

"Has Marcus given you the grand tour? Then go, go. Show her how she may dine in the pool without ever getting wet. Show her the birds and the fish. Show her everything."

Marcus took her outside to the garden and bade her sit on a white marble couch in the pool. Jets of water gushed from beneath the couch as if forced out when she reclined against the pillows, but there was an underground outlet, so the pool filled but never overflowed, and the couch seemed to float.

"When you dine here, the heavier dishes are set by the ledge of the basin, but the lighter dishes in the shape of boats and swans float on the surface and turn round and round."

Boxwood trees were cut into the shape of animals, and roses bloomed in great abundance. "Beyond the three outdoor bathing pools is a private suite of rooms with enchanting views over the gardens. The bedchamber is soundproof and excludes all light and noise. Adjoining it is a private dining room. Once we are married, we can spend time there."

"I realize we will have to occupy separate suites until we are married. We must not be indiscreet in your father's house."

"He would lecture me severely if I did not treat you like a vestal virgin."

They went back inside. "Please don't ask me to show you the jeweled frescoes or the family temple or the library tonight. There is something else I want you to see."

"Where are you taking me?" she asked innocently as they climbed the marble and ivory staircase.

"To see my chamber."

Diana was much impressed with the grandeur of his suite. The walls were painted with a series of pictures showing the campaigns of Alexander. The massive bed was carved with rams' horns, and a balcony looked over the garden and the ornamental fish ponds.

"It suits you. It is completely masculine. Perhaps I shouldn't be here, Marcus."

"Did my father not tell me to show you everything?"

"Yes, but—oh, what are you doing?" she cried in dismay as he began to strip off his clothes.

"I'm showing you everything," he said with a wide grin.

"You are a devil, Marcus Magnus. You know we must sleep apart!"

He threw back his head and his laughter rolled about the chamber. "No power on earth could keep you from my bed tonight. All too soon I'll be off with Julius on official business. He agreed to let me come home to see my father on condition that I would stay with him for a week or two while we entertain the senators, individually as well as en masse. His summons could arrive as early as tomorrow."

She came to him shyly as he sat naked on the bed. "Do you honestly think you'll get permission to marry?"

"Julius assures me it's just a formality. If the wheels of officialdom grind too slowly, I'll oil them with a bribe, never fear. I'm sorry to desert you, love, but there will likely only be enough time to make preparations for the wedding feast and have a wedding dress made. I have the most magnificent ring tucked away and my father will likely give you jewels for a marriage gift."

She reached up to unwind the ribbons from her curls. "Are you bribing me to be complacent about the bacchanalia you will be attending?"

He opened his knees and drew her against him. "To say nothing of the orgies," he teased. When he saw her innocent look of vulnerability, his face softened. "The only activities I plan to indulge in are visits to the games and the races at Circus Maximus, to which all Romans are addicted, I'm afraid."

"Enjoy your city without feeling guilty, Marcus. You know I would hate those things."

He slipped off her stola and tossed it to the floor. She stood before him adorned in only her sandals and her gold half-coin. When he unclasped the delicate chain and refastened it about her tiny waist, she shivered. Marcus' eyes smoldered at the erotic picture she made. "Tonight we'll do only those things you love with a passion," he said huskily.

When Marcus arrived at the Procurator's residence, he learned that Julius Classicianus had arranged to take a half-dozen senators to the games that afternoon. Also invited was a military administrator who could provide Marcus with official permission to marry.

"I'm sorry I didn't bring my brother, Petrius, with me, Julius. The young devil disappeared into the bowels of Rome the moment we arrived. Once he's indulged all the vices of youth, I'm sure he'll show up."

"He already showed up, my friend. I took him to court last night and introduced him to the emperor. He and Nero took to each other immediately. I expect it was your brother's beauty that attracted Nero. But I believe Petrius has a certain amount of cunning he'll use to our benefit. We are fortunate to have him in our arena."

Marcus devoutly hoped so. Petrius would use his cunning to benefit himself, but if he was willing to exploit Nero's vices, it could save them all time and trouble.

When they arrived at the Claudian Amphitheatre, Marcus was amazed to see Petrius sitting with the emperor and his friends. They were laughing together with such intimate ease, one would have thought Petrius a longtime member of the inner circle.

Julius took Marcus forward to meet the emperor and he hailed him with a military salute, rather than exchanging the kiss of greeting that was gaining favor throughout the city.

"Another Magnus brother, though not of the same mold. Welcome back to Rome. Tomorrow there is to be *venatione,* in my name at the Circus Flavian. You and Julius must honor me with your presence. I guarantee you have never seen anything like it. As well as lions and leopards, there are to be bears. They have been busy for a week designing mountains and caves and they have even put in a small forest."

"That should be quite a spectacle, Emperor," Julius said with the necessary enthusiasm.

Petrius hailed his brother with an insolent wave of his hand. The look he gave Marcus clearly implied that he could influence Nero to do his bidding. And indeed, Petrius was thoroughly enjoying his new position of prestige.

The gladiator bouts were many and varied, with several at a time taking place to entertain the thousands who were gathered in the amphitheatre. The masses loved the games, which were free to all. They cheered the valiant, booed unsportsmanlike behavior, and made wagers as to the outcome. The most interesting combats were between the *retiarus,* who fought with nets and tridents, and the *secutors,* who fought with the traditional helmet, sword, and shield.

Marcus surreptitiously watched his brother and the plump Nero continuously whisper to each other. He wondered what they spoke of so earnestly, but if he had been able to hear them, he would have been sickened.

"Are you enjoying the games?" Nero asked, twirling the rings on his pudgy fingers.

"I like more bloodletting," Petrius replied with a gleam. "When a defeated gladiator begs for mercy, the crowd always obliges."

Nero smirked. "I, too, like to see men die, but I have to be satisfied with the wounding; I cannot go against the masses."

"You do not realize your full power, Emperor. I wager that if you turn thumbs down on the next man defeated, it won't be long before you sway the thousands gathered here.''

The two gladiators before the emperor's eagle-decorated box fought on and on. They were well matched, but finally the larger man disarmed his opponent and placed a victorious foot on his neck. The crowd went wild, cheering and collecting their wagers. When the fallen man lifted his arm for mercy, Nero suddenly turned thumbs down on him. The collective voice of the crowd protested, and Nero's hand wavered.

"Courage!" Petrius urged and stretched out his own hand with the thumb turned down.

The victorious gladiator plunged his short sword into the fallen man's heart. The crowd gasped. When the victor withdrew his weapon and held it on high so that the blood dripped down his arm, the crowd began to cheer.

Nero grinned at Petrius with delight. When the next gladiator fell, the masses turned thumbs down on him and cheered with bloodlust when the victor slashed the defeated man's throat wide open, so that his lifeblood spurted into the sand.

"It feels good to kill," Nero whispered, sexually aroused.

"It feels even better when your hand wields the sword."

"You are a centurion. It is easy for you; difficult for me," Nero said, placing his pudgy hand on Petrius' solid thigh.

"Difficult, but not impossible, Emperor." Petrius' eyes lingered on Nero's rouged mouth. "Why don't we retire to a more private place where I can suggest many things that will appeal to your appetite."

Nero's hand squeezed his new favorite's knee. "Just one more bout?" he whispered avidly.

Marcus Magnus felt a great sadness come over him. He wanted to get his young brother away from the deviate Nero. But it was too late. Petrius was the one doing the corrupting, and if he could teach depravity to one as evil as Nero, he was beyond redemption. With Petrius it wasn't about sex, it was about power. Marcus knew he was in his glory manipulating the Emperor of Rome. To see them walk off together after the bouts put a great sadness in his heart.

In Nero's opulent chamber the air was heavy with perfume sprayed from jets in the high ceiling. At twenty-five, Nero was no longer aroused by women. He had turned to men, but the limp-wristed slaves available by the score did not have much appeal. They abased themselves too easily and could not bear much pain or cruelty, either to themselves or to others.

The young emperor preferred more muscular partners, who were not squeamish when he wished to flagellate them and were also strong enough to hold a victim powerless while he inflicted more inventive tortures. They were ugly devils, both unemotional and insensitive, with bovine intelligence, but their large physical attributes brought him release.

Petrius Magnus was different. Nero hadn't been this excited about a lover in years. The young man had the beauty of a woman and the hard body of a centurion. He also understood the narcotic of bloodlust. He was that rare being: a beautiful brute.

Nero sprawled upon his purple silk couch while Petrius undressed him. They indulged in arousing talk to keep the emperor erect. "A few weeks ago I decided to experiment with one of those deranged Christians. I had his prick tied with a leather thong, then I made him drink and keep on drinking. I was curious to see what would happen when he became overfilled, but couldn't relieve himself by pissing."

"Was it arousing?" asked Petrius, slowly removing his own tunic.

"Not really. I thought his prick would swell to enormous proportions. It was slightly amusing, though. He became drunk on plain water. When he began to run around, screaming, he kept falling down. But his bladder burst and he died much too quickly.''

Petrius was naked now, except for a black leather sheath he wore over his cock, held in place by a strap about his lithe hips. Some centurions wore them for penile protection in battle. Nero became stiff the moment he laid eyes upon the black obscenity. Petrius, however, wanted Nero aroused to madness before he gave him release. So he described in detail how many bloody wounds could be inflicted and exactly where, and how to hold off death for hours while the blood oozed and seeped.

When Nero was panting with need, Petrius pushed him back upon his couch and fellated him. There was no way he was going to take Nero's short, fat prick into his body. Nero looked down upon him with adoration as Petrius' long silken lashes swept his cheeks and his beautiful mouth sucked him dry.

Then Petrius ordered Nero on his knees. The power that surged through Petrius' body when the Emperor of Rome obeyed his command was like nothing he had ever known before. This was pleasure! And before Petrius was done with him, Nero would obey all his commands, not just for sexual purposes. He would take control of Nero's very soul. That would be power; that would be glory!

Chapter 26

Marcus received official permission to marry before the day was over. He sat down that night to write to Diana and impart his good news. She had been worried that consent would be withheld, which proved that she longed to marry him. An unnamed urgency within him told him to secure her. He reasoned that once she was legally his, she could not go back whence she'd come, nor would the gods snatch her away from him.

He had never written a love letter before and found he could not pour out his heart on the wax tablet. Consequently, it read like a military communiqué. When he re-read it, he grimaced at the authoritative tone and forced himself to add a flowery sentence or two.

> *Each day apart has a hundred hours; each*
> *night a thousand. Make all necessary prepara-*
> *tion so we can be wed the moment I return.*
> *My heart is in your keeping.*
> > *Your husband, Marcus.*

He was beginning to see things as Diana saw them. Where once he would have enjoyed gladiatorial games, he could now see that they illustrated completely the pitiless spirit and carelessness of human life, lurking behind the pomp, glitter, and cultural pretention of imperialism.

He and Julius had spent the evening wining and dining certain senators, and tomorrow night would be more of the same. Marcus felt drained. This was far more exhausting than a fourteen-hour day training legionaries to cross a raging river. Petrius had not attended the banquet and Marcus tried to keep his thoughts from how his brother was spending the night.

As it turned out, Petrius was introducing Nero to another of life's evil pleasures. The streets of Rome were dark and dangerous at night. There were no street lights, and after sundown, silence blanketed the elite avenues that earlier had swarmed with life.

The Subura's squalid streets and alleys, however, were filled with rumbling carts and wagons bringing in food supplies. They were forbidden from Rome's congested streets during daylight hours. Ordinary citizens usually did not stir outdoors at night, for in spite of the watch, there were sneak thieves, cutpurses, and open bandits known as *siccarii,* or dagger men.

Wealthier citizens who spent their evenings dining with influential friends were accompanied by slaves with torches. The upper classes could not resist braving the darkness for dinner, which was the crowning event of a Roman's day. So it had recently become fashionable for lawless young nobles to indulge in the evil pleasures of ranging the dark streets and beating harmless and poorly guarded citizens.

Petrius, Nero, and a select number of the emperor's Praetorian guards who were also his intimates donned masks and armed themselves with bludgeons, daggers, and other assorted weapons. Petrius promised Nero that when he bloodied his first sword the thrill would be orgasmic. As an added fillip to their game, they would have a treasure hunt. At dawn they would compare the souvenirs they had collected and see who had won. Points would be given for fingers, ears, and noses, with the highest number of points awarded for the ultimate prize: a severed penis!

* * *

Livi and Diana's other female slaves described to her all the details of a Roman wedding. She would be married in a *tunica recta,* a garment woven in one piece, a robe of extremely good omen. About her waist would be a sash tied with a complicated Knot of Hercules for her bridegroom to untie. She could wear nothing beneath the robe, but would wear a flowing veil over her hair with a garland of flowers to hold it in place that must be picked by her own hand and interspersed with sprigs of the sacred herb verbena.

The ceremony itself was a simple civil affair, with no religious rites required. However, there was always a sacrifice with a soothsayer to examine the entrails to see if the signs were favorable. At the altar, the groom himself, with no priest or official, would put the direct question, "Will you be my *mater familias*?" Then in turn the bride would ask, "Will you be my *pater familias*?" Amid the cries of congratulations, they would place cake and wine upon the altar and dedicate them to Jupiter and Juno.

Livi told her there was always a wedding procession, where the bride clings to her mother and the groom tears her away and carries her to his house, followed by flute players who lead all the guests after the newlyweds. The custom was a remembrance of the rape of the Sabines.

Titus Magnus asked Diana to describe to him exactly what she wanted in the way of wedding finery and he would have Lucas order it. When the sandalwood boxes arrived and Diana saw how beautiful the garments were, a lump of gratitude came into her throat, and her eyes became liquid with tears. He had told her the veil could be any color she desired, so in a moment of recklessness she chose red, the antithesis of what would be *respectable* for a Georgian bride.

The gauzy, flame-colored silk veil she lifted from the box had been imported from distant China and was worth its weight in gold. The cream-colored tunica recta was indeed woven in one piece, but it was embroidered with creamy roses that had crystals scattered across the petals like drops of dew. The cream leather slippers were encrusted with pearls.

Diana found Titus in his library, and when he learned how delighted she was with his simple gifts, he longed to see the look upon her face when she received the jewels he had chosen for her. Rome's most famous jeweler had visited that morning and Titus had chosen diamonds for his new daughter. He wanted a large amethyst added to the center of the necklace to match her lovely eyes and paid extra to have the work done immediately.

The older man and the younger woman found they were most companionable. The library was their favorite room in the villa. When Titus asked her to read to him, she was more flattered than she had ever been in her life. Titus loved a glass of Setinian wine, which Diana poured from the decanter on the library sideboard, rather than call in a slave to disturb their privacy. They repeated this ritual in the afternoons and again in the evenings. It was a poignant reminder of the precious days she had spent with her own father.

"Livi has given me all the details of a Roman wedding. It is amazingly similar to our own in Britannia, except in one detail." Diana hesitated, then plunged ahead. "Must there be a blood sacrifice?"

"It is a time-honored custom. The guests would be disappointed; the slaves would whisper that it was a bad omen."

"Life is precious. I don't wish anything to sacrifice its life because of me," she said earnestly.

"Do you not eat meat and wear leather shoes, Diana?" he asked quietly.

"Yes, I do." She smiled apologetically. "I know I'm being irrational."

"Join me in a glass of Setinian."

When she poured the wine and handed him his glass,

he took her hand. "If the slaves wish to examine entrails, they will have to do it on the animals slaughtered for the feast. I will not see you unhappy on your wedding day. It should be the happiest day of your life."

"I hope the guests realize there will be no procession."

"Of course there will. We'll have a procession all through the villa and out into the peristyle to the garden suite. The pillars to the entrance will be wound with wool and the door touched with oil, the emblems of plenty. Marcus will lift you over the threshold to avoid an ill-omened stumble, then present you with a cup of water and a glowing firebrand to show that you are entitled to the protection of his family gods."

She smiled at him. "Marcus is all the protection I shall ever need."

Marcus' eyes widened when he saw the transformation that had taken place inside Circus Flavian. It was exactly as Nero had described it, with mountainous caves and a forest. Though no animals had yet been released for the hunt, their growls and roars could be heard all over the arena.

Julius sat between two influential senators, as did Marcus. The emperor's box was surrounded by Praetorian guards, but Nero and his intimates had not yet arrived. Since the *venatione* was being given in the emperor's honor, the hunt could not begin until he arrived.

When the crowds became restless, a troupe of musicians brought out dancing apes on long chains. They were trained to do circus tricks and it held the attention of the masses for some time. When this began to pall and the crowds screamed for action, the *bestiarii* gladiators who would hunt the animals were paraded around the arena. The audience began to select their favorites and place bets. Their weapons were varied. Some carried spears, some bows and arrows, while other gladiators preferred swords or nets and tridents.

Finally Nero arrived, and when he stepped to the front of his imperial box and raised his arms, the crowd went wild. Petrius sat down behind Marcus and leaned forward to whisper to his brother.

"The fat swine thinks they worship him, when in reality they are in a frenzy for the bloodsport to begin."

When Marcus turned to look at his brother, the pupils of Petrius' eyes told him he had taken a heavy dose of narcotic and wondered if he had taken it for pain.

"How is your arm?" Marcus asked.

Petrius made a fist. "I can't feel a thing. Don't look so worried." He let his fingers fall open. "I have him in the palm of my hand."

And that was exactly what was beginning to worry Marcus. Petrius was unstable. Perhaps he should speak to Julius about him. The young son-of-a-bitch needed locking up somewhere before he did irreparable damage. Marcus decided to take him aside and have a word with him after the games.

Suddenly, a deafening cheer reverberated about the arena as the animals were released. Pandemonium reigned as lions, leopards, and bears began attacking each other. Male lions fought each other, huge bears tore into leopards and tossed them across the arena floor. Cunning female lions hunted the bears in packs and the carnage was horrific. The gladiators had an easy job slaughtering the wild animals while all their instincts were focused on surviving attacks from the other species of animals.

Marcus was disgusted. He had expected an exhilarating hunt where man was pitted against prey and survival depended upon courage, quickness, strength, and intelligence.

Julius and the senators with Marcus seemed to find this appalling spectacle as distasteful as he did. Marcus could not help voicing his disapproval.

"I think we've seen enough," Julius said as they filed down to the front of the box to take leave of the emperor.

He seemed displeased at their departure.

"Surely you are not leaving? Midday is reserved for executions. I have devised some spectacular tortures for the enemies of Rome."

One of the senators from an old patrician family spoke up. "The Senate is sitting this afternoon, Emperor. We are on our way to the Curia now."

Nero knew better than to object when a venerable senator spoke. Though he was emperor, the senate enjoyed such prestige and moral authority that Nero paid them lip-service. They could depose him if they so chose. Though the army and the emperor were powerful, the supreme power of the empire rested with the Senate.

When Marcus saw that Petrius intended to stay on with Nero to enjoy the executions, he fixed his brother with an intense look of authority. When Marcus jerked his head, indicating that Petrius attend him, he obeyed immediately.

Marcus walked Petrius a distance away from Julius and the senators before he vilified him. "I covered for you when you deserted your military post, and if you wish to prostitute yourself for Nero, that is your affair, but do not bring shame upon the House of Magnus or bring sorrow to our father by feeding your narcotic addiction in his villa. Get yourself clean before you dare to enter his house again!"

When Petrius returned to the emperor's side, Nero saw that he was shaken. "What troubles you, my love? Tell Nero, so he may put it right."

"My brother, Marcus, and I are very close. He is to be married soon to a Briton and he fears she has betrayed him. He has heard a rumor that she is a Christian spy working for the Celtae tribes, sent to seduce him. Marcus fears for our father while he is absent with the procurator and the senators. He begs me to return to our father's villa to watch the traitorous bitch until he can deal with her himself."

"Stay by me. I'll send a Praetorian guard to arrest her," Nero urged.

"Nay, he has no proof of her perfidy yet, but it is comforting to know that you are ready to help and will personally mete out a fitting punishment if she lifts a hand against the House of Magnus."

"At least stay for the executions. I have devised what I call a *living torch*. It is quite spectacular!"

Diana spent the morning in the garden learning how to make a bridal wreath of flowers and verbena, then she had a delicious lunch in the pool. On her way to the library to read to Titus, Tor stopped her to plead for a respite from his unexpected duties. "Lady Diana, please find duties for Livi and the other girls. They won't leave me alone."

"You look exhausted. Didn't you get any sleep last night?"

Tor shook his head. "When you are in the library with the general's father, I am at their mercy."

"There is an office next door to the library. I'll inform them you must write some letters for me."

"Lady, I cannot read and write," he said miserably.

"They don't know that," she pointed out.

Diana summoned Livi, who was idling behind the pillars, waiting for her to enter the library. "I need Tor to handle some correspondence for me this afternoon. Take your girls upstairs and tidy my chambers." She winked at Tor. "Rest while the opportunity presents itself."

Diana found Titus in a talkative mood, full of reminiscences of his own marriage, the birth of his firstborn, and what Marcus was like as a boy. Diana could have listened to him praise Marcus forever, and hoped she would be able to give her husband a child in his own image.

She poured Titus a glass of Setinian and sat down on a stool beside his couch. She was wearing a deep magenta-colored gown that made her eyes a darker shade of amethyst and contrasted so beautifully with her pale gold hair. Titus was admiring her over the rim of his glass. Suddenly, his throat burned like fire. He clawed at it and the glass fell from his fingers.

Diana's eyes widened in horror as she watched the wine stain his snow white toga and heard the hideous gurgles that came from his throat. She felt paralyzed. She knew he needed immediate assistance, yet she knew also it was too late. She tried to cry out, but it was a silent cry she emitted. She stumbled toward the door to summon Lucas, but it was Petrius who strode into the library with an accusation already on his lips.

"You have poisoned my father!"

"Nay!" she gasped, turning back to Titus, who lay still upon his couch, a grotesque grimace of pain frozen on his face.

Petrius drew his dagger and advanced toward her.

"Tor!" Diana screamed. He burst through the door immediately, his hand upon the hilt of his sword, but before he could even draw it from its sheath, Petrius plunged his long dagger into Tor's belly and ripped it open.

Diana screamed again as she watched the nightmare unfold before her eyes. As Tor writhed on the mosaic tiles, desperately trying to prevent his intestines from spilling out onto the floor, Petrius knelt and slit the boy's throat.

Lucas and a dozen household slaves crowded in at the door. Petrius turned to them with cold deliberation. "She poisoned my father! Her slave tried to kill me."

"No!" Diana sobbed. "He did it!"

Lucas knew that Marcus' bride and Titus loved each other. "Nay, she would never harm him!" Lucas protested.

Petrius was unbelievably calm. With unnerving calculation, he said, "If she did not poison the wine, it must have been one of the slaves. You know what happens when a slave murders his master . . . the entire household is put to death."

Lucas stepped back in horror. Only last month a household of two hundred were crucified for murdering their cruel master.

"Lucas, send immediately for the *Praefectus Vigilum*. I will secure her in the strongroom until he arrives."

Diana was grieving for Marcus. He would be devastated over his father's death. Petrius grabbed her by the hair. He brandished the knife still dripping Tor's blood.

"When my brother learns what you have done, it will break his heart." Petrius smiled.

"Marcus would not believe such unspeakable evil of me." Tears of pain and distress streamed down her cheeks. He dragged her to the cellars where the strongroom was located. It had a heavy door, barred windows, and a set of stocks and manacles for locking up disobedient slaves.

He forced her to her knees and manacled her wrists to the floor. Then he took her chin in his hand, compelling her to look at him.

"You were too fine to spread yourself for me. You and Marcus conspire to rob me of my father's land and wealth, but I shall get it all, and you, my beautiful bitch, will get your just deserts."

When he locked the door, fear almost suffocated her. She knew now that he must be insane. He had poisoned his own father for gain and planned it so she would be blamed. When she thought of Tor, lying dead because he had run to her aid, her burden of guilt doubled.

She tried to swallow her fear and think rationally. Marcus would have to be informed of his father's death. Of course Petrius would fill his brother's ears with his filthy lies, but Marcus would know she was innocent of murder. Diana could not rid her nostrils of the metallic smell of blood. A sob escaped her lips. Marcus would come. Marcus would protect her, from the entire world if necessary. Hadn't she told Titus that Marcus was all the protection she would ever need?

Chapter 27

Diana couldn't stop trembling. Her throat was raw from screaming her innocence, her head throbbed from Petrius' vicious hair-pulling, and her hopes of being delivered from her nightmare were fading away.

When the *Praefectus Vigilum* arrived, he believed every word the vile Petrius Magnus uttered. Diana made so many denials she began to babble. Petrius insisted she was his brother's slave, and as a result she had been transported to the *ergastula,* the underground slave prison where the very scum of slave criminals were fettered each night in what could only be described as kennels.

The stench of human misery made the air fetid. There were hundreds of prisoners, some no more than children, but most of them were men either sentenced to hard labor or sentenced to death. They stared at her elegant magenta stola and her pale golden hair as if she were some sort of freak, and within the first hour she was thanking God for her manacles and those of the other slaves. They were the only things that stood between her and total violation.

Petrius returned to Nero the moment he left the *ergastula.* The blood rushing through his veins was almost singing. This had been the most exhilarating day of his life, and it was not yet over. When he anticipated tomorrow, his blood rushed even faster. It was exactly like a play unfolding upon a vast stage, which had all the elements of a Greek tragedy. Not only was Petrius the leading actor, he was also the author!

He threw himself upon the emperor's breast, allowing the anguish to flow from him. His suffering and pain seemed so real, it greatly excited Nero.

"I cannot tell my brother of our father's death, I cannot . . . I cannot!" he sobbed.

"She shall be sentenced to death. Her suffering shall be greater than yours. I can have her brought here tonight, if you wish. Torture her, and as you watch her die, it will assuage your pain."

Petrius was sorely tempted. He'd like to fuck her to death! But Diana's suffering was not his ultimate goal. Petrius wanted revenge against Marcus. He wanted his brother's suffering to be purest agony.

"Nay, my pain matters little. It is the thought of my brother's pain that consumes me. He is to attend the races at Circus Maximus tomorrow. He has looked forward to seeing them for years. I cannot tell him of our father's death unless I can assuage his pain. His need for revenge upon the woman he brought into our father's home must be satisfied immediately. If I could give Marcus this gift, it would help me repay him for all he has done for me."

"Petrius, that is an excellent suggestion. She shall be put to death in the morning at Circus Maximus. It will be spectacular. Half of Rome will be there to witness justice. I will turn her into a living torch!"

"And lions, I should like lions." Petrius could see that Nero was becoming aroused.

"Yes, yes. It shall be another race the people may wager upon. Which will reach her first, the starving beasts or the flames?"

"How may I thank you, Emperor?"

Petrius need not have asked. Nero was already on his knees.

Magnus found that sleep eluded him. Earlier, he had spoken before the senators at the Curia and had done so with eloquence. When he spoke of Britannia and Aquae Sulis, his words were from the heart. He felt passionately about that corner of the empire, where he had spent so many years, and every senator present felt that passion and knew the sincerity of his words.

After his speech, Julius Classicianus, Britannia's procurator, added the weight of his own words, and as they mingled with the senators after the meeting, they felt confident that they had accomplished their mission in persuading the senate to recall Paullinus as governor of Britannia. Already they were suggesting names of men who could replace him.

Over dinner, Julius told Marcus he was well pleased with what they had accomplished. He was acquainted with Petronius Turpilianus, the name that had been put forth most often. He had long experience in the military and had been a successful governor of Nimes in Gaul.

"It won't happen overnight, the mills of officialdom grind slowly, but we have set the wheels in motion and a change for the better is inevitable. I deeply appreciate your help, Marcus. If you hadn't accompanied me to Rome, it may have taken forever. How can I repay you?"

"By attending my wedding. You will be one of the few guests Diana knows."

"I expect you are anxious to return to your lovely bride."

Anxious doesn't describe what I feel. I am empty without her.

"After the races tomorrow, I intend to return to my father's villa. I can wait no longer to be married. If you need me further, I will be happy to return, *after* the fact."

"How impetuous you are. Still, love is so fleeting, you must grab hold and savor it while it lasts."

As Marcus lay abed, he reflected upon Julius' words and realized he disagreed. *True love, the kind of love I have, is everlasting,* Marcus thought. *I will love Diana throughout eternity.* He stretched his limbs. The bed was so empty without her. Not only the bed; he, too, was empty, almost bereft.

He closed his eyes and breathed deeply in an effort to assuage the ache of loneliness. Her scent stole to him and then a vision of her face filled his head. She had a radiance about her that was unique, special. The ache became sharper. Now he wished with all his heart he had gone to her tonight. He could manage without Circus Maximus a lot easier than he could manage without her. In the quiet of the night he imagined she called to him as he drifted into a light sleep. "Soon, my love, soon," he murmured.

As Diana crouched in fear and misery, gradually she heard the words of the slaves about her. They spoke of beatings, lashings, and brandings. She saw that many had letters burned into their foreheads. At dawn each day coffles of slaves were taken to grist mills, chained to the grindstones, and driven by the lash to toil like donkeys. Other chain gangs, many of them male children, worked the fields until darkness fell. Others hauled concrete, stone, and marble fifteen hours a day to fill the constant demand for new buildings.

They spoke of loaded whips with leaden balls on the thongs and flesh-eating carp, kept in ponds behind the slave pens. There was also talk of a slave revolt. The one led by Spartacus over a hundred years ago had never been forgotten, but Diana heard the apathy and hopelessness in their voices and knew a revolt would never come to pass.

All wished they could be sold to train as gladiators, for most of them knew that this way they would only end up in the arena to give sport to the bears or lions. At least as gladiators, they would have a chance of victory. Finally, they spoke of crucifixion and the more common death on the *furca,* where the victim's head is placed at the opening of two V-shaped beams and the professional floggers lash them to death.

Diana could bear no more and blocked out their voices. Did Romans not realize slavery's brutality was soul-destroying to master as well as slave? She should never have come to Rome. She had known it all along. The refined luxury of the fortunate few was purchased by the squalor and lifelong suffering of the brutalized many. How could Romans close their ears to the discordant sounds of misery, the clink of fetters, the snap of whips, the groans of human cattle?

"Marcus . . . Marcus," she whispered, hope still flickering in her heart.

At dawn the slave pens were emptied except for the handful who were to be executed that day. When two Praetorian guards came to fetch her, hope soared inside Diana's breast. When she told them she was to wed Marcus Magnus and begged them to take her to him, they replied, "We know you are a special prisoner. The emperor himself has given us our orders."

They took her to the prison bath, where she was allowed to bathe and brush the tangles from her golden hair. She had no choice but to don the magenta stola once more, and when she was dressed, the guards placed her in a litter and set off with the crowds that were streaming toward the Palatine.

"Where are you taking me?" Diana asked uncertainly.

"Circus Maximus," came the curt reply.

Circus Maximus? Marcus would not attend the races with his father lying murdered. There must be some mistake!

"You must take me to the villa of Titus Magnus on the slopes of the Esquiline."

"We have orders from the emperor," was the only reply they gave.

Perhaps Marcus had gone to Nero himself to get her released. That must be it! Again hope soared in her breast. But once again it was dashed to pieces as she was taken to a cell beneath Circus Maximus and locked inside. The air was heavy with the pungent odor of horse droppings.

She was filled with dire apprehension and could not comprehend why she had been brought to this place. Her throat was so parched and sore, she could not swallow. She longed for a sip of cool water. Because she did not know what was going to happen to her, her imagination had begun to conjure the most terrifying scenarios.

As Diana clung desperately to the bars of her cell, she saw magnificent chariots embellished with silver and gold being pulled along the wide underground passages. She called out to the men, but they would not even look in her direction. They avoided eye contact as if she were somehow loathsome.

Next came majestic horses in teams of four in every color imaginable—jet black, bay chestnut, roan, gray, cream, and pure white. The animals were restive and hard to control. She dimly realized these were the horses used in the chariot races. They could not wait to unleash their pent-up energy in the vast arena.

Would she be taken in one of these chariots to Nero? It seemed such a remote possibility, and yet all that had happened in the last twenty-four hours seemed remote and impossible.

Marcus arrived at Circus Maximus early. Some of the most famous charioteers were racing today and he greatly admired their skills. He knew firsthand how difficult it was to control a team of four horses as they thundered down the track and took the turns. To win a race, so many factors came into play. Not only the temperament and training of the horses, but the weight of the chariot, the grease on the axles, the length of the reins, and the condition of the track were vitally important.

The prime element necessary to win a chariot race, however, was the attitude of the driver. It not only took skill, courage, and determination, it took recklessness and an iron will to never accept defeat; it took balls!

As Marcus watched the chariots and horses being brought up from the underground stables, he felt his excitement build. Though it was only morning, it promised to be a glorious day. When the races were done, he would leave immediately and surprise Diana. This definitely promised to be one of the most exhilarating days of his life!

Because he lingered with the charioteers, he was late arriving at the Imperial Box. All eyes were focused upon him as he entered and hailed Nero. He flashed a smile of apology. His features were so strong and darkly powerful, Nero wondered how he had thought Petrius the one with beauty.

Diana gasped at the size of the guard who unlocked her cell. He was naked, save for a loincloth and a burning torch. The muscles on his massive body gleamed with oil, and she shrank back in alarm when she saw his face. He had an ugly, hard face that was totally devoid of emotion. His eyes looked dead, they were so impassive. He looked like an executioner!

And suddenly, she knew her nightmare had only just begun. So that he would not lay hands upon her, she stepped from the cell and nodded to him. As she followed him into the arena, she began to pray. Deep in her heart she knew her cause was hopeless and so she sought the help of Saint Jude.

"O holy Saint Jude, apostle and martyr,
Great in virtue and rich in miracles,
Near kinsman of Jesus Christ,
The faithful intercessor of all who invoke
    Your special patronage in times of need.
To you I have recourse from the depths of my
    heart,
And humbly beg you, to whom God has given
    such great power,
To come to my assistance . . . ."

The size of the crowd staggered her. The babble of their voices was so loud it hurt her ears, and then it faded away and all she heard was the pounding of her own heart in her eardrums. She could not swallow, and the pain in her throat had spread to her heart.

Diana walked as if she were in a trance. She had nowhere to go but forward. Even if she were able to cry out, no one would hear. If she ran, she would be cruelly dragged back. She knew that if she begged and groveled, it would avail her naught. All she had left was her dignity. She approached the waiting stake with every shred of it she could muster.

She lifted her chin with disdain as her guard lashed her wrists and ankles to a seven-foot, tarred stake. But when he set the top of it ablaze, she began to tremble like an aspen leaf. Though she faced the Imperial Box, the sun mercifully blinded her and she closed her eyes to block out its brilliance.

The great unease in Marcus' breast escalated to alarm as he saw the look of pity on the faces around him. Finally, Nero spoke. "We are sorry to give you tragic news on such a glorious day, General. Your father is dead, poisoned by the woman who betrayed you."

"No!" The denial was loud and firm, not yet filled with anguish. Marcus' accusing eyes swung to Petrius. His brother stepped forward and raised his arm to indicate the center of the arena.

"This is my gift to you, Marcus."

He swung around and saw her. He knew instantly that it was Diana by her lovely pale gold hair. She was wearing his favorite magenta.

"No!" The cry this time rent the air. The mixture of anger, pain, and fear were palpable. Icy fingers closed about his heart and squeezed until all the breath left his body.

Marcus ran to the front of the box and vaulted down to the floor of the arena, twenty-five feet below. He bent his knees in anticipation of the impact as his feet hit the packed earth of the track. He was running before he came out of the crouch. The moment he landed, a gate on the far side opened and a pair of lions, starved for a week, sprang forth.

The crowds were on their feet screaming their encouragement. Here was sport! A three-way race to see who could reach the female first—the warrior, the lions, or the flames.

Marcus had a will of iron. He was a man who would not acknowledge defeat even when it stared him in the face. He drew his gladius sword and willed his powerful legs to cover the ground faster.

Marcus and the lions reached their goal at the same instant. One sprang at him, while the other lunged at Diana. Even as his sword thrust into the lion's vitals, killing it, he heard her tortured scream.

He flung the carcass away and plunged his weapon into the second lion. Mortally wounded, it fell away from his beloved, but not before a swipe of its great claws had torn open her breast and shoulder and throat.

"Marcus . . ."

With horror he saw that her hair was already afire as the tarred stake burned about her head. He held her agonized gaze with his fierce black eyes. "I'll love you forever, and beyond," he vowed as he raised both arms and plunged his sword into her heart.

Chapter 28

The jolt Diana's body experienced had the power of a lightning bolt. One moment she was burning hot; then she was freezing cold. She felt as if cool air were rushing past her. Her eardrums felt as if they would burst. She experienced the sensation of falling, and awoke with a cry of terror on her lips, trembling uncontrollably.

The first things she saw were the peach-colored covers of the bed in which she was lying. Diana thought she was back in her own chamber in Aquae Sulis. Then she felt Marcus' powerful arms about her and realized she was safe. Her relief was overwhelming.

"Marc . . . Marc . . . Marcus," she sobbed. "I had a terrifying nightmare that I was being put to death at Circus Maximus. Thank God I woke up!"

"Hush, hush," came the deep soothing voice.

"Oh God, it was unbelievably real. Just hold me . . . I feel so safe in your arms."

As his arms tightened, she rubbed her cheek against the muscles of his chest. It felt like solid rock and she clung to him desperately. Even the familiar scent of his body was comforting to her. His hand stroked her hair until her trembling lessened. On a shuddering sob she whispered, "Darling, I can't go to Rome with you, please don't ask me, Marcus. Please understand."

"Lady Davenport, do you know where you are; do you know who I am?"

Diana's eyes widened. Her glance traveled about the chamber and it slowly dawned on her that it was the Elizabethan room she had occupied at Hardwick Hall. She closed her eyes to steady herself. When she reopened them and still found herself in the peach-colored room, she whispered, "Dear God, I'm back."

The man who held her loosened his arms and pulled back so that he could see her face. His black eyes bored into hers intensely, as if he were trying to read her thoughts.

"Yes, indeed, you are back. The question is, back from where?" the Earl of Bath demanded.

Diana did not want to be back in her own time, yet she certainly did not wish herself back in Rome. She had had a miraculous escape. Then she realized time or place had nothing to do with her deep longing. It was Marcus from whom she could not bear to be separated. But, of course, she wasn't separated from him. He was here, holding her. Mark Hardwick was Marcus Magnus. She knew it as surely as she knew she was Diana Davenport. The only problem was, *he* didn't know it!

She searched his face. Except for the scar, he looked exactly the same. She knew this man more intimately than any woman had a right to. Surely he would believe her story. Diana took a deep breath and let it out in a tremulous sigh.

"It all began when I went into an antique shop and found a Roman helmet. When I put it on, I was swept back to the time when the Romans occupied Bath. It was called Aquae Sulis—"

"I know it was called Aquae Sulis," he said dryly. "I am an archaeologist."

She smiled at him. "Everything Roman fascinates you because you actually lived in Aquae Sulis. Your name was Marcus Magnus. You were a general who trained legionaries before they went to fight in Wales."

The earl looked at her incredulously, as if he were dealing with a liar or a madwoman. He stood up, towering above her in a threatening manner. "You've been gone for months. Have you any idea the trouble and the scandal you caused by disappearing?" His dark face hardened. "When you are ready to tell me the truth, I shall be willing to listen." He strode to the door.

"You insufferable, pig-headed devil! At least you might have the courtesy to listen to my story before you dismiss me as a crackpot! Where are you going?" she cried.

"To summon the doctor who is attending you. You've been unconscious all night."

Diana turned her face into the pillow. The shock of all that had happened to her in the last hours, coupled with the fact that she had been torn from Marcus Magnus so cruelly, were too much to bear. Tears flooded her eyes and spilled down her cheeks as she quietly sobbed, "Marcus . . . Marcus."

As the Earl of Bath reached the door, the plaintive sound of Diana's crying stopped him in his tracks. The longing and quiet desperation he heard in her voice touched a chord deep inside him, and hearing her cry transported him to his childhood and the dim remembrance that his grandmother had always called him Marcus.

The doctor came the moment he was summoned. He had attended university with Mark Hardwick and the two men were well acquainted. Mark met him at the door.

"Charles, she's regained consciousness. It happened quite suddenly. She was lying still as death, then she shot up in the bed so distraught I didn't quite know what to do. When she calmed down, I asked her where she had been and she concocted some ridiculous tale about being transported back in time."

"Really?" Charles Wentworth asked with great interest.

"She's been crying for someone called Marcus."

"Isn't that *your* name, old boy?"

"Well, yes, but I can assure you Lady Diana isn't crying for me. The two of us rubbed against each other rather abrasively whenever we met."

"Well, I'll have a look at her. I think I'd better go in alone. We don't want to upset her further."

Mark nodded his understanding. "I'll wait down here, Charles."

When he opened the chamber door, he smiled at the beautiful girl in the bed. "Good morning, I'm Dr. Wentworth. Don't be alarmed, I'm just going to make sure you're all right, after your ordeal."

He had thought her lovely when he had seen her unconscious, but now that he saw her eyes, the color of violets drenched with tears, he found her beauty breathtaking. Before he examined her, he wanted to talk with her. If he could gain her confidence, perhaps she would tell him where she had been and what had happened to her.

"My ordeal? You saw me last night, I understand?"

"Yes. Apparently Mark went to an antique shop up on the heights last evening to pick up a Roman helmet they had acquired for him. He and the proprietor found you unconscious on the floor. Since you were engaged to his brother, the earl put you in his carriage and brought you to Hardwick Hall. They sent for me immediately. I gave you a cursory examination, found no bones broken, and advised them to keep you in bed, keep you warm, and have someone sit with you. I told them to summon me the moment you regained consciousness."

He put his first question very gently. "Do you remember what you were doing before you lost consciousness?"

"I remember exactly, Doctor. I was browsing through the antique shop up on the heights, when I saw an authentic Roman helmet. I was so thrilled to see it, to touch it. I couldn't resist trying it on. I forgot I was wearing a wig and somehow it got stuck on my head and I couldn't get it off. I remember I felt quite ill, as if I were about to faint, but when I fell, I didn't fall to the floor, I just kept falling—I felt a wind rushing past me. I can't really describe the sensation, I have no adequate words, but I was transported back in time to when the Romans occupied Britain."

The doctor watched and listened to her intently. "You went into the antique shop yesterday?"

"No, I'm afraid not, Dr. Wentworth." She smiled wistfully. "It was in the summertime—months ago, I imagine. By the snowflakes drifting past the window, I can tell it must be winter now."

"Early spring, actually. This was a late freak storm. So you fainted in the antique shop on a summer's day and Mark found you there unconscious the following spring, and you have no recollection of what happened in the months between?"

"Oh no, Doctor, I recall every moment! I went back in time to when the Romans occupied Aquae Sulis. I lived in the villa of Marcus Magnus, a legionary general." She stopped herself before she blurted out that Marcus Magnus and Mark Hardwick were one and the same. "You must think I'm mad! None of this can possibly make any sense to you."

"No, no, Lady Davenport, I don't think you mad at all. You are convinced that this happened and I urge you not to suppress it. The only way you can work through it is to talk about it. Obviously you've suffered a great trauma. Are you feeling ill at all?"

"No, I feel quite well—a little shaky perhaps. Is my hair all right?" Her hand went to her head. "Is it burned or singed?" she asked apprehensively.

"Not at all, your hair is quite lovely. I'll just listen to your heart." He unfastened the buttons on the high neckline of the starched white nightgown she wore and folded it back, so he could listen to her heartbeat.

Diana stared down at the expanse of creamy, unblemished flesh. Her fingers came up to touch her shoulder and throat where the lion had torn her open, then they trailed down across her heart where Marcus had plunged in his sword to put an end to her suffering.

"I seem to be all in one piece," she whispered shakily.

"All in one piece," Dr. Wentworth confirmed. "Your pulse is rapid, but I'm sure it will settle down if you try to stay calm and get lots of rest." He closed his black bag and gave her a reassuring smile. "I'll be back to see you tomorrow."

When the doctor descended, he found Mark Hardwick pacing the front hall.

"I can't find anything physically wrong with her, but she has obviously suffered some sort of trauma."

"Did she give you any sort of explanation where the hell she's been since summer?"

"She's convinced she's been right here in Bath, or Aquae Sulis as it was called in Roman times."

"Good God, man, did she try to fob you off with that ridiculous tale?"

"Mark, I know how utterly implausible it sounds, but to her it is very real. Perhaps it was her way of escaping from a situation she found intolerable. Let her talk. Encourage her to get it all out, every detail. It's the only way she'll rid herself of this obsession. Having someone listen to her without poo-pooing her will be therapeutic, cathartic even. Once her mind unloads itself of the burden she's carrying, perhaps she will begin to recall what really happened to her and where she's really been for the last nine months."

"If this is the mumbo-jumbo of medicine, I'm glad my consuming passion is archaeology. I wouldn't have the bloody patience to be a doctor!"

"Well, patience is exactly what you're going to have to exercise with Lady Diana, Mark. None of your bullying, autocratic tactics."

"Me? Bully? I am the epitome of a gentle man."

Charles rolled his eyes ceilingward. "I'll be back tomorrow."

As Mark strode back to the stairs, he encountered his cook with a tray of food in her hands.

"Why didn't you tell me the young lady was awake? She's had nothing to eat since yesterday, Your Lordship. Why are men so thoughtless?"

"No lectures, Nora, I beg you. I've just had one from Dr. Wentworth. I'll take the tray up. Thank you for your thoughtfulness."

When the earl reentered the chamber, he caught a look of infinite sadness on Diana's face, as if she longed for a love, lost forever.

The pain of losing Marcus was so sharp, Diana thought she might die of it. In fact, she mourned him so deeply, she wished she had died. And then the chamber door opened and he walked in. Her breath caught in her throat and her heart started to hammer erratically.

Why couldn't Mark Hardwick remember that once upon a time he had been Marcus Magnus? Once upon a time—it sounded like a fairy tale. Surely it was more than that? Diana cast away all doubts. Marcus was Mark. He simply didn't remember. It would be up to her to make him remember. The question was, did she want to?

She loved Marcus Magnus with all her heart and soul. She did not love Mark Hardwick. She wasn't sure she even liked him! Seventeen hundred years of civilization under his belt had masked his good qualities and magnified his flaws.

"You must be hungry," he said, putting the tray down beside her.

"I'm thirsty. My throat is very dry. Thank you."

He took a chair beside the bed and stretched his long legs before him.

Diana fingered the high neck of the nightgown she wore. She looked into his black eyes and asked directly, "Did you undress me?"

The Earl of Bath licked lips gone suddenly dry. Her words and the vision they provoked made him shift in the chair to accommodate his arousal.

"Nora undressed you." He cleared his throat. "Most of the servants at Hardwick Hall are male; Nora is my cook."

She began to sip the broth he had brought her. His eyes followed the spoon to her lips. "Did she make this? It's delicious."

"She's a Frenchwoman. I'm lucky to have her." As he watched her eat, his mind went back to last night when he found her unconscious. When he lifted her into his arms, an icy finger of fear had touched his heart. An overwhelming protectiveness arose within him that still lingered. He had thought it stemmed from her vulnerability and helplessness, but now he wasn't so sure.

His mind drifted back to the first time he ever saw her, dressed as a goddess. He had been instantly attracted to the beautiful young girl, which was odd, because he preferred older women of experience. Perhaps it was because she was dressed in the Roman style. He had always had an inexplicable passion for anything Roman.

Whatever it was, he had known instantly that he wanted her. When he propositioned her, she had thrown champagne in his face. Mark Hardwick's mouth curved with wry amusement as he remembered mistaking her for a cyprian. How the hell he could have done that was beyond his comprehension. She had had such an air of innocence about her, a man of his experience should have known better.

Wishful thinking on his part had blinded him to her unmistakable air of breeding. If he was being honest, it was a hell of a lot more than wishful thinking, it was hot lust! When he had offered her carte blanche, he remembered her words exactly: *You are too arrogant, too cocksure, and far, far too old for me, Lord Bath.*

Also remembered vividly was the feeling of rage that swept over him when he had walked into his bedchamber and found her in Peter's arms. When his brother told him they were engaged, he experienced such a sharp sense of loss, he realized he had been on the brink of falling for her. In that moment he hated his brother and coveted her shamefully.

The problem was he still coveted her. When he had found her unconscious in that antique shop, he had resented bringing her to Hardwick Hall and Peter. He secretly hoped that Peter would reject a fiancée who had been missing for months, but his brother had been overjoyed that Diana was found, and had rushed off to London at dawn to inform her aunt and uncle.

What no one knew, save himself and Nora, was that in the middle of the night the earl had come to this chamber and told Nora he would stay with Lady Diana as she lay unconscious in hopes of being there when she awoke.

As he watched her, lying so still and pale, her beauty overwhelmed him. Just thinking of her had been a strong enough lure to bring him to her bedside. Once he was in the same room with her, desire gripped him by the throat. He was drawn close to her by some compelling force that played havoc with his willpower. His hand reached out to touch her of its own volition. He brushed the golden tendrils back from her brow and was instantly lost.

Desire flared in him, flooding his brain, his heart, his loins. A longing to make her his consumed him. He took his hand from her as if it had been burned, then moved his chair back from the bed. Yet it had not diminished his desire. He was fully aroused and his body remained in that blatant condition all night.

He felt extremely possessive about her, as if she had belonged to him and he had lost her. Throughout the long, quiet night he had received fleeting glimpses of . . .

what? Another time, another place? The sensations were similar to déjà vu, yet were so ephemeral and fleeting, he could not hold on to them. He had had these feelings before, whenever he held a Roman artifact in his hands.

Where the hellfire had she been for nine months? Jealousy consumed him. Yet he knew he had no right to be jealous. Lady Davenport was engaged to his brother, Peter. Had she run away because she did not wish to marry Peter? He found himself wishing it were so.

When Diana finished the broth, she drank a full glass of water, then reached for the pot of tea.

Mark Hardwick cleared his throat. "I'm sorry I was so brusque before."

Diana cast him a sideways glance. "It almost chokes you to apologize."

He bristled at her words and Diana felt a flicker of satisfaction.

With effort, he hung on to his temper and said most reasonably, "If you will tell me about your ordeal, I promise to listen. You must tell someone."

"And that someone ought to be you? How patronizing. And when I've finished my tale, you'll pat me on the head and pop a sugarplum into my mouth. Then you'll relate everything I've told you to your friend, Charles Wentworth, and you'll both laugh your bloody heads off!"

"For God's sake, Diana, give me a little credit. I am quite capable of being open-minded."

"Diana, is it? What happened to Lady Diana?"

"That's what I'd bloody well like to know! Whatever happened has robbed you of your sweet air of innocence."

Diana began to laugh. "Innocence?" she gasped. "That was the very first thing I lost. I lived with the decadent Romans. I was captured by General Marcus Magnus. When he saw me naked, he ordered me bathed and perfumed and sent to his couch. And I became his slave!"

Chapter 29

Mark Hardwick's jaw almost fell open. Her words painted such an erotic picture, blood surged in his veins, hardening his already swollen shaft to marble. His skin-tight buff riding breeches made his condition most uncomfortable. He stood up in an effort to conceal his arousal, but her amethyst eyes slid over the enormous bulge knowingly.

Was she openly admitting that she'd had a lover? The idea shocked him. She was a young, unmarried, *titled lady.* It was unheard of. His mind searched for another explanation.

"Are you trying to tell me you were raped, Diana?" he asked grimly.

"No! But you must understand that I was a slave in his household. He had absolute authority over me."

Mark thrust his hands into his pockets to stop his fists from clenching. "So you yielded to him?"

"No! I refused to obey his orders; refused even to acknowledge that I was his slave." The corners of her mouth lifted. "You were absolutely livid! Sorry . . . Marcus was absolutely livid."

"Did he beat you?"

"Marcus? Good heavens no. He had a slave master with an enormous flagellum to whip his slaves for him."

She's making this up, and enjoying every moment, Mark thought silently.

"He gave orders that I was to be put to work mopping his tile floors until I was ready to yield to him."

"That is when you surrendered?"

"No! I mopped the bloody floors."

"But you told me you lost your innocence; by that I assume you meant your virginity?"

"My virginity." Her mouth curved in remembrance. "It absolutely fascinated you—I mean him."

The earl ran his tongue over his top lip. Christ, she was so titillating, he wanted to push her back in the bed, remove the prim white nightgown, and thrust between her thighs.

"Since he owned me and had total authority over me, I knew that sooner or later I would have to obey him; it was inevitable."

"So you yielded."

"No! I did something you taught me to do; I negotiated."

His mind flew back to the time he had carried her up to his town house to negotiate.

"You taught me quite a lot that night. I learned that when a man wants sexual favors from a woman badly enough, he will agree to any terms."

Mark Hardwick felt his anger begin to rise. Diana had refused his proposition, but now she was going to tell him she had accepted another man's.

Diana ran her fingers through her disheveled hair and pushed it back from her shoulders. The earl's fingers curled inside his pockets. He wanted to bury them in that pale golden mass.

"I told Marcus Magnus that I would pretend to be his slave in the presence of others, if he would allow me freedom to say what I pleased when we were alone, and if he agreed to treat me as a lady. He reluctantly agreed."

"In return for what?" Mark demanded.

"In return for my virginity, of course."

"So he did rape you?"

"Ah no, I gifted him with it. Not immediately, of course, not until he had wooed and won me."

"Do you expect me to believe a barbaric Roman would woo a woman?"

"Marcus wasn't a barbarian." She closed her eyes remembering. "He was a patrician. The general was a stern military man with little time for women. He was no depraved voluptuary. Yet he wooed me as no other woman was ever wooed. He was physically magnificent, his body so lithe and powerful, he made me weak just looking at him. Seeing him in his breastplate and armor was like an aphrodisiac to me. Our lovemaking was too precious and private for me to share with anyone. Suffice it to say that when we consummated, we ravished each other."

Mark Hardwick could never remember being so highly aroused in his life. Being in this bedchamber with Diana Davenport was like being in a high-class brothel while a courtesan related an erotic sex fantasy. Only Lady Diana was no strumpet, she was a young, unmarried, titled lady. One with tantalizing sexual experience. The earl's black eyes dilated with desire.

"And you believe that I was this Marcus Magnus?" he asked huskily.

"I know you were." Her glance swept him from head to foot, lingering on his mouth, the width of his shoulders, the blatant bulge of his groin. "The years have not been kind to you, Lord Bath."

He stiffened, insulted. "What the devil do you mean?"

"Oh, you have the same arrogance as Marcus, the same authority and command, but seventeen hundred years of civilization have put a veneer upon you that is unattractive. You are sophisticated, cynical, and selfish; vain, egotistical, and bored. Perhaps even profligate. In other words you have become jaded, Lord Bath, and it is most unappealing."

"Then I shall relieve you of my odious presence!"

"Good! I should like to get dressed now. I am not an invalid."

"You'll do no such bloody thing! You most assuredly are an invalid. You haven't begun to recover. You're still—"

"Delusional?" Diana asked sweetly.

"Yes, delusional. I shan't mince words with you. You will stay in bed, or else."

Her chin went up. "Or else what?" she challenged.

"I shan't call my slave master. I'll beat you myself." His black eyes had a definite hint of wildness that warned her the earl was capable of any recklessness, even violence.

Diana slid down in the bed. It felt wonderful to hear the total authority in his voice. It was both familiar and comforting to listen to his deep male voice issuing commands, and know she flaunted them at her own risk.

Mark had the doorknob in his hand when he turned back to her. "You haven't asked about Peter."

"Peter?" she asked blankly.

"Your fiancé, Peter Hardwick. You do remember him?"

Was the edge in his voice sarcasm? "Unfortunately," she said candidly.

His spirits soared, yet perversely he reprimanded her. "You put my brother in a hell of position when you disappeared. It was all over the newspapers. He instigated an exhaustive search for you. Peter was overjoyed when I found you, so obviously he feels the same about you as he did, in spite of everything."

"There is absolutely nothing between your brother and me. I didn't deny the engagement the night you found us together because I felt he had compromised me. I was that innocent!"

"You are not in love with Peter?" he asked sharply.

Diana laughed. "Peter is a boy. I have known a great passion since the last time I saw your brother. I am not the naive child that I was, allowing myself to be trapped over a few kisses. Since then I have experienced the love of a man, a real man.''

Mark Hardwick came back toward the bed. "Peter left for London this morning, in spite of the snow. He's gone to tell your aunt and uncle of your return. Naturally, they will come back with him. I expect them tomorrow night unless the roads are bad.''

"Ugh! Prudence!" Diana said with a shudder. "I suppose she must be faced.''

"Are you afraid of her?''

Diana considered for a moment. "I was. She kept me on a very short leash. She dominated me, and when that didn't work, she manipulated me with guilt, playing on my sympathies by pretending to be an invalid. She will soon learn I am no longer a biddable girl, but a woman.''

"The gossip your disappearance caused wasn't pleasant for her.''

An impish look of delight crossed Diana's face. "Her god is respectability. Oh, how I wish I could have witnessed her discomfort.''

"Your aunt and uncle are still your legal guardians,'' he cautioned.

A look of dismay replaced her delight.

"I thought you weren't afraid.''

"Prudence will punish me dreadfully for this, but after the fear I've experienced, Prudence will be no more than an irritation.''

He raised an eyebrow of inquiry as dark as a raven's wing.

A lump came into her throat and she began to tremble. "Don't ask,'' she whispered. "I cannot speak of it . . . not yet.''

"Get some rest,'' he said brusquely. He closed the door quietly. *What the devil is she hiding?* he asked himself. She fascinated him much more now than she had in the past. Now, an air of mystery surrounded her, and cou-

pled with the unconventional things she said, he was drawn
to her like a lodestone.

Apparently she intended to withdraw from the engagement, which wouldn't sit very well with Peter, who had
dashed off to London, probably to inform her guardians that
plans for the wedding could proceed. Mark Hardwick felt
relieved that she had not given her heart to his brother, and
not only for personal reasons. An exquisite woman like
Diana deserved better than a profligate young hellraiser like
Peter.

As he had expected, when Peter Hardwick got halfway
to London, the snow turned to rain. In spite of the weather,
he was in good spirits. He had fallen so deeply in debt from
his gambling, he had begun to feel like a hunted man. His
markers were piling up at every gentleman's club in London and he knew the only reason they hadn't been called
was because his brother was the Earl of Bath.

More pressing debts had had to be paid, however. His
losses at cockfights and pit bull fights were staggering, and
those men would have broken his legs, at the very least, if
he had not paid up. As a result, he had fallen into the hands
of the moneylenders. This had postponed his troubles, but
by no means had it solved them. Fleet Prison loomed very
real on Peter's horizon, and his only hope to avoid it was to
throw himself on his brother's mercy and confess all. This
was an indication of just how desperate he was, for he hated
Mark with a vengeance, and would do anything to avoid
that arrogant son-of-a-bitch's contempt.

Then at his darkest hour he had been saved by Diana
Davenport. She had reappeared as suddenly as she had mys-
teriously disappeared. He didn't give a tinker's damn where
she had been. All that mattered to Peter was that his wedding to the heiress could now go forward.

It had been eight months since he'd spoken to Richard
and Prudence Davenport. They had remained in Bath for a

month while a lengthy search had been carried out, but eventually had no choice but to return to London.

The hour was late when he arrived in Grosvenor Square, and he found Richard Davenport and his wife at home. When the majordomo took his caped greatcoat and ushered him into the drawing room, Peter said, "I know you will forgive the lateness of the hour when I tell you the news. Diana has been found!"

No joy registered on either face. They looked as if he had dropped a bombshell.

"Found alive?" Richard demanded.

"Mercifully, yes. She's quite safe at Hardwick Hall."

"But we assumed she was dead," Prudence blurted out. She and Richard exchanged what could only be described as a look of guilt.

A red flag went up in Peter's mind. Being a devious bastard himself, and human nature being what it was, he suspected them of chicanery. With his face a mask, his voice bland, he said, "Plans for the marriage can go forward immediately."

"Not so fast," Richard interjected. "Our precious agreement is no longer in effect." Richard's mind darted about like quicksilver. Diana was presumed dead and he had proceeded accordingly. Naturally, without a body, a number of years must pass before the courts declared her legally dead, but Richard was in complete charge of Diana's money, and by clever manipulation and maneuvering, he had managed to transfer the bulk of her fortune into his own accounts.

Peter Hardwick's mind easily kept apace with Richard's, especially when money was involved. The only reason this pair of vultures would declare their arrangement of 60-40 null and void was if they had high expectations of keeping it all.

Peter smiled. If Richard Davenport had done something illegal, he had him by the short hairs. "As Diana's fiancé, I believe I will advise her to look into how her estate has been managed while under your guardianship. My brother, the earl, enjoys the services of London's finest barristers.''

"I shall inform Diana you are only interested in her money,'' Prudence threatened. "She will call off your engagement immediately!''

Peter's smile reached all the way to his eyes. "Regardless of whether she marries me or not, your time is running out. In two short months she will come of age and inherit. Will that be sufficient time to restore the money that is missing?''

Prudence and Richard exchanged swift glances.

"Ah, I thought perhaps it wasn't,'' Peter said affably. "It appears your agreement with me is the lesser of two evils, after all.''

Peter could see that although it was clearly a struggle, both Richard and Prudence knew the only thing for them to do was put the best face on it they could. Richard turned to Peter and said, "I shall come to Bath at once. Did the wretched girl say where she had sloped off to all these months?''

"Actually, no. The earl found her unconscious in an antique shop and carried her to Hardwick Hall in his carriage. Naturally we called a physician. He found no bones broken and expects her to recover without delay.''

"Why didn't you tell me she was hurt?'' Prudence demanded, reverting to the role of caring aunt in the blink of an eye.

"You didn't bother to ask,'' Peter said dryly. "I think it best if we marry in Bath. I shall be returning tomorrow and can take you in my carriage if that would suit?''

"Thank you, but I believe we shall take our own conveyance, Mr. Hardwick,'' Richard said decisively.

As soon as Peter had departed for the town house in Jermyn Street, Prudence said, "That was a wise decision to take our own carriage, Richard. I wouldn't trust him as far as I could throw him."

"I thought we'd seen and heard the last of my dearest niece. God damn and blast it all! Everything was going along so smoothly; too smoothly apparently. Prudence, you are right not to trust Peter Hardwick. I believe he could prove to be a very nasty customer. We must go very carefully with him and try not to antagonize him. The very last thing we want is an investigation of Diana's assets."

"Richard, he did say Diana was found unconscious. She may not recover, you know."

"Prudence, you are building castles in the air. The chit is too damned obstinate to conveniently die. I was convinced she had met with foul play, but apparently your suspicions were closer to the mark. She must have run off with some lover, and now that he's deserted her, she's come running back."

"It's absolutely disgusting! She ought to be put in a home for wayward girls. Perhaps we're fortunate Hardwick's still interested. Perhaps the best thing is to get her married off quickly."

"Well, we shall assess the situation when we arrive at Bath. We are still her legal guardians for the next two months and even the earl himself cannot deny our full authority!"

Chapter 30

At Hardwick Hall a chambermaid put fresh linen on Diana's bed while Nora ran a bath for her.

"Thank you, Nora. This isn't your job. I'll manage just fine."

"You'll do no such thing. Who will do for you if I don't? Mr. Burke likes to think he controls Hardwick Hall, but what good is he in a situation like this where a young female guest is confined to her bed?"

"I'm sorry to be so much trouble."

"You're no trouble at all. I'll just get you a fresh nightgown and you can pop back into bed."

"Whose nightgown am I wearing?" Diana asked curiously.

"Why mine, of course. I have some lovely ones, all from France. I put you in a plain white one because the doctor was coming, but I have some with lace, and some cambric ones fine as spiderwebs. I'll pick something pretty and be right back."

The moment she left, Mr. Burke put in an appearance. He brought her a decanter of wine and glasses. "If there is anything I can do to make you comfortable, Lady Diana, please let me know. It was remiss of me not to have a ladies' maid on staff, but we have been a household of bachelors for some time."

"Nora has been very kind to me."

Mr. Burke didn't exactly sniff—such behavior was beneath him—but he said, "She's a Gaul, you know."

Diana's eyes widened. Mr. Burke reminded her of Kell. And it suddenly hit her—of course, Nora resembled Nola, the woman of Gaul. Diana shivered. It was all rather uncanny and gave her the most uncomfortable feeling.

Nora returned with the nightdress just as Mr. Burke departed, and handed it to Diana.

"This color matches your eyes."

"Oh, it's lovely." The pale lavender nightdress had lace around its high neck and cuffs, making it look prim, while the sheerness of the material made it alluring. "It's naughty and nice at the same time."

"Yes, the French have a knack for such things. Now, into bed with you and I'll fetch you a tray when dinner's ready."

Diana already felt lonely for Mark Hardwick's company. She hoped he would dine with her. "Does his lordship dine at home tonight?"

"He's gone riding in this inclement weather. Over the fields at the back of the property the Archaeology Society has what they call a 'dig.' Spends hours there sometimes, but he definitely said he'd be back in time for dinner."

Diana slipped into bed anticipating Mark's return, but all she could think of was what she would say to Prudence.

When the earl came striding into her bedchamber, Diana's spirits soared. She pretended complete indifference, of course. He hadn't joined her for dinner and she was almost finished when he arrived. She tested the water by referring to the food of Aquae Sulis. When Mark did not dispute that she had been there, she relaxed, knowing she did not have to pick and choose her words.

Though the earl enjoyed her company, he knew he must keep his mind occupied or his thoughts would focus on how much he wanted to make love to her. "Do you play chess?" he inquired politely.

"Yes, I used to play with my father."

As Mark set up the board between them, she said, "The last time I went shopping in Aquae Sulis I bought a Roman board game called Robbers."

Mark was immediately interested. "I've heard of it, but I could never learn the details of how it was played."

"Well, I'm not very good at it. It's similar to chess, but more abstract with very elaborate moves. The men are 'soldiers' and 'officers,' and mine were made of crystal."

"I wonder . . ." Mark said thoughtfully.

"What?" she prompted.

"Well, one or two silver soldiers have turned up from time to time in Bath. I assumed they were children's toys, but perhaps they are game pieces from Robbers."

"Nora told me you have an archaeological 'dig' on your property."

"Yes, but that's not the only one. There are two or three in the surrounding district. I'm starting up a museum. I have a display of artifacts here at the Hall, but so many are turning up, I think they should be in a museum where the general public can see them."

"That's a good idea. I'd love to see your artifacts and I'd like to see your dig."

"I rode out there this afternoon. I wanted to give the dogs a run. A friend of mine gave me a pair of young mastiffs a couple of weeks ago."

"Oh!" Diana cried. She knelt up in the bed and reached across the board with her hand. Then she covered his mouth. "Don't tell me their names!" she warned. "I'll tell you."

The moment she touched his face, desire shot through him like molten lava, making his blood hot and demanding.

"Romulus and Remus!" she said with delight.

"How did you know?" he demanded. "No, don't tell

me. Marcus had a pair of mastiffs called Romulus and Remus.''

Diana slid back beneath the covers. "Exactly!" she said with deep satisfaction.

He cocked an eyebrow at her. "Mr. Burke could have told you. He greatly admires those dogs."

"But he didn't," she insisted, "and here's something else that's uncanny—I firmly believe Mr. Burke was your slave master, Kell."

"The one with the flagellum?" he asked, amused.

"The very same. I can laugh about it now, but he terrified me in the beginning."

"Burke has that quality—he terrifies me sometimes."

She laughed. "Liar. I doubt very much if anything terrifies you."

His mind did not seem to be on the chess game, and yet he took her knight and then her castle. "When you went back in time," he said carefully, "what year was it?"

"It was 61 A.D. Boudicca had led the uprising of the Celtae tribes and burned Londinium less than a year before. As a result, Paullinus, who was in charge of the Roman army, was systematically wiping out the Britons, tribe by tribe." They both forgot the game as she became absorbed in her story.

"Julius Classicianus, the Procurator of Britannia, wanted to get rid of Paullinus. He needed a more statesmanlike leader to restore the support of the Britons. Marcus and Julius were very much in agreement on this issue, so Julius asked him to go to Rome and speak to the Senate." Her voice trailed off, and a look of great sadness came into her eyes. "I should have stopped him from going."

He didn't want her to cry, so to take her mind off her sadness, he thought to provoke her by challenging her story. "You actually make it sound credible."

Diana glanced at the chessmen, saw she had no possible way of winning, and abruptly moved her legs beneath the covers to scatter the pieces.

Mark's black eyes danced. "Willful little vixen," he murmured. "You like to play games but you don't like to lose."

"I'm telling the truth, not playing a game!"

"Between a man and a woman, Diana, it is always a game."

"Ohmigod, I said that to you. You've waited seventeen hundred years to give me back my words."

For one brief second he experienced déjà vu. He dismissed it instantly, not wanting to believe her. Yet it was easy to believe they'd been lovers. If he had waited seventeen hundred years, it was to give her back more than words. He had to exercise an iron control to stop himself from snatching her into his arms. Her scent stole to him and he found it irresistible, and faintly familiar. He needed to taste her too, and hold her breasts in the palms of his hands, and anchor himself deep within her, and arouse the wild passion he knew she was capable of.

Stop it! he told himself. *The girl has bewitched you.* He studied her for long minutes. "I'm curious. What did this Marcus Magnus make of you when he first saw you? Surely he didn't believe you were from the future?"

"Indeed he did not. I remember I was wearing this hideous dress with panniers and an equally hideous powdered wig. He thought I was a misshapen old woman until—"

Until he saw you naked, Mark added silently.

"For quite a long time he was convinced I was a Druid priestess sent to spy on him."

"That would make sense considering your peculiar form of dress," Mark teased.

"That would make sense considering my high degree of intelligence!" she countered.

"You're quite well read; I'll concede that much."

She shrugged. "You saw my father's library—and coveted it, I might add."

"Among other things," he murmured suggestively.

Diana blushed, proving that she knew exactly what else he coveted.

"You probably studied the Romans extensively, as did I," he suggested.

"No, that's the strange part. I was never much interested in the Roman period. I often had fantasies about other times in history. I much preferred the Elizabethan or medieval period to our Georgian times."

"Why?" he asked curiously.

She gave him a scathing glance. "You haven't the least notion how restrictive life is for a young, unmarried lady. I have no freedom of dress, no freedom of speech, and would have no freedom of thought if Prudence had her way."

I'm a fanatic about freedom myself, he thought. *It's the most precious thing we have.*

"If you compare our effeminate dandies who emulate Prinny with Elizabethan or medieval men, surely there is no need to ask me why I prefer those times in history."

"Well, thank you very much."

"Oh, not you, of course. You're what a real man should be like, but seldom is."

So there is a mutual attraction, he thought.

"Tell me," she said matter-of-factly, "how do you keep in such superb physical condition?"

His mouth curved, flattered that she noticed. "I exercise, swim, ride, and sometimes quarry stone. There's nothing like physical labor to shape a man. It's good for the mind as well as the body."

She cast him a provocative glance. "It certainly seems to be good for yours."

"The things you say are wildly unconventional. I find the quality attractive."

"Not only the things I say . . . I could teach you things you've never dreamed of."

"You are more than flirting with me," he accused. "You are being deliberately seductive!"

"Part of the game." She smiled her secret smile.

"When I play with you, it will be according to *my* rules," he warned.

She laughed in his face. "If you believe that, Lord Bath, you don't know as much about women as you think."

Lord God, the pleasure I'm going to have mastering her.

She glimpsed the dark wildness in his eyes and feared she had driven him too far. "Since I intend to get dressed and leave this room tomorrow, perhaps I'd better get some rest."

"You may only get up if Dr. Wentworth and I agree," he said firmly.

"We'll see," she said lightly as she escorted him to her door.

"If you think I'll let you have your own way about everything, you don't know me very well."

"I know more about you than any woman has a right to," she said softly, luring him on again before closing her chamber door in his face.

When she was alone, Diana walked over to the tall, mullioned windows. She pulled back the heavy drape and stood gazing out at the landscape. A fine dusting of snow covered the ground and lay along every limb of the stark black trees. The pale moonlight cast eerie shadows in every direction. The beauty of the night had a coldness about it. She had never known Aquae Sulis in winter, and she somehow felt cheated. They had left for Rome before the snow came. It had been cold, though. Her mouth curved as she remembered the fur leggings. Marcus had found them extremely erotic.

Marcus . . . Marcus. He was the reason she felt cheated. It had nothing to do with the season, nothing to do with Aquae Sulis. How would she get through the rest of her life without him? How would she get through tonight? Her fingertip traced his name on the wet windowpane. She sighed heavily. Daylight had effectively banished her fear, but in the darkness it crept back. Diana began to shiver. She ran back to the safety of the bed and pulled the covers high.

In his own chamber Mark Hardwick lay supine on the bed with his arms folded behind his head. He tried to relax, but found it almost impossible. His eyes traveled down his body to his sex, still in a state of arousal. Damn her, no wonder he couldn't relax. And yet it wasn't just rampant desire that made him tense.

The moment he had entered his chamber he had searched among his Roman history books to find the time period she had spoken of. The books verified everything she said. The Governor of Britannia was Seutonius Paullinus; the Procurator, Julius Classicianus. She had even called Boudicca by her authentic name, rather than Queen Boadicea, which everyone used today.

He searched the encyclopedia for a reference to the game of Robbers, but found nothing. He finally found the volume where he'd seen it mentioned, but all it said was: *A Roman boardgame whose exact details could not be recovered.*

Without referring to history books, he knew that Nero had been the Emperor of Rome at that time. Though everything Roman fascinated him, Mark's gorge rose whenever he thought of the atrocities Nero had committed. At the inauguration of the Colosseum, nine thousand animals were reportedly killed. Nero was a madman who committed suicide, but not nearly soon enough. Mark's mind shied away from contemplating what he had done to Christians.

Sleep was a million miles away. He left his bed and put on a robe, then he went to his desk. He was writing a book about the history of Bath that began when Claudius invaded Britain and established a spa for the military fed by hot natural springs that were called Aquae Sulis.

Mark pulled out a map he had drawn of Aquae Sulis

and began to study it. Whenever he worked on his Roman projects, they absorbed him completely. As his body began to relax, his mind began to review the questions he had never been able to answer. Why did he have a consuming passion for all things Roman? Had he lived in the time when the Romans occupied Britain? He had always been open-minded enough to believe it was a possibility.

Now, however, new questions arose. Had he been a Roman? Had he been a general called Marcus Magnus? He liked the name. It seemed to fit. He threw down his pen and ran his fingers through his hair. He was being fanciful. He wanted to believe this fantasy because Diana was a part of it. He wanted to believe they had been lovers, so they could be lovers again. He was being ruled by his cock!

He'd been in a state of arousal so long, his testes ached. He glanced over to his bed and pictured her lying there. His imagination didn't stop at the bed. He pictured her nude, lying in her bath, her golden hair floating about her creamy shoulders as she languidly soaped her beautiful, half-submerged breasts.

This was the result of a day of denial and restraint; what the hell would he be like after a long night of the same? He knew the only way to get her out of his system was to make love to her. It was midnight. The house was asleep. He could go down the hall to her room and carry her struggling to his bed. She tantalized him so much, he stood up from his desk and contemplated the door, his urgency almost bringing him to flash point.

Beneath the covers, as she began to get warm, Diana contemplated the long lonely night ahead of her, fraught with fear. And then a most comforting notion came to her. If she fell asleep, perhaps she would dream of Marcus. The thought was irresistible, luring her to drowsiness, then finally sleep. She tumbled deep into the abyss immediately and slept undisturbed until almost midnight. Then slowly she began to toss about.

Where was she? Dear God, she was back in the slave pens. She was fettered, and so were they, but close enough that they could reach out to touch her! She pulled away frantically, not wanting their loathsome touch. As she moved out of reach of one, another made a grab for her. "No, no," she moaned desperately, tossing and turning this way and that to avoid the cruel hands.

By the time the massive guard came to take her to Circus Maximus, she was trembling uncontrollably. *Dear God, don't let this be happening! Why have I gone back in time again?* She had gone through this once, now she had to face it all again, only this time it was worse. This time she knew what awaited her in the arena! Half mad with fear, she began to scream, and then by some miracle she broke away from the executioner and began to run.

Mark heard her scream of terror. He strode swiftly across his chamber and threw back the door. Diana was running down the darkened hallway that led from her room to his. She ran straight into his arms.

"I went back, I went back," she cried, her body shaking so badly her teeth chattered. Her body was freezing cold, he could feel it beneath the fine cambric of her nightgown.

His powerful arms tightened about her and she clung to him desperately. "Diana, you're safe. It was a nightmare." A wave of protectiveness swept over him. He knew a deep need to protect her with his life, even if it was only from the darklings.

Chapter 31

He lifted her and carried her to the fire. Her arms about his neck clung desperately.

"Marcus, help me," she begged.

"I'm Mark," he said firmly, lowering himself into a chair before the fire, still holding on to her.

She was trembling like a frightened animal snared in a trap. She pressed her face into the hollow between his neck and his shoulder, and he stroked her hair and her back with a firm hand to imbue her with some of his strength.

"Diana, do you know where you are?" he demanded. His voice was deep, almost harsh. Instinctively he knew she needed his strength, not his gentleness. It felt as if she nodded her head. He loosened the stranglehold she had about his neck and held her hands in his. Her eyes were wide with fear, her breathing labored as if she'd been running for her life.

"Answer me!"

"Yes," she whispered.

"Who am I?"

"M . . . Mark."

"Then you know you are safe. I won't let anything or anyone hurt you!"

She reached out her hands to feel the slabs of muscle in his chest, then she spread her hands apart as if measuring the width of his broad shoulders, then she brought her palms down and gripped his powerful biceps as if she were testing his strength.

She looked into his black eyes. "You're just the same, just as big, just as hard. You're such a powerful force against evil. I need you to hold me."

Forever, he thought. "For as long as it takes," he promised.

She held on to him just as firmly as he held her. She drew on his strength, giving herself over to him completely. As the warmth of the fire and the heat of his body seeped into her, she began to feel safer. Slowly, her panic began to recede. Gradually, her trembling ceased and she lay quietly and trustfully in his arms.

As he held her in his lap, he marveled that the seductive woman of a few hours ago was now a very young girl. He had never nurtured and protected a female before. It was a heady sensation to feel so all-powerful. Strange as it seemed, when she drew upon his strength, it doubled, making him feel omnipotent.

She had given him her confidence and her trust. He knew there would never be a better time to get the rest of her story from her. "Talk to me—tell me what happened."

"In the nightmare?"

"No, Diana. What happened in Aquae Sulis?"

She nestled against him. "Marcus and I fell in love. How can I describe how deeply, how completely? So many things stood between us—our beliefs, our attitudes, our religion, even time itself, but our love overcame everything. We became bonded. We were soulmates."

Her murmured words touched his heart with loneliness. He had never known what she described. His arms tightened and she rubbed her cheek against his rock-hard chest.

"He didn't want to go to Rome without me, but Marcus considered it his duty. He wanted us to be married, but needed permission from Rome because he was a career soldier who had signed on for twenty-six years." She moved her cheek so that she could feel his heartbeat.

"I was terrified to go to Rome. I had read about Nero's atrocities, so I made up my mind to use my seductive powers to keep Marcus from going. I reckoned without love. He had to go, so I set my fears aside and went with him.

"His father welcomed me as his daughter. Titus Magnus and I grew to love each other in the short time we had together. Marcus left me at his father's villa while he and the procurator used their influence with the senators to get Paullinus replaced as governor of Britannia . . ." Diana's voice trailed off.

"No matter how dreadful, you must face it. Trust me to keep you safe." His lips touched her temple.

She drew back and looked up into his eyes. "I trusted Marcus completely. I believed he was all the protection I would ever need. He was the strongest, most physically powerful man that any age of history could ever produce, but it wasn't enough."

"Let go of it, Diana!" It was a command.

"Titus was poisoned and I was blamed." She began to sob, and everything came out in a rush. "I was taken to the slave pens—it was a living nightmare. Marcus kept hope alive within me. I was certain he would come. I was taken to Circus Maximus to be executed while Nero watched from his imperial box. Marcus was with him. He must have learned of his father's murder at the same time he saw me staked in the arena."

She drew a shuddering breath that convulsed her whole body and held on to Mark Hardwick as if he were her salvation. "The lions, the flames, and Marcus all reached me at the same time. Marcus loved me enough to plunge his sword into my heart to end my agony!"

Mark closed his eyes, feeling her pain, reliving Marcus' tortured anguish. It was as if he experienced his own death. "I saved you," he murmured joyfully.

Diana stopped sobbing and looked at him.

"Marcus saved you. When he plunged in his sword, you came back to your own time."

"Yes."

She touched his face, so heartbreakingly familiar, so beloved. "Thank you." The shared moment was private, intimate, for them alone. She moved back against his heart and he enfolded her in his arms. She felt boneless, melting against his strength, which she knew would endure forever.

He didn't move until he knew she was asleep. Then he carried her to his bed and laid her gently on top of the covers. He stared down at her, his brows drawn together in perplexity. She had told her story so convincingly, he had experienced it along with her. There were so many questions and so few answers, but of one thing he felt certain—their lives were entwined.

He stretched out beside her on top of the bed, watching over her like a dark avenging angel.

She sensed his presence and turned from her back so that she lay half on him in her favorite position, one of her legs between his, one of his between hers.

She thinks she's in bed with Marcus, his brain cried out.

"I know it's Mark," she whispered as if she read his thoughts. Her hands skimmed over his hard muscles once, and then she was asleep.

When Mr. Burke opened the chamber door with the earl's shaving water, Mark Hardwick's eyes flew open guiltily. As the beautiful girl stirred in his arms, he said, "Mr. Burke, you didn't see this."

"Of course not, my lord," Mr. Burke said calmly. He set down the water and departed as he did every other morning.

Diana, using his ribcage to lever herself up, blushed profusely. "I'm sorry, my lord."

"I'm not; it was my pleasure." His black eyes

brimmed with humor. "And now that we've slept together, I think you can stop calling me *my lord*."

She didn't smile. "I want to thank you for helping me. I was terrified and you banished my fears for me." She was in earnest, and covered with embarrassment.

He lifted his arms behind his head, stretched his muscular thighs beneath the velvet robe, and allowed his eyes to roam over her at leisure. "If I am Marcus Magnus, why are you embarrassed? Surely awakening in my arms is familiar to you?"

Her embarrassment was immediately replaced by a spark of anger. He was mocking her. "But totally unfamiliar to you. I remember every detail, you remember nothing!"

"I remember last night," he said seductively. "Perhaps you can rekindle my memories. Let's see, when you awoke with Marcus, your bodies entwined, surely he made love to you? Why don't you let me—"

"Dream on," she said sharply, tossing back her hair and scrambling off the bed.

He cursed low beneath his breath at the reaction of his body to her merest touch. Quitting the bed, he turned his back upon her to tend the fire.

He suspected she knew exactly how tempting she looked in the sheer lavender nightgown with that silken mass of gold shimmering about her shoulders. He was about to accuse her of running to him in the night on the pretext of a nightmare, but stopped himself in time. He knew her terror had been genuine. But now that daylight had arrived, so had her confidence and she was back to being a saucy baggage.

When he turned from the blazing fire, he saw that she was examining the map on his desk.

"This is wrong."

He stiffened. "What the devil do you mean?"

"This map of Aquae Sulis is wrong. Who drew it?"

"I did," he said aggressively.

She lifted her lashes to give him a pitying glance. "Oh dear, your memory is abysmal."

He closed the distance between them immediately. "I didn't draw it from memory, I drew it from research."

"Then your research is as faulty as your memory."

"What's wrong with it?" he demanded.

"The fortress covered a much larger area than you have drawn. The baths were inside the walls. They were built for the legionaries."

The earl was about to contradict her, but suddenly what she said made complete sense to him.

"The fortress covered at least thirty acres. As well as housing soldiers, a huge barracks ran along the wall that housed slaves."

His finger followed the path hers traced across his map. "Slaves?"

She looked up at him frankly. "They were your bloody slaves. Who the hell do you think built the roads and bridges? Not the Romans, though they get all the credit!"

"My engineers were the finest in the world!" He stopped, aghast at what he had been goaded into saying.

"You *do* remember!"

They were standing so close, their thighs brushed. Diana suddenly realized how revealing her nightgown was. "Oh lord, I forgot the doctor was coming," she mumbled.

Diana was barely back in the peach-colored chamber before Nora came sweeping through the door. "Your bath's ready and here's a more respectable nightgown to pop on before the doctor arrives."

Bathed and shaved, immaculate in buff breeches and bottle-green waistcoat, Mark Hardwick greeted his friend, Charles Wentworth.

The doctor lifted an eyebrow of inquiry. "Did you encourage her to talk?"

"Yes, she's talked at great length."

"Without coercion, I trust?"

"Dammit, Charles, you talk as if I'm incapable of being gentle with a woman."

"Mmm, well, I suppose there's always a first time for everything. Has she changed her story?"

"No. She's absolutely convinced she traveled back in time."

As they ascended the carved Elizabethan staircase, Mark asked, "Do you ever get the impression that you've lived before, in another time?"

Charles examined his friend's dark face to see if he was serious. He was. Charles laughed. "To tell you the truth, yes. When I graduated university and went on my grand tour, I visited Egypt. It was as familiar to me as London. More familiar. I experienced such strong déjà vu wherever I went, it couldn't possibly have been the first time I was there." He pulled a deprecating face. "Physician to the Pharaohs sounds like the rambling of a madman."

Mark shrugged, "Sounds normal enough to me, old man. Now I'll leave you to your patient."

Charles entered Diana's bedchamber saying, "Good morning, Lady Diana. You are looking much better; radiant in fact."

"Thank you, Dr. Wentworth, I'm feeling quite rested. May I get up today?"

"Not so fast, young lady. I have a couple of questions first. Have you experienced any pain?"

Only in my heart. "No, none at all, Doctor."

"Good. Have you experienced any faintness or dizziness?"

"No."

The door swung open and Mark walked in. "Has she told you she experienced a terrifying nightmare last night?"

Charles's eyes sought hers for confirmation.

"One so real she thought she'd gone back in time again," Mark continued.

Diana glared daggers at him.

"That's interesting," Charles said. "Not altogether bad in my opinion."

"Bad enough," Mark said grimly.

"No, I meant instead of being repressed, it's coming out both consciously and subconsciously." He glanced at both of them. "Apparently you feel comfortable discussing this with Mark and I think that's the best therapy."

Diana bristled. "If you'll keep your mouth shut, the doctor will let me get up today."

Mark towered over her. "I don't object to you getting up. I've seen you in bed so much, I'm beginning to believe you really were my mistress!"

Charles grinned. "By God, the two of you don't need me to encourage you to communicate, unless it's as referee."

Diana blushed faintly. "I'm sorry, Dr. Wentworth, but Mark can be so impossibly arrogant."

Charles's eyes danced. "I take it you've known him for some time."

Only seventeen hundred years.

"You may get dressed if you don't overtax yourself, and if you promise to have a rest this afternoon. Same time tomorrow."

"My aunt and uncle should be here by then. Lord, I'm not looking forward to the inquisition I'll get."

"I'll be glad to speak to them, Lady Diana. Give them all sorts of dire warnings about what could happen if they press you too hard."

"Thank you, Doctor."

"Peter should be back by then too?" Charles said, giving Mark a look that warned he'd better get his feelings for the lady sorted out before his brother returned.

Mark walked Charles to the front door of Hardwick Hall and held it open for him. "Charles?"

"Yes, Mark?"

"Mind your own damned business."

Charles grinned with delight, not the least bit offended.

As soon as she was alone, Diana slipped from the bed and opened the wardrobe. There hung the hideous beige pannier dress and, beside it, the old-fashioned corset. Her glance then fell on the trunk she had left behind the morning she had run away from Hardwick Hall. She knelt down to open it and memory of her pretty new clothes came flooding back.

Here was the saucy red half-corset and the jade velvet gown she had bought at Madame Madeleine's. She shook out the velvet folds and hung it up, then did the same with her other dresses. Diana tucked the nightgown she was wearing beneath the pillow and donned the corset. It certainly wasn't as exotic as her Roman garments, but she was willing to bet it was the most daring article of clothing in modern-day Bath.

She put on her smart black riding habit, then twisted her long hair into a chignon at the nape of her neck. When she couldn't find the earl indoors, she wandered out toward the stables. He was saddling a horse, and when she asked him to saddle one for her, he frowned.

"The weather isn't conducive to a sedate ride in the park, Lady Diana."

He was back to addressing her formally. She wondered if it was because of the severely cut riding habit. "I don't ride sedately. I have learned to ride neck or nothing, as I have learned to do most other things. It's so much more exhilarating."

"The doctor advised you not to overdo it."

She lifted her chin with *hauteur*. "You are not the only one who needs the outlet of a wild ride every once in a while. Being caged indoors makes me, too, long for freedom."

He relented and saddled the horse for her. Apparently they shared the same feelings about freedom. He took her to the back of his acres to the site of the dig, where she dismounted and plodded about in the mud, as fascinated as he was himself with the archaeological project.

From there they rode to the stone quarries, where he noted she asked the workmen scores of intelligent questions. It dawned upon him that she was not pretending an interest to flatter him, as most women would do, she was genuinely curious.

When they stopped at an inn for a bite of lunch, the earl did not dare to order a private room. They kept a cool distance between them while they ate and talked, as if they had declared an unspoken truce. They avoided personal topics, they avoided antagonizing each other, and they avoided any reference to last night.

Their politeness continued on the ride back to Hardwick Hall. When they arrived, both were pleased with themselves. They had spent time together without once losing their tempers. It was a relief to both of them that they could act in such a civilized manner.

Diana went to her room, determined to take a nap so that she would not be overtired later this evening. It was possible that Prudence, Richard, and Peter could arrive tonight if the roads were passable. She removed the riding habit and hung it in the wardrobe. Tonight she would wear the jade gown to give her confidence. She did not wish to be at a disadvantage when she faced Prudence.

The chamber door swung open. "Diana, I—"

Mark's black eyes took in the long legs, the succulent breasts, and the saucy red garment in the space between. The picture she made was such a contrast with the one she had presented in the severe riding habit that he lost control.

His hands closed about her tiny waist and he lifted her against him for a kiss.

"Oh dear heaven, don't kiss me—once we start, we can never stop," she breathed.

Chapter 32

Holding her in his arms brought such a heady sensation, Mark Hardwick couldn't have stopped if he'd wanted to. When he held her in the night, she had been genuinely terrified and his protective feelings had outweighed his desire. Now, however, Diana wasn't afraid of anything unless it was the intensity of her reaction to him.

His mouth on hers was hard, demanding, and she responded hungrily as if she were starving. *Don't stop—don't ever stop,* her brain cried out.

One kiss was not enough. His lips brushed her eyelids, temples, cheekbones, then slanted against her mouth once more, forcing her lips open to accept him inside her. Her tongue played with his deliciously, endlessly, until he mastered her and she yielded willingly, generously.

They kissed until they were both panting, kissed until their need for each other was ravenous. He picked her up, and her arms slid about his neck and clung possessively. Her smallness excited him, as did her passionate surrender. She would hold nothing back—she would allow him to be as wild and dominant as he pleased, endlessly taking from her, as she endlessly yielded.

Diana moaned softly as his powerful hands roamed her curves, remembering, remembering.

With his mouth still possessing hers, he carried her

down the hall to his own chamber and kicked the door closed behind them, shutting out the world.

Diana was in a frenzy to see him naked, to run her hands over the slabs of muscle in his chest, to feel the hot slide of naked male skin against her soft flesh. She knew Marcus' body completely; Mark's not at all. They felt the same, but she needed to see him, to taste him, to explore to the full his powerful maleness.

Her fingers were on the buttons of his shirt but his impatient hand brushed them away. He stood her on the bed while he tore off the shirt and flung it away. Her eyes widened as she saw the gold half-coin gleaming against the dark expanse of his muscled chest. Her fingers trembled as she lifted it.

"Mark, your Caesar coin! Marcus always wore it!"

The pupils of his eyes dilated with need. He would put his indelible stamp upon her to obliterate all thought of Marcus. He reached for her, but she stayed his hands.

"Where did you get the coin?"

"I've always had it," he said thickly. Again his hands reached out for her. His powerful fingers splayed beneath her breasts and he dipped his head to devour her.

"Wait! Wait! I have something to show you."

He closed his eyes and groaned. The last thing on earth he wanted to do was wait. Because she held him off, his hands fell to the waistband of his riding breeches and he stripped them from his body.

Diana's eyes filled with love. Naked, without his modern clothes, Mark was Marcus. She hadn't lost him, he was here for the taking. It was up to her to make him remember. Diana smiled a secret smile. She would have to ensnare him. Mark Hardwick was compulsive about his freedom. He would be easy to seduce; almost impossible to marry. In that moment, Diana made up her mind to have him. There was no way in heaven or hell she was going to lose him a second time!

Slowly, with tantalizing fingers she unfastened the corset and stepped from the scarlet lace. His black eyes smoldered as they traveled from her creamy breasts to the golden curls of her high mons. Around her slim waist she wore a gold chain that added a most erotic touch to her nakedness. She slipped her fingers beneath the half-coin and lifted it.

"This is the other half of Caesar. We fit together perfectly."

She had his attention now. She unfastened the clasp and put the other half of his priceless gold coin in his hands. Mark lifted it to his own half-coin. When he saw the two halves fit together to form a perfect Julius Caesar, he sat down upon the bed stunned.

"I've been searching all my life for this. It's probably the reason I have a passion for archaeology and Roman artifacts. I've had my half-coin since my earliest memory. I assumed it came from a great-grandfather. How did you get yours?"

Diana knelt down on the bed beside him. A faint blush dusted her cheeks as she remembered. "The coin was whole when Marcus wore it. After the first night we spent together, he took it off and placed it about my neck so I could have it all day to remember him, while we were apart."

"After he made love to you?"

Her lashes fanned her cheeks. "No. The first night he wanted to keep me virgin longer."

"He must have been mad," Mark said hoarsely.

"After that, whenever we made love, we passed it to the other, taking turns wearing it. The Caesar coin medallion was precious to him. When he asked me to marry him, he gifted me with half of it, to wear forever."

Mark fastened the tiny clasp and lifted the chain over her head. The half-coin dipped into the deep valley between her breasts.

"Do you believe now that you were once Marcus?"

"I'm beginning to," he admitted in a voice that

sounded like black velvet. He reached out a calloused fingertip to trace the swell of her breast. Diana shuddered. "I don't think I have the willpower to keep you virgin any longer."

"But I'm not virgin. You made love to me every night," Diana whispered.

He cupped her shoulders with gentle hands and pressed her back upon the bed. She yielded, doing whatever he wished to do. Their eyes met and held as Mark trailed the back of his fingers along the inside of her silken thigh. She did not resist his touch, but rather welcomed it as her thighs fell open to aid his searching quest.

As he ran his fingers through the gilt tendrils, she arched her mons in pleasure. His touch was hypnotic. Again she marveled that such large, powerful hands could be so tender when they caressed her female flesh.

One finger only stroked her cleft; a drop of woman's mist formed instantly, luring him on, easing his way. One finger only circled and separated her pink petals. One finger only slid up inside her.

Diana wet her top lip with the tip of her tongue. His black eyes followed its glistening trail. She wanted his fingers inside her, she wanted his tongue inside her, she wanted him to sheath his great gladius sword. She was drowning in need and he was obviously in a mood to draw out their loveplay until she was on the edge of madness. She swallowed hard, her throat aching with desire. It had to be just the way he wanted it this first time. How else could she enslave him?

She reached for his other hand, dropped a kiss upon it, then took one finger only and dipped it into her mouth. She began to suck upon him seductively and Mark felt the erotic sensation all the way to the tip of his marble-hard erection.

Diana was scalding hot and tight upon the finger of his other hand. When he imagined what she would feel like on his shaft, it began to pulse and buck of its own volition.

The problem was, he could clearly feel the barrier of

her hymen pressing back against his finger. He withdrew it slowly and made a decision. He would not tell her she was still virgin. She believed otherwise. She had an innate female sensuality that had nothing to do with age, and she was eager for his lovemaking. He did not want to see fear in her eyes. He wanted to see her pleasure, he wanted to feel her passion, he wanted to fulfill her every expectation of her woman's sexuality.

He simply could not resist what he did next. He went down on his knees, dipped his head between her thighs, and began to make exquisite love to her with his mouth and tongue.

Diana, with half-closed eyes, looked down at the beloved dark head between her thighs. He still made love in exactly the same way, thank God. She arched her mons into his mouth, raked her fingers through his black hair, and pressed him closer to show him how much blissful pleasure he was gifting her with.

She peaked in an amazingly short time, but Diana needed more, much more. She needed to feel his weight upon her, needed him to fill the emptiness inside her, needed the complete domination and submission of lovers who mated for life.

Mark moved up onto the bed. As he stretched out beside her, the disparity in their size was emphasized. The backs of his fingers brushed her cheek. "You are utterly lovely," he murmured softly, curbing his fierce lust so he could savor her as she deserved.

His fingers threaded into her golden mass of hair that crackled at his touch. He wanted to wrap himself in the silken tendrils, he wanted to bury himself inside her. He had never felt so greedy in his life. He wanted everything. He pictured taking her in every position known to man and then some, but not this first time, his inner voice cautioned. She was small and delicate, and he knew she would experience pain when he deflowered her.

Mark could not resist her lips for long. He moved over

her possessively, his mouth making love to hers endlessly. They began softly, sweetly, then progressed to sensual kisses, arousing kisses that spurred them on to wild, fierce, and savage kisses, until her lips were love-swollen. Then he began the cycle all over again, softly brushing her lips with his until she was writhing with need. Only then did his mouth move down her throat, trailing a hot path to her aching breasts.

Diana reached down and closed her hand around his sex. Dear God, she had forgotten how enlarged he became in their loveplay. When she clasped him tightly with the fingers of both hands, Mark knew he could delay no longer or he would spend.

"Wrap yourself around me," he urged hoarsely.

Diana needed no instruction. Her long legs slithered high about his back as he thrust deeply. A short scream burst from her throat. Mark went still to allow her to get used to him. The pain was so sharp, it was unendurable, but it was over in seconds, replaced by a fullness that stretched her to the limit.

Diana slowly realized her fingernails were digging into his shoulders, and then he was moving with long, slow thrusts, then gliding faster, building one exquisite sensation after another. Her hands caressed his shoulders now, as he whispered love words she'd never heard before. His hot whispers aroused her until her whole body was atremble. She arched against him once, twice, three times, and then she climaxed.

As her pulsations began to recede, he cried out harshly and she felt his white-hot seed pour into her. At that moment, she experienced something that had never happened to her before. She climaxed again, hard and fast and hot.

They clung to each other possessively, not wanting to separate. He rolled his weight from her, but took her with him so that she lay sprawled upon his body. He was still impaled in her voluptuous splendor. It was what both of them wanted. They were oblivious to the outside world.

This night belonged to them. Though darkness had not yet fallen, they would stay abed until dawn.

It was fortuitous that Peter spent the night in a gaming hell with his profligate friend Barrymore, and Prudence and Richard were forced to put up at an inn twenty miles from Bath because of a heavy deluge of rain that made visibility impossible once night had fallen.

The weather took its toll on Prudence's patience. When she learned that only one room in the inn was available, with one double bed, she became downright sullen and vindictive.

Richard left her to her own devices while he went to the taproom in search of an amenable wench. His quest was unsuccessful and he returned within the hour. Now both of them were sullen and vindictive.

"That wretched niece of yours was visited upon me like a biblical plague of locusts."

"That wretched niece of mine has made it possible for you to live in Grosvenor Square. Her money allows you to live in the lap of luxury!" Richard retorted.

"Well, if you had amounted to more than a starving solicitor, we could live off your money!"

"You are a bitch, Prudence, and the poorest fuck I ever had in my life!"

Prudence gasped. She was struck dumb that a man would sink so low as to use obscenity to a respectable wife.

"Why the hell I stay with you is beyond me. I should have divorced you long ago!"

Prudence stiffened. Dear God, the scandal of divorce would kill her. "You wouldn't dare! I know too much about your shady dealings. You'd bilk your own grandmother if you had the chance!"

Richard smiled. It was not a pretty sight. "And you, my dearest Prudence, would help me spend her money. We are two of a kind, and in this together whether we like it or not. I suggest we find a way to rub along together.''

He eyed her opulent breasts. "Get into bed, lie down, and above all, shut up," he ordered.

With stiff fingers, Prudence snuffed the candles and began to remove her layers of clothing. Men were beasts and sooner or later demanded their marital rights. Submitting to Richard's disgusting fumbling in the dark was far less traumatic than facing the world as a divorced woman in broad daylight.

After a horrible two days on the road, they arrived in Bath, where they decided to rent a house of their own rather than be obligated to the hospitality of the Hardwicks. It was afternoon before they arrived at the earl's magnificent Elizabethan hall in the midst of its own parkland.

As she stepped from the carriage, Prudence's lips narrowed at the thought that someday this would probably belong to Diana if she married Peter Hardwick. Still, that would keep her away from the house in Grosvenor Square —the house that Prudence had come to think of as hers.

Mr. Burke led them to the drawing room, where Diana awaited them with trepidation. Prudence stared hard at Diana, examining her for changes. And changes she found. The girl before her in the jade velvet gown seemed older with far more poise and composure than she had ever witnessed in her niece before.

Diana smiled at them. "I am so sorry for the worry I have caused you both, though my disappearance wasn't deliberate, I assure you. Thank you for searching for me and worrying about me. You will both be happy when I come of age in a couple of months and you are relieved of your responsibility."

The girl was deliberately pointing out that their authority would soon be at an end. Prudence and Richard exchanged an alarmed glance. Diana smiled again. "You mustn't worry about me; as you can see I am quite well."

Prudence looked closer. She appeared decidedly fatigued; her eyes had a slumberous look about them. Yet she seemed divinely happy. "Where were you all these months?" Prudence demanded.

Diana had debated with herself over what she should tell Prudence. Should she tell her some plausible tale, should she concoct some scenario that her aunt could swallow? In the end she had decided to tell the truth. Neither Prudence, nor Richard either, would believe her, of course, but that really wasn't her problem. No matter what story she told, Prudence would believe exactly what she chose to believe.

Diana stated the facts without embellishing them. "When we left Hardwick Hall that morning I was in a dilemma about marrying Peter. I took a walk up on the heights and went into an antique shop where I came upon a Roman helmet. I tried it on and it became stuck. I believe I fainted. When I woke up, I was in the same place, but in a different time period. I cannot explain how, but I was transported back to when the Romans occupied Britain."

"Rubbish!" Prudence said flatly. Diana had run off with some man. By simply looking at her, Prudence could tell she had lost her innocence. "Richard, I should like a word alone with Diana, if you would excuse us, dear."

He obliged Prudence, thinking as she did that Diana had been with her first lover and couldn't possibly admit such a thing in his presence.

"You have behaved scandalously!" Prudence accused when they were alone.

Diana put her head on one side as if considering her behavior. "Actually, I have, Prudence. The things I wore were scandalous, the things I said were scandalous, and the things I did were quite depraved. Quite deliciously depraved."

Prudence turned an unbecoming shade of carmine. "You have been gone for *nine months*. Did you have a child out of wedlock?"

Diana gasped. "Leave it to your respectable mind to

suspect such a thing. No, I'm sorry to say, I did not have a child, and it is the one thing in all this I deeply regret!''

"Oh! You will show some respect when you speak to me, young lady, even though you obviously have no respect for yourself!''

Prudence turned and stalked toward the door, yelling out for her husband. "Richard, I refuse to deal with your ward. She is out of control. She is not in her right mind!''

Richard, hearing Prudence's shocked hysterics and reading between the lines that Diana had been ruined, said hastily, "When Peter arrives, I think we'd best have the wedding as quickly as possible.''

Diana stood up. She wanted to tell them that was impossible, but she knew she must tell Peter first. She owed him that courtesy. "Whether we marry or not is between Peter and I. It is none of your business.''

"It most assuredly is our business, young madam,'' replied Prudence. "You are under our control for the next two months. Tell her, Richard.''

"That is true, Diana, whether you like it or not,'' Richard confirmed.

"I am under your *guidance,* not your *control,*'' Diana replied, raising her voice to match theirs.

In the front hall Charles Wentworth and Mark Hardwick looked at each other with concern. "Shall we intervene?'' asked Charles.

"We shall,'' replied the earl decisively.

Chapter 33

The raised voices ceased immediately and silence filled the air as the two men entered the drawing room. Mark broke the silence.

"This is Dr. Wentworth, who has been caring for Diana since I found her unconscious. Charles, this is Prudence and Richard Davenport, Diana's guardians."

Richard stepped forward to shake the doctor's hand. Prudence nodded stiffly.

"I'm very pleased with Lady Diana's progress, but I feel I should advise you that she is not completely recovered."

"In what way?" Prudence demanded.

"She has suffered a trauma. Luckily she has recovered physically."

"But not mentally?" Prudence cut in.

"There is nothing wrong with her mental state," Charles said firmly. "She has not fully recovered emotionally. She needs time for that."

"What about the lies she's concocted to cover up the truth of where she's been all these months?"

"I would not call it lying when she firmly believes what she has told us."

Diana opened her mouth to protest. They were speaking about her as if she were invisible. Mark put a finger to his lips and reluctantly she obeyed him.

"Claptrap and rubbish!" Prudence declared.

Charles Wentworth summoned all his patience. "We don't have all the answers, but with time and understanding Lady Diana will recover completely, and surely that is what all of us want."

"Pack your things. We have taken a house in Queen Square."

Mark's black eyes bored into Prudence. "That is entirely unnecessary. Lady Diana may stay here until Dr. Wentworth feels she is recovered."

Prudence pretended outrage. "That would be highly improper. My niece is an unmarried lady, Lord Bath."

"Are you suggesting I would compromise her?" Mark Hardwick demanded with cold arrogance.

Diana stood up, suddenly tired of all the arguing. "I shall come to Queen Square as soon as I've spoken with Peter. I'm sorry about all of this, Prudence."

Thinking to smooth over the awkward situation that had arisen, Charles said, "Diana will be just fine. I shall be happy to come to Queen Square to keep an eye on her."

"Dr. Wentworth, your services are no longer—"

"Prudence, that's quite enough!" Richard cut in. "Dr. Wentworth has been most helpful." He shook the doctor's hand. "I am indebted to you, sir, for the care of my niece. I shall indeed send for you to Queen Square." With that, Richard and Prudence took their leave, followed by the doctor.

"Why the hell did you cave in to her bullying?" Mark demanded.

"I haven't the faintest intention of going to Queen Square. I just said that to get rid of her. I had to do something before you came to blows."

"That is the most odious woman I have ever encountered."

Diana began to laugh and cast him a sideways glance. "Imagine her insinuating that you would compromise me."

He closed the space between them in two strides, clasped her firmly about the waist, and lifted her high. "Let me do it now."

"Absolutely not."

His dark brows drew together in disappointment. She kissed his frown away. "It's my turn to compromise you!"

It was long after dark when Peter Hardwick finally arrived. Diana had cajoled Mark into letting her talk to his brother alone, against his better judgment. She sat reading in the library, knowing in her bones that he would come tonight.

Mr. Burke took Peter's greatcoat and told him Lady Diana awaited him in the library. He swept into the room like an ardent suitor.

"Darling girl, how wonderful to see you recovered." He lifted both her hands to his lips, then tried to draw her into his arms.

Diana stepped back from him. "Peter, we have to talk."

He held up his hand. "No confessions, Diana, I insist. What's done is done, and it really doesn't matter to me where you have been. All that matters is that you've come back to me."

He was behaving so gallantly, Diana was consumed with guilt. "Peter, I'm withdrawing from the engagement."

"I shan't allow you to do any such thing. We will be married immediately."

"Peter, you are not listening to me! I cannot marry you!"

At her tone, Peter wrenched his high neckcloth from

his throat with savage fingers, as though it were choking him.

"Is there someone else?" he demanded.

"Yes," she said quietly, "there is someone else."

His lips curled in rage. "I have a written agreement with your guardians that cannot be broken."

"I know nothing of this," she told him truthfully.

"You also know nothing of the fact that they want your money and petitioned the courts to have you declared dead!"

The book she had been reading dropped from nerveless fingers. "What are you saying?"

"I am saying they are vultures who already have their hands on your money. If you marry me, they will no longer have control of you."

Diana's eyes widened. "You want to marry me for my money!" It was a revelation. How utterly naive she had been. "There is no need for me to marry, thank God! I come of age in two months and will control my own money."

"There'll be nothing left. Two months is ample time for Richard Davenport to bleed you dry."

"I won't listen to this. I shall go and confront them immediately!"

"Your safety lies in this house and in marrying me. Don't put yourself in their hands. Diana—"

"Leave me."

"Oh, I'll leave you for now but you can be assured that you won't get free of your agreement this easily," said Peter as he stomped from the room.

Diana sat down at the desk. Could there possibly be any truth in the things he was saying? Prudence and Richard were after her inheritance? Peter Hardwick was willing to marry her for her money? They had a written agreement? It was true that Prudence had pressed her continually to marry Peter, but how could that benefit her aunt and uncle?

Icy fingers stole about her heart; the written agreement

must carve up her fortune between them. Diana's thoughts swirled about, trying to piece things together, trying to make some sense of it while at the same time denying that all the people who professed to love her loved only her money.

Richard had tried to sell her father's priceless library. What motive could he possibly have had but money? Mark had wanted to buy it. Dear God in Heaven, was he in on the agreement?

Peter Hardwick flung open his brother's bedchamber door. "Mark, you've got to help me."

The earl had been trying to work on his book about ancient Aquae Sulis, but of course his mind was on other matters. He would have preferred to be with Diana when she gave the news to Peter about breaking their engagement. After all, he felt totally responsible. He stood up from his desk and indicated the chairs before the fire. "Sit down, Peter."

"When I arrived in Grosvenor Square to give the Davenports the good news about Diana, they wanted to kill the messenger. Richard had petitioned the courts to have her declared dead. I have reason to believe he had already siphoned off her money to his own accounts."

"That is a very serious charge, Peter. What makes you think he would do such a thing?"

"He said our agreement for me to marry Diana was off. Mark, the only reason he would call off such a profitable arrangement was if he had a way to get *all* of her money."

"Are you telling me you were being paid to marry Diana?" Mark's black eyes were riveted on his brother's handsome face.

Peter shot up from the chair. "You make it sound like some sort of crime! Mark, for Christ's sake, I'm over my head in debt. The moneylenders are closing in on me. I'll see the inside of Fleet Prison unless I marry Diana Davenport."

Mark Hardwick's fist smashed into Peter's jaw. The shorter man fell to the floor like a ton of bricks. Mark took a deep breath to curb his impulse to pummel his brother senseless where he lay.

"You profligate young swine. The sight of you makes me sick!"

Holding his jaw, Peter crawled onto his knees, then using an overturned chair, pulled himself upright.

"You self-righteous bastard! Because you were first-born, everything was handed to you on a gold plate embossed with strawberry leaves—the land, the title, the money. It's easy for you to look down your arrogant nose at me because I'd marry for money, but you haven't even the guts to marry!"

Mark ran his hand through his hair to prevent him from smashing it into Peter's face again.

"You have a generous allowance, which would be adequate if you didn't run wild with those debauched friends of yours. I'll settle your debts one last time. If you fall into debt again, I'll let you rot in prison. Now get the hell out of my sight before I kill you."

The thick walls of the Elizabethan manor prevented Diana from hearing the argument, but when Peter Hardwick came rushing down the staircase and crashed the front door closed behind him, she came out of the library to see what on earth was happening. She went to a front window and drew aside the drape in time to see a carriage and horses thunder down the driveway.

When Diana went back to the entrance hall, Mark was standing at the top of the stairs. Even in the half light, she could see he was in a towering rage.

"Was that Peter?"

"Come upstairs," he ground out.

Diana was suddenly afraid. "I'm sorry I've made such a mess of things."

"Come upstairs," he repeated. The sound of his voice told Diana he was as upset as she had seen him throughout this entire ordeal.

Her chin went up. "I haven't broken his heart," she said defensively. "He was marrying me for my money, but obviously you knew that—everyone but me knew that."

He came down the stairs like a panther stalking its prey. Hair on the nape of her neck raised in alarm and a shudder passed over her. *Run!* her inner voice cried, but she was rooted to the spot, mesmerized by the dark force of the powerful male who advanced upon her.

He swept her up in commanding arms that brooked no refusal and carried her up the staircase. She struggled against him, but his brute strength and anger were so great she could not escape his iron grip. He strode into his bedchamber and kicked the door shut behind them.

"Marcus . . . Mark!" she gasped. "Please don't do this."

His black eyes gazed into hers in disbelief. "Are you afraid of me?"

"I . . . I am afraid of your anger," she whispered.

He sat down before the fire and gathered her against him. "My anger is not at you, it's at what they've done to you!"

Diana sagged against him, grateful for his strength.

"How will you ever trust anyone again, when they've all betrayed you?" He clenched an iron-hard fist. "You were even afraid of me. I want to kill them!"

She took hold of his fist and drew it to her cheek. His fingers opened and he brushed them across her temple and caressed her face tenderly. Centuries of civilization had wrought changes. Marcus would have killed them; Mark controlled his bloodlust. "What did Peter tell you?"

"He said Richard and Prudence were embezzling my money. He said my only hope of escaping their control was to marry him. He had some sort of written agreement with them to divide up my fortune. I told him I would go and confront them."

"No. You mustn't do that. I'll have my barristers start an investigation immediately."

"What did Peter say to you, or more to the point, what did you say to Peter?"

"When he admitted he wanted to marry you for money, I let my fists do my talking for me."

"Poor Peter."

"You're not sorry for the young swine?"

"In a way. He'll never be able to measure up to you. You set a formidable example."

"You exaggerate, but I love it." His lips touched her earlobe. "Tell me more."

"You are noble and honorable and—"

"I'm a bloody fool. I told him I'd settle his debts. I'll have to go up to London tomorrow and buy back all his markers. I can't just give him the money, he's completely untrustworthy." His arms tightened about her. "Come with me?" Mark knew it was a lot to ask. If they traveled to London together, openly, she would be completely compromised. The ton would descend upon her like a pack of ravenous beasts and devour what was left of her reputation.

"I'd rather stay here," she murmured against his throat. While he was safely in London, Diana fully intended visiting Queen Square for a showdown. She didn't need Mark to fight all her battles for her. In fact, she was quite looking forward to a confrontation with Prudence.

"Perhaps that would be best," he said ruefully. "You'll be perfectly safe here. Peter isn't likely to return for some time, but if he does, I'll have Mr. Burke forbid him the house."

"I'm not afraid of Peter. So long as I have you, the whole world and everyone in it can go to hell."

His lips claimed her possessively. Between kisses she whispered, "Why don't you look for a pair of Roman din-

ing couches while you're in London? Food and lovemaking
are a delicious combination.''

She was the most fascinating, unconventional woman
he had ever known and he utterly adored her. He cursed that
he had to leave her tomorrow, but he would make up for it
tonight.

The following morning when Charles Wentworth was
summoned to Queen Square, he was mildly surprised. Prudence Davenport had hated him on sight and did not want
him treating Lady Diana. Richard Davenport must have
overruled her. Though it wasn't apparent, Davenport must
have the upper hand in the marriage.

When he arrived, Dr. Wentworth was greeted by Richard and it was obvious that Prudence, sitting quietly in the
drawing room, had been told to mind her manners.

"Thank you for coming, Dr. Wentworth. We need to
understand more fully what happened to Diana and learn if
she is to recover."

"Well, it's a rather baffling case, of course. Your niece
disappeared for months. Only she knows where she was,
but she has suppressed this knowledge. Lady Diana believes she was transported back in time to when the Romans occupied Britain. It's a form of amnesia. The mind
has a blank space that is terrifying in itself, and so it substi-
tutes a plausible story."

"Plausible?" Prudence could apparently hold her
tongue no longer.

"Plausible to Diana. All the answers lie hidden. If she
is allowed to talk about it openly, I believe she will get it all
out of her system and the truth will surface."

"You have no guarantee of this, Dr. Wentworth. Is it
possible she will always be delusionary?" Richard asked
quietly.

"I wish I could tell you otherwise, but as you say,
there are no guarantees. However, she functions normally in

every other way and most of us have eccentricities. May I see my patient?''

"I'm sorry, Doctor, she hasn't returned from Hardwick Hall yet," Richard replied. "I just wanted to clear up a few things before she arrives."

"Dr. Wentworth, I would appreciate it if none of this went any further," Prudence said stiffly.

"Mrs. Davenport, I assure you I wouldn't dream of discussing my patient with anyone. Only the fact that you are her legal guardians allows me to even discuss the matter with you."

As Richard closed the front door, Prudence opened the door that led from the drawing room into the dining room. A barrel-chested man stepped across the threshold.

"Were you able to hear everything, Doctor?"

"Indeed I was, madam. It appears you have every reason to be alarmed."

As Richard joined them, he was most gratified to receive a look of admiration from Prudence. The idea had come to him out of the blue, not when Diana began rambling about Romans, but when Richard realized she was going to refuse to marry Peter Hardwick. Why share her fortune when they could have it all?

He could pay the right doctor to have her certified insane and institutionalized. He would manage her legal affairs and her estate once she was declared incompetent.

"Why Richard, dear, you are brilliant," Prudence declared when he explained his plan. "Our consciences will be perfectly clear because Diana is truly deranged. She needs to be put where she will be guarded twenty-four hours a day. For her own protection she must not be allowed to wander off again."

"We cannot have a doctor from Bath or even the County of Somerset. The earl has far too much influence here."

"Surely in all your dealings with the law you know of a doctor who could be persuaded?"

Suddenly Richard thought of the perfect man for their plan. No wonder the scheme had come to him so readily. Two years before he'd been involved in a similar situation. A prominent family had the heir who inherited declared incompetent, and Dr. Clayton Bognor of Wiltshire had signed the papers to have him committed. Chippenham, Wiltshire, was only twenty miles away and Davenport had no difficulty persuading the honorable doctor to return with him to Bath.

Richard looked up at the tall man gravely. "I'm sure when you see and hear the patient for yourself, Dr. Bognor, you will agree with my wife and I that our niece is unlikely to recover."

As Prudence put on her fashionable bonnet and firmly anchored it with a jet hatpin, she cautioned, "We may meet with resistance when we try to remove her from Hardwick Hall, Doctor."

"Have no fear, dear lady, I anticipate no difficulty. The law is completely on our side."

At that moment the doorknocker rapped loudly and Prudence looked out the front window to see who the unwanted caller was. "It's Diana," she hissed at Richard.

"How very convenient," he replied.

"Perhaps I should go back into the dining room for the time being. She'll be much more forthcoming if she finds the two of you alone," Clayton Bognor suggested.

Chapter 34

When Richard opened the door, Diana swept in with great authority.

"No servants? I'm amazed, especially since I'm paying for all this. Prudence, you usually can't manage without half-a-dozen lackeys at your beck and call."

Prudence flushed darkly. "You will speak to me with respect, young lady!"

"Respect has to be earned, Prudence. All you and Richard have earned is my suspicion, my anger, and my contempt!"

"You are not in your right mind, Diana," Richard said. "You have turned into another person."

"One not quite so gullible and naive. Peter Hardwick returned last night, and when I informed him that the wedding was off, he disclosed the secret financial agreement he had with you."

"We have no secret agreement with Peter Hardwick. He is lying!"

For one brief moment she wanted to believe her uncle. But in her heart she knew it was true. The blindfold had been removed from her eyes and she saw clearly what a scheming pair they made.

"Then you won't have any objection to an investigation of how you have administered my finances," she declared triumphantly.

"None whatsoever," he said grandly. "In two months time when you come of age, I will turn everything over to you and you can investigate to your heart's content. I shall be glad to be shut of the whole responsibility."

Prudence knew she must bring her back on track. "Diana, have you remembered where you have been all these months or are you still insisting you were swept back to Roman times?"

Diana swung around from her uncle to face Prudence. "For such a respectable woman, you have decidedly obscene thoughts. You are simply panting for me to confirm that a lover got me with child and I hid away for nine months. But that simply isn't true, Prudence. I went back in time to when the Romans occupied Aquac Sulis. The general who enslaved me, Marcus Magnus, was Mark Hardwick, the Earl of Bath. And yes, Prudence, we were lovers!"

Richard pushed open the door into the dining room. "Have you heard enough, Doctor?"

The burly man stepped through the doorway. "She is completely delusional. I'll sign the papers."

"Who the hell is this?" Diana demanded, furious that they were deceitful enough to conceal someone so that their conversation could be overheard.

"This is Dr. Clayton Bognor. He has agreed to take over your case."

"I'm under the care of Charles Wentworth. Do you seriously believe I'd accept a doctor of your choosing?"

"You have no say in the matter. You are a minor."

"Step aside!" Diana was almost choking with fury.

Her uncle did not step aside. He and the doctor closed in on her and held her firmly by the arms.

Diana struggled fiercely. "Take your hands from me, you scheming swines!"

Dr. Bognor clamped a cloth to her face. Diana gasped,

breathed in heavy, noxious fumes, and slumped into her uncle's arms.

Diana felt herself being lifted. She opened heavy eyes and realized she was being carried into a large building that looked like a stately home, except it had bars on the windows. The two men who carried her were Dr. Bognor and her uncle Richard. Dear God, it was another nightmare that was not a nightmare. Was she losing her mind?

No, it was really happening. She could feel the fingers of the doctor digging cruelly into her soft flesh as he carried her, and her head ached vilely from the substance he had used to render her unconscious. Prudence was nowhere in sight, but Diana knew she must have approved this abduction.

When they took her inside, anger momentarily overrode fear. As they set her feet to the floor, she shook off Richard's hold on her. "Where am I?" she demanded.

"You are in a hospital," he replied soothingly, as if dealing with a hysterical child.

"I'm not staying! There's nothing the matter with me!" She tried to shake off the doctor's hold, but he held her in a viselike grip.

"Of course you're not staying; as soon as you are well, you may come home," Richard promised.

Fear was slowly gaining the upper hand. Diana knew what they were doing. They were going to confine her here indefinitely, so they could control her money. Panic choked her. She must escape! She saw Bognor's hand gripping her arm and in a flash she sank her teeth into his flesh and bit down hard.

He cried out in pain and released her immediately. Richard made a grab for her, but she darted away to stand behind a huge mahogany desk between them. The matron who had been sitting at the desk jumped up in alarm. Diana picked up the chair the matron had been sitting on and hurled it at Dr. Bognor. It missed him and crashed into the wall, making an ugly hole in the plaster.

Diana snatched up an oil lamp. "If you don't let me out of here, I'll take this bloody place apart, stone by stone!" She had been imprisoned before; this time she wasn't going meekly.

"She's insane, call for attendants!" Dr. Bognor ordered the matron.

Diana smashed the lamp and threw it onto the papers stacked on the desk. It blazed up immediately, and the three people in the room fell back. Diana immediately made a rush for the door, but to her utter dismay she found it locked.

Two large, athletic-looking women in striped uniforms came forward. With a shiver, Diana thought of the bath slaves in Aquae Sulis.

"We have no alternative," Bognor said, beating out the flames with his coat. "Put her in a straitjacket."

"Nooo," Diana wailed as the females easily subdued her frantic struggles.

They took her upstairs to a small room that had no furniture. A window, set high in the wall, had bars across it. Diana breathed deeply trying to hang on to her sanity. She knew she must escape from this place, but no plan suggested itself. She could not do it with physical strength; therefore, she would have to use her wits.

The women began to undress her. She eyed the canvass jacket with its straps and buckles and began to tremble. "Please don't put that thing on me, please. I'll behave myself. I won't give you any more trouble." Diana might as well have been talking to the walls for all the effect her pleas had on the hospital attendants.

Within minutes she was naked, save for the gold half-coin about her neck. In a flash she covered it with her hand and backed away from them. She knew she hadn't a hope in hell of keeping it, but a desperate idea came to her.

"Listen to me, both of you. This half-coin is solid

gold. It is a priceless antique. It's Julius Caesar from Roman times. Don't give it to the doctor. Nobody knows I have it!''

The women looked at each other with meaning. Diana could see they were tempted to keep it for themselves. ''If you pawn it, they'll give you a few pounds; if you sell it to an antique shop in Bath, they'll give you maybe a hundred guineas. But its value is absolutely priceless. The Earl of Bath once offered me half a million pounds for it.''

The women exchanged a look of disbelief that said they knew they were dealing with a lunatic. Diana's heart sank. She'd priced it too high. They couldn't comprehend that kind of money. One of the women forced open her hand and took her most beloved possession from her. Each of them looked at it without saying a word, then one of them slipped it into her pocket.

The women then forced her arms into the canvass sleeves, crossed them about her body, and buckled the straps at the back. Another strap went between her legs and fastened at the back onto the others.

Diana talked quickly, trying not to babble. ''How much money do they pay you here? A pound a week, two? If you sold that gold coin to the Earl of Bath, you'd never have to work again!''

They went out and locked the door. There was no bed to lie on, no chair even to sit upon. Diana slid down the wall until she touched the floor. Why hadn't she gone to London with Mark? Why had she allowed herself to become a victim again? It was because once she was back in her own Georgian times, she thought she was safe. But evil was the same in any age. Evil was timeless. Since the world began, there were certain people who would do anything for gain.

She closed her eyes to try to prevent the tears from rolling down her cheeks. *Don't give up hope, or they have won.* Love, too, was timeless. ''Mark,'' she whispered, ''find me . . . help me.'' Diana was terrified to escape into sleep, for sleep might bring worse nightmares. *Mark will come.* The thought was the only thing she had to sustain her and help her hang on to her sanity.

The Earl of Bath made the rounds of every fashionable gentlemen's club in London, buying back his brother's markers. After only one day he realized he did not wish to be there. Without Diana, London held no appeal for him.

It was the early hours of the morning before he sought his bed, yet still he could not sleep. Memory of her filled his senses. He felt almost bereft without her. His bed was too empty, as was his heart. It was brought home to him that for the first time in his life he needed someone. Another thought nagged at him relentlessly. What if she needed him? If Diana had a nightmare during the long, dark hours, she would not be able to seek the sanctuary of his arms.

Mark arose early. Dawn had not completely dispelled his vague apprehension about Diana. He decided to return to Bath immediately, and to that end paid a visit to the chambers of his barristers, Chesterton and Barlow. He instructed them to pay off his brother's debts and asked them to start an inquiry into Lady Diana Davenport's inheritance from her late father.

"Your lordship, this is a delicate matter. For the record, our hands are tied while the lady in question is still a minor. Off the record, we can begin an investigation on the QT," Johnathon Barlow explained.

"She comes of age in less than two months," Mark Hardwick provided.

"Good. What we need is a deposition, signed by the complainant, and also one signed by you as a witness. We'll do the preliminary investigation so that the day she comes of age we can legally proceed."

Armed with the proper papers for a deposition, Mark was on his way home by midmorning, and rather than stop at a posting inn, he decided to drive straight through. He knew he could not possibly arrive before midnight, but the anticipation of surprising Diana and rousing her from sleep spurred him on mile after mile.

When he turned into the long driveway of Hardwick Hall, he saw that the lights were still blazing and he sensed immediately that something was wrong. He drove directly to the stables, left explicit instructions regarding his lathered team of horses, then raced to the house.

Mr. Burke had not yet retired. "Lord Bath, I've been consumed with worry and didn't quite know how to proceed."

"It's Diana, isn't it?" Mark demanded, throwing off his greatcoat and heading for the stairs.

"Lady Diana isn't here, sir."

"Where is she, Mr. Burke?"

"That's just it, sir. We have no idea. The coachman drove her into town, ostensibly to do some shopping. She told him to wait for her at the Abbey, but she never returned to the carriage."

"Did Peter come back?" Mark demanded suspiciously.

"No, sir. I haven't seen hide or hair of him."

"Her aunt and uncle are staying here in Bath. In all likelihood that's where she will be." Mark cursed himself for leaving her behind.

"I took the liberty of calling round to Queen Square this morning, my lord. There was no answer."

A cold suspicion took hold of him. Diana had left Hardwick Hall for propriety's sake. He took the stairs three at a time. His bedchamber was immaculate. The red lace corset was no longer on the carpet where she had dropped it. He was about to curse again when his eye fell on her earrings, which she had left on his bedside table. He picked them up and slipped them into his pocket.

Next he went down the hall to the peach-colored chamber. He was relieved when he opened the wardrobe and saw her dresses hanging there. She hadn't packed and left him after all. His relief was short-lived. Obviously she'd had every intention of returning. A woman did not leave her clothes and her earrings behind unless she intended to return.

He ran his hand over her pillow. Tucked beneath it was her nightgown. He lifted it to his cheek absently, and her unique scent stole to him. All his senses told him that Diana was as attracted to him as he was to her. She would not remain apart from him voluntarily. Prudence and Richard must have forbidden her to return to Hardwick Hall. His mouth curved grimly. Diana was willful as ten strong men. What Prudence forbade would have little effect on her. *They must be constraining her forcefully!*

"Mr. Burke, get me a dry coat," he called as he came running down the staircase. "I'm going to Queen Square. After all, I am a justice of Bath; if necessary I'll swear out a search warrant."

Mr. Burke knew it was useless to point out to the earl that it was three in the morning. Mark Hardwick was a man who made his own rules.

The coach barreled across Pulteney Bridge and along Bridge Street. As it turned onto Barton, the coach driver was stopped by the watch. The watchman lifted his lantern to peer at the driver. "No carriages allowed in this part of town. What's your business at this hour of the night, anyway?"

"Out of the way, man! Don't you realize whose carriage this is?"

"I don't care if it's the Earl of Bath himself. No carriages allowed!" He shone his lantern inside the carriage and was taken aback. "Sorry, yer lordship, that were just a figure of speech, ye understand."

"No, no, quite right. I'm most pleased you are doing such a diligent job." He gave the watchman a sovereign and told his driver to carry on.

At Queen Square he hammered on the door, but no

light went on inside, and after about ten minutes, he reluctantly accepted that there was no one at home. He decided to return at dawn and question the neighbors. In the meantime he directed his driver to take him to Charles Wentworth's residence.

Fortunately the good doctor was used to being roused at odd hours of the night. The gentry cared little about a doctor's sleep, when gout or indigestion prevented their own. When Charles came downstairs and found Mark pacing up and down his entrance hall, he asked, "Is it Lady Diana?"

"She's gone, Charles. I was hoping you had seen her."

"Come into the library, Mark. The embers of the fire should still be giving off a little heat. Let me get you a brandy; you look as if you could use one."

"You do know something!" Mark said with hope.

"Not really. Two days ago I was summoned to Queen Square and went immediately to see Diana. Richard Davenport and his wife met me in the drawing room and said they needed to understand more fully what had happened to Diana and if she would recover. I again explained that their niece believed she had been transported back in time. I advised them to encourage her to freely express herself and not suppress her memories. When I asked to see my patient, they said she was still at Hardwick Hall."

"That's all that was said; nothing else?"

"Well, Prudence asked me to keep everything completely confidential. I gather she'd rather be buried alive than be the butt of gossip."

"They want the whole bloody business kept quiet because they're up to something!" Mark cursed vilely.

You're in love with her, Charles thought. *It's finally happened.*

Mark drank off his brandy. "I'll find her." He said it with such determined conviction, Charles believed him.

"If I can help in any way, just ask."

By five-thirty, Mark was knocking on the other doors

of Queen Square. All he found out was that the Davenports neither brought their own servants nor hired the staff that usually came with the rental property. No one had seen a young lady arrive or leave.

The earl's next stop was the rental office. When they proved most reticent about answering any questions regarding their clients, he took another tack and rented the house for a month. With the keys firmly in hand, he returned to Queen Square and searched it from top to bottom, looking for some proof that Diana had been there.

He found nothing. There was, however, a peculiar odor in the downstairs rooms that he couldn't immediately identify. He had encountered it before, but could not recall where. It was a medicinal smell, not exactly noxious but definitely unwholesome. With reluctance he locked up the house and slipped the key into his pocket.

When his hand touched Diana's earrings, he closed his eyes, remembering the moment she had removed them. He wanted her back in his bed, back in his life. She had become a part of him. Deep down he was convinced she would not leave him of her own volition. If she had run away, it was not from him, it was to escape either her guardians or Peter.

Mark Hardwick decided to make the rounds of every coaching inn in Bath. Transportation to London, Bristol, and every other large city was available on a daily basis. If Diana had bought a ticket anywhere, he would find out. He began at the Christopher in High Street, then moved on to the Bear and the White Hart. By the time he questioned the coach drivers at the Saracen's Head in Broad Street, he was beginning to think his quest was hopeless.

At the Angel in Westgate Street, where they had extensive facilities, he learned that the Davenports had stabled their own horses and coach there. No one, however, recalled seeing a young woman.

He ran a savage hand through his hair in frustration. Then suddenly it came to him. Opium! What he had smelled in Queen Square was similar to the cloying fumes of opium! God in Heaven, what had they done to her?

Chapter 35

Diana spent the night huddled against the wall. By morning she had tremendous difficulty breathing. The straitjacket crossed her arms over her chest so tightly, she felt as if she were suffocating. She swore that if it was removed from her, she would not behave in a reckless manner that would give them an excuse to put it back on.

Finally, the same two women who had attended her the night before unlocked the door and brought her wash water. They removed the straitjacket and left her naked. Diana waited until they left before she gave herself a sponge bath. She remembered the advanced bathing facilities in Aquae Sulis, reliving the laughter and joy she and Marcus had enjoyed in his bathing pool. Compared with the Romans, the bathing facilities of the Georgians were almost squalid.

The women had taken the straitjacket with them and she prayed she had seen the last of it. She much preferred being naked. To most people that might be humiliating, but Diana had learned to accept her unclothed body as beautiful. Nudity of herself or others no longer intimidated her.

When the women returned, however, they brought a brown smock and a pair of canvas shoes.

"What is this place?" she ventured in a calm voice.

The women exchanged a cautious glance, then one of them said, "It's a private asylum."

Asylum? Dear God, they've put me in the madhouse! "How many other patients are in here?"

"There are more than fifty inmates," came the reply, "but you won't be allowed to mix with the others until you learn to behave yourself. You are to be kept in solitary confinement for the first few weeks."

Weeks? Dear God in Heaven, don't let me be here weeks! she cried silently. But Diana realized her chances for escape were very slim while they kept her isolated. They took her from the room and put her in another down a long passageway. It was furnished in a Spartan manner with a cot, a commode, a table, and a chair.

Diana's knees went weak when she saw the tray on the table. It contained a jug of water, a bowl of gruel, and a thick slice of bread. She was ravenous and so thirsty her throat was sore. She heard the key turn in the lock when the women departed, but all Diana could think of was food.

After she ate the last mouthful of gruel and licked the spoon, a dull, lethargic feeling came over her. She found it difficult to think coherently and it gradually dawned upon her that they had drugged her food to keep her docile. She crawled onto the cot and lay staring at the ceiling. "Mark . . . please. You're the only one who can help me," she whispered. Sleep beckoned. She tried to keep her eyes open, tried to fight the sedation, but it was a losing battle.

Mark Hardwick was not about to squander valuable hours sleeping, as long as there were still avenues to investigate. Mr. Burke packed his valise while Mark changed his clothes. Within the hour he was on his way back to London. He took one of his coachmen along so they could share the driving on the hundred-mile journey from Bath.

In Grosvenor Square they pulled up before the Davenports' elegant house, where the Earl of Bath ran up the steps and gave his calling card to the majordomo. His discerning eye noted the servant was not the same man who had opened the door to him almost a year ago when he came to buy the library.

He was shown into that library now and the minutes stretched out while the servant went to inform the Davenports of their caller's identity. Mark Hardwick relived the encounter with Diana when sparks had flown between them. Her presence was almost tangible in the room and his hope soared that she was close by.

The Davenports' entrance broke through his reverie.

"May I be of service, your lordship?" Richard asked formally.

"I've come to see Lady Diana," he stated bluntly, crushing the urge to take Davenport by the throat.

Richard caught his wife's eye before he answered.

"I'm afraid she isn't here. She didn't return to London with us."

"May I inquire where she is?" Mark Hardwick challenged in a tone that clearly said he would not be put off.

"Lord Bath," Prudence said stiffly, "I don't want this bruited about, so it is in the strictest confidence I tell you that she has gone again."

"Gone where, madam?" he said implacably.

"Why, gone wherever it was she went to when she disappeared before, I presume."

The woman was lying; Diana would never leave him of her own free will. He was not going to play cat and mouse with this pathetic pair. "I believe you are concealing her whereabouts," he stated flatly.

"That is a lie!" Prudence cried. "The girl has been a sore trial to me since her father died. I am trying to live down the scandal of her first disappearance. Why would I stir it all up again?"

"If she is not here, you should not object to a search of the premises."

Richard straightened his shoulders. "Lord Bath, my profession is the law. In this country a man's home is sacrosanct!"

"But this is not your home, sir. This house is Lady Diana's, and therein lies your motive!"

"Motive?" Richard looked affronted. "I could sue you for slander."

"You do that. Perhaps you could explain to the judge why I smelled opium in the house in Queen Square."

"Opium!" Prudence looked shocked enough to faint. "My good sir, I am a martyr to hip pain, which is the reason I went to your wretched town of Bath in the first place. What you smelled was laudanum. I cannot sleep without it."

Laudanum! Christ, she has an answer for everything.

The Earl of Bath realized the futility of interrogating them further. He quit the house, but not the vicinity. He questioned the neighbors about Diana. All agreed they had not seen the young woman for almost a year. Mark Hardwick waited about most of the day hoping to question the servants who worked for the Davenports. Finally he spotted their coachman, James, and took him to a pub in Shepherd's Market for a couple of pints of best bitter.

"My digs is over the coach'ouse, ye understand, not in the 'ouse, so I rely on gossip from t'other servants. When young Peter come an' told 'em Lady Diana had been found, I drove 'em to Bath. It rained cats 'n' dogs, so we stopped at an inn in Chippenham about twenty miles away."

"Did you drive them to Hardwick Hall the next day?" Mark inquired.

"I did, yer lordship. It was after they rented the 'ouse in Queen Square, and from the way they talked, they intended to take Lady Diana from yer place back to Queen Square. Mad as fire they were when they left without 'er."

"When Lady Diana came to Queen Square two days later, did you drive them anywhere?"

"If she showed up, I never saw 'er."

Mark was clearly disappointed. "She didn't return to London with you?"

James shook his head.

"What about Lady Diana's maid? Do you think she will be able to throw a light on her whereabouts?"

James bent toward Mark Hardwick confidentially. "Lady Muck give Biddy her walking papers when Lady Diana run away the first time. Biddy was thinking of coming to Bath to see if she could get 'er old job back."

The earl clearly saw that it was fruitless to pursue the servants further. He slipped James a ten-pound note and headed off toward Allegra's studio, which was close by.

After the earl departed, James wondered if he should have told him about taking Richard Davenport back to Chippenham in Wiltshire. He shrugged. The gov'nor had been alone, he certainly hadn't taken his niece with him, so James decided the information would be no use to his nibs.

As the Earl of Bath walked along the iron railings in front of the tall house, Dame Lightfoot approached from the opposite direction. When they arrived at the front door together, the earl tipped his hat. "I'm here to see Allegra. Does she still reside here, ma'am?"

"I'm Dame Lightfoot. Pray come in, sir, and be seated. The lady you seek will be with you in a trice."

Mark assumed the gray-haired dragon with the tall walking stick was a relative of Allegra's, but thought what an odd pair they made. After ten minutes he became impatient that he had been left alone to cool his heels. Didn't these damn women realize he had no time to waste?

Finally, Allegra sailed in, all jet curls, rouge, and décolletage. "Mark, darling," she said huskily, "you haven't been to London in eons."

"Allegra, I'm at my wit's end. I'm searching for Lady Diana Davenport. She's disappeared."

"At least ten months ago," Allegra said dryly.

"No, no, I found her, but she's gone again. Have you any idea where she might be?"

Allegra smiled at him. "What an utterly delightful creature I found her to be. Obviously I'm not the only one. Unpredictable, unconventional, and wholly spontaneous

. . . I can see you are smitten and I'm happy to hear she is giving you a run for your money!''

"Damn it, Allegra, I'm frantic. I fear something's happened to her.''

Allegra's eyebrows elevated. "I believe she is perfectly capable of looking after herself. She was a dancing pupil of Dame Lightfoot's, you know. Even she couldn't intimidate her.''

"Then perhaps I should talk with the old dame?''

Allegra began to laugh. The sound was throaty and not without an earthy allure. "Mark, don't you know?''

"Know what?'' he demanded impatiently.

"Dame Lightfoot and I are the same person.''

For a moment he stared at her blankly.

"As Dame Lightfoot, I have the entree to the homes of the ladies of the ton, and their innocent daughters. As Allegra, I have the gentlemen in my pocket.''

Mark Hardwick was not amused. His black eyes swept her from head to foot. *Just when you thought you knew everything there was to know about women, one of them makes a bloody laughingstock of you. Perhaps more than one of them.*

Allegra took pity on him. "I'll keep my ears and eyes open, darling. In fact, both of us will.''

The Earl of Bath had nowhere to go but Jermyn Street. He hadn't slept in thirty-six hours and his frustration was taking its toll on his temper.

He used his own key to open the door of his town house and came face to face with the butler-cum-valet that he kept on staff, whether he was in residence or not.

"Good evening, your lordship.'' The look he gave the earl was one of dismay mixed with relief.

"Is something the matter, Jefferson?'' he asked irritably.

The servant hesitated, then informed him that his brother, Peter, was at home.

Mark was in no mood for a brotherly encounter. He was about to go through to the library when he heard what sounded like a whimper coming from upstairs. *Splendor of God, has the young swine abducted Diana to force her to marry him?* As he gazed up the staircase, he heard the unmistakable sobs of a woman. Mark's fury exploded. *I'll kill him!*

He took the stairs three at a time and flung open the chamber door. What he saw sickened him. A young drab was tied to the bedpost, while Peter lashed her naked flesh with his riding crop. Peter's rampant sex shriveled as the black eyes of his hated brother swept him with contempt. The earl did not need to speak; his look said it all. He stood there until Peter untied the prostitute and she began to dress.

Mark went to his own bedchamber and locked the door so that he would not unleash his full fury. He picked up a decanter of brandy and took it with him to a leather chair. He tipped the decanter and took a deep swallow. The brandy burned all the way down and blossomed in his chest. He'd always known Peter had a dark side. The young swine was addicted to bloodsport and apparently it didn't stop with animals.

Cynical thoughts crowded in on Mark as he again raised the crystal decanter to his lips. Did everyone have a secret, shameful side to their nature? Peter, Allegra . . . Diana?

He kicked off his boots and unfastened his waistcoat. The whole bloody world was a cesspool. *Fuck it and everybody in it!* he thought cynically. He had every intention of draining the decanter and proceeded to do so.

The next morning he had a brandy hangover. He decided to skip breakfast altogether and went into the library to write some checks. When Peter strolled in, Mark grit his teeth. Nonchalance was an art with Peter.

"Don't suppose you could spare me some blunt? The girl was well paid for her services."

"When I burst in on you, I thought it was Diana."

"Diana?" Peter's eyebrows shot up. "Don't tell me she's taken off again? Wait a minute, do I detect another Hardwick casualty here?" He saw that Mark's face was haggard. "Well, I'll be damned."

Peter sat on the edge of the desk and swung a booted foot. "If it's any consolation, I think you've had a lucky escape. Granted she has the beauty of a goddess, but she is completely cold. More than cold, she is a bloody ice queen. I'm not one to take no for an answer, but she always kept me at arm's length with her touch-me-not virginity."

In spite of the hangover, Mark suddenly felt better. He surveyed Peter with a speculative eye and changed the subject. "Did it ever occur to you to *earn* some money?"

"No, never," Peter replied with utter candor.

"I'll give you a job either at the stone quarry or on one of the barges I own."

Peter's lips curled. "My brother, the reformer. No thanks, your lordship. I'm engaged at Almack's tonight, dancing attendance on Lady Edwina Farnsworth-Peniston, heiress to Peniston Railway. And you thought I wasted all my time whoring and gambling."

When Peter left, Mark was convinced his brother had no further interest in Diana. His day stretched ahead of him endlessly. Other than tailing Richard Davenport, no brilliant ideas occurred to him. He had been convinced her guardians knew of her whereabouts. Now, however, he wasn't so sure. What if Diana had simply decided to leave? She was a feisty young beauty who could assuredly survive until she came of age. Then she'd come sailing back, scoop up her inheritance, and thumb her nose at the world.

The ache in his heart was almost unendurable. He ruthlessly ignored it and picked up the morning *Times*. His eye caught the write-up of an archaeological find. Some massive stone walls, thought to be Roman in origin, had been discovered beneath the cellars of Bush Lane, off Cannon Street. He went immediately to investigate. Many of his friends from the London Archaeological Society were there. It was one of the most exciting finds ever discovered.

But Mark found that, without Diana to share it with, the whole afternoon felt flat and almost pointless. The earl stayed in London three more days. He followed Richard Davenport each and every time he set foot outside Grosvenor Square. The solicitor visited his law office during the day and a Mayfair brothel in the evening. Finally, Mark Hardwick accepted the hard fact that Davenport would not lead him to Diana. On the fourth day, with all hope gone, the earl returned to Bath.

Diana lay on the cot, her eyes fixed on the high barred window. Freedom, it was almost as necessary as air. The idle hours crawled by sluggishly, making the days interminable and the nights endless. She thought dully that if she hadn't been mad when she arrived, she may well be raving mad before she ever got to leave.

Diana begged her attendants for some sort of work, hoping she would be taken to the kitchens or elsewhere, but they ignored her pleas. She asked for something to read, but it was like talking to the walls and she was wearied of doing that. She began to live inside her own mind, until it became realer than her actual surroundings. Often she was back with Marcus in Aquae Sulis, but more frequently she daydreamed of Mark and the lovely Georgian town of Bath.

Diana had no idea how long she had been confined. At one point she made marks on the wall with her spoon, until it occurred to her that she was veritably sticking her spoon in the wall. Because they dosed her food, she ate very little. She became thin and pale and listless, but deep down she clung on to hope. Without hope she feared she would die.

Mark would come. She loved him more now than she ever had before. He was her dream lover; he would be her salvation. She closed her eyes and drifted into sleep, floating from dream to dream, from caress to kiss, always longing to awaken and find herself safe in his powerful arms. But it never, ever happened that way.

Diana had fallen into a trancelike state, and then suddenly, one day, she began to vomit. When she was still vomiting on the third day in a row, her attendants informed Dr. Bognor.

He was alarmed. The drugs they were putting in her food to sedate her must have been poisoning her system. He had seen it before in small women. He ordered all dosing be stopped immediately. Bognor knew her guardians would care little about the girl's death, but he would have to answer to the Wiltshire County Board of Councillors and the coroner.

Gradually, Diana's stomach settled down until she vomited only occasionally. She could tell that they had stopped drugging her food and her appetite increased. Though she was no longer getting sick, she was still assailed by nausea each morning and a dreaded suspicion began to gnaw at her.

Chapter 36

Mark Hardwick's answer to worry and frustration was work. As the Earl of Bath, he headed the Bathonian Corporation, which was made up of the mayor and aldermen as well as attorneys, physicians, brewers, vintners, saddlers, and shopkeepers. They had hired a surveyor, Thomas Baldwin, to draw up plans to clear a congested area for better access and build five new streets. The plans called for an appropriately named Union Street to join the upper and lower town by demolishing the Bear Inn. The plans also included a proposal to rebuild the Great Pump Room.

Mark Hardwick gave final approval to the plans and loaned the corporation twenty-five thousand pounds to get the work started. Now all he had to do was persuade Bath's wealthy patrons and patronesses that *city bonds* were a safe investment. His days were filled with business, but his nights were filled with emptiness. The hours stretched out endlessly, keeping pace with his sleeplessness.

His magnificent Elizabethan bedchamber, where a queen had once slept, now only evoked the memory of one woman, Lady Diana Davenport. Just as flowers left some of their fragrance in the hand that bestowed them, Diana had left a trace of herself upon the very air he breathed. His thoughts were filled with her; his memories only went as far back as the day he'd met her.

In the darkness he fantasized about her, and when Morpheus did lure him to sleep, his dreams were wildly erotic. Mark searched his mind relentlessly for someone to question, for someplace to investigate, for something he had overlooked. He knew he was becoming obsessive, but until he found her, he would know no peace.

Diana, too, had come to focus all thought upon one thing. She knew she must have been confined for more than a month, for every instinct told her that she was with child. She lived in dread of the day one of her attendants discovered her secret. It had nothing to do with the shame that was heaped upon a female who bore a child out of wedlock. If she had not been incarcerated, she would have rejoiced that she was bearing Mark's child. But every instinct told her that if the doctor discovered her condition, her baby would be in danger.

They would never allow her to keep it, and indeed, even she herself did not want her child living in a madhouse. But the fear that they would separate her from her baby and give it away terrified her. But even worse than that was the fear that the evil Dr. Bognor might give her a drug to rid her of the baby in order to save them all a great deal of trouble.

The Earl of Bath pored over his account books all morning. He had a man of business who dealt with the clerical side of the quarries and the barges that transported his beautiful stone to Bristol, but he kept a strict tally of expenses and profits, even though he found it a tedious business.

By the time he had finished, he felt caged and knew he needed a physical outlet for his excess energy. He saddled his favorite stallion, Trajan, and rode out across his lands. Mark was amazed to see that spring had arrived. He had been too preoccupied with his own dark thoughts to even notice. He felt at odds with the season. How callous that life went merrily on; that winter ended and spring brought its promise of renewal.

He moved off toward the river, drawn by a stand of copper beeches that had come into leaf. He dismounted and looked about him at the beauty of this particular spot. There was something deeply, disturbingly familiar about his surroundings. What was it he almost remembered?

His eye caught sight of an unusual object sticking up out of the soft earth of the riverbank. When he bent to examine it, his pulses speeded up. It looked like a Roman artifact, one of those writing tablets they often buried. He used his fingers to dig it out from the ancient roots of the tree. Most of the wood had rotted away, but the lead was intact.

Mark brushed away the clinging soil and clearly saw the name *Marcus.* His heart began to pound as he made out other words. It definitely said *Aquae Sulis,* followed by the word *loved. Yes, by God, it says* Diana *followed by the date* A.D. 61.

As he held the mud-encrusted tablet in his hands he knew with a certainty he and Diana had buried it together. It had happened one glorious afternoon when they had made love, here by the river. The pain in his heart became almost unendurable.

He clenched his fists as a renewed surge of determination flooded through him. Centuries ago they had loved each other and he swore a vow that they would be lovers again.

"Hold on, Diana, I'll come for you," he whispered with reborn hope in his heart.

When he arrived back at the hall, Mr. Burke informed the earl that he had a visitor who had been waiting in the library for over an hour. When Mark recognized Mr. Dearden, a shop owner, he assumed he had come regarding corporation business.

"Good afternoon, my lord. Yesterday, I had a woman come into my antique shop with a half-Caesar gold coin."

"My God, man, was she young, blond?" the earl demanded.

"Ah, you are as excited as I was when I examined it and decided it was authentic."

"Yes, yes. The woman. Who is she? Where does she live? I must speak with her."

"I'm afraid I don't know, your lordship. She was a tall, well-made woman, certainly not young, but not old either. I offered her a hundred pounds, thinking she would take my arm up to my elbow for such a sum, but she was reluctant to part with the artifact. I then told her I might possibly be able to give her more after I'd consulted with a client who had a keen interest in such things." Dearden coughed. "That was you, of course, though I was careful not to mention you by name."

"You let her get away?" the earl demanded.

"She indicated she might be back, your lordship," he offered lamely. "I'm very sorry, sir. I shouldn't have bothered you until I had something definite to offer."

"No, no! You did exactly the right thing by coming to me." Mark ran his hand through his black hair in frustration. Disappointment followed on the heels of elation, but it was the first lead he'd had in over a month, and tenacious as a terrier, he wasn't about to accept defeat.

"If she returns, I must know who she is. Send for me immediately or follow her yourself if necessary. The woman's whereabouts are a thousandfold more important than securing the half-coin. I appreciate this, Mr. Dearden. You will be well paid for your services to me."

Mark Hardwick rode into Bath immediately to make the rounds of all the antique shops. Perhaps one of them had offered more than Dearden and learned the identity of the woman. Every shopkeeper he questioned replied in the negative except one. He told the Earl of Bath that the woman walked out when he offered her fifty guineas. He had no idea who she was. The earl told every dealer that he was offering a reward for the woman's identity and to inform him immediately if anyone came in offering to sell a half-Caesar coin.

A week went by, during which he heard nothing further. The earl could not sit idle. He again made the rounds of the coaching inns, since it was possible the woman lived out of town. Bath antique shops were famous for their Roman artifacts and that was what had drawn the woman. The drivers had many female passengers, but they could not recall any who had asked about antique shops.

Deep down, Mark felt that if he was patient, someone would see the woman again. The trouble was that patience wasn't one of his virtues. His hopes were dimming hourly, when suddenly Fate smiled upon him.

A strange woman came to Hardwick Hall and asked if it was possible to speak with the Earl of Bath. Mr. Burke led her to the cheery breakfast room, where large windows let in the sunlight and purple crocus and paper white narcissus bulbs bloomed in earthen pots on the windowsills, and then left to summon his master.

Mark Hardwick took a deep breath before he went in to her. Though he had the inclination to put his pistol to the woman's head, he knew intimidation would get him nowhere at this point.

"Good morning, Mrs. . . ." His eyebrows raised in question.

"My name is of no matter, my lord. I was told you collected Roman artifacts."

"Indeed I do, madam."

"I know someone who has a Roman coin for sale, or I should say a half-coin. I believe it bears the head of Caesar."

Mark's heart soared. With studied nonchalance his fingers drew forth his own half-coin from about his neck. "Is it anything like this?"

The woman looked startled. "Why, yes it is."

"Well, as you can see, I already have one and unfortunately have no need of another. However, there's an antique dealer in town who might give you as much as a hundred pounds for one of those medallions."

The expectant lines of the woman's face fell in disappointment. She had just walked four miles for nothing and would now have to return the same four miles into town, where she had left her sister safeguarding the treasure.

"Order the coach! The one without the crest," Mark directed Mr. Burke the moment the door closed behind the woman. The Earl of Bath had no idea what lay ahead of him, but he was prepared for any eventuality. He went to his safe and took out money, then he opened a leather case and removed a pair of onyx-handled pistols. Now he realized why he had chosen black over ivory or silver. They looked so much more menacing. Black carried its own deadly authority. He chose a black cloak rather than a greatcoat, thankful that the winter chill had left the air.

When the closed carriage thundered past the woman who had visited the hall, Mark was amazed that she had already covered over two miles on foot. She was athletically built and he wondered curiously what she did for a living. She reminded him of a bath attendant.

His first stop was Dearden's Antique Shop. The earl explained that the woman who had the half-coin for sale had paid him a visit and that he told her he wasn't interested.

"I'm certain she'll be back for the hundred pounds you offered her." He counted out two hundred pounds and gave them to Dearden. "The other hundred is for your trouble."

The Earl of Bath told his driver to wait for him at the Angel in Westgate Street, then he crossed the street and went into the tobacconist shop. He had no idea how long he would have to keep watch. The rich aroma of tobacco leaves permeated the air and he couldn't resist selecting a mixture and having it rolled into cheroots. When the cigars were ready and the woman still had not put in an appearance, he schooled himself to patience and pondered a selection of cigar cases.

To his surprise, he saw two women who were almost identical approach the antique shop. By the time he had selected a cigar case and paid for his purchases, the sisters were leaving the shop. He watched them walk downhill toward the lower town, then he strolled across the street and retrieved Diana's coin.

He followed the pair, keeping quite a distance between them and himself, knowing two women together would be difficult to lose. They went into a pastry shop and came out with a large box.

Already spending their ill-gotten gains, he thought cynically.

He watched them head straight for the Christopher Inn in High Street and knew they were going there to catch one of the coaches. A hundred questions came to mind. Was Diana staying with friends outside Bath? Had she asked the women to sell the coin for her because she had no money? The answers came back a resounding NO. Marcus had given it to her. It was the only thing she had been able to bring back with her. Mark knew it was so precious to her she would never voluntarily part with it.

He walked over to the Angel, two streets away, and told his coachman to go over to the Christopher and find out the women's destination. The coachman came back with the information that they bought tickets to Chippenham. Mark swore. He had no jurisdiction outside Somerset.

"Coach doesn't leave until five o'clock. There the two of 'em sit eatin' cream cakes, fer gawd's sake!"

"Might as well order some food; we might not get dinner tonight."

"Pint of bitter, sir? Surveillance is thirsty work."

When the coach left Bath, the sun was setting and they were able to stay well back. They had crossed the county border from Somerset into Wiltshire by twilight, but by the time they reached Chippenham at seven o'clock, it was full dark.

Mark Hardwick sat up on the box beside his driver. They followed the two women from the coaching inn for perhaps half a mile. The sisters were obviously nervous as they walked swiftly along the dark road for they looked over their shoulders a couple of times when they heard the coach and horses behind them.

The women turned into the long driveway of what looked like a Georgian mansion. Mark spoke very low to his driver. "When we turn in the driveway, they will start to run. They are carrying a hundred pounds and will think they are being robbed. I want to talk to both of them inside the coach. You catch the one on the right."

The sisters, who thought they were safe this close to their destination, found out otherwise. They were strong women, who fought their assailants hard, but the Earl of Bath soon subdued his quarry, then helped his driver hustle her sister inside the coach. When Mark lit a carriage lamp, the woman who had been to Hardwick Hall gasped, "It's the Earl of Bath!"

In the flickering shadows, his dark face looked menacing. When he spoke, his voice matched.

"I suspect the lady who owns the half-coin is within those walls. Am I correct?"

The sisters looked at each other with alarm.

"What is this place?" he demanded.

"Woodhaven Asylum."

Christ, the bastards put her in an insane asylum. I never would have found her!

"Have you any idea how much trouble you are in? The lady in question is an abducted heiress. You two have stolen and sold a piece of her jewelery. I happen to be a justice of the county." He knew they would have no idea that his authority did not reach into Wiltshire. He let them sweat for a few minutes, then he offered them a way out of their trouble.

"If you cooperate with me, I will see that you do not take the fall for the crimes that have been committed here."

The sisters exchanged glances, then nodded their assent.

Mark handed one of his pistols to his driver. "Here's a barking iron. Keep it on her until we get back." He turned to her sister. "You will lead me to the lady, very quietly. Is there a back door?"

She nodded.

"After tonight, I have never seen you and you have never seen me. Is that understood?"

She glanced at the pistol he pointed at her. "Yes, sir," she croaked, her voice cracking with fear.

The woman unlocked the back door with one of her keys, and proceeded along an ill-lit corridor between laundry rooms and kitchens. Creatures of the night scuttled away from their feet into the deeper shadows, then the woman led him up two sets of steep stairs that took them up to the third floor.

They encountered no one, but cries of distress, moans of despair, and an occasional deranged laugh came from the locked rooms. The Earl of Bath pinched his nostrils against the odors of cooked cabbage, carbolic soap, and stale urine. The fury within threatened to explode, and he knew that if anyone challenged him, anyone at all, he would put a bullet in their brain.

Diana awoke from a fitful dream and heard her door being unlocked. A dark figure loomed in the doorway. Dear God in Heaven, she had known Bognor would come for her, but she hadn't expected him in the night. "No!" she cried out sharply. "Don't touch me."

At the sound of her voice, Mark's heart turned over in his breast. He had finally found her. He wanted to warn her to be silent, but all he could say, as he drew close to the bed was, "My sweetheart."

"Mark?" she whispered, not fully trusting her ears.

"Yes, love," he murmured low, taking her hand to his chest, where his half-coin rested over his heart. As her questing hand slid over the hard muscles, his deep voice hushed, "Try not to make any noise."

As he lifted her in his powerful arms, she thought her heart was hammering so loudly it would waken the dead. She clung to him tightly, knowing God and Saint Jude had granted her a miracle. He carried her down three flights, then along the passageway to the back door. He gave the woman a final warning. "I will release your sister immediately. If I were you, I would not sound the alarm, I would lock the door quietly and retire."

On the ride back to Bath, Mark slipped his arms about Diana and drew her back against him. With gentle hands he brushed her tangled hair back from her temples. "Try to relax; we have a private two-hour drive ahead of us."

"You are so clever; how did you find me?"

"Nay, love, it was your own wits that led me to you. Only you could have planted the seed for them to bring the half-coin to me."

"Oh Mark, they put me in the madhouse." She shivered uncontrollably.

He drew her inside his cloak so that the heat from his body would warm her. Gradually, she told him what happened from the moment she had decided to confront Prudence and Richard. When she finished, she asked, "How long was I locked away?"

"Forty days and forty nights. How did you bear it?" he said very quietly.

"I knew you would come."

Diana's words were so sure, so certain, he hated to cast a shadow upon her peace of mind. But facts had to be faced. "Diana, you are still legally under the control of your guardians for another three weeks."

When she flinched in his arms, he said, "The law is on

their side and they will be able to take you away from me the moment they learn I have abducted you.''

''Please, don't let them put me back in that place.''

He hated to hear her beg, and offered the only solution he could think of. ''If we marry, you will be under my authority.''

Diana's heart soared. This was what she wanted more than anything in the world, yet she knew the thing Mark Hardwick treasured most was his freedom. Her heart overflowed that he was willing to make the supreme sacrifice to keep her safe. ''Thank you,'' she whispered.

''Don't thank me, love. It is only a temporary measure. They will go to the courts and have it annulled because I do not have their consent to marry you. All we can hope is that it takes them three weeks to get the marriage set aside.''

Chapter 37

It was after ten o'clock when they arrived back at Hardwick Hall. Diana had the feeling that the house welcomed her, as if she had come home. Mark felt so protective of her, he wanted to sweep her into his arms and carry her upstairs. Why should she walk when he could carry her? But he knew she had been so closely confined she needed freedom of movement.

She paused at the foot of the newel staircase, appreciating its carved beauty. As they climbed the steps together, her fingers wound their way about his. "I love to hold hands with you," she admitted shyly.

He closed the door and moved into the room to light the lamps. She stayed by the door to watch the room come alive as it was bathed in the soft glow. The four-poster held all her attention with its beautiful green velvet curtains, embroidered with small golden crowns and lions. "I love this chamber. I'll never leave it again."

He turned to speak and the words died on his lips. In the ugly brown smock and canvas shoes, she looked pale unto death. He swallowed the lump in his throat and swore a silent vow. If anyone ever hurt her again, he would kill them!

"I know it's late, but we must be married tonight, so I'm afraid you're going to have to leave this chamber."

"I need a bath," she said softly.

"How would you like a tub before the fire as they bathed in Elizabethan times?"

Within minutes the chamber was filled with bustling servants who dragged in a large porcelain tub, followed by buckets of steaming water. Mr. Burke and Nora arrived, one to see to his master's toilet, one to look after her. The Earl of Bath said politely but firmly, "We would like to be alone for a while."

Diana pulled off the smock and canvas shoes and slipped into the scented water. Mark bent down, bundled up the discarded things, and opened the chamber door. "Burn these," he ordered the first servant he saw.

"Whatever will I wear?" Diana worried.

"Does it matter?"

"Of course it matters; I'm getting married. Even if it is only for three weeks," she added wistfully.

Mark drew close, his black eyes caressing her with love. "You can wear this," he said, fastening the half-coin about her neck.

"Did it cost you the earth?"

"Hardly anything. I told the woman I had one and didn't need another." He reached into his pocket and pulled out her earrings. "And you can wear these. I've carried them about with me the whole time." The only reason he wanted her to wear the earrings was so that he could watch her take them off when they went to bed.

She looked up at him, knowing he surrounded her with his love. "You sent Nora away, so you'll have to help me."

When she was done, Mark wrapped her in a Turkish towel and lifted her from the water. He knew if he sat down and drew her into his lap, they would never get dressed. "How would it be if I went to your chamber and chose something from your wardrobe?"

Diana smiled a secret smile. When he was Marcus, he had chosen her clothes. She remembered how shocked she had been at the loin dress. She nodded her assent and opened the towel so that the fire warmed her flesh. How delicious it felt to be free to do whatever she wished.

Mark came back with the jade velvet. "This holds special memories for me, and this," he said, holding out the scarlet corset. He helped her to dress. When he fastened the gown, he saw how much weight she had lost. Starting tomorrow he would insist she get lots of food and exercise. He didn't like to see her looking so pale and fragile. He wanted her glowing and brazen, able to give as good as she got. He wanted her to be able to hold her own against him, both in bed and out of it.

She tried not to stare as he shaved and changed his linen, but she was greedy for the sight of him. His dark face was so strongly masculine, he looked rugged even in formal dress clothes. He looked up and saw her watching him. Did he dare to hope she felt possessive of him?

"I have no ring," he suddenly realized.

"What would a sworn bachelor be doing with a wedding ring?" she teased.

He twisted his favorite ring on his finger, an emerald cut in intaglio. "We'll use this one. Mr. Burke and Nora are coming with us as witnesses." At last, when he was fully dressed, he dared to touch her. He cupped her face with his hands, lifted her mouth to his, and cherished her lips. "Are you sure you're up to this?"

Diana nodded. "Very sure." She didn't want him for three weeks, she wanted him for eternity, but even if they only had this one night, she felt more blessed than any other woman in the world. Fate had allowed her the gift of falling in love with this man twice over.

It was after midnight when the small party gathered in the parlor of a Bath justice of the peace. The civil ceremony was short, the most important part being the signatures on the marriage license rather than the words spoken.

On the carriage ride back to the hall, the earl explained to the servants that the marriage almost certainly would be annulled by Diana's guardians, but in less than three weeks she would turn eighteen and come into her inheritance. When they arrived home, Mr. Burke and Nora discreetly disappeared within.

At the front entrance, Mark swept her up in his arms. "We have to obey all the rules," he said as he carried her across the threshold.

"This is a Roman custom. The groom lifts the bride over the threshold to avoid an ill-omened stumble. Then you present me with a cup of water and a glowing fire brand to show that I am entitled to the protection of your family gods."

Once more they climbed the gracefully curved staircase together. When they entered the master bedchamber, they saw that Mr. Burke and Nora had set out wine and sweetcakes for them. Mark helped her off with her cloak, then removed his coat, vest, and intricately tied neck cloth.

"I have a gift I think will delight you." He brought the lead tablet inscribed with their names and placed it in her hands.

"Oh, Mark, Marcus, you found the proof!"

"It was down by the river beneath the copper beeches, where we once made love."

"You remember!" Her face was so radiant with joy, he felt a lump in his throat. He quickly moved to the cabinet and poured them wine.

"Let me propose a toast to Diana, Countess of Bath."

"Good Heavens, am I a countess? It sounds so formal and stodgy! I have a much better toast." She slipped out of her gown, tossed it aside, and flung herself backward on the bed in her scarlet corset. Then she flung her legs in the air and kicked them wildly. "I propose a toast to freedom!" she cried joyously.

Mark was delighted with her abandon. He had been half expecting tears, fears, and bad dreams, and was prepared to soothe them all away. The need to protect her rose up strongly in him. He had no intention of making sexual demands on her tonight. "Drink your wine and let me tuck you into bed. It will be daylight in less than four hours."

She obediently lifted her glass to her lips and lifted one leg at the same time. "Take off my stocking." He slipped it off her leg and kissed her toes before he lifted her other leg to repeat the pretty gesture. She finished her wine and unhooked the fastenings on her corset. When she looked up at him, he hadn't started to remove his clothes.

"Hurry," she urged, stretching wantonly on the drift of snowy sheets.

He swallowed hard, wondering how he was going to deny himself.

"My favorite thing in the whole world is lying naked together and kissing," she informed him.

Mark removed his shirt and trousers slowly, delaying the torture that awaited him. "Kissing is all you're going to get," he warned.

She looked at him to see if he was teasing. He wasn't. He fully intended to deny himself for her sake. He was being noble. She decided to change his mind.

"Well, you're the master, and I did promise to obey you." She reached up and slowly removed her earrings.

Mark could stay away from her no longer. His side of the bed sagged under his weight and Diana rolled against him.

"I'd forgotten how muscular your chest was," she said, running her hands over him.

"We'll wait until you are stronger, sweetheart. A few days of good food and exercise and you'll be fully recovered from your ordeal."

She moved over him so that her pale breasts lay on his darkly furred chest. "I know a wonderful exercise, but I did promise to obey you."

"You're cock-teasing," he whispered between kisses.

She moved her hand down his body. "It's working." She moved once more, so that now her bottom half also lay atop of him. "When you carried me across the threshold, you said we had to obey all the rules. Isn't consummation the cardinal rule?''

Mark groaned, then said hoarsely, "I'm trying not to be selfish.''

She moved against him erotically. "Oh please, darling, be selfish!''

Their kisses deepened dangerously. To distract her, Mark asked her to describe a Roman wedding.

"It's a long story, and it will be my pleasure to describe all the intimate details . . . after.''

"After?'' he asked huskily, knowing he was going to give in. He had the strangest feeling they had exchanged these exact words before. He knew if he allowed her to remain in the dominant position, she would exhaust herself. He rolled with her until they were on their sides, then lifted her knee so that it rested on his hip.

She kissed his heart, then stretched so that her lips rested against the powerful column of his throat. She offered up a prayer of thanks that her baby was safe between their hearts. She wouldn't tell him tonight. She would embrace her secret a little while longer.

Because he had tried to deny himself, Mark was iron hard and throbbing. He rubbed the engorged head of his shaft along her silken cleft, slowly. Each time it caressed her bud, heightening the sultry sensations until she became taut. When she closed her eyelids, all was black shot with silvery light; as she became aroused, the dazzling silver turned to gold, then changed again to crimson when he thrust all the way into her. The beautiful red color stayed with her, bringing her as much pleasure as his thick phallus sliding in and out in a rhythm that matched their heartbeats. Determined that this loving would not turn savage, Mark made it deep, slow, and sensual. Finally, the color beneath her lids intensified to deep purple and she licked and sucked his neck as her pulsations began and seemed to go on and on endlessly. When he spent, she climaxed again.

Mark withdrew and turned her so that she lay in the

curve of his big body, spoon-fashion. She sighed with repletion, marveling that she could feel so luscious without
even exerting herself. His hands caressed her breasts and
belly. "You have such loving hands."

He threaded his fingers into the golden curls on her
high mons and cupped her with his palm, in complete possession. "Tell me about a Roman wedding," he whispered.

She described all the lovely things she had planned for
her wedding to Marcus, then she told him of the customs.
When she finished, he tightened his arms about her and
confessed, "These last few weeks I secretly feared you had
gone back in time again . . . back to Marcus."

"Darling, you are Marcus."

"I know that now."

"I can never go back. That time is finished. Our time
together is here and now."

"I love you," he whispered.

"I love you," she whispered back. She realized that
love was far more important than marriage. Marriage was
wonderful, but love was better. She had always hoped she
could convince him. It was the most precious wedding present he could have given her.

They spent the morning riding in the spring sunshine.
They left the parkland of Hardwick Hall behind as they
rode out across fields filled with wildflowers. Diana took
him up the heights of Landsdown, where the track for chariot races had been laid out, then they rode up Hay Hill into
what was left of the vineyards.

On the way back to the hall, she insisted on racing.
When she arrived at the stables, he was there awaiting her
with uplifted arms. She went down into them for a kiss, her
hair in a golden tangle, her cheeks blooming with roses.

"When you win the race, I'll know you are fully recovered."

He made her eat a decent lunch, agreeing to spend the afternoon shopping only if she had second helpings.

"I'm still stodgy from breakfast," she complained. "If I'd known you were a dictator, I wouldn't have wed you!"

Their first stop was the jewelers, where they selected a wide gold wedding band. As he slipped it onto her finger, he said, "Now you can give me back my intaglio."

Her face fell. "Oh dear, whatever did I do with it? Don't tell me I lost it." When she saw the look of dismay on his face, she said, "Just a minute, feel down in here." She opened the top three buttons of her afternoon dress in saucy invitation. Mark dipped his fingers into her décolletage and drew out his emerald intaglio. The jeweler's mouth gaped that the Earl of Bath and his lady were openly indulging in sexual byplay. He couldn't wait to spread the news that at last the earl had chosen a countess.

"I never did buy those dining couches you suggested; however, Dearden has a pair in his shop. Would you care to have a look at them?"

"No, but you must grab them. I'm off to Madame Madeleine's. Do you remember the costume of Goddess Diana I was wearing the first night we met?"

He rolled his eyes heavenward. "How could I forget?"

"We'll dine in the Roman style tonight."

He laughed. "I refuse to wear a toga."

She went up on tiptoe and whispered in his ear, "Just bring your flagellum."

He was reluctant to let her go off on her own, but knew he must overcome his apprehension. Diana needed complete freedom at the moment.

The Earl of Bath only bought the couches on the condition they be delivered immediately. When Dearden offered him congratulations on his marriage, Mark knew it wouldn't be long before the news spread to everyone in town.

"Lady Diana, how lovely to see you again," Madame Madeleine enthused, avid for a snippet of gossip about the girl who had disappeared into thin air, then reappeared so strangely.

"How lovely that you remember me," Diana said with a straight face.

"How could I ever forget that you won the battle over the jade velvet gown?"

Diana smiled. "Not only did I get the gown, but I ended up with the earl as well." She held up her hand to display her new wedding ring.

"Oh, your ladyship, how may I be of service?"

"Well, you do such lovely work; how would you like to create some rather unconventional garments for me?"

Mark and Diana decided to turn the dressing room adjoining their bedchamber into their own private dining room. Mr. Burke carried up a small table, which he set between the couches, then searched the other rooms for the reclining and elbow cushions Diana described. When Mark was out of earshot, she confided in Mr. Burke. "The costume I intend to wear is rather revealing. Would you mind terribly if I asked Nora to serve dinner tonight?"

"Not at all, your ladyship. Just remember she has more gaul than grace."

Diana took her boxes from Madame Madeleine's down to the peach-colored chamber so that Mark wouldn't see what she planned to wear.

He fully expected to see her in the short, white tunic of the Roman goddess, Diana, and decided simply to wear his black velvet bedrobe since the dinner was to be a most intimate affair. To make her laugh, he carried a whip that resembled a flagellum. When he opened the adjoining door that led from their bedchamber, Diana was there ahead of him, posed upon her dining couch.

His black eyes widened with shock as they swept over

her reclining figure with one impudent breast fully exposed. She was as composed as only a woman who was sure of her beauty could be. While his body reacted in a most pronounced manner, the earl wasn't sure he wanted his wife to display herself in such a bold and wanton fashion.

He strode toward her without hesitation. When Diana saw the disapproval writ plainly on his dark visage, she lifted her arms and her lips for the kiss of greeting. He towered above her without touching her. "I'm not sure a countess should—"

She serenely lifted her lips to within an inch of his and said, "Don't think of me as your countess, think of me as your slave."

He groaned and covered her mouth hungrily. He pulled his mouth away. "You've done this before."

"Mmmm," she responded sensually.

He thrust his angry tongue into her hot, inviting mouth and felt his anger melting away. His cock stood up like a ramrod, lifting the black velvet.

Diana took the flagellum from his fingers. "You don't need two weapons."

His eyes were smoldering now as he reached out his hand to fondle her breast.

"No! Behave yourself and go to your own couch. I'll join you for dessert."

At that moment, Nora came in with the dinner and Mark helped her take the platters from the tray and place them on the small serving table, placing himself between the servant and Diana. He was much too modest to let Nora see her lady in this state of undress! "We'll serve ourselves. That will be all, thank you, Nora." Mark went to his own dining couch.

"Come over here," he commanded.

"No! I told you I would join you for dessert."

"If you are my slave, you had better learn to obey my orders." His voice held a tone of total authority. "Come over and show me how to place these cushions."

She went slowly, never taking her eyes from his. "Recline upon your side." She placed the large cushion at his back. "Now tuck this small cushion beneath your elbow."

She stood beside his couch, nervously running her hands along the handle of the whip she had taken from him. A shaft of desire pierced his loins as he watched her fondle the flagellum. He undid the tie on his robe so that the black velvet fell open to reveal his naked splendor.

"Pleasure me," he commanded.

Chapter 38

In that moment he was so darkly dominant Diana was almost regretful that she was not his slave. He made her weak with desire. But both knew they were only playing a love game.

She moved her hand up and down the phallic handle with mock innocence. "You are very demanding," she said softly.

"I am a man. I give the orders, you obey them."

Both were becoming aroused without even touching the other. Beneath the banter was a note of total authority that made her want to behave shamelessly with him. She trailed the leather thongs of the flagellum across one flat, bronzed nipple, moved it slowly down his ribcage and across his taut belly. When she gave his erection a tap on the head, he snatched it from her roughly.

Her lashes swept her cheeks, all contrite. "I'm sorry," she murmured, and slid to her knees beside his couch. She bestowed a kiss upon the carmine crown of his jutting manhood, heard the intake of his ragged breath, then with the tip of her wet tongue delicately traced every inch of him.

When he opened his eyes, she had retreated to her own couch. She gave him a sultry look that promised him paradise. "That was just an aperitif until we get to the main course."

"Little vixen," he growled. "If you have a taste for teasing games, I shall give you a few lessons."

The following morning saw them again racing across the fields. When Diana lost once more, Mark grinned at her and said, "I intend to mount you better this afternoon."

"Surely you couldn't improve on last night's mounting?" she drawled outrageously.

"I can always try," he said, winking. "You know what I mean. We'll go shopping for a mare for you this afternoon."

"Why can't I have a stallion?"

"You can have anything you desire, but I'd prefer to be the only male in your life, and a mare would make Trajan exceedingly happy."

"Your stallion in Aquae Sulis was named Trajan."

Mark smiled into her eyes. "Coincidence doesn't quite explain it, does it my love?"

He took her to a breeding farm at Avebury and let her have her pick. Diana chose a young mare with a blond mane that rivaled her own. "Do you think she's too young to breed?" she asked her husband.

Suddenly, Mark wasn't thinking of horses at all. He was overcome with the fierce desire to plant his own seed in his beautiful young wife. "I think she's absolutely perfect." He hugged her to his side and dropped a quick kiss on her golden head.

They didn't arrive home until twilight, where Mr. Burke awaited them with news they had been expecting. While they were at Avebury, Richard Davenport had delivered a legal paper he had filed with the courts to have his niece's marriage annulled on the grounds that written consent had not been obtained from her guardian. The case would come to court at the Easter Assizes, four days before Diana turned eighteen.

She tried not to show how upset she was, but Mark knew her too intimately not to feel her distress.

"It's a damn good thing I wasn't here," he cursed. "I would have set the dogs on him."

Diana was thankful her husband had not been at home, for she knew he was capable of much more than setting the dogs on her uncle.

In bed she clung to him, needing his strength to face not only the scandal of annulment, but the reality of it. She had hoped Richard and Prudence would let well enough alone, after what they had done to her. She had hoped that once she was married to the Earl of Bath, they would let it stand and gracefully accept the fait accompli. How naive she was.

"What will we do?" she whispered desperately.

"My sweetheart, once the annulment is granted, I shall simply take you where they cannot find you until your birthday."

She wanted to ask *and then?* but she couldn't. He had not suggested that the day she turn eighteen, they marry again. Diana was fully aware that it was only a temporary arrangement. Her hand briefly caressed her belly. If she told him of the child, she had little doubt that he would offer remarriage to protect her. But she desperately wanted him to marry her from choice, rather than necessity. How perfect it would be if he didn't feel compelled.

She sighed, wishing things were otherwise. Then she turned her face into the hollow of his throat. She knew how precious his freedom was to him. And it really didn't matter, so long as he loved her. Hadn't she decided that love was infinitely more important than marriage?

To Mark, the thing of paramount importance was for Diana to be in charge of her own inheritance. Once her guardians were no longer holding the pursestrings, she would be able to slap them with all sorts of lawsuits, but not until she was of age. He did not want to do anything that would jeopardize her legal rights. All they had to do was exercise patience for another fortnight.

As he lay contemplating their situation, he stroked her hair and her back, both as smooth as satin. The problem of the annulment was a little more complicated. When the king introduced the Marriage Act to keep Prinny in line, the age of consent to marry became twenty-one. That was a distant three years away, and though Diana might be content simply to live together, Mark was not. For the first time in his life he wanted a wife, he wanted children, and he wanted them legitimate.

What it all boiled down to was, even when she became financially independent, Diana would still need Richard's consent to marry. The Earl of Bath's face turned hard. He would force Davenport to consent, he decided ruthlessly.

Diana stirred restlessly. She needed something to divert her. "I've been thinking that we need a private bathing pool. You can help me draw up some plans."

"Indoor or outdoor?"

"Well, if it were outdoors, we wouldn't be able to use it year-round. How about inside a glass conservatory with trees and plants?"

"It sounds divine."

"I can swim, you know."

"That's something I'd love to see."

"Let's go to King's Bath tomorrow," she suggested. "I can't wait to see you in those canvass trousers."

When they arrived at King's Bath the next afternoon, Diana was surprised at how quiet the usually bustling Stawles Street was.

"I'll see you inside," Mark said as they separated so that he could enter on the men's side and Diana could go to the ladies' dressing room.

There was only one female attendant, to her surprise.

"I can't believe how quiet it is today; the baths are almost deserted."

As the bath lady helped her into the high-waisted, brown linen dress, she said, "Didn't you know? The Earl of Bath has rented it for a private swimming party today. The galleries are closed so that spectators won't be able to observe you."

When Diana went through to the bath, Mark was cutting through the water, naked as the day he was born.

"You devil! I wanted to laugh at your canvass drawers, but it appears I'm the figure of fun here."

"There's none here but us. Are you daring enough to disrobe?" he challenged.

"Bathing nude isn't a novelty to me," she assured him with *hauteur*. But only when she had scanned the galleries to make sure her display was for his eyes only did she unfasten and remove the respectable linen gown. She slipped into the warm water to show him that she could swim. "This is the breaststroke," she informed him.

"It certainly is," he agreed, watching her porcelain globes float on the water's surface.

They played and teased for over an hour, but Mark kept a protective eye on her. She was no longer pale, and she certainly wasn't timid, but she still looked unbelievably fragile to him. He swam underwater and brought his body up against hers as he surfaced. She slipped her arms about his neck and lifted her mouth for his kiss. Suddenly their laughter fell away and they became serious. "Let's go home," he whispered.

When they arrived, Diana was overjoyed to see that a large box had been delivered from Madame Madeleine's. She rushed upstairs with it and called over her shoulder, "We'll use the private dining room tonight."

Mr. Burke remarked to the earl, "With Lady Diana at Hardwick Hall, there's never a dull moment, sir. I suppose you'll want Nora to serve?"

"The countess is so unconventional, I think that would be safest."

Diana was putting the finishing touches to her cascading curls when Nora came in search of her. She stopped, aghast, in the doorway of the peach-colored chamber. "You cannot wear that, your ladyship."

Diana had fastened her gold chain about her waist and the crimson loin dress about her hips. "Why not?" Diana asked, amused.

"Well, I have liberal ideas, being French, but this is too shocking."

Diana smiled her secret smile. "It may shock a Frenchman, but not a Roman. Were you able to find me that incense burner?"

"I put it in the dining room."

"In Aquae Sulis it was called the triclinium."

"Is that where they held their orgies?" Nora whispered, knowing Diana was an avid student of Roman history.

"Among other places," she confirmed.

Diana had decided that this was the night Mark would ask her to remarry him, once their present marriage was annulled. She was determined to overcome his obsession with freedom.

Hoping to shock and surprise Diana, Mark came to dinner wearing only a towel. When he came through the adjoining door from their bedchamber, Diana was putting a lighted taper to the incense. His eyes licked over her curves displayed so erotically in the crimson loin dress. "Two minds with but a single thought," he said huskily.

"This is a Roman custom. Frankincense is an aromatic to recall records of the soul."

His nostrils flared. She was lovelier than any goddess. What had he done to deserve this gift from the gods?

When Nora came in with dessert, they didn't even see

her. They were curled together on one dining couch, feeding each other with their fingers. She left the sweets and fruit and departed.

As Diana licked his fingers, he murmured softly, "What fruit would you like—passion fruit?"

"I'm particularly partial to plums," she murmured, slipping her hand beneath his towel and rolling his testes together shamelessly.

"What else are you partial to? Let me fulfill all your desires." He picked her up and carried her into their bedchamber, leaving the towel and the loin dress draped over the dining couch.

"Tantra."

"Tantra?" He had no idea what it was, but it sounded almost forbidden, the sultry way she suggested it. "Show me."

"Not on the bed, on the floor. I sit in your lap, face to face, so every part of our bodies receives pleasure. Your slow, sensual thrusting must stop on the brink of climax, so you can begin again . . . and again."

Mark was lost. He sank to the rug and pulled her into his lap.

Two hours later when she was soft with surfeit, he kissed her hair and whispered, "What would you like for your birthday?"

She held her breath, hoping he would offer her a permanent marriage. The silence was like black velvet. Finally, she whispered, "Guess."

He searched his mind, but he was too full of her; too love-drunk to think coherently. "Rubies, diamonds?"

She stiffened in his arms, then deliberately climbed off his semihard erection. "You are a damned devil! You know what I want more than anything in the world, but your bloody freedom is too precious to you!"

His black brows drew together to warn her of an impending storm. "I'll give you anything; what the hell is it you want?"

"You're so bloody clever, figure it out for yourself!" She departed their bedchamber unmindful of her nudity.

Mark stared angrily at the door she slammed. How could she be so loving one moment, and like a spitting vixen the next? *Bloody women!* This was the thanks he got for lavishing his attention upon her. She was a spoiled little bitch, and if she wanted to sleep alone, he would let her!

They didn't speak for two days, but each of them paid a price in loneliness and misery. On the third day he went into town without her, then closeted himself in the library upon his return. Diana was ready to beg his forgiveness. She knew his towering pride would never allow a man such as Mark to beg for anything, and of course that was exactly the way she wanted him.

At dinner she asked for a tray and carried it to her own room, wishing she had an excuse to go to him. There on her pillow sat a velvet box. She opened it, excited as a child at Christmas. It was a silver torque, encrusted with brilliant blue lapis. She ran lightly down the curved staircase, then opened the library door without knocking. He was addressing a stack of envelopes, but covered what he was doing when he saw her.

She held up the velvet box. "Your apology is very beautiful."

"It isn't an apology, it's a peace offering," he growled. Diana saw the glint of amusement in his dark eyes.

She said lightly, "You see, you knew what I wanted after all."

He stared at her, then murmured, "It took me a while, but finally I read your mind."

"Put it on for me."

"Upstairs."

"I have food."

"Let's eat it in bed."

Their sexual hunger was blatant, but beneath the lust was a love that knew no depth. Each one's happiness lay with the other. Like the two halves of their coin, they were not complete unless they were together.

On the very first day of the Easter Sessions, the court found the marriage of Mark Hardwick, Earl of Bath, and Lady Diana Davenport null and void on the grounds of consent. When the legal notice was brought to Hardwick Hall, Mark and Diana were ready to depart for Bristol aboard one of the earl's vessels.

As she stood at the rail watching the swirling waters of the River Avon, Mark turned her to face him. He cupped the curve of her cheek with his long fingers. "My sweetheart, I'm sorry the marriage is dissolved, but we knew it would happen."

She pressed her cheek into his palm. "They're just pieces of paper . . . marriage certificates, annulments . . . they cannot declare our love null and void."

Diana was putting the best face on it and he wanted to divert her. "After we've bought out all the ladies' shops in Bristol, I think we should go to London. We can be there on your birthday, in time for you to enjoy a little revenge."

"Oh Mark, that's perfect! I shall go to Grosvenor Square and take back my house. Will you come with me?"

"I wouldn't miss it for the world. Between now and your birthday, they will be scouring the country looking for you. They have only four days left to play fast and loose with your money. I intend to stay closer than your shadow. I may no longer be your husband, but be assured I am still your protector."

That night, long after Diana had drifted off to sleep in his arms, Mark lay awake trying to decide how he would get Richard Davenport to give written consent for Diana to marry him. Her uncle would be in financial difficulties, so he would jump at a bribe. But Mark could not bring himself to reward a man who had subjected Diana to an insane asylum.

He could force Richard at gunpoint, of course, but that would leave them open to another challenge in court, and Diana had been through enough. Mark would simply have to coerce the vultures into capitulation.

He glanced down and saw her lashes lying against her cheek. He had already bought her wedding finery and addressed the invitations. He couldn't wait to see her amethyst eyes deepen to violet when he proposed remarriage.

On her eighteenth birthday, Diana awoke in the big bed at the Savoy Hotel in London. Had the management known their marriage had been annulled, they would never have given them a suite, earl or no earl. She decided to wear red for her confrontation with her aunt and uncle, since Prudence believed no woman in red could be respectable.

Diana fastened the braided frogs on her spring walking dress, adjusted the ostrich feather to curl beneath her chin, and chose a frilly red parasol, just in case she needed a weapon.

Their first stop was the chambers of Chesterton and Barlow, where Diana affixed her signature to half-a-dozen legal documents, then a short carriage ride took them to Grosvenor Square.

The Davenports had spent the last week in Bath. Four days ago, when the court annulled Diana's marriage, they descended upon Hardwick Hall to resume the guardianship. When Mr. Burke informed them Lady Diana was not there, they wasted a whole day obtaining a search warrant, which failed to flush the quarry.

When Mr. Burke let it slip that the bird had flown to Bristol, they followed on what proved to be a wild-goose chase. The odious Burke was obviously laughing up his sleeve at them. Now, when it was too late, Diana had the boldness to walk in and have the butler announce her!

"Good afternoon, Richard. Good afternoon, Prudence; how's the old hip?"

The Earl of Bath's black eyes glittered with appreciation at the way Prudence's mouth fell open, then compressed into a lipless line.

"How you have the audacity to flaunt yourself when you are the scandal of both London and Bath is beyond me."

"I always had audacity to spare, Prudence." Diana smiled. "You did your best to suppress me, but as you can see, none of your pathetic little schemes worked."

Prudence lifted a haughty chin and looked down her long nose. "At least I had the satisfaction of having your marriage annulled!"

Damn you to hellfire, Prudence, you still have the ability to hurt me.

"A word in private, Davenport?" the earl said quietly.

Alone with Prudence, Diana was determined to hide her vulnerability. "Marriage is just a piece of paper, Prudence, not really very significant to me."

Prudence smiled cruelly. "Not when it's declared null and void by a more significant piece of paper called an annulment!"

"Since you have such a fascination with pieces of paper, I have one for you." Diana reached into her reticule and presented her with a document.

"An eviction notice?" Prudence screamed.

"There's no hurry, just so long as you vacate the premises by midnight."

"You little bitch," cried Prudence, taking a threatening step in her direction.

"Watch it, Prudence, or I'll give you a Dognor injuction."

"What?"

"That's where I stick this parasol up your arse and pull it down open!"

Chapter 39

The earl was also enjoying himself at Richard Davenport's expense. He held a handful of legal documents that were as lethal as any pistol.

Richard eyed him warily.

"Let me satisfy your curiosity. This deposition authorizes a full investigation into the handling of Lady Diana's finances."

Richard blanched.

"This one charges you with unlawful abduction; this one with unlawful incarceration and interment."

"We were within our legal rights of guardianship."

"Not without just cause."

"The girl was insane, believing she had gone back in time."

"Only you and I and Dr. Wentworth heard her say anything about Aquae Sulis, and the doctor and I will deny it."

"Dr. Bognor is a witness," Richard asserted.

"Dr. Bognor is in even more trouble than you, Davenport. I'm afraid his days as a doctor are numbered, as are yours as a solicitor. Oh, I forgot to mention this deposition charging you with embezzlement. Being a man of the law, you will know the penalty that carries."

Richard's face turned ashen and he began to perspire. The earl allowed him to sweat for a few minutes.

"I might be able to persuade Lady Diana to forget about pressing some of these charges, if she were my wife."

Richard's hands were trembling. "Prudence will never give written consent to the marriage."

"Fortunately, you are Diana's legal guardian, not Prudence."

When the gentlemen rejoined the ladies, Diana said sweetly. "We mustn't keep you any longer, you will have a deal of packing to do."

Prudence, vindictive to the end, said triumphantly, "You still need our consent to marry until you are twenty-one years old. Do you think you can sustain your position as mistress for three more years?"

Diana's heart constricted with pain; Richard's sank with dismay; Mark's soared with triumph.

On the carriage ride back to the Savoy, Diana's smile never dimmed, but Mark noticed that it didn't reach her eyes.

"Would you like to go out for a birthday supper tonight?"

"I'd much rather have a private supper, if it wouldn't disappoint you, Mark."

"I've already ordered it, so staying in won't disappoint me."

Diana took her bath and chose a white negligee trimmed with gold ribbon to set off her deep blue lapis torque. When she emerged from the bedroom, the dinner cart had already arrived. She lifted the heavy silver cover from the first dish and gasped with delight. Mark had ordered her pale blue orchids. She turned into his arms. "You think of everything."

His lips brushed her brow. "Let's go home tomorrow."

She sighed wistfully. "It isn't my home," she said softly.

He pressed a paper into her hand. "It soon will be."

She opened the crackling parchment and read that Richard Davenport consented to a marriage between Lady Diana and Mark Hardwick, Earl of Bath. Suddenly she was laughing and crying at the same time. "Are you truly asking me to marry you?"

"You had better say yes; I mailed the invitations this afternoon."

The corners of her mouth drooped. "Oh Mark, I've caused such scandal, no one will accept. I'll be ostracized by polite society and you along with me."

"Rubbish! Society is anything but polite. I'm an earl, for God's sake. People will be fighting for a chance to come to Hardwick Hall, and dying for the opportunity to observe my outrageous bride."

"You really did know what I wanted for my birthday."

"You are transparent as Venetian glass, and just as delicately lovely. Why don't we forget the food and go straight to bed?" he murmured.

"Are you mad? I'm starving to death! First I want dinner, then I want you for dessert."

"Deferred pleasure is twice as passionate." He dipped a piece of lobster tail in the drawn butter and lifted it to her lips. "I shall gratify all your senses before the night is through."

She licked her lips. "You are so damned cocksure."

Mark smiled his secret smile.

Hardwick Hall, ablaze with spring flowers, had never looked lovelier. Even the weather cooperated for the wedding. The food was being catered so that Nora was free to attend the bride.

The night before, Mark and Diana exchanged wedding gifts. She bought him a magnificently preserved Roman gladius sword and he gave her a diamond necklace with a flower of amethysts at its center to match her eyes.

"Oh, I forgot this," he said, bringing out a huge box from beneath the bed.

When Diana opened the box, her eyes became liquid with tears. There lay a creamy *tunica recta,* woven in one piece, and a pair of cream leather slippers encrusted with pearls. The wedding veil was flame-colored Chinese silk.

"Mark, you must listen to my stories most attentively."

"Why would I not? I love you for much more than your beauty. Your intelligence and your humor delight me."

Diana wondered how many centuries it had taken him to learn to appreciate a woman for all of her attributes.

"Have you enough courage to wear a red veil?"

"I have courage enough for anything!"

Now, however, as she stood in front of the cheval glass while Nora fastened it to her hair with a wreath of verbena, Diana wasn't sure. Last night she had been convinced they would have no guests. Today, carriages had been arriving for the last two hours.

"It's too late for me to act the respectable countess at the eleventh hour, Nora. The ton has come to scrutinize me, so far be it from me to disappoint them."

A light tap on the chamber door told them Mr. Burke had arrived to escort her to Hardwick's own chapel. Every pew had been decorated with lily of the valley. The small chapel overflowed with guests, whose faces were just a blur to Diana. The only one she was acutely aware of was the dark face of her beloved awaiting her at the altar.

She listened attentively as the minister joined them in holy wedlock. She was startled when the groom took her hand and said, "I, Marcus, take thee, Diana, to my wedded wife . . ."

When it was her turn, she used his full name, "I, Diana, take thee Marcus to my wedded husband . . ." When she'd finished the traditional vow, she added softly, "Will you be my *pater familias*?"

Mark squeezed her hands, telling her he would be anything and everything she wanted him to be. As they left the chapel and were showered with rice, Diana hugged her secret to her for the last time. Tonight she would share it with her husband.

The afternoon sun shone so brightly, the doors were thrown open so that the guests could explore the gardens of the lovely old Elizabethan hall.

Diana was surprised that she knew so many of the guests. Dr. Wentworth and his attractive wife were there, and Diana was amazed to see Dame Lightfoot, who had arrived with the Melbournes.

"Allegra couldn't come?" Diana asked wickedly.

"She'll be here later when things liven up and the dancing begins," replied Dame Lightfoot with a straight face.

Lady Emily Castlereagh and her husband, the Marquis of Londonderry, who had been such close friends of her father, had joined the Granvilles for the drive to Bath. William Lamb, one of her disappointed suitors, arrived with Caro Ponsonby, and Diana was almost sorry to hear that the couple were engaged. *She'll lead him a dog's life. Poor William!*

The eccentric Countess of Cork was holding court in the drawing room when Diana and Mark strolled in to mingle. The old girl pinned her to the wall with her piercing gaze. "So, where was it you disappeared to all those months, Lady Diana?"

The room fell silent as Diana gathered her wits. "You know how men always have a grand tour before they settle down to married life? Well, I decided that was completely unfair to the female sex, and took a trip to Rome."

"Bully for you, my girl," cheered the countess, and

the rest of the ladies in the room seemed all in favor of equality.

Mark opened his cigar case and offered it to the man beside him. "Do you ladies mind if we smoke?"

"Not if we join you," said Diana outrageously, reaching for a cheroot. Dead silence followed, then the Countess of Cork reached for one, held it to her nose, and said, "Turkish blend. Actually I prefer American."

When Mark and Diana moved on to the next room, she gave him back the cigar.

"You love to shock people," he accused.

"Not all all. Save it for me and I'll smoke it later."

As the evening shadows started to gather, Diana found Mark. "I'm going upstairs to take off my veil before we go up to the ballroom for the dancing."

"Good, your hair is far too beautiful to hide."

"It has been an absolutely perfect day. You have all of my heart." Diana couldn't wait until they danced together in the magnificent Elizabethan ballroom, while the music drifted down from the minstrels' gallery.

He took hold of her hands and lifted them to his lips. He longed to kiss more than her fingers, but knew if his mouth began to explore hers, he would not be able to stop.

Diana went into Mark's bedchamber, which had once been used by a queen, and was now theirs. When she turned from closing the door, she looked straight into the eyes of Peter Hardwick. How in the world had he gotten in here? Then she knew. He had used the secret passage so none would know he was there.

"Peter, what do you want?"

"You were too fine to spread yourself for me. You and Mark conspire to rob me of my father's land and wealth. Until you came along, I was his legal heir, now he thinks to breed heirs on your body. But I shall get it all, and you, my beautiful bitch, will get your just deserts."

"Petrius!" she cried out in horror.

"I shall take you up to the roof, where of your own accord you will jump off! None know I am here, and none shall ever know."

When he lunged for her, Diana did not waste time screaming. She reached for the door and had it open when his cruel hands took possession of her. She wrenched away from him with all her strength. Her red veil came away in his hands, but her feet were already running along the hallway to the staircase. Peter was behind her; she could hear him breathing.

Then she saw Mark at the foot of the stairs with Charles Wentworth. Before she could cry out his name, she felt a brutal shove from behind, then she was tumbling helplessly down the long curved staircase.

A look of horror came across Mark's face as he watched Peter push Diana down the stairs. Mark bent and picked her up in his arms, his heart thundering inside his ears. He was a stranger to fear, but he felt its hammer blow now as he searched his beloved's face.

"I'm all right, Mark . . . it was Petrius!" she gasped.

Charles Wentworth took her from Mark's arms. "I'll look after her—get him!"

With murder in his black eyes, Mark took the stairs three at a time. He did not hesitate, but went straight to the master bedchamber and the secret passage that led to the roof. Peter had fled on this course before when they were boys and he had done something brutal to one of Mark's horses. He hadn't caught him then, but he intended to trap him now.

Peter pressed himself against the tall chimney in the deep shadows. He had planned to fling Diana from the roof, but this was even better. Mark was the real impediment to his future. Hatred and bloodlust rose up within him; it was the most ecstatic feeling he had ever known.

Mark stood absolutely still until his eyes became accustomed to the darkness. His gaze slowly moved across the pitch and gabled roof and along the parapet walk. When he saw nothing, he knew Peter must be behind him on the other side of the chimney stack. Very deliberately, he walked out onto the open parapet, where he knew that he would be visible.

"Come out." It was a command.

For the space of perhaps two minutes, there was no sound, no movement, nothing. Then suddenly Peter was hurtling himself toward Mark at full speed.

Ancient memories flooded Mark's consciousness. Petrius had poisoned their father and had made Nero turn Diana into a living torch!

Mark's powerful fists felled him. As Peter went to his knees, he suddenly lost his balance and went hurtling backward over the crenellated stones. The impact was fatal.

Mark stared down at his brother's body sprawled lifelessly below. It had happened too quickly for Mark to reach out for him. *Would I have saved him if I could?* Mark could not truthfully answer, but he knew that Peter was evil incarnate and carried within him the seeds of his own destruction. The Roman wedding had been celebrated with a sacrifice after all.

Mark found Diana in their chamber, where Dr. Wentworth had carried her upstairs to examine her. His black eyes sought those of his friend, Charles, and held.

"Diana will be all right if she stays off her feet for a few days. She was very lucky she didn't lose your child."

Mark was startled, yet not. "Thank you, Charles. You'll be needed downstairs, I'm afraid."

Mark sank down on the edge of the bed. "Are you really all right?" His insides felt like jelly.

"It was Petrius—"

"I know, my love. He can never hurt you again."

"It's very wicked of me, but I'm glad he's dead."

"He deserved to die. It's over."

Diana lifted his hand to her cheek, then pressed a kiss into his palm.

"You are so slim, are you sure you are having a child?"

"I'm very sure."

He kissed her brow. "Rest. I'll take care of everything else."

As the door closed softly, she knew that this man was all the protection she would ever need.

On a warm night in May, Diana and Mark sat facing each other, submerged in the large porcelain tub.

"The bathing pool will be finished in a couple of days. This old tub can be relegated to the attics."

"Not in a million years. I've become rather fond of it," she said, inching her toes along the inside of his iron-hard thigh. Mark's feet were imprisoned beneath her buttocks so he couldn't do wicked things with them.

"How would you like to play master and slave tonight?"

"How would you like to play mistress and slave?"

"Not in a million years!" But he knew in his heart this woman had enslaved him.

"Let's negotiate," she suggested playfully, her toes only a fraction away from their goal.

"I'll let you call me Marcus," he tempted.

Diana loved to have the last word and knew she was blessed to have a man who would allow her to have it, once in a lifetime. Beneath half-closed eyelids she murmured, "I'll obey your every command if you wear the gladius sword I bought you." Then she punctuated her offer with a silken slide of toes.